HORROR STORIES FOR HALLOWEEN

TONY WALKER

D1565972

CONTENTS

1

MY NIECE ALISON

My niece Alison was always a strange girl. Maybe a little more than strange to be honest. My brother, before he died, called her otherworldly, and when he'd gone, I simply felt a responsibility for her. She had too many tragedies too young — losing her mother and now her father at such an age. My wife, Laura, felt sorry for her but never actually liked her — even when she was tiny. Laura said there was something about Alison that unnerved her, though she could never explain exactly why.

Alison and I always got along well, though. We were both into spiritual things, and I used to take her to the Buddhist place up past Langholm on meditation courses. We even went to the Spiritualist Church four or five times. She got messages from the dead, but I didn't. All that stuff used to drive Laura nuts. She would say, 'I don't even know why you go,' and I'd reply, 'Because I want to know the answer.'

She lifted and eyebrow and looked at me. 'The answer to what?'

I knew she'd think me stupid, but I said it anyway, 'The answer to what happens after you die.'

Laura rolled her eyes and told me it was tea-time.

THE YEARS ROLLED ON. Against my better judgement, Alison went a long way away to University. I wasn't sure she was emotionally tough enough to go where she knew no one, but she insisted. She went to study Fine Art at Aberystwyth, and I heard nothing from her until the end of October just before Halloween.

The phone call came late at night — just before midnight. I was up reading. Phones that ring in the middle of the night usually bring bad news, so I was relieved when Alison said, "It's me, Uncle David."

Her voice sounded very distant. She wished me a belated happy birthday and apologised for not sending a card. Her problem was that she was moving from the town to a farmhouse she had rented, and she had no car; would I come and help her move?

It was about two hundred miles away and a difficult time of year but, as I said, we had always got on. I arranged to travel down the last week in October. Laura wasn't happy. I asked her whether she wanted to come down with me — joking that maybe we could have a rainy break in Wales.

She said, "We live in Cumbria, David. We have sheep, mountains, lakes and rain here. Why would I want to go to Wales?"

I set off on 30th October from Penrith. I have a big estate car, and I took very little so there would be more room for Alison's things. I drove down the M6. The rain on the motorway was terrible — large trucks spraying water across my windscreen. My only comfort when overtaking blind was that I was relatively sure there wouldn't be any traffic coming towards me.

I stopped for a sandwich near Manchester. Just short of an hour after that, I crossed the border, passing the *Welcome to Wales* sign and heading down through Mid Wales to Llanidloes. Quick to describe but long to drive in the unfriendly weather.

The landscape all around was a washed-out green. I drove past woods stripped bare by the oncoming winter. Small towns sped past. Having my foot always on the accelerator gave me cramp. I found somewhere to park, got out, stretched and strolled over to get an organic coffee and some hummus on toast in the Great Oak Café, which was the only place open.

And after that, going through the Cambrian Mountains the weather was appalling -- worse than it had been. I feared the mountain streams tumbling down the hillsides would break their banks and wash away the road. I was prepared at any time to run into floods as I headed west along the A44. My windscreen wipers could hardly keep the rain off. Not surprisingly, there was little traffic.

The day was dark, and the light faded early. Soon, all I had was the sinuous road snaking through the bare hills, cats-eyes in the road glinting with my reflected headlights, asphalt shining in the rain. Occasionally another vehicle came in the opposite direction. But they were few and far between.

After what seemed a long time peering forward into the receding dark, I reached the Nant yr Arian forest centre and found it was closed for the winter break. There being nowhere else to stop, I went on and began to descend gradually towards to coast.

I had Alison's address, and I had written out rudimentary directions from the map I studied before I set off. We didn't have Google Maps in those days. It was very remote. Basically, I had to go all the way into Aberystwyth and then back up into the mountains. It would have been shorter as the crow flew from where I was, but there were no crows flying that night.

I arrived at Aberystwyth quickly enough on the main carriageway and made my way slightly north to Penrhyn-coch. Then I got lost. The roads were tiny from here, the landscape dark and unbothered by lights. As I peered through the darkness, it seemed there were no people about at all.

I got onto a narrow mountain track. The wind blew wildly, juddering the car, and I worried I would get swept off into some dark ravine. Where there were signs, the names were strange to me – the Welsh words danced before my eyes as I stopped and strained to read them in the head-lights. At one point, I came across some sheep sheltering behind a stone wall. I was glad I was not them.

I turned a corner, and the road pitched steeply down. Before I knew it, I ran into a flood. In a moment's panic, I thought it would mount up and drown the engine, but the car spluttered and ploughed through. I imagined breaking down in that place and wished I had had the vehicle serviced as it should have been.

Then the road climbed again. It was a single track with grass growing in the middle, grass blasted and bent by the wind and rain, but managing somehow to survive in that wild, empty place. The single track split. Going off to the right was a stony trail, hardly fit for motor vehicles. But a wooden sign said *Pant y Garreg Hir*. That was Alison's house. Taking a minute to steel myself, but realising I had no option for I didn't relish retracing my steps; I turned the wheel and attacked the slope. The wet stones slipped and jumped under my wheels, the engine roared, but I wasn't getting anywhere, and then suddenly there was traction. The car sped up the incline and then down into a depression — ahead of me, I could see the cold, wet shape of a dark house.

There were no lights on. I looked at my watch and saw it was 9:20 pm. The journey from Aberystwyth had taken hours. My phone had no signal. I was hungry and disappointed that Alison wasn't home. I opened the car, and the elements swept in — threatening to tear off the door and blowing the cold and rain in with me. I closed the car door behind me and walked up to the front door. The house was obviously empty, but I knocked anyway. I even knocked twice, but there was no reply. On the glass in the door was a sticker, like a car bumper sticker, that said: "*Witches do it on Broomsticks.*"

I shone the torch I'd taken from my car into the window. Through the window, I saw the kitchen had a table and some chairs. Otherwise, the place looked like a house that was awaiting a new tenant. I could see a card on the table that I could partially read and then guess enough of the rest to work out it said, "*Welcome to Your New Home*".

The wind got wilder. I went back to the car and waited. And I lingered, and no one came, and I knew that in that weather no one was going to appear. I half decided to go back to Aberystwyth then I imagined the roads even more flooded than before, the full wild streams, the endless buffeting wind. It was stupid to take the risk in the dark. I huddled in my car. Unexpectedly, I slept.

In the middle of the night, something rapped at my car window.

I woke in sheer terror, my heart hammering. I slapped

down the door locks and peered out. It was still raining, and I could hardly see; the windows streaming outside and misted with condensation inside. Looking at my watch, I saw it was 2 am. I wondered if a neighbour had seen my car, and come to check what I was doing there. But I'd not seen any houses nearby and who would go walking at that time, in that weather?

Then I wondered maybe it was a branch, broken and blown from the trees that clustered around the house. That must have been it. Ridiculously, I wanted to leave right then. I was frightened of the wind. My rational brain told me not to be stupid. It told me to wait for Alison, or morning, whichever came first.

I SLEPT AGAIN, and I woke to a grey morning. Not raining but with broken clouds streaming from the sea to the west. I got out of the car and stretched. The wind, though weaker, still took my breath away. I looked around for any broken branch that might have stuck my window but could see no obvious candidate. Then I went up to the house again. It was unchanged. The card still sat on the table in the otherwise empty kitchen. I walked around the back, and for the first time, I noticed an ancient-looking standing stone. I guessed it was something from the Bronze Age or earlier. I rubbed my fingers along it, but it was featureless rough stone. Its only decorations were small growths of moss in indentations and grooves.

I then walked out of the depression where the house lay to get a better view of the barren hills that stretched all around. They inclined higher behind and dipped lower towards the coastal strip. A few farmhouses dotted the moors far and away with odd stands of trees, but otherwise, the landscape was empty. I was starving hungry, and I had no phone signal — neither was there any sign of Alison, so I decided to head back into Aberystwyth.

The town was pleasant, by the sea and full of students. I had my brunch at a beautiful pizza place where they hand made the dough in front of me. I washed the vegetarian pizza down with elderflower cordial. The shops and cafes were festooned with the usual Halloween stuff; pumpkin lanterns in the windows, cut-outs of witches and spooks in coloured paper on the doors. The bookshop had a section on local Welsh folklore and Halloween customs.

I should've liked to have a more extended look around the town, at the Castle and the Old College, but the rain started up again. The wind whipped the tops off the waves and drenched me in saltwater, making me hurry indoors. Not wishing to go back to that bleak house just yet, I spent some time in one of the bookshops, then in a café, rang Laura and told her about my adventure.

"Well, where is she?" she said.

"I don't know. Alison doesn't have a mobile phone, so I was counting on meeting her there." I grimaced. "I'm sure she'll turn up. I'm going to head on back up there soon, after taking the precaution of booking a B&B for tonight here in town."

"Take care and hurry home soon. The silly girl doesn't deserve your help".

"Aww, come on, Laura. You know I'm all she's got."

She could never forgive Alison. "She's got no sense of responsibility."

I sighed. "I'll be back home tomorrow, whatever happens."

"Love you, David, hurry home."

When I got back to Pant y Garreg Hir, there was a

removal van parked outside. Three men sat in the cab at the front, one of them reading a paper. They didn't open the window immediately. I tapped on it. A big ginger man wound it down and said, "Yes?"

I wondered what he thought I was doing there, but I asked him if they had furniture for Alison Bragg.

"Are you her dad?" he said.

I shook my head. "Uncle."

"Well, we've got her stuff. But she was supposed to be here. We have waited, but it's a good job you turned up, or we would have just unloaded it."

The men got out of the van, and two of them opened up the back. They spoke to each other in Welsh. The leader came with me and said, "You got a key?"

Again I shook my head. "I was expecting to meet her here. She said she wanted me to help move her stuff. But she obviously hired you too."

"Yes, we went to her old place, and her landlord opened it up. I know him anyway — Euros Morris; went to school with him."

"But how will we get in?"

He tapped his nose then went over to the plastic rubbish bin to the left of the front door and pulled it off the flat slate it rested on. He lifted the stone and picked up a door key. "People always leave them in places like this."

"I must admit I'm beginning to get a bit worried about where she is," I said.

He laughed and opened the door. "You go first in case she's dead in there!" Then he looked serious like he might have offended me, and said, "No offence."

I stepped into the quiet house. It was cold and felt damp. If she had been here at all, it hadn't been for long. Behind me, the men started to bring Alison's furniture in.

"Where do you want it?" They asked.

"I don't know. Wherever there's space."

"We'll put the bedroom things in the bedrooms, the bathroom things in the bathroom. You get the idea," said the leader.

The day was darkening already. As I stepped inside, I switched on the light. It was a gloomy 60-watt bulb, but at least there was electricity. I saw there was an open hearth and beside it some chopped logs, matches and kindling wood. I knelt down and began to make a fire. Soon it was roaring and filling the kitchen with warmth.

"It's a spooky old place," said the removal man. "Have you seen the standing stone in the garden?"

I nodded.

"That's what the name means — Pant y Garreg Hir — 'Hollow of the Standing Stone.' I wouldn't like to stay the night here. Just saying. On Halloween too!"

"Thanks," I grinned trying to be light-hearted.

"And you've got your own well too, but you have to be careful with the water up here; there's lots of old lead spoil around from the mines. Best stick to the tap."

"Thanks for that advice," I said.

"Well, we're about done now." He reached out to shake my hand. "Geraint Jenkins by the way. Removals. If you ever need anything shifted."

"I'm not from round here. I live up in Cumbria."

"Just rain and sheep and hills up there from what I've heard," said Geraint, smiling.

I grinned back. "That's about right."

He paused. It took me an instant to realise what he wanted. "How much was it again?" I said.

"We agreed £150, the girl and me."

Embarrassed, I reached for my wallet. "I don't have that much cash on me."

"Don't worry. I'll take a cheque. You seem an honest man."

He waited while I wrote out a cheque.

"I can see why she hasn't turned up now," he laughed.

I was puzzled.

"So's you'd pay, good boy! Don't worry; I'm sure she'll be back soon."

THEN THEY DROVE AWAY, leaving me to the wind and the old house.

But she wasn't back soon. Alison had clearly been in the house because there was some food in the cupboards, and one bed had a duvet and pillows on it. There was enough wood to stoke the fire to keep me warm while I made a rudimentary meal out of some pasta and a can of tomatoes with herbs. I had brought a book with me, and I sat by the fire reading until I felt my eyes beginning to close. It wasn't late, but I was tired.

I woke later. It was dark. Still, Alison wasn't back. I considered driving down to Aberystwyth to the B&B, but the weather had closed in again, and the trees thrashed like crazy things in the wind and rain. The wind whistled around the house, and it felt like the roof might lift off. I couldn't face the journey on those dark windswept roads, but I couldn't phone the B&B to cancel. I would just pay tomorrow and apologise about not letting them know.

I got ready to go to bed. I pulled the iron fireguard around the dying fire and made my way up the slate stairs to the bedroom. I went into the room that had the duvet. I guessed it was Alison's room, but she wasn't here, and there were no bedclothes in the other bedroom. The room was cold, and I took off my shoes but slept in my shirt and pullover. I lay there for a long time listening to the storm outside and thinking how far I was from anyone who knew me, and how distant I was from anyone who could help. But then I wondered what I needed help for.

I had an awful dream. As I lay there in the bed, I dreamed that I heard someone coming up the stairs. In my nightmare, the door was pushed open. I sat up in fear and silhouetted against the open door; I saw a young woman. She was dripping wet.

"Alison!" I shouted in my dream.

"Hello, Uncle David," she said. "I'm glad you've come."

"Alison — have you been out in the rain?"

She ignored my question and instead came walking towards me. The water dripped from her. She was so cold and white. I pressed my back against the headboard, but she kept on coming. And when she was close, she leaned into me. I felt the water dripping off her hair onto my face. She came close to my ear and whispered. "Uncle, do you want to know a secret?"

And I knew it was the secret of what happens after you die.

WHEN I WOKE, all I could hear was the wind howling outside, knocking the window, threatening to break in. I got up and went and shoved a chair against the door, pushing it and jamming and wedging it under the door handle so the handle wouldn't turn. I know it was irrational.

I went back to bed and lay there trying to sleep, but the cold terror of nightmare still lay heavy like bitter liquor in my veins. The dawn seemed a long time away.

Minutes ticked by, maybe hours, while the dark lay heavy on the house. I don't know what time it was. Not yet dawn.

And then, as I lay there, I heard someone downstairs.

I leapt out of bed, my breath coming in gasps while I went to listen at the door, holding the chair ready to stop anyone coming into the room. Someone was moving downstairs.

As I listened, not daring to breathe, I heard them mount the stairs.

Whoever it was, came up a step at a time, slowly, slowly, but not pausing. Inexorable. Like they couldn't be stopped.

The wind howled outside, my heart thumped in my throat as I listened to the sound of those cold dragging footsteps.

There was nothing in that house. Nothing at all. There was no reason for the footsteps to come upstairs, except for me.

I thought of opening the door and challenging whoever it was. I thought of going out, brandishing the chair in front of me.

But I didn't. Fear held me fast.

And then, whoever it was, whatever it was, stopped, just outside the door. My skin prickled and I dared not breathe. I just stood, hearing the silence of someone waiting.

My hands trembled. I put all my weight on the wedged chair so they couldn't open the door. But still, I heard nothing. And then, I told myself I'd imagined the whole thing: imagined the sound of someone climbing the stairs; imagined those slow dragging footsteps.

I told myself that it was only the wind; that it was only the creaking of an old Welsh house. I told myself it was only imagination. I convinced myself there was no one out there.

No one waiting.

No one standing behind the door.

No one at all.

Only the sound of the wind scouring the empty moors.

No steps.

No breaths.

No one. Actually, no one could be there. I had the house key. The only key. Unless Alison had hidden a second key as casually as the first, a key easy for anyone to find, a key easy for anyone to pick up, unlock the door, and come in.

I knew I should open the door from my room. I would open the door just to calm my nerves, see no one. Then I would sleep until the morning. I would drive to Aberystwyth, go to the Police and report Alison as a missing person. And so, I finally convinced myself and kicked the door of my room wide open.

There was no one.

At first, I was relieved. I laughed at my stupidity, my voice echoing in the empty house.

And then I stopped laughing.

Soaking wet footprints led down the stairs into the kitchen. I pushed the door suddenly closed and lodged the chair hard against it. I shoved my back to the door, panicking, my eyes wide with fear. I looked around the room, looking for I don't know what. As if by opening it the door, I had let something in—something invisible. Something that would lurk in the shadows, waiting for me to sleep.

Of course, I couldn't sleep. Not even when the dawn light made everything visible and ordinary: the dusty pictures of old women in Welsh stove-pipe hats on the walls, the rumpled duvet on the bed — my discarded book.

Before it was properly day, I hurried out to the car and

drove down to Aberystwyth. As I drove away from Pant y Garreg Hir, I did not look in the mirror.

I found the Police Station. There I filed a missing person's report. The sergeant wanted to accompany me back to Pant y Garreg Hir. He said, "My grandparents lived in Cwmsymlog nearby. I've never been in that house. It's supposed to be haunted by a girl who drowned in the well. I always wanted a nosey inside," he laughed.

I put my hand to my throat. "I don't really want to go back there."

"It's up to you, but I could do with getting some of her things – for the dogs if we do a search."

And so out of obligation, I agreed to go back to the house with him. And I thought -- at least he had his radio. The journey up in the Police 4x4 was more comfortable. We got out of the car, outside the house. "I haven't been up here for years," he said. "It's a bleak place. Hardly anyone lives in these hills anymore: just hippies and mad old farmers too crazy to give up."

He wandered around the back to look at the standing stone. He tapped it and strolled over to a circle of stone mostly overgrown with bleached mountain grass. "And here," he said, "is the well."

I didn't go over. I just stood there while the policeman looked down.

I saw it on his face before he spoke. He came and took my arm and led me to the car. Then he spoke into the police radio rapidly in Welsh. He turned to me. "I'm really sorry."

"She's in there?"

He nodded.

Alison was found drowned in the well. At the inquest, the Coroner recorded a verdict of misadventure, but the papers said she'd killed herself.

Most of the time, I am all right. I sleep moderately well when I forget about those footsteps. But sometimes I lie awake while Laura sleeps. I'm too frightened to close my eyes in case I hear Alison coming up the stairs, coming to tell me what I've always wanted to know.

What she promised to tell me in my dream: the secret of what happens when you die.

2

THE CATACOMBS

A city of the dead lies under the streets of Paris. Down there, countless tunnels twist under the metropolis, lined with skulls and bones, some in neat piles, some in geometrical patterns, and others in careless heaps.

This all began in Paris, just before Halloween. Stephanie and I decided to give ourselves a scares. It was all just fun; yep, fun is all it was, until it wasn't; until it transformed into the strangest and most unnerving experience of my life.

Halloween isn't as prominent in France as it is in the Anglophone countries, but it's growing, and they have 'All Souls Day' where good Catholics visit cemeteries to pray over their dear departed.

At the green kiosk at the Catacomb's entrance, I paid for my ticket. With nervous giggles and and feet ringing on the cast-iron steps, we descended the iron staircase down to the caverns of the dead.

The Catacombs' entrance lies close to the Denfert Rochereau Metro Station. I went with my friend Stephanie. We were teachers of business English: Stephanie was an

Australian, and I come from Atlanta, Georgia; though I don't sound like I'm from Atlanta, apparently.

I'd majored in French and Spanish at UCLA, and was living in Paris for two years before I ever visited the Catacombs. I knew of them, of course, but something held me back from going. It was Stephanie who said we should go. She'd been before she said. She said it would really freak me out. She wasn't wrong.

So there we were on the narrow iron spiral stairs, hand on the rail, stepping carefully, so we didn't trip and fall. From the bright sunlight of modern Paris, we descended into the dark of the past. Though the flesh must have long since rotted, the place was still somehow filled with a damp miasma of death.

When we got to the bottom of the staircase, there were bones. The bones around us were brown, broken and pitted and heaped in awful piles. The leaflet said they were dug up from the city's graveyards when land got expensive inside the city proper, and people wanted to build houses where the graveyards were. So the bodies were dug up, though at that was left was bones, and the bones had been stored here and were turned now into a macabre tourist attraction.

You can go with a guide, but we'd taken the cheaper option of navigating our own way with a leaflet. The map on the leaflet was poor definition and small and hard to read, especially in the poor light. We were warned it was easy to get lost. I joked about leaving a trail of crumbs.

Stephanie wasn't listening to my jokes; she was too wired being down there.

"Switch your flashlight off. I've got the candles," said Stephanie in her sunny drawl. Like all Australians, she liked doing crazy things.

I was more hesitant. "Are you sure?"

"Of course. It'll make it really spooky."

"It's already spooky enough for me."

But she wouldn't listen. She rode roughshod over my fear.

We lit a candle each and switched off the flashlights. The flames flickered in a breeze that blew down the tunnel while shadows danced in the empty eyeholes of a thousand skulls.

I knew I was being stupid, but I couldn't help the shudder that ran down my spine. Stephanie was killing herself, laughing. "Follow me, Scooby-Doo!!"

She set off through the labyrinth of tunnels. She had the map, so I had to keep up with her.

It was cold. I'd expected it to be warm somehow even though it was October. The atmosphere was eerie and very heavy somehow. The fluttering candlelight made the bones seem to move all around us. We were walking so fast that the flame guttered and I had to shield it with my hand. Stephanie abruptly stopped and peered at the map by the light of her candle. "This way, I think."

I raised my eyebrow. "You think? You only think?"

I didn't like this.

"It's fine. Just a tiny bit lost. It's easy to get lost down here."

I had a strange sense of foreboding. "I want to go back."

"Just calm down," said Stephanie. "I can navigate in the Australian bush, so I can sure find my way through some smelly French tunnels."

Then she pointed, apparently at random. "This way."

I followed her as she hared off. There was a movement of air down the passage in front. I had to race to keep up with her. Because I was going so fast, the candle flame flickered and went out.

"Hey, wait up," I called.

In the dark ahead, she shouted, "Hurry up, Laura."

At first, I could see her silhouette and her dancing candle, but then she turned around, and I could see nothing. I shouted.

"I can't see you! Come back!"

I struggled to get the flashlight out of my bag. I wished I'd kept it in my hand. I could see nothing as I scrabbled in the impenetrable dark. Then I stopped and stared.

Behind me was a light. But it wasn't the warm yellow light of a candle or even the beam of a flashlight. It was a cold light; luminous, white and fearful like the luminescence that comes off dead things. I backed away, but it grew brighter, condensing into a shape in front of my eyes. It was a girl of about seventeen who had a thin, sad face, big green eyes and yellow hair. I could see right through her.

Stephanie found me standing there, shaking. The flashlight was in my hand, but I hadn't turned it on. "What's up?" she said.

"I just want to get out of here."

I didn't tell her what I'd seen.

"Ok, spoilsport," she said.

Using the map, we managed to find our way back to the stairs. She obviously knew there was something wrong with me, but I wasn't in the mood for talking. I knew what I'd seen. But how could I believe it? It scared me.

I WENT HOME to my one-room apartment in Auteuil. I sat and poured a glass of wine from the cheap supermarket plastic bottle I'd bought on the way back. I tried to read, but I couldn't concentrate; my mind kept returning to that silent figure in the Catacombs. I was scared of her, but I felt sorry for her, and I dreamed up some romantic fiction about her being a girl who'd gone down there and got lost. I had the wacky idea I could help her. But then I told myself to get a grip.

I put my book down. I wasn't reading it anyway. Then I turned on the TV, and after flicking through some channels, turned it off again. To distract myself from these weird thoughts, I picked up a pen and some paper and started to write a letter back home to my mother.

As I held the pen, my hand started to shake. My hand twitched as if there was some electricity inside it and then as I watched, horrified, the pen began to write on its own.

It spelled out an address: "rue des Prairies 47b".

I threw down the pen and stared at it on the floor as if it might start moving on its own. But it lay there still, as dead as roadkill. The electricity had gone from my hand, and I was alone again. Something wanted me to go to that address.

I hardly slept that night, keeping my eyes on the door as if the girl's ghost might come through it at any time.

At first light, I got up. It was Sunday, and outside my window, the street was deserted. I got dressed and made my way down the stone staircase and let myself out.

RUE DES PRAIRIES was in the east part of the city. I took the Metro and got off at Place Gambetta, the nearest station, and I walked down the street to number 47. It was a fairly ordinary building. There was a column of bell pushes with names written in various colours of ink alongside them. 47b belonged to someone called Herault. But I was still far too early to visit, so I went into a café and ordered a cappuccino and a croissant. At nine o'clock I went back and pressed the bell.

A voice said, "Hello?"

In French, I said, "Hello, my name's Laura Richards. I'm an English teacher. I wonder if I could speak to you?"

The voice sounded suspicious. "What do you want?"

I paused for a long time. "I know this sounds crazy, but I think I saw a ghost in the catacombs. I also think it wanted me to come here." My voice was shaking.

I expected her to tell me to get lost.

"Come up." I heard a buzz as she opened the door.

47b was to the left of the main entrance hallway. My heart pounded as I knocked on the door, not knowing what to expect. Why had she invited me in? I'm pretty sure I wouldn't have invited up a freaky stranger who came talking about ghosts.

A young woman opened it straight away. Standing there, in her dressing gown, was a sad-looking girl with red hair and green eyes. She was identical to the ghost.

I drew my breath in sharply.

Quietly she said, "You look frightened."

"No," I stammered, "it's just that you look..."

She tilted her head to one side. "I know. I look just like her. She was my twin sister."

She made me a cup of coffee as I sat on her sofa. "This is so strange," I said.

"You're not the first. Marguerite appears to anyone she thinks will be sympathetic."

She told me that her twin sister had died three years ago in the Catacombs from an asthma attack. They both suffered from asthma, but that day her sister Marguerite had forgotten her medication. She'd been with a girlfriend so that maybe explained why she'd appeared to me. Marie sat down in the chair opposite me and watched me drinking my coffee. "So you see, it's sad, but nothing to get alarmed about."

I finished the coffee and got up. The girl smiled, but without emotion. As I walked through the door, I glanced back, she was staring at me. Walking back to the Metro, I thought a modern ghost story — a curious but inconsequential mystery. But still, I felt there was something unresolved: as if there were secrets yet to penetrate.

On my way back home, I was still so bothered about Marie's story that I made a diversion and called into one of the big public libraries. I got a CD of all the articles that had appeared in *Paris Soir* for the year Marie's sister had died. I searched for Marguerite Herault, and sure enough, there was the tragic story of a seventeen-year-old girl who'd died from an asthma attack in the Catacombs.

That was it. I ejected the disk and got up. But something still nagged me, so I put the CD back in and found the name of the journalist who'd written the piece. I then got the telephone number for *Paris Soir* and phoned her. She remembered the event very clearly,

"Yes, a terrible thing. So young. What's your interest, if you don't mind me asking?"

I hesitated. "I know her sister."

Her voice changed. "No, that can't be."

"I'm sorry? Why not? I saw her sister only this morning."

"No, Marguerite was an only child. That's why it was so hard on the parents."

MARIE CAME to me in my dreams that night. I tried to ask her what had really happened — who her sister really was, but she wouldn't reply. All she did was hold up a skull in her hands, and I knew she wanted me to go back to the Catacombs.

I WAITED at a café on Place Denfert Rochereau until about half an hour before the Catacombs were due to close. The shops and cafes around the square were draped with witches and goblins. Tonight was Halloween.

I checked my watch. It was time. I finished my cold coffee with a gulp, then got up and went over to the kiosk.

I bought my ticket. A man with a tired and creased face sold me a ticket and looked at me oddly. There was a special tour later on for Halloween, but I would be finished by then.

I suppose not many young women choose to go to that place on their own. I got to the top of the spiral staircase and waited. I was nervous; I felt it in my throat, but this was a mystery I needed to solve, for the sake of my own sanity if nothing else.

The temperature dropped with every clanging step I took down. The smell of old death coated me like damp dust. Then I was at the bottom.

I walked about fifty yards into the labyrinth, turned down a corner away from the orderly rows of skulls and into a place where long bones had been piled carelessly out of sight. I waited there, switching off my flashlight until my nerves would bear it no longer and I had to turn it back on for a second. In the light, the skulls backed off and stopped moving, but when I flicked off my flashlight again, my imagination brought them leering forward.

I looked at my watch. The Catacombs were now officially closed. I waited, and I knew she would come. A soft, quiet glow grew to the right of me, and I turned and saw Marguerite's red hair and sad green eyes.

In a voice that sounded like a dry wind through a forest of bones, empty and pleading, she said, "Save me."

"How can I save you? What must I save you from?"

But only the faint whispering voice came again, "Save me."

Then I heard footsteps behind me—quiet, deliberate steps, but light, like the tread of a young woman. Marguerite began to drift away, the glow fading. A terrible sadness filled me; she thought I'd failed her.

The footsteps came closer. There was no doubt, but they were heading for me, unhurried and precise. In the darkness, whoever it was knew where I was.

Heart in mouth, I stepped back onto the main corridor from where I was lurking, and then, turning, I saw dead Marguerite's double; her double, her doppelgänger, her place taker–Marie, though Marie wasn't its real name either; it never had a real name.

I knew the doppelgänger had come for me, had lured me down into the halls of bones, and I realised that by pretending to be Marguerite's non-existent sister, it had fooled me into thinking I was helping somehow.

My heart went crazy. My throat was dry. If it caught me here, it would kill me and take my place, stripping the soul from my body and leaving me lost to wander the catacombs like poor dead Marguerite.

I panicked, but instead of running away into the maze of tunnels where it would surely find me, some instinct made me run *at* it. It hadn't expected that and it started back.

This move only bought me a few seconds, but I pushed past it, and sprinted down the corridor to the stairs and leapt up them three at a time.

Seconds, not more than seconds, surely not a minute and I was up there, my heart slamming my ribs.

I snatched at the door, but the door was locked. I hammered the old wood, all the time feeling the doppelgänger at my back, all the time not daring to look, and all the time knowing it was climbing the stairs one after another, after another, after another, until it came close enough to snatch me, and pull me screaming down into the boneyard below.

No answer yet to my frantic knocking, I dared glance over my shoulder and there only feet away, it stood, lips drawn back over white teeth, looking at me with hunger in its yellow eyes.

The a sound of a key turning in the door was my salvation.

Hearing the promise of my rescue, the doppelgänger darted forward, grabbing at my leg. I hurled my flashlight at it. The flashlight struck it heavily in the face, and it backed off snarling into the darkness below.

But then it started up again. It moved quickly, sinuously, like a serpent.

I pressed myself against the exit door, hammering, and the handle turned.

It was nearly at me now.

The ticket collector opened the door. Behind him was an astonished crowd of Halloween revellers in costume. The man looked astounded.

At the sight of all those people, the doppelgänger fled down back into the dark.

The ticket man was frowning. "You are fortunate, mademoiselle, that we have a special party here tonight; otherwise you would have had to spend the night among the bones."

I pushed my way through the door and through the amazed crowd, not speaking. They just stared after me. The ticket collector yelled as I left, "There's nothing to be frightened of down there, mademoiselle. Just old bones."

I COULDN'T STAY in Paris. I packed and was gone within a week. That was months ago, and now I work as a tourist guide in Savannah, but I only sleep in snatches, by daylight, or with the light on.

Believe me, it's not for me that I'm frightened. I'm a long way from Paris, but I can't rest because I know that in the sunken depths that lie under that city, the doppelgänger waits for another girl, another girl like me.

Maybe you've seen him too, seen him but didn't recognise him. Well, I've got some advice for you: if you can't hide from him, run from him. And if you can't run, go so still he won't know you're there and maybe he'll pass you by. Wait, and be quiet. Stop breathing. Wait without knowing if he's really coming, wait with bated breath and wait days, weeks, hours, until you're certain he's not there. But of course you can't be certain. Not really. Not ever.

And if you ever consider going to Paris, and if you ever wonder whether a descent into that dark palace of dead bones might be fun, and if you're ever on the edge of buying that ticket. My advice to you is: don't.

3

THE WOMAN AT THE DOOR

They say a wise man knows when he can't win, and that a fool will never beat his fate. What does that make me? I moved halfway across the world to get away from mine, but always with an eye over my shoulder, always expecting it to catch up, and always hoping it wouldn't.

You see, last year, my wife and son were killed in an automobile wreck on the Beltway. That's the major orbital highway of Washington DC. That's it, plainly put. I've said it, got it out the way. It was hard.

After they died, I went as far away from where that happened as possible. My father originally came from Scotland. Maybe that's why I went there. My father was a significant influence on me. You could say that he was behind everything that happened in my life, everything major at least.

I looked for property to buy through the Internet. The Scottish Borders were wild and empty and cheap, and I found that I could afford a fortified tower house dating from the Middle Ages. The internet picture showed it made of red sandstone, surrounded by trees in some bleak landscape with low windswept hills in the background.

By profession, I'm a doctor, so I had some cash, and I knew my house in Bethesda would sell quickly. And that was that. You might say that I wasn't thinking straight, but I just bought the Tower and went to the middle of Scotland.

I had enough money left so that I didn't have to work. I got some from the life insurance on my wife. I haven't mentioned, but my father died the same week as my wife and kid. That was a hell of a blow. He left me a sizeable inheritance. The money from my wife's insurance and my dad's will felt dirty. But I took them both. Being sensible, I had to, of course.

So, like I said, I didn't have to work. At first, that felt like a blessing, and later like a curse. I realise now that it isolated me. I saw no one — I was with no one. If it hadn't been for the radio, I would have gotten unused to the spoken word.

For the first weeks, I used to lie in my bed at night listening to the wind howling around the Tower and imagining the emptiness about me.

Scotland feels mostly unoccupied: there are mountains and marshes and forests, but nobody lives there. The highways are empty too, twisting through bare glens or thick plantations of pine trees. My house was vacant. The centuries echoed in it. I had a bed, a portable CD player and some books that lay in piles on the wooden floors gathering dust. The previous owners had left lots of plates and cutlery behind, so at least, I had something to eat with and on. When I ate at all. I got my food from the convenience store in the small town five miles away. I ate tuna from cans and drank strong coffee.

I bought some canvases and oils in the tiny local art shop and started to paint, but the images I drew became frightening to me. They were dark, and always I got the impression that something was waiting in them; just waiting for me to paint it and bring it to life.

And when that feeling grew almost overpowering, I left the painting. Feeling almost overpowered with anxiety, I sat for hours looking out of the window from my bedroom on the second floor, gazing over the bleak moorland in the direction of the invisible ocean. I felt alien there. But it wasn't that I'd made a wrong move; it wasn't Scotland that unnerved me — there was no place on earth that I would feel comfortable in.

The electrical supply in the Tower was pretty unreliable. The lights flickered all the time. And when they finally went out, sometimes they'd be off for hours. I always had candles ready.

Of course, there were noises — the place was six hundred years old. But then I started to almost see things out of the corner of my eyes. There was never anything when I turned to stare.

ONE SUNDAY MORNING towards the end of September, the wind dropped, and the silence of that empty landscape dragged at my nerves. I was standing by the window, looking out. The atmosphere was so electric, I gripped the counter-top, wishing for something to happen.

Abruptly, the knives and forks in the kitchen drawer started to rattle. The jangling metal sound sent me rushing to the kitchen. The drawers were still closed, but I could see them shaking and banging. I began to tremble, and the hair stood up on the back of my neck. The temperature dropped suddenly. Something unnatural was happening.

And in the middle of it, I heard a hammering on the

front door as if someone was coming to get me. I stood there, half in half out of the kitchen, watching the drawers shake and listening to that knocking, repeated again and again: summoning me.

And then the knives stopped their infernal racket. I stood cold but sweating, and I realised the knocking on the door had stopped too. I ran and yanked it open. I heard a car driving off, and there was nobody there.

I DIDN'T SLEEP that night. I just lay there in bed listening for the knives to start rattling again, looking at the electric light frightened it would die away. When morning came, I felt unwell with lack of sleep. I rose and went for a walk over the wild moorland, watching the wind bend the reeds, listening to the mournful cry of the curlew.

When I got back, there was a car parked in front of the Tower. The woman opened the car window as I got close. She was about thirty-five years old, straight dark brown hair down to her shoulders. Her face tapered to a determined-looking chin and she had dark eyes and strong eyebrows.

There was something about her that was very familiar, but I couldn't say what. It was as if I knew her; her name was continually at the tip of my tongue and out of reach. In the end, I gave up trying to remember who she reminded me of.

She looked at me and spoke with a Scottish accent. "I came yesterday, but you were out," she said.

She got out of the car. She was wearing clothes made for hiking — a waterproof jacket and a thick roll necked black sweater. "I'm Alice Bell, your neighbour." She extended her hand.

I shook her hand. "I didn't know I had any neighbours."

She laughed. "A couple of miles, but I'm the closest."

I guessed she was only being neighbourly. I'd been lost in my own thoughts for so long, I'd forgotten how to behave. Suddenly remembering my manners, I said, "Come in. You want a coffee? I haven't got any milk, I'm afraid."

"Black's fine." She smiled. She seemed calm and somehow detached.

She sat down, gazing around at the emptiness of the kitchen. I opened the drawer quickly and pulled out a spoon.

She laughed. "Do your drawers bite?"

"Excuse me?"

"You looked like you thought the drawer was going to bite you."

I smiled without humour. It was too close to the truth. I put the coffee down on the table in front of Alice. "Sorry, the place is so bare. I haven't gotten round to buying any furniture yet."

She shrugged and took a sip. "What do you think of Scotland?"

"Very beautiful. A bit lonely."

"It's empty here. It's the sort of place that people come to escape. Did you come to escape, Tom?"

"How do you know my name? I haven't said it."

She pointed to some letters on the mat. They'd fallen through the letterbox, and I hadn't bothered picking them up.

"Dr Tom Fisher," she said.

I found her easy to talk to. She had a way of getting me to tell her things. I hated myself for even realising she was attractive so soon after Elise, but I told her everything.

She put her hand on mine.

"I'm really sorry," I said, trying to laugh but I couldn't hold back my emotion, and it came out like a dam bursting.

I wanted to control myself, but I felt wails of grief rising out of me. I told her about Elise and my son. She lent me a handkerchief — pitying me. She kept staring at me as if she knew more than I'd told her.

Then, after she'd calmed me, there was a long, peaceful silence until she looked at her watch. "I have to go."

I watched her drive away, and I felt better than I had for a long time. I listened to music through my headphones until it was time for bed. The next day, I painted a land-scape. In it, I drew a lone male figure, walking across the moorland, coming in my direction. He was too far away for me to recognise.

But later, that night, as I washed at the hand basin in the chill bathroom, I looked up at the mirror in front of me. In it, I saw the face of my dead father. He was standing behind me in the bathroom as if he was close enough to touch, but I didn't dare turn round. I closed my eyes, and when I opened them again, he was gone.

After the first time, I saw my father all around the Tower. Unexpected, he would come, and I would look up from my book to find him at the bottom of my bed, or turn round as I was going out of the door and see him standing behind me. I shouted at him to go away.

He just stood flickering like an old fashioned projector film, vanishing and returning. I was terrified of him. I thought of leaving, but it wasn't the Tower that was haunted - it was me. So I stayed there and waited for him to return.

ALICE CAME AGAIN, and I said nothing to her about the ghost.

We started to see each other often: the only two living people in that empty land, or so it seemed. I stopped painting because what I drew frightened me. Instead, I took to reading detective novels. It was easier than thinking; it didn't threaten to turn over any stones and reveal what was hiding there. I didn't destroy the painting, I couldn't. It was like it wouldn't let me - like it had more to show me. But I turned it to the wall so I couldn't see my father, walking towards me across that bare land.

I had no interest in driving, so Alice drove me every-where — to the sea, to the long white unpopulated beaches. The beauty of the place was almost unbearable. It didn't care about us; people didn't matter to it. As she drove, I watched her silently, looking at the way the soft dark hairs curled up from the back of her neck where it lifted up to pull into a ponytail.

And at night when she was gone, he would return, standing there silently. I picked up the novel from the table beside my bed and hurled it at him. But it just flew from my hand and banged off the door. There was no one there.

And then at 3 am, I got up and started painting again. I sat at the easel in my pyjamas, frantically filling in the canvas. I tried to keep to the landscape — painting the grey sky and the bleak hills. But my hand was drawn to paint the figures that walked towards me. And as I painted, I saw with horror that it was a woman and a boy.

I threw down the paintbrush. I went to the kitchen and poured myself a whisky in a glass tumbler. That's one thing Scotland has a lot of; my father's country has whisky.

I managed to sleep eventually; I managed to convince myself that somehow my subconscious was playing tricks on me.

And then, from the middle of nightmares, I was dragged awake. A colossal weight sat on my chest. I could hardly breathe. It pressed down on me, and I stretched out my hand for the bedside lamp switch. Whatever it was, it sat corpulently on me, seething and hissing, whispering obscenities in my ear. I flicked the switch, but the light didn't come on.

I pushed up with my hand and felt long hair and a woman's face. It bent down towards me again and said, "It's me — it's Elise".

The old terror gripped me again. It's true what they say; hell isn't a place. It's a state of mind. The horror of it rendered me unconscious.

After that, there were always two of them, both my father and Elise. And I heard the boy, whispering from outside the door, whispering from the attic.

I couldn't face seeing Alice. There were things I didn't want her to know. So when she came round, I would stand quiet while she hammered on the door. She must have known I was in, but eventually, she gave up and went away. I slept during the daylight and sat up all night with the lights on. But then every night the electricity would go, and they would come again.

I hardly ate. I didn't wash; I talked to myself to break the silence that they invaded. He was always there now, but she only came when it was dark. It went on and on, night after night.

I knew that they wanted me to kill myself. I thought I needed to get help. But who would help me? The only person I knew was Alice. But she didn't come.

I got so weak from hunger that I thought I might die. I left the door open in case anyone saw it and came in, someone who could save me. But no one did.

And then Alice returned. I had almost given up hope. I thought she had gone and would never come back. The day she returned to save me, it was Halloween. She came in through the door that was permanently unlocked; I wasn't frightened of anyone outside, only those who were within.

She found me asleep on the couch. "You look dreadful. What on earth's the matter?"

I wanted her to ring a doctor, but she told me it wouldn't help. She told me that she would look after me. That night she cooked me a meal, and all the while kept asking me what the matter was. Finally, I told her.

I told her the truth about my son and wife; I expected her to hate me, but instead, she turned to me with a smile and said, "There is no escape, Tom. Not from what you did."

As I looked at her face, the awful sense of familiarity came back. I still didn't know who she was. I said, "Alice, you're scaring me."

She laughed and stared at me. The awful sense of familiarity came back. Who was she?

And Alice opened her mouth, and in place of her teeth and tongue, there was only an awful hole; a hole that went down to hell itself. She came towards me, opening her mouth wide, and said, "Alice went away. You didn't open the door to her. Maybe she could have saved you, Tom. But it's too late now."

I stammered. "What do you mean? You look like Alice."

She shook her head. "No, Tom. I'm not Alice. I'm Elise. Come to take you home."

TOM FISHER WAS FOUND dead in the Tower three days later. He had hanged himself. The postman who had come to deliver one of his now rare letters from America was suspicious of the open door.

The area seethed with gossip when first the local Police and then the FBI came to the Tower. The story eventually leaked out to the press. It transpired that Tom Fisher found out his father and wife were having an affair.

Later, he tampered with the brakes of the family car. His wife and son were killed in an automobile accident. He then went and told his father and watched while the older man slit his wrists. The boy was his father's not his.

Some say he was justified — that it was a crime of passion — that his wife and father were guilty. But Tom took their lives, then he took their money. In his rage, he also took the life of the innocent boy.

Tom Fisher tried to escape from his mortal sins; he crossed the world to get away from Elise, but in the end, she came to take him back.

The dead you wrong will not rest; they will come to you in dreams; they will come to you in lonely places; they will come to you at the end of your journey when you have nowhere else to run. There is no escaping from the dead, and, if in your heart you know you have done them wrong, then I warn you that there is an Elise who will come for you too.

4

DARK WATER

It was October 1920 when we visited Paul's father. We were on disembarkation leave after returning from the Army in the Ruhr and at a loose end. Paul's father was a vicar and had a parish in Radnorshire in Wales. The weather was beautiful as we motored up from London in Paul's Ford through the dusty market towns, taking turns to drive and declaim verses from Houseman's *The Shropshire Lad*.

Poetry was the only means I had of breaking through the fixed mirth that formed the surface of our relationship. Paul rarely spoke of anything serious, not because he shied away from it, but rather because it wasn't in his nature.

Like many young men of my generation who had survived the trenches, I owed my life to someone else. In my case, it was Paul to whom I owed the debt. After the event, he never mentioned that he had crawled with me on his back across no man's land returning to British lines. A naturally brave man of few words, I don't suppose he regarded it as any more than anyone else would do. I was glad I'd never myself been put to the test.

·   ·   ·

THE VICARAGE WAS old and rather sombre in appearance. Houses often reflect their owners and Paul had hinted that his father was rather severe — more so since his mother died. The Reverend Gordon was a tall thin man, and he greeted his son formally with little warmth and me with brittle politeness. The only one to show any enthusiasm was the dog "Digger" who frolicked and fawned around Paul's feet.

Later, over dinner, Paul bubbled with his usual good humour, recounting stories of the doings of our friends in the Army. Paul and I, at least, were much amused, even though I had heard and told the same stories a hundred times. Reverend Gordon seemed distracted. He smiled thinly, and after the meal quickly excused himself and went to his library.

Paul suggested that we visit the local hostelry. He had been away to school and followed his father through a succession of parishes in rural England and Wales. Paul hardly knew the local area and was not recognised by its inhabitants. Before we went out of the door, Paul made a point of asking his father if he would care to join us. I was not surprised when he refused.

"I knew he wouldn't come," said Paul lighting a cigarette, "but I thought I'd ask him anyway."

It was a chilly Autumn evening, and the prospect of the quarter of a mile walk to the pub was quite refreshing after the muggy atmosphere of the house. The pub itself stood in the centre of the few houses strung along the road that made up the hamlet of Llantrisant. It was an old building; the black wooden panelling attractive, if a little worn, against the white plaster rendering of the outside wall. The windows were closed but through them seeped the sound of laughter and talk into the night. Paul pulled the heavy door to allow me in. As soon as the door had begun to open, the chatter stopped, and we were confronted by a gallery of hard country faces, their expressions more hostile than curious.

There were a few roughly carved turnip lanterns on the window ledges and above the fire. Candles flickered ominously through their jagged eyes and mouths.

Paul strode into the room and clapped me on the shoulder "My treat. A pint of bitter for you I take it." They began to talk again, but not the laughter and jokes that had prevailed before we entered. Instead, a low, angry whispering issued from all corners of the room. After I had drunk my pint, I was keen to go. Paul at first wanted to stay for another, as if he was oblivious to the atmosphere in the pub. But when I insisted he came out with me.

Just as we were nearly at the door, a large man barred our way. I could see from the ugly smile on his face that he was playing to the audience. "You're the vicar's son, aren't you? Your daddy know you're here, does he? Keeps himself to himself, the vicar."

A low laugh ran round the room. Our tormentor continued. "Just as well. He doesn't belong here, and neither do you. Only he knows it, and you don't seem to."

Paul was a strong man — the star of the Regimental rugby team. I had in the past needed to handle myself as well, but there were an awful lot of them. Paul straightened his back and stared the man in the eye.

I put my arm on his and said: "Come on, Paul, I can't say that I particularly enjoy their company anyway."

We pushed past the big man, and he let us go.

The moon sailed high above, and we walked home by its

light, along the road, through the dense woodland on both sides. We joked as we went along, made braver and stronger by the beer, as we relived our altercation.

"I should have punched his head in, the lout."

"Just as well you didn't Paul. Your father's vicar here. What would the bishop say when he read it in the local paper?"

Just then there was a sound from the undergrowth where the trees came very close on both sides of the road. I started — my imagination already effected by the baleful moonlight. From the inky blackness, I heard it again. Something was moving in the wood. It was not the sound itself that alarmed me, but the heaviness of the noise; otherwise, I would have shrugged it off as a fox or a badger.

It was too big to be either of them. It had sounded like something dragging itself through the broken branches on the forest floor. But when I listened again, I heard nothing. Paul hadn't stopped and was some paces ahead. "Did you hear that, Paul?"

"No. Come on, there's whisky back at the house."

THE NEXT DAY WAS SUNDAY. Paul must have explained to his father that I was an atheist because they let me sleep while they went to church.

They were longer coming back than I had anticipated. I ate breakfast, and then I found my way to Reverend Gordon's well-stocked library. Shelves of dark spined books on theology and related subjects pressed in on the room from all sides. In its centre were a massive oak desk and a leather-covered chair. I traced my finger idly along a row of books. They were not just in English; many were in German,

Greek and Latin. I picked up one about ancient heresies. Perhaps some invisible hand guided me to it.

Reflecting afterwards, I could see no other reason why such a title should catch my interest. But maybe it was some perception that the book was out of line with the others, that it had been removed and read more recently than they had. The book smelled damp. It was mid-Victorian in date, and the inner binding and frontispiece were speckled brown with age. Its contents were turgid enough, but as I leafed through it, a sheaf of hand-written notes fell from within it to the floor. I must confess I was far more intrigued by these than by anything else in the library. The chance to peer discreetly into someone else's private thoughts has always been tempting to me.

I placed the book on the desk and unfolded the notes. There were several thousand words of a neat hand-written script; somehow, the look of the writing matched what I knew of the Reverend Gordon's personality. I was convinced that he was the author, and despite the age of the book, the notes appeared relatively recent.

Quickly scanning the words, with one ear open for the return of my host, I tried to make sense of them. They seemed to refer to the worship of some dark deity — some ancient cult that still persisted from the nightmares of mankind's past. Hardly a topic for a churchman. Not that he in any way condoned the sect; the notes were bitterly condemnatory.

I would have said that they were the thoughts of a man terrified by the words he put down on the paper in front of him. Although I did not read them in great detail, I could plainly see that they became more disjointed as they went on, till, in the end, the train of thought seemed smashed and replaced by random, ghastly images.

The object of the worship was called "Lord of Dark Water", but it was difficult to understand what kind of thing exactly it was.

I heard the front door open, and Paul's voice greeting the maid. I put the book with the notes in it back in its place and went to meet him. He and his father were hanging up their hats. Paul looked up at me as I entered.

"Hello, old boy, have a good kip?"

"Yes, thanks for letting me sleep on." I glanced, half-embarrassed at Paul's father and said, in what I intended to be a pleasantly cheery tone,

"I've been looking at your books, sir."

He made some comment, nothing of much importance, but his eyes caught mine and in their depths, I could have sworn there was a flash of fear. Then he resumed his brusquely polite air and excused himself.

Paul was merry enough and suggested we muck around with a cricket bat and ball in the garden. The afternoon was hot, and we passed it in a friendly fashion.

The next day we mooched around and then on Tuesday when we were both becoming a little bored, we decided that we would drive to Shrewsbury. With his usual skill, Paul got chatting to a couple of nurses out for the afternoon in the park. On our journey home, we stopped for a meal at a pub in Craven Arms. It was Halloween.

We arrived back to some commotion. Jenkins, the gardener and handyman, appeared as we were garaging the car. He seemed to be in rather a state. "What's the matter, Jenkins? You look a bit glum," said Paul stepping out of the car.

"Digger's gone missing, sir."

Paul was concerned to hear about the dog. "Oh, dear. Where? When?"

"Your father was walking him by the old wood, and he must have gone after a rabbit or something. He hasn't come back."

"Didn't Reverend Gordon look for him?" I asked.

Jenkins became quiet.

"There's a superstition about the wood. The locals won't go near it," explained Paul. "My father, for some reason, has caught the same bug. Well, we'd better go and get the dog. He could be stuck down a hole."

"Don't go in the dark, sir," said Jenkins, looking actually quite afraid.

"He's right, Paul. We'll never see anything now. Better leave it till first light."

Paul was naturally a man of action, but he could see sense in what I was saying. "But Digger was my mother's dog. He's been with us for eight years."

"We've got more chance of finding him in the light. We'll get up at dawn; I promise."

I SLEPT LIGHTLY and somewhere in the middle of the night, I got up to go to the bathroom. As I switched the light on, I was astounded and more than a little startled to find Reverend Gordon standing by the window. He had been standing there stock still in the dark. He was fully dressed, and his eyes had an odd vacant look. I would have assumed he was drunk if Paul hadn't told me previously that he was tea-total.

I attempted to give some normality to the situation by greeting him. "Shame about the dog, sir. Paul's very upset. But we'll get up at dawn and go looking for him."

My words sounded stilted even to myself, but he hadn't heard them. He just stared at me. I thought then that perhaps he was sleepwalking. But then he said, "It's coming for me. I heard it in the trees."

I was utterly dumbfounded and could see nothing I could practically do. The man seemed mentally ill as if he held onto his reason by his fingernails alone.

Leaving him, I went on to the bathroom, and when I came back, he had gone. Paul knocked on my door, almost on the dot of five o'clock. There was already some light in the sky. We pulled on our coats, having decided to postpone breakfast until we returned. "Do you know where the dog went missing?" I asked him.

"Yes, I asked my father last night. I know where he means well enough. It's not actually that far."

I wondered if I should tell him of my strange meeting with his father, but decided against it. We left the house and made our way onto the road. The previous day's sunshine had been replaced by low grey clouds. It had rained during the night and was promising more to come. We followed the road to the village until we entered the wood a little before the place I had heard the noise.

"This is the quickest way — if we cut through the trees here." He stepped onto the first bar of the gate and lightly swung his body over.

I followed, but my skin began to prickle with some unknown dread as we left the roadside.

The gloom of the trees was oppressive — the leaf mould was thick and soft underfoot and made me often stumble as we trudged through the trickling damp of the half over-grown path. Nettles and rank weeds came up to our hips, and all the time, I kept expecting to hear something moving in the bushes behind me. Paul started calling out the dog's name over and over again into the trees. We were walking uphill, and I was panting slightly and watching Paul some yards ahead.

There was a noise, and then something jumped out of the undergrowth and seized him. It happened very quickly, but I was left with the almost photographic memory of a half-naked man covered in tattoos savagely beating Paul on the side of his head.

Then I felt an enormous blow to my own head. I was scrabbling in the twigs on the wet ground with leaves and dirt scratching my face. There was a weight on my back. I struggled to get up but was forced down again. I pushed upwards, my knees straining and feet slipping on the oozing floor.

I heard Paul scream as if he was being hurt, and I was filled with fear that I would also be. They held me tight and shoved Paul along in front of me. His face was streaming blood.

I yelled at him, asking him if he was all right. He answered, but the words were inarticulate, choked in his own blood. The men who were herding me struck me again from behind with something substantial. Whatever it was knocked the wind out of me, and stinging blood ran into my eye from a wound on my eyebrow blinding me.

We stumbled on through the woods along a distinct path. I stole glances at our captors. Their faces underneath the blue tattooed whorls and spirals were similar to those of the men in the local pub. The swirling patterns reminded me of drawings I had seen of the ancient Picts.

Then we stopped. To the left, a path led away from the main trail down into a cleft in the rock. Below, I guessed, was some kind of cave. An overwhelming terror filled me that these painted men would drag me down into the hearth.

Paul halted. He dug in his heels. They had to shove him forwards, but he held back, fighting them. They heaved, two of them at once, and he fell. Down on the ground, his weight was more difficult to move, and his guards shouted back to the men who were pushing me.

It seemed so oddly out of context that their voices had the same broad vowels as local farmers discussing the cattle auctions. Perhaps they were local farmers — underneath the bucolic comfort of the market scene was the filthy bestiality and violence that filled these painted men.

Paul slipped further down the slope and banged his head against a rock. I heard the thick noise of a blow against the bone. Two of the three men who had been with me went down to help manhandle him.

I saw my chance. The one left with me was barely more than a boy underneath the face paint. With the strength that only pure terror can engender, I lashed out. My fist connected solidly with his mouth, and he went reeling. I ran, leaving Paul behind me.

I ran through the trees, the spiky twigs tearing my face and catching my clothes. Blind with panic, I tried to put as much ground as possible between them and me. My blood pumped in my ears as I crashed through the wood, but in my imagination, I heard and saw them close behind me.

Only when my lungs were on fire, and I could no longer make one leg follow the other did I fall to the ground. If they caught me now, I no longer had any power to save myself. I lay there in the mulch, and as my breathing subsided, I was alone with the unnatural silence of the forest and my own dumb terror.

I do not know how long I lay there, but eventually, I got up and sometime later struck upon the road. I was terrified that someone from the village would see me and take me back to the painted men, so I slunk along like an animal, blood dripping from the cuts and scratches on my face and hands. I imagine that I looked quite appalling when Jenkins found me in the grounds of the vicarage.

He took me to Reverend Gordon. I garbled out the story of what had happened, gradually correcting myself and repeating myself until I had explained it as cogently as I could.

Reverend Gordon's reaction showed me that he understood what had happened long before I got to the end. His face revealed, not concern for a lost son, but rather horror for his own safety. He began to walk away from me, and I followed. I yelled at him. I kept on shouting till he reached the library door which he slammed in my face.

I stood outside, hammering on the door. "Sir, your son is at risk. His life is in danger. You must come and help."

All I heard was him saying weakly, "I can do nothing."

"So you'd leave him?"

But this time he was silent. In disgust, I turned away. Jenkins stood in the hallway.

Jenkins suddenly said; "He did try and fight it once, sir. But the terror of it mastered him." Jenkin's face was hollow. "Either you follow it, or you hide from it. You can't beat it, sir. People either leave this village or become slaves to it. Either way, they never talk. But he found out sir, the Reverend did. He tried to fight it, but he couldn't."

Jenkins saw I was in no state to listen to him and he left me alone, sobbing, standing there in the hallway. Through all that, I knew that I couldn't leave Paul. He had gone to the edge with me on that day in France. I must go to the edge with him, never mind how deep the abyss.

In the games room, on the wall were some hunting guns. I took down a rifle. Paul told me he had hunted with it himself, so I knew it worked. He had even shown me where the bullets were. I loaded the gun and filled my pockets with them and then made my way outside.

The trail to the cave was easy to find again. It took me about twenty minutes to get to where we were taken. As I got closer and saw the cave mouth, my heart raced with fear, but there was no one there. I entered and followed it as it twisted and turned into the earth. The light was shut out behind by the bends in the tunnel, and I lit my lighter. Its feeble flame was threatened by every gust of wind from the unseen depths before me. Then I turned another bend and saw lights ahead.

There was a large cavern, lit by three paraffin lamps. Darkness reigned outside the circle of flickering yellow light. Inside the cave, five painted men knelt in adoration. They gazed at a black pool which filled most of the cavern. Paul was there also, a broken insect in an angular heap at the edge of the dark lake.

The painted men were chanting and intently watching the water. And then the pool heaved with a sick motion. The liquid rolled again. This time, when the waves subsided around the lip of the pool, something was there. Something arose from the undisturbed depths. Like some mixture of pitch and vomit, the flaccid shape pulled itself half out of the water towards Paul. The chatter of the painted men increased, and I heard Paul cry out as he saw what was approaching him. One of the painted men got up and moved as if to push Paul's body closer towards the thing.

It felt its way like an enormous slug. I realised that this thing was their god and that they and their ancestors had worshipped it since before history was written. The painted man pushed Paul again towards his greedy god. I raised the rifle to my shoulder and aimed.

My first shot took the man in the back, and he pitched forward towards the thing. It paused and then began to move in the direction of the painted man as if it, in its loathsome coldness, it could smell his hot blood.

The others turned to see where the shot had come from. I fired again and hit another. They ran for cover like frightened rabbits, and one painted savage missed his footing and slipped into the pool. The feeding slug slid over the victim of my first shot, digesting him alive. It shot out a tongue, like a frog catching a fly. It rolled the fleeing man and pulled him towards its pulsating body.

There were still many of the painted men. They saw me and came at me, brandishing ritual stone axes, their faces twisted with hate. A stone flew in from the side and hit me on the shoulder. I yelled in pain and dropped my rifle. Now I was defenceless.

I spun and saw a savage running at me. The cultist swung his axe at my head. It would have brained me, but I stepped back but in doing so lost my balance and slipped. I fell full length, backwards onto the muddy ground, knocking the wind out of me. I lay there helpless, and the cultist stood above me, preparing to swing down the axe, a terrible grin of triumph on his face.

I felt I would die. But then there was a shot. Someone fired a rifle from the shadows, and it struck the savage in his chest. He fell to the ground, dying, dropping the axe. I didn't know what was happening, but the rifle rang out again. Taking advantage of the confusion, I rolled onto my knees, the pain in my shoulder was tremendous. The unseen shooter fired again. The cultists screamed, but in the dark, I couldn't clearly make out what was happening.

Then there was another scream, more terrible than any I had heard. A shout, and then silence.

I waited there, expecting the slug thing to drag its way towards us and ready to run. But it did not come.

Eventually, gathering my dazed wits, I stood painfully and ran towards Paul. Pulling him up on my shoulder, he was still conscious as I lifted him. I managed to get him out of the cave and into the trees. On a patch of grass, I examined his wounds. There was nothing life-threatening.

We rested a while, and then I helped him onto his feet. We had to pass by the mouth of the cave on our way out of the wood. I was pretty confident that the painted men were no longer a threat, but I wanted to be sure there was no one around. I listened for a while before we approached the cave mouth, but there was no sound.

As we turned around the corner and the cave mouth came into view, I saw something; some bundle of dark clothes by the entrance. It looked as if had been squashed or emptied; the soft tissue sucked out of it.

Although I did not want to, I left Paul and went over to investigate. The slug thing had been here, looking for us. But instead of us, there, at my feet, was the half-digested body of Paul's father, a useless hunting rifle still clutched in his mangled fingers.

It seemed the old man had finally found his courage.

5

THE HOUSE IN THE FOREST

The rain streamed over the windscreen of the now stationary car, and Rebecca blurted, "It's all my fault. I'm sorry." She was almost in tears.

"No, don't worry, lass. It's not your fault; it's this crappy car," said Gavin, the driver.

They'd just met. Rebecca was hitchhiking in desperation to get home as there were no more trains. Her mother was ill back in Carlisle, and Rebecca had to get down from Stirling where she was studying. She'd rung mum to tell her she'd got a lift, but not to wait up because she was going to be late.

Like everyone else, she'd been told about stranger danger but she wasn't scared of Gavin, even out here in this dense wood. Gavin had an honest face, plus his thirteen-year-old daughter, Emma, was sitting in the front seat.

She'd stood by the road for ages in the rain, thumb out until after about a hundred cars, one stopped. Rebecca ran to catch up as they pulled in down the road. Gavin and his daughter, Emma, were on their way home from a dancing competition back to where they lived in the Scottish

Borders. That was before, and now they were all stuck in the middle of nowhere.

"I don't like it here," said the kid, Emma, gazing out through the misting windows.

"The spark plugs have got damp," Gavin muttered. "It's a known problem with these Fords. In bad weather, the moisture runs down and collects in the plugs."

Rebecca hadn't noticed engine misfiring, though Gavin started to complain about it five miles back. Finally, he pulled over by the side of the dark highway. Now they were broken down, and this was just the worst place to be broken down.

They'd been driving through the National Park and entered the vast forest about twenty minutes previously. The fir trees huddled close to the road, and there was no sign of an end to their dark ranks. Through the rain-soaked windows, Rebecca saw the shady trees crowding on both sides of the two-lane highway. There was precious little traffic on the road either; it was late, and the weather was awful. Rebecca knew she should have stayed in town, but she had little money to spare for a room, and she wanted to get home to her mother.

"I'll walk to the nearest garage," Gavin said.

"No, dad!" shouted Emma in a voice that was a cross between a scared little girl and the petulant teenager.

Gavin gave Emma a look that Rebecca didn't get. But they were family and knew each other's body language and things. Anyway, he smiled and ruffled her hair, which Emma obviously hated.

Gavin's hair was shaved short, but not completely bald. What hair he had was ginger, and he wore a red puffer jacket which set it off. Emma was slight for her age. She had unfortunately coloured curly hair, not the Titian or Auburn beloved of the pre-Raphaelite painters, nor even the Copper that kids hate —and grown women covet—but carrot red.

"Em, we can't sit here all night," said Gavin. "We'll freeze to death."

"I'll look after her," Rebecca offered. "If you go."

Gavin smiled at Rebecca, and she looked away. Rebecca knew she had to be careful with men. She had long, straight blonde hair, blue eyes with a corona of gold around the pupil like spring flowers and a very curvy figure that turned heads at a hundred paces.

Gavin clicked the car door open, allowing the weather to come howling in. The cold wash of drizzle and the strong pine smell of the forest took Rebecca's breath away.

"Daddy, please, no!" said Emma.

"How far is it, Gavin?" said Rebecca. Emma's voice had made her nervy.

He said, "From the map, there's a hamlet and a garage in about five miles."

Rebecca frowned. "It's a long way."

He shrugged. "On a night like this. But it'll take me maybe forty-five minutes there, and then I'll get a lift back on their repair truck."

"Are you sure they'll have the parts?" said Rebecca.

"It's a Ford. They should, and out of the way communities like this always have mechanics."

"I don't want you to go, daddy," said Emma.

"I'll be back within an hour."

Rebecca didn't want to be there all night, and he wasn't asking her to walk. He should go. "It'll be okay, Emma," she said. "I'll take care of you."

"Okay," said Gavin, "I'll be back soon," and he shut the door.

The rain drummed on the roof as Gavin's red-coated figure walked off down the road. Rebecca didn't envy him.

Emma leaned forward to turn on the radio. There wasn't much on; a Country and Western Station and a voice reciting the Shipping Forecast.

"Turn it off. We don't want to make the car battery flat," said Rebecca.

"I want to listen to something," said Emma.

Rebecca said, "Don't worry, there's nothing to be scared of."

Emma turned round. "What if there is?"

"There isn't." Kids always imagine things, Rebecca thought. She'd just have to keep Emma calm by distracting her until Gavin came back.

BUT GAVIN DID NOT COME BACK SOON. Rebecca checked the time on her phone. There was no signal in that place, and she only had 15% battery. She switched off the phone, and as its blue light winked out, it was tar-black dark.

Gavin had been gone an hour and a half. From her breathing, Rebecca thought Emma had drifted off to sleep. She didn't know how she could; because even with her coat and scarf on and her hood pulled up, it was freezing. The wind and rain howled outside and an eternity went by as she sat under the endless downpour. Only one car went by in that whole time, and it didn't stop.

Emma woke with a start. "Where's dad?" she said. Rebecca thought she heard misery in the teenager's voice. "What if he's hurt?"

Rebecca said, "I doubt that could happen. There's nothing out here."

"I want to go and find him."

"No, that's stupid; we should stay in the car. What if he comes back and finds us gone?"

"No, I'm going to find him." Emma shoved open the car door and stepped out into the stream of water that was running down the road.

Rebecca sighed, but she couldn't let a thirteen-year-old walk five miles on an empty road in the middle of the night. Out in the weather, the rain drenched her, and the cold pierced her coat.

Trees stood tall and black on either side. Rebecca thought she saw Emma's small figure hurrying some way ahead, but shadows moved in shadows, and her eyes could have been seeing what she wanted them to see, rather than what was. She had to catch Emma up. Rebecca broke into a run, shouting Emma's name and almost ran into her in the dark.

Emma strode forward, her head down against the weather. Rebecca took her arm, and the girl didn't shrug it off. She realised that Emma was crying.

"Hey, what's up?"

"I want my dad," snivelled the girl. "He should have come back, and he hasn't. I'm worried about him."

Rebecca held Emma tighter. "He'll be okay. He must have just got delayed. There's no phone signal for him to phone us."

"I just want to see him," Emma said.

"We should go back to the car," Rebecca said.

"No, I want to find my dad."

"Really, Emma..."

"No! You don't care. He's not your dad. I want to find my dad."

Rebecca sighed as they walked together in silence, their shoes clumping and scraping on the rough country road.

Rebecca's socks and feet were wet, and the rain had also soaked through the legs of her trousers.

"I'm freezing," said Emma.

"Let's go back to the car."

"No, I want my dad."

Then the shadows changed ahead. The trees to their left fell back. There was a wall of slate about four feet high and a gateway. Beside the dark stone of the left pillar of the gate posts was a sign:

Armboth Hall

"A house," said Emma. "Maybe he went there for a telephone." Her voice seemed suddenly keen.

"Yes," said Rebecca warily. There was something ominous about this dark drive that led deep into the forest that moved and sighed in the wild wind.

"*They will* have a phone," said Emma.

"Maybe, but it's the middle of the night. They'll be asleep."

"How far have we walked?"

Rebecca shrugged. "I don't know. Maybe a mile."

"Then it's another four to the village. Can we see if the people who live here will help us? Please? We're just two girls. They won't be scared of us."

"I might be scared of them," Rebecca laughed.

Emma shook her head. "You needn't be. They live in a hall. They'll be posh." She tugged at Emma's rain-soaked hand. "Come on. Please?"

Rebecca hesitated. A dull sense of foreboding took hold of her, but Emma tugged her arm forward.

The rain was still sheeting down. It was pretty awful out

here. Maybe the people here would have a phone. Or even a car.

The two girls walked down the drive, the dirty gravel crunching underfoot. On either side trees reared up; larches and pines, but they could only see the first rank of them; the gloomy forest depths were invisible, brooding out of sight. Rebecca had the strangest feeling they were being watched from within the trees, and she squeezed Emma's hand tighter as if she was reassuring the girl rather than the other way round.

If Emma noticed her companion's gradually increasing anxiety, Rebecca was pleased to see that she didn't show it. Emma was walking faster, Rebecca guessed she was anxious to get out of the rain.

The hall drive was about a quarter of a mile long. Then the forest opened out, and an old house loomed up, looking like it had been there for hundreds of years. It may well have been. It certainly appeared as if it was built for a past age of war with battlements rising high above, and rows and rows of windows like lines of blind eyes.

Even in the gloom, Rebecca saw the hall was not well kept. If they'd hoped to find a wealthy family with a Mercedes Benz conveniently parked outside, their hopes were now disappointed.

Emma pointed to the first floor. "There's a light on." It burned a faint yellow, not like electricity, more like the gleam of an oil lamp.

Before Rebecca could stop her, Emma ran to the door and lifted the rusted knocker, an iron ring held in the mouth of an ancient iron wolf.

She hammered it down: Bang. Bang. Bang.

The dull noise echoed inside the house.

For some reason, Emma shuddered; it felt like they were

summoning something from inside the house. When no reply came, Rebecca was relieved, but Emma lifted the ring to knock again.

"Don't," said Rebecca.

Emma turned. "Don't what?"

"Don't bother knocking again. Let's go."

"Maybe they didn't hear."

"They heard okay."

"How do you know?"

"Anyone would have heard."

There was an awkward tension, Rebecca wanted to leave. "Please," Rebecca said, holding out her hand to the girl.

Emma shook her head. "No. I want to go in. It's cold and raining. I'm not waiting out here."

"There's no one in," Rebecca said.

"The light," said Emma, pointing again. "There is."

Emma went to knock, but Rebecca stretched out to stop her. Her nerves wouldn't bear that noise again. For some reason, fear filled her when she thought about who might answer the door.

But it was too late; someone moved on the other side, fiddling with the lock. Rebecca stepped back. She wanted to leave, but she didn't know why. She said, "Let's go. Run."

"What?" said Emma said, laughing. "You're daft. There's someone here now."

"I know, but..."

"But what?"

"I don't like this place."

"You're stupid," Emma said.

And then the door opened. A woman stood there. She was tall and thin with black hair streaked with grey. Her cheeks were hollow, and her eyes were so dark they looked like holes in her face. The woman didn't speak.

Emma grinned. "Our car broke down."

"Yes," said Rebecca, standing behind Emma, putting her hand on the younger girl's shoulder, as if to guard her.

"We thought you might have a phone?" Emma said.

Finally, the woman spoke. "Yes, I have a phone."

"Great," said Emma. She stepped forward. Rebecca tried to hold her back. Rebecca said, "Can we use it?"

The woman nodded and moved aside. "Enter. If you want. Enter my house."

Emma stepped through the door, but Rebecca hesitated. "Emma..." she stammered. Emma turned round, a smile on her face. "Come on. You're a lot older than me, but you're being a baby."

The woman closed and locked the heavy door behind them. "I'm Mrs Lukas," she said. She smiled, but her smile held no welcome.

THE HOUSE LOOKED OLD, and it smelled old. Centuries hung around in corners, pressing themselves against the dark stone walls loitering on the old wooden furniture. The floor was stone-flagged, and a dim, underpowered light bulb burned in a dirty lampshade above their heads. Emma said, "My dad's gone to the village - to the garage. Do you know the number?

Rebecca explained, "My phone doesn't work here."

Mrs Lukas stood with her back to the front door. "No, there's no mobile phone coverage here."

"But you have a phone."

"I said so, yes."

"If you could show me it and the phone book."

"I'll ring them for you," said Mrs Lukas.

Rebecca brushed her blonde hair from her face, dark now with rain. "I don't mind ringing them. Then I'd be sure—"

"I'll ring them."

"Oh, okay." This wasn't going well. Rebecca tried to be gracious. "I hope we didn't wake you."

Mrs Lukas stared at her. "I don't sleep."

"Not ever?" Rebecca said.

Mrs Lukas didn't answer.

"It's okay. If you just ring then we'll be gone," said Rebecca.

Mrs Lukas turned the key in the door, as if to make sure she'd locked it.

Rebecca's heart jolted. "Why did you lock the door?"

Mrs Lukas said, "You never know who's out in the forest."

Rebecca really wanted to phone the garage herself, if only to speak to someone from the ordinary world. She didn't want to step any further into the house.

"This is old," said Emma, guessing her thoughts. She looked down the dark corridor with its black and white Victorian tiles that disappeared into the darkness. An old wooden staircase led upstairs. There were doors on either side. Mrs Lukas opened the door to the right. "Go in here."

Emma went blithely ahead. She flicked on the electric light. Once again, it was a weak bulb. Rebecca thought it was only about 40-Watts. She imagined Mrs Lukas as a mean old woman who'd rather sit in the gloom than pay for a bright bulb.

The furniture was old fashioned. There was a horsehair sofa covered in faded green satin and two chairs with the same upholstery. Their legs were scuffed and kicked. A threadbare rug lay in the centre of the floor on floorboards that had once been varnished. Emma pulled a face at the old chairs but went to sit in one.

"I don't suppose you have a towel?" said Rebecca. "We're very wet."

Mrs Lukas didn't answer at once but then said, "Of course." Then she turned and left.

"I don't like this room," said Emma. "I even think grandma would find this old-fashioned."

"It's horrible," said Rebecca.

Emma sat there swinging her legs, kicking her heels against the wooden legs of the chair.

The noise went right through Rebecca. She barked, "Stop it!"

Emma looked affronted. "You can't tell me what to do," and she kept on kicking. Rebecca thought if the kid kept doing that she would get up and give her a smack.

Then Mrs Lukas returned. She held two grey towels and gave one to Emma and one to Rebecca. Rebecca turned hers over in her hand. She guessed the grey towel was supposed to be white, but at least it was clean. Rebecca stood and took off her coat. She felt Mrs Lukas's eyes boring into her back and half-turned. The old woman was staring at her.

"Did you phone?" said Rebecca.

Mrs Lukas nodded.

They waited for Mrs Lukas to say something more.

"And?" said Rebecca, failing to keep the irritation from her voice.

"He had left."

"Dad had left?" Emma said.

"Where did he go?" Rebecca said.

Mrs Lukas fixed the girl with her black eyes. "He's coming here."

"You told him we were here?"

"Of course," said Mrs Lukas.

"It's not far, is it?" Emma said.

"Not far."

"So, he'll be here soon."

Mrs Lukas smiled. "You have nothing to fear."

"What do you mean?" Rebecca said.

"I'm not frightened," Emma said.

Mrs Lukas put her hand on the door. "Shall I close it after I leave?"

"Yes, please," said Emma.

"No," said Rebecca simultaneously. "Where are you going anyway?"

"I'm going to sit and wait."

"Sit and wait?"

"That's what I said."

Emma darted a look at Rebecca. Without another word, Mrs Lukas turned and left, closing the door behind them.

"I wish we hadn't come here," said Rebecca.

"Don't worry. Dad will be here soon."

OUTSIDE IT WAS STILL RAINING. Old fashioned lace curtains that Mrs Lukas hadn't bothered to draw hung at the window. The room smelled so musty that Rebecca wondered whether it had been used in years. Time went by until Emma grew quiet, and Rebecca felt her own eyes grow heavy. Then after drifting, she forced herself awake. The room was still lit by the dull bulb and rain still fell, streaking the window. Emma was still asleep. Rebecca checked her phone. It was nearly two a.m. so Gavin should be here by now. She only had 8% battery left. Soon her phone would switch itself off, and she wouldn't know what time it was.

She dozed and awoke in a flash of panic. She looked at

the room door and saw it was open. She sat suddenly, staring at it. Surely, Mrs Lukas had closed it when she left.

Emma's eyes were wide. "What time is it?"

"It's late. Your dad's not here yet."

"He'll be here soon," Emma said and sat up too. The room felt colder now. It was past the middle of the night.

Rebecca got up and walked to where she'd dropped her coat on the chair. The coat was still very damp, and it wouldn't do for warming her. Then she stood at the window. She could see nothing outside, but she imagined the endless forest and that long ominous drive up to the house.

Rebecca turned suddenly. "What if Mrs Lukas didn't ring your dad?"

"Why would she lie?" said Emma.

Rebecca said, "I don't like her. She's odd."

Emma said, "She's just a weird old woman. Dad will be here soon. Don't worry."

"I hate it here," Rebecca muttered.

Emma said, "It won't be long now. Soon dad's headlights will come shining up the drive."

"I hope so," Rebecca said,

Minutes went by. "I'm going to go and look for Mrs Lukas," Rebecca said. "I'll find the phone, and I'll ring the garage myself just to make sure…"

"They'll be shut now," said Emma.

"Probably get call outs all night. And they might be with your dad," Rebecca said. "I'll just go and look. You stay here."

Emma said, "Please don't leave me alone."

"I'll go and find the phone. It'll be okay. You just close the door. You'll be fine here. Mrs Lukas is just a stupid old woman."

"I don't want you to go."

"I have to."

"You don't."

"If I can speak to someone on the phone, I'll be reassured," said Rebeca. "Just wait."

Emma came up and grabbed Rebecca's wrist. Rebecca gently took the girl's hands off her arm again and walked to the door. She hesitated and turned back. "If I can't find the phone, we'll just leave."

"It's still raining."

"But it's better than this horrid place."

Emma said, "No, I'd rather wait here than go outside."

Rebecca said, "If I can't satisfy myself that she's really phoned, we're leaving."

Then she closed the door behind her.

THE HOUSE outside the room was deathly quiet, but Mrs Lukas had left the hall light on, inadequate as it was. Rebecca's feet echoed on the tiles as she walked to the entrance hall. She put her hand on the doorknob of the room opposite the one Emma and she had been in. As she did so, for some reason, she stopped. What could be behind that door? This place just creeped her out, but downstairs near the front door was the kind of place phones usually were. Rebecca turned the knob and pushed the door open. Inside, the room had the same smell of must as the other room and felt equally unused. Sliding her hand up the wall, she found the light switch. It looked like the house was wired in the 1930s and had never been updated since. She flicked the switch, but nothing happened.

It seemed Mrs Lukas was too mean to even put a bulb in this room. The room was very dark. She took out her phone and put on the flashlight function, even though it would drain her battery. She saw more old furniture and a bookcase filled with ancient-looking books. She couldn't read the titles from the door, and she didn't want to go in. There was no phone there, anyway. She turned and got a cold prickling up her spine like someone was watching her. She glanced around the hall, shining her phone beam down the corridor. Then she switched off the light. She couldn't afford to waste battery.

As she walked, she thought she saw movement at the top of the stairs.

"Hello?" she said.

There was definitely some kind of shuffling.

Rebecca backed towards the front door. "Hello?" she said again, studying the stairs in case anyone descended. "Mrs Lukas?" she said hesitantly. Who else could it be?

But whoever was up there wasn't coming down. Rebecca swallowed. Her heart beat fast, and her throat was tight. If she couldn't find the phone, she'd just get Emma, and they would leave.

But something really was there at the top of the stairs. Rebecca's pulse thumped in her ears. The old freak woman was watching her, standing in the shadows. "Mrs Lukas!" she shouted.

Still, there was no answer. From outside, they'd seen the only light on the floor above. That's where Mrs Lukas lived. It was stupid being scared of the old bat. She didn't believe Mrs Lukas had rung the garage for whatever reason of her own. Rebecca would just go and find the old woman's room, knock on the door and demand to use the phone herself.

But she hesitated, her hand gripping the bannister. Then, gathering her courage, she mounted the steps, first one flight, then a turn to the left and then another flight. After the third flight, she was on the landing. There was hardly any light up here, but she saw that a corridor ran down the length of the house. She guessed the layout would match that of the floor below.

She found the light switch and turned it on. Above her, a brass chandelier had room for three bulbs, but only one was fitted. In the dim electric light it gave off, the rugs were old and faded. On the wall behind her, above the window, was a stuffed animal's head: a black wolf. She thought wolves had been extinct here for centuries.

Then her spine tingled, and she spun around, once again convinced someone was watching her—this time from down the corridor.

Mrs Lukas's room must be down here. She had decided she was going to demand to use the phone, but something held her back. A primal instinct of self-preservation didn't want her to go down there. She wouldn't let the freaky old woman scare her, so she straightened her back and stepped forward. A glow came from under a door to her right. That must be the old woman's room. There she would be "sitting and waiting" — whatever the hell that meant.

Rebecca wouldn't be rude. She wouldn't accuse her of not phoning the garage —she would merely insist on being shown the phone and make the call herself. She knocked on the door, but no sound of movement came from inside the room. Maybe the old bat had fallen asleep after all. Rebecca knocked more insistently this time, but there was still no response.

With her heart going crazy, Rebecca turned the door handle and edged the door open. Inside, she glimpsed an old-fashioned bedroom. A water ewer stood on the table with a jug. Rebecca shoved the door wider until she saw the foot of a bed. She cleared her throat. "Mrs Lukas," but no one answered. An oil lamp burned on the table beside the bed. That was the light they'd seen from outside. But the bed was empty — it hadn't been slept in. Then she heard a noise from outside the room, down the corridor. Someone was playing hide and seek with her.

Rebecca ran from the room and to the top of the stairs. Her breath came in frightened gulps as she stood there, peering down into the hall. She'd forgotten the phone now; they were just going to leave. She'd go and get Emma and get out of that place.

She ran down the first flight, the second then stopped. The door of the room where Emma had been, stood open. Rebecca felt dizzy.

"Emma!" she shouted, but there was silence. She hurried down the last few stairs but even from the stair bottom, she saw the room was empty.

Maybe Emma had left the house. Perhaps she'd been scared and just left. Rebecca ran to the heavy wooden door with its big iron latch and below that an empty iron keyhole. She lifted the latch and pulled at the door, but the door was locked against her.

Rebecca was petrified now. Again, she turned, convinced someone was watching her. "Emma!" she yelled desperately into the house, and her voice echoed down the silent passage and up the empty stairs.

Rebecca grasped her throat. The front door was locked. Panicking, she thought of smashing the front room window and climbing out. Rushing into that room, she yanked the cushion off the chair to protect her hand. She got to the window, steeling herself to strike, and then saw Emma's coat on the chair.

Emma wouldn't go out without her coat, so the little girl must still be somewhere in the house; somewhere with Mrs Lukas.

Rebecca went back out into the hall and again called

Emma's name, but her voice was quiet, almost whispering as if frightened of something in the house.

She'd have to go and find her. She had a cold feeling between her shoulder blades. She would have to check all the rooms. What if Mrs Lukas had Emma bound and gagged? There was something seriously mentally wrong with that woman; Rebecca wouldn't put anything past her.

There was a room there to the right. Rebecca opened the door, but all was in darkness. Another room lay on the left, also old and unused. It felt like the house's owners had died and the place had been covered in drapes. Rebecca couldn't believe that Mrs Lukas actually owned this place. She must be a caretaker or something, but even then she felt wrong like she'd come in from outside.

Around her, as Rebecca walked, the house slept and suffered its nightmares.

At the end of the corridor, there was a T-junction. Rebecca flicked the light switch, but again nothing happened, so she turned on her phone light and pushed open the door to another room. There was a smell of old books here. Amazingly, this light worked, and she saw the room was lined with bookshelves. There was even a reading desk with a seat. On the table was a leather-bound tome.

Abruptly, Rebecca's phone died. It was useless as a brick now without power. At least this room's light worked. Rebecca went over to the table and flipped open the book to read the first page. It was old — a journal, written in Victorian copperplate handwriting. The ink was once black but was now faded to brown. She flicked through the pages. It covered the years 1840 to 1845 and was written by a woman called Elizabeth. She must have been the mistress of the house because she talked about her daily doings — servants' wages, cook's recipes, and ideas for the garden.

As Rebecca turned the pages, she came across pressed flowers — dried out blooms from summers over a hundred and seventy years ago. Maybe the journal would be interesting for another time, but not now.

But Rebecca still thumbed through the rest of the pages, the yellowed edges brushing her thumb like playing cards. Then she saw something about a wolf. She remembered the wolf head on the wall.

Elizabeth reported that her husband shot an enormous male wolf. Apparently, it was the last one in the hills roundabout. Elizabeth's husband had the head cut off and mounted. That must be the one at the top of the stairs. The last sentence on the page said:

The servants talk about how the house is haunted by the spirit of a wolf.

That intrigued Rebecca, so she read on. Elizabeth wrote that, in fact, though they said the wolf her husband shot was the last, the great alpha wolf had a mate; a black she-wolf, and that it was her spirit the servants were scared of. They babbled that it had come into the house and it would not rest until it took revenge on all humans there. Rebecca shuddered. The journal ended abruptly about a month later, so she flicked it shut.

A banging noise started from above. Rebecca almost jumped out of her skin and stared at the ceiling while dust fell with each thud. Someone was knocking on the ceiling.

Rebecca's heart turned over. Maybe she could leave and come back in the morning. Go back to the car. Sit there and wait. Maybe Gavin was still there, tinkering with it. Perhaps they could get a lift to the garage and come back when it was light. It would be easier to see.

But she knew she couldn't leave. How could she explain to Gavin how she'd left his thirteen-year-old daughter in this house of horrors?

Emma hadn't gone out. What if she'd gone into the house looking for Rebecca? Maybe it was her banging after she'd got herself stuck in one of the rooms. That would be simply done with all the disused rooms and their rusty locks.

Rebecca really didn't want to do this, but she had to. Emma wasn't in the rooms she'd searched downstairs. It must be her banging after she'd got herself locked in upstairs.

Rebecca found the bottom of the staircase. She went up slowly, dreading each step. At the top of the landing, she hurriedly flicked the light switch. The wolf head hung behind her on the wall; its glass eyes staring through her. Rebecca ran her fingers nervously through her hair. The hammering kept coming, but she told herself it was stupid to be so scared. It was only an old house. It wasn't like there was anything really dangerous here. "Emma!" she shouted. "Is that you?"

Maybe the girl hadn't heard her. Rebecca stood back outside Mrs Lukas's empty room. The lamplight still glimmered under the door, but it didn't mean the old woman was inside. With a gulp of air, Rebecca hurried past Mrs Lukas's room. She went to the end of the hallway and saw another staircase leading up. This one was narrower and looked older — ancient even.

The banging became a hammering. "Emma!" she shouted. "Are you up there?"

The staircase opened in front of her, leading to the top floor of the house. The banging was directly ahead; it must be coming from there. Rebecca put her foot on the first wooden stair. It creaked. Anyone could hear, but having no choice, she stepped on it anyway. The hammering went on and on. It was destroying her nerves. "Emma, for Christ's sake, answer!"

Rebecca took out her phone and then remembered it had no power. The banging became louder and more frantic. Emma really must have gone upstairs and got herself locked in, but why would she go upstairs into the pitch darkness?

Rebecca pushed her hair behind her ears. She imagined the girl trapped — desperate but now thinking no one would hear her. She went as quickly as possible up the stairs. The landing light from below gave vague illumination behind but ahead was blackness so thick she could taste it.

She shouted into the dark. "Emma, baby. I'm here. Please answer."

There were two thumps. That was all, just two, and they came from directly ahead.

Rebecca couldn't see anything so she could trip and break her ankle so easily. She put her hands out in front and fumbled for a light switch on the wall to the right or left. The walls were papered here. They felt damp and cold.

A hand grabbed her wrist.

Rebecca screamed and pulled back, stumbling and then tumbling against the wall, just catching herself.

Mrs Lukas stepped out of the dark with her black dress, her face in shadows, her eyes looking like holes dug all the way to hell.

Rebecca screamed and struggled, and Mrs Lukas let her go. For the first time, Rebecca noticed an odd dog-like smell on this level of the house.

Rebecca cried in fear. "What are you doing standing here in the dark?"

"I was waiting."

"Waiting? In the goddam dark?"

Rebecca couldn't see the woman clearly, but she heard the smacking of her lips. "Yes, in the god-damned dark."

"Where's Emma? What have you done with her?" Rebecca heard her voice shaking. She stepped back, away from Mrs Lukas. A light came up from the landing below, faint but enough to make out the shape of the old woman. Mrs Lukas stepped closer. Her mouth was half-open, and Rebecca saw her teeth were yellowed and moist.

"I don't like your kind," Mrs Lukas whispered. "I don't like them at all."

Rebecca screamed and ran. Somehow, in her blind panic, she got down two flights of stairs and arrived at the front door. Rebecca pulled at it, but it was still locked, and she had no key.

Mrs Lukas was coming for her. She heard light tread behind. Rebecca yanked and heaved at the door, but it was useless. She felt as if her heart would burst. She ran through to the room she and Emma and been in. The cushion was still there, but she saw the dead hearth and the cast iron grate. She reached and heaved it, and hurled it at the window where it smashed the glass into shards. A ring of pieces like sharp ice surrounded the hole she'd made.

The wind blew into the room, cold and damp and Rebecca picked up the cushion and used it to break off the jagged bits of glass. She was beside herself with panic. Mrs Lukas was right behind her, she was sure.

Rebecca made the hole as safe as she could so she didn't rip open her legs as she stepped out. She climbed out of the window and down onto the wet gravel outside. Then she glanced towards the window where Mrs Lukas stood grinning. Mrs Lukas's eyes were empty coals, her teeth long and yellow. The woman came no further. Even so, Rebecca fled. She sprinted down the drive until her lungs burned and her legs would work no longer.

THE BRIGHT HEADLIGHTS of a car blinded her, and Rebecca put her hand up to her eyes. The car crunched to a halt. "Rebecca!" It was Emma's voice, shouting out of the wound-down window of the car. How had Emma got back to the car? It was Gavin's car. There was no doubt about that so he must have got it fixed. She was so relieved to see them that she ran to the car, and Gavin wound the window down. "Rebecca, you look terrible."

"I got out of the house. The door was locked. Mrs Lukas locked me in, but I smashed the window." Then she looked at Emma. There was something she couldn't figure out, but there was no time for that now. The car worked. She just needed to escape.

"Let me in, please!" she said, hardly able to speak correctly from fear. All the time she looked over her shoulder to see if Mrs Lukas had followed her down the drive.

"Sure, sure," Gavin said. "Just calm down, Rebecca. It's all okay now."

Rebecca yanked the car door open and pushed herself inside, slamming the door closed behind her. "What time is it?" Her phone didn't work.

"Don't worry, Rebecca," Emma said. "You can stay at our house tonight."

"Okay, thank you."

Gavin started the car. The wheels moved, and the vehicle crunched on in the direction of Mrs Lukas's house. Rebecca panicked at first then she realised it was probably because he couldn't turn the car around on the gravel drive, it was too narrow. He'd have to go to the house and turn on the space in front of it. Rebecca pressed down her door lock for extra safety, but it was all fine now. She'd been rescued. Her heart began to slow. She sighed in relief, but she wouldn't fully relax until they were out on the main round and away from this place.

Rebecca smelled that weird dog smell inside the car. That was odd. Maybe she'd brought the smell with her from the house, but she had no time to think of that now. She was so tired.

Gavin finally got to the turning circle in front of the old Armboth Hall. The broken window gaped, but Mrs Lukas wasn't standing there anymore. But, as they got closer, Rebecca saw, to her horror, that Mrs Lukas was opening the front door, and lurking there in her black dress, silhouetted in the dim electric light of the entrance hall.

Rebecca buried her face in her hands. "Oh, no! She's there. Please, drive fast!"

"Nothing to worry about," Emma said. She said it almost like she was laughing at Rebecca's nerves.

Rebecca couldn't look. She just wanted Gavin to drive off. Why didn't he drive off?

Emma grinned. "Hey, Rebecca. You never asked us our family name."

Rebecca pulled her hands away from her face. She frowned. "What?"

"Yeah," the girl smiled even more broadly. "Our surname, our family name, you know?"

Rebecca stammered. This was confusing. "I don't know what you mean."

Emma said, "Well let me introduce myself formally:

Hello, I'm Emma Lukas. This is my dad Gavin Lukas, of course, and I think you know my grandma."

Rebecca tried to get out but she'd locked the car door, and while she struggled to unlock it, Gavin's strong hand gripped her shoulder so she couldn't escape.

Emma Lukas said, "Armboth Hall, yeah it's the family home. Sorry for not telling you before, but we were hungry."

Gavin Lukas smiled. His eyes were yellow, and his face was lupine.

Grandma Lukas ran over yanked open the car door. She licked her doggy lips. "Lots of tasty flesh on this one."

6

THE MIRROR

That Autumn, we took a road trip to Northumberland. Since we both retired, we had plenty of time to go and see places we'd long wanted to visit, and we didn't have young kids so we could avoid the school holidays and go when it was quieter. We got some bargains that way. It was the end of September, getting colder and probably our last break before Christmas.

Northumberland is a beautiful place: England's most northerly county, bordering Scotland to the west and the cold North Sea to the east. The coast is a long sapphire necklace of yellow sand beaches, stone-built fishing communities, ancient castles and rocky islands.

Lindisfarne, or Holy Island, was the home of a Dark Age monastery, and the monks are still there. The castles such as Bamburgh, standing on its rock above the sea since at least the 6th Century, are breathtaking. Inland are the rolling barren hills of the National Park: more curlews than people: empty glens echoing to the memory of ancient bloodshed and long-dead feuds.

We drove up the coast and then found our way back towards Wooler. The Autumn day was bright but cold. There was a wind from the east as we made our way inland.

We stopped at a magnificent castle, still lived in by the family who built it centuries ago as a bastion against Scots' raids, and a springboard for attacks of their own into Scotland. The times of the Border Reivers were bloody and lawless, and thank the Lord, long gone. The Castle was impressive, though we couldn't be shown round all of it as the family were there in their private rooms. Our guide was knowledgeable, and I enjoyed the tour. But somehow the cold seeped into my bones from that old place, and there was a feeling about it I didn't like.

My husband, George, didn't seem to notice the atmosphere. He wanted to stay and take some more photographs, but it was about 4pm. That meant it would be getting dark soon. I managed to drag George away by reminding him he wanted to go to the second-hand bookshop in Alnwick. It's built-in an old railway station, and it's enormous. It's famous all across the north, and he'd wanted to see it for some time.

We got there just before it closed. I was glad the place had a coal fire in the sales area, and I sat down on a leather chair there while I waited for George to browse. The place smelled of old books. I don't like that musty smell. If I'm going to buy a book, I want it to be crisp and new. Or better still, an ebook that I can carry around in my Kindle and which weighs nothing!

George was gone a long time. I'd occasionally see him down the rows and aisles, picking up a book to add the pile already in his arms. Sometimes he put them back, retracing his steps to make sure he got them in precisely the place he'd taken them from. That was George—a thoughtful man.

Eventually, I got bored, and I went to peruse the Antiques section. The girl behind the counter told me that they were just venturing into antiques. It was mostly furniture. I guessed they got it at auctions and then stripped down the wood, cleaned it up and re-varnished it. There was a lovely big oak table, but it was hundreds of pounds. I was standing there looking at the furniture when George returned.

"About ready?" he asked.

"Just looking at this table."

I could tell he didn't care for the table. He nodded and glanced around, still clutching his books. He inclined his head and said, "That's nice."

It was a mirror. The kind that stands on its own legs, I think they call that a cheval mirror. It was about four foot high, and you could angle it. The silver mirroring was spotted a little as it was so old, but it was a beautiful piece. It was more than we could afford.

I told George that, but he said, "Margaret, It's lovely, and we deserve a treat now and again. Don't forget we can leave it to the children as an heirloom!"

He wouldn't be dissuaded. It wasn't that I disliked it, but he loved it, and he was happy to part with his cash. The girl behind the counter was lovely, accommodating—a pretty little thing with long auburn hair and a Scottish accent.

"It's a bit big to wrap!" she joked.

"No, we'll just put it in the car," said George. "Thanks for your help."

OUR LONG WEEKEND in Northumberland came to an end, and we were back home. At first, things seemed to be much as they were before. Then I noticed that George was spending more time in his study. He had his computer there, and he was doing a bit of family history research. He usually went in there with his books and papers. I knew he looked up things on the Internet and discovered long-lost cousins in Canada, but since we'd come back from our trip, he was always there. He stayed there long into the evening when we had previously sat and watched TV together.

I even grew suspicious, and one time, when the weather outside was howling, I walked up to the door of the study and listened. I heard George talking. It was as if he was having a conversation, but I couldn't hear the other person. I guessed he was speaking with his sister Jean in Auckland on Skype. If he had headphones on, I wouldn't hear her — only him.

When George eventually came back through, I said. "Is Jean okay then?"

He frowned. "My sister Jean? You're making me feel guilty now. I haven't spoken to her in weeks."

It was my turn to be puzzled and a little jealous. I had the idea it was a woman. "Weren't you on Skype before? I heard you talking to someone."

"Me? No. Just been looking up surname histories." And he sat down to watch TV.

The next time I noticed something wrong was when I woke in the middle of the night. I don't know what disturbed me, but I realised George wasn't in bed. I sat up. He must have just gone to the bathroom, I thought. But he was a long time. In the end, I put on my dressing gown and went to look.

He wasn't in the bathroom, but I saw the light was on in his study. Curious, I went to the door and pushed it open. George span around guiltily. He was just standing there in the middle of the floor. I said, "George, what on earth are you doing?"

The computer was off, so it wasn't that. I felt slightly relieved.

He said, "Nothing."

I wondered if he was getting ill or confused, something to do with his age. Then I saw that he'd moved the mirror into his study. It was right there, tilted so he could look into it, which struck me as odd. I knew he liked the mirror, but to get up and admire it in the middle of the night? That was peculiar. Eventually, he came back to bed with me.

I made an appointment for him to go to the doctor. Our daughter Nicola and I accompanied him. Sitting in his clean little surgery room, the doctor asked him what the problem was? George said there wasn't a problem.

I told the GP that I'd heard George talking to himself and then found he had got up in the night and was just standing in the middle of the room. The doctor seemed to find this significant, and he got out a memory test question-naire. George scored perfectly. The doctor then took his temperature and a urine sample. They were all fine.

"I can't find anything wrong," said the doctor.

I felt George had made a liar of me.

The doctor said, "We'll take a blood sample in any case. Just to make sure we catch anything that isn't obvious. All I'd say is that you look a little pale. How are your energy levels?"

"I feel a bit drained, but I put that down to getting older," said George.

After the consultation, Nicola and her father went out, talking to each other. I followed along behind. They had always been close. When I was younger, I was jealous of their relationship, but she was such a daddy's girl and always had been. Our son John was different, but he was in London and was rarely in touch.

That night I woke again to find George wasn't in bed. I was angry this time. I marched down to his study, and he was standing there. As I approached the door, I tried to be quiet. He was talking again — having a conversation, and it almost seemed he was flirting. He had adopted the tone of voice that a man assumes when he's talking to a pretty woman. It was ridiculous, the old fool. I stepped into the room, blazing angrily. "George, what the hell are you doing?"

He stood facing the mirror. It was that he'd been talking to.

He turned on me, his face twisted in rage as if I'd interrupted him. I was suddenly frightened. For a second I thought he'd strike me. I stood my ground. "George, I'm worried about you. Who are you talking to?"

He snarled. "You wouldn't understand." And when I looked in his eyes, I saw something strange. Something that wasn't him. Not George. There was a kind of reflected evil in his eyes. I stepped back.

"Come to bed, George, please." I reached out and touched his arm. Warily, as if my touch was not welcome, he let me take it. Gently I tugged him. "Come on, please."

He let me drag him away. When I awoke again, just before dawn. He wasn't in bed. I knew where he'd be, but I couldn't face hearing him muttering still, talking to someone who wasn't there.

The next time I went to the doctor, it was just Nicola and me. I didn't want George to know, and I left him at home in his study. The doctor referred him to a psychiatrist.

The psychiatrist thought he might be suffering from a psychosis and said he would ask the local psychiatric crisis team to call around and interview him. That frightened me.

I didn't want them to drag him off and tie him up in a straight-jacket. But when they came, they were charming. It was two girls. They didn't wear nurses uniforms. They just asked him a lot of questions: did he hear voices? Did he see things that other people couldn't see?

He denied it all of course, but I told them about him getting up in the night and me finding him talking to that odd mirror. They suggested he come into the hospital for a couple of days, but of course, h refused. They let him decline the admission, and I didn't want them to have to get the Police. I just hoped that they'd give him some medication and he'd get better at home.

Their psychiatrist prescribed him something, but once they'd all gone, he wouldn't take it.

That night, I found him in his study. I said quietly, "George, you need to take the tablets they gave you."

He snapped at me. "No, I don't. I'm not mad."

"I'm not saying you're mad. Just you're not totally well. I mean George —you talk to people who aren't here. That's not normal."

He looked at me with an icy glare. "You don't understand. You never understood me. She knows me better than you ever could."

"She? Who is she?" It made no sense that he was having an affair. Who with? He hardly ever went out these days, and very rarely alone. I would know.

He didn't answer. A faint smile played on his lips as if he had some kind of secret.

"It all dates from you buying that mirror," I said.

He stared at me.

"I think we should throw it out. Sell it. I just don't like it," I said.

He pointed his finger at me and said, "If you touch that mirror, I will take a knife and cut your throat."

The shock of him saying that was like a punch. I was devastated, shattered. He'd never spoken to me like that in all the thirty-five years of our marriage. I admit I burst into tears. I turned and ran and shut myself in the bedroom. He never came to see if I was all right. He didn't come to bed either.

Eventually, I slept, and I had a dream of a woman in white. She had a cruel face, skin the colour of bleached bone, long black hair, lustrous as the feathers of a carrion bird and a mouth as red as blood in the snow. She watched me as I slept. I woke with a start and had the faint idea that there had really been someone in my room. George's side of the bed was cold. I knew where he'd be, but I didn't dare to go and find him.

In the morning, he was still in his study. He hadn't eaten. His cheeks were hollow, and there were black rings under his eyes. He hardly acknowledged me. He just kept staring at the mirror.

"I'm going away for a few days," I said.

George didn't look up.

"You're frightening me, George. You need help. I'm going to stay at my sister's."

And still, he said nothing. He was stroking the mirror's frame as if it was something beloved to him.

I RANG Nicola and told her to go round and see her father. I told her she could ring the Crisis Team and they would come out. They might even take him to hospital. She asked me where I was going, and I said I had to find out about the mirror.

The first thing I did was ring the place we bought it. There was no one there who remembered it. I described the girl who'd been there at the counter.

"Ah, Sally? She's on her day off," said the man.

"Will she be in tomorrow?" I asked.

I could hear him turning over the pages of a book, presumably with their rota on. "Yes," he said.

"What time do you open?"

"Nine thirty."

I put the phone down. There was nothing much I could do but wait. I wasn't going to my sister's I was going to go back to Northumberland. I drove all day and got myself a bed and breakfast in Alnwick, where the shop was.

I rang Nicola, and she said she'd gone round. Her dad was much the same. Sitting in the study staring at the mirror. She managed to get him to eat something, and she called the Crisis Team, but he didn't really listen to them. They did get him to take some of his tablets, and they said they'd come back the next day.

Nicola said she'd stay there overnight with her dad. I could tell she felt I was running out on him. I didn't tell her that he'd threatened me. It was only because he was ill and I didn't want to do anything to make her think less of him. I even felt I was running out, but then I told myself that all this was something to do with the mirror and I had to find out about its history.

THE NEXT DAY, I was there at the antique and book store before it opened. It was a frosty morning, and I stood there in my coat, my breath making clouds, waiting for them to unlock the door.

"You're keen," said the owner — presumably the man who answered the phone.

I pushed past him. "Is Sally in?"

"Yes," he said frowning. "Why?" Then he realised. "Ah, you're the woman who was on the phone yesterday. You've come in person. I got the impression you lived miles away."

"I do. But I have to know about the mirror."

His frown deepened. "Sally handles the antiques. I focus on the books. You'll have to ask her."

Sally was as helpful as I remembered her. "What's the matter with it?" she said. "It was a nice piece."

I said, "Did you not think there was something odd about it?"

She laughed. "Well, I did get it at an excellent price. I joked with the woman who sold it to us that it seemed like she wanted to get rid of it."

"Where did you get it from?"

She could see I was deadly serious. Her expression froze. "It came from the Castle."

It was the Castle we had visited. I said I knew it. "Do you remember the name of the person there?"

"Yep. Dan Hetherington. He handles the visitor side of things. The owners have no commercial sense, so they leave it to him."

"Thank you," I said and hurried out back to where I'd left the car.

IT TOOK me fifteen minutes to drive to the Castle. The weather was heavy with low clouds and grey everywhere: it matched my mood. The Castle loomed ahead of me. I had to pay to take the car in, though I didn't intend to take a tour. My hand shook as I paid the man at the gate and then wound the window back up and drove through. I parked, got out and pulled tight my coat. At the entrance, I asked for Mr Hetherington. The guide there told me I needed an appointment. I even thought of bribing him, but in the end, I just told him how important it was. He could see I looked upset.

Eventually, Dan Hetherington, who was a kind man, agreed to see me. "It seems urgent," he said, extending his hand.

I shook it, and Mr Hetherington asked me to sit down. He inquired whether I wanted a cup of tea, but I was in too much of a state to drink tea.

I blurted, "I've come about the mirror."

"The mirror?" he said.

I nodded. "You sold a mirror at a knockdown price to the antique and book place in Alnwick."

His expression changed. He said, "Are you a journalist or something?"

"No."

He sighed. "I don't believe in all that kind of thing you know."

I was inquisitive now. "What kind of thing?"

"The so-called cursed mirror."

"I didn't know it was cursed. But my husband hasn't been well since we took it home. It's almost as if it's given him a breakdown."

He pursed his lips. He paused and then said, "I don't know if it'll help, but maybe you should speak to Mrs Eliot."

I was bewildered, but if he thought it would help, then I'd speak to anyone.

. . .

MRS ELIOT WAS one of the general castle staff. She did a bit of cleaning and a bit of cooking for the tourists — baking cakes, making sandwiches and chips, etc. It turned out her family had been in employed by the Castle for decades if not centuries. Her grandfather was a ploughboy in the days before tractors. Her husband had been the night security man for the Castle.

"Does he still work here?" I asked. Mr Hetherington shook his head and was about to speak, but Mrs Eliot said, "He's dead."

I felt a cold hand grip my heart. "I'm sorry to hear that," I said. "How long ago did your husband pass away?"

"About a year ago now." She looked at the ground. "It was the mirror."

Mr Hetherington raised up his hand. "We don't know that, Diane. He had a heart attack. I don't think it had anything to do with the mirror."

She turned sharply on him. "You don't know, but I do."

"Please tell me about it," I said.

She told me that her husband had been night watchman and security guard at the Castle. He'd previously worked in the forestry but had an injury with a chainsaw so he couldn't do that anymore. The family had moved him inside. "It was kind of them", she said. "They could have just fired him."

He liked the work, explained Mrs Eliot. She used to bring him a flask of tea and sandwiches about ten pm, to get him through the night.

She said it all happened the previous winter. The days were short, and the nights were long and dark. The Castle kept cold in it — a chill that almost felt unnatural as if its centuries of blood weighed heavily.

·   ·   ·

MRS ELIOT SAID that there was a story that one of the family had married a woman from away. She was Scottish or Irish or something, but she wasn't English, and the local people hadn't taken to her. It was long ago — like a fable.

Mrs Eliot told me the story. "The woman was pale and cruel with long black hair and a red mouth as if her lips were painted in blood. But Sir Humphrey had loved her. In fact, he was besotted with her. He never wanted to leave her side, and eventually, he stopped eating, and he sickened. All he would do was stare at her. When he died, the local people said she was a witch, or worse, and that she'd killed him with black magic. That she'd sucked out his soul."

"But that didn't stop her. She didn't care what they thought of her. She used the money and the Castle she'd inherited to do what she pleased. And it pleased her to bring men there. Young men, middle-aged men, old men, they all fell for her beauty. And they all disappeared."

"And so eventually the countryside was in an uproar, and the magistrate had to act. They came and knocked at the castle doors that had been kept locked for so long, with only her having the key. But this time the doors were open. The magistrate and his men hesitated before they entered. There was such an air of foulness and despair about the place. Eventually, they went in, but there was no sign of her. She was gone."

Hetherington coughed. "But that's just a silly old story. You're frightening our guest."

I was terrified, but I couldn't stop listening. It was as if something in the story Mrs Eliot told would supply the key to understand what was going on with my own husband.

"But she did exist," said Mrs Eliot.

Mr Hetherington nodded. "Some kind of 16th Century gold-digger. In any case, Sir Humphrey's brother came back from the wars in France and took over the Castle, and everything was fine."

Mrs Eliot interrupted. "But she was still there all the time."

"Where?" I asked.

"In the mirror."

Mr Hetherington said, "Of course it's absurd. But that's what the people believe round here."

"But what did that have to do with your husband?" I said.

Mrs Eliot said, "Not long after he started being there on nights, he began to talk about a woman that walked in the Castle. At first, I thought he meant one of the family or their guests, but then he was talking about seeing the woman when they were all away at their house in London. The times when he was the only one in the Castle. I told him he was being stupid, but he insisted. He started telling me how he talked to her. How she would come to him, and they would chat. And from the way he spoke, it was as if he was falling in love with her — this pale-faced woman with black hair and a red mouth."

"My mother said to me I had to get him away from the Castle. It didn't matter if he was unemployed. She said the woman was old Sir Humphrey's bitch; the woman who got all those men and ate them."

"Ate them?" I said.

"This is beyond absurd," said Mr Hetherington.

"What happened to your husband?"

Mrs Eliot said, "I talked to him time after time, and I even went up with him to the Castle and sat all night, even though I had my own job in the day. And he would get up and go walking away from me, saying that she was calling him. But I wasn't going to give up without a fight. I called her out, the evil witch. I even think I saw her once, but I can't be sure. Women don't normally see her."

Mr Hetherington let her talk.

"And so, I got him to quit the job. The master of the Castle said he'd find him another job because he was looking so ill, it was obvious that the constant night shifts didn't suit him. He stayed home with me, but I would wake to find him out of bed, just standing at the window, looking up at the Castle."

"And then one night, he got up and opened the door. I grabbed him. I held him back. I asked him where he was going. He said he was going to her, his mistress. He said she wanted to take him into the mirror. I screamed at him and tried to hold him back, but he was too strong, and he ran out of the house, into the night. It was pouring down."

"I got my coat and ran after him, but when I got up to the castle gate, he was already dead. The gate was locked, and he couldn't get in, but the woman took him anyway. My only comfort is that she didn't take him into the mirror-like she did with all the others, and so his soul was safe, and she didn't take him into that place where she eats them."

"My God," I said. I was trembling.

Mr Hetherington tried to calm me. "Whatever Mrs Eliot thinks, there is a rational explanation. There are no such things as ghosts."

Mrs Eliot, sitting behind him, shook her head. "She isn't a ghost."

"Then, what is she?" I asked.

"She's a demon."

I PHONED Nicola and said I was driving back. I'd be about three hours. She sounded worried and told me her dad hadn't been eating. She said she was pleased I was coming back. I could tell she didn't know what to do. I told her to ring the Crisis Team at once, they could maybe get him to hospital. By force if necessary — anything to get him away from that woman in the mirror.

When I got home, Nicola met me outside. "Oh, mum," she said. "He's locked himself in his study. I can hear him in there, but he won't come out."

The Crisis Team nurses were there. A middle-aged, dark-haired man of theirs said apologetically. "I'm sorry, I can't get him to come out. I think we're going to have to call the Police and break down the door."

"Just do it," I said. I hurried through the house to the study door. I banged on it. "George let me in. It's Margaret. It's your wife."

I could hear him in there, talking. Talking to that thing in the mirror, and I knew the woman would be trying to persuade him to come into the mirror with her.

I shouted, "Don't listen to her, George. Come back to us. Come back to your wife and daughter," but he didn't answer. He just kept talking to her, listening to her whispers and promises. I knew he was at least half in love with her would believe her in everything.

I banged on the door until my fist hurt. But George didn't stop talking to her.

By the time the Police came, there was silence. "Are you sure he's still in there?" asked the policeman. "It's very quiet."

"He's in there," said the man from the Crisis Team. "He must be."

Nicola was standing there, a look of sheer terror on her face. "I saw him go in. There's no other way out. Are you okay, mum? It'll be all right."

But I knew it wouldn't.

The Police smashed the door in. Splinters of wood flew everywhere, and the door sagged off his hinges. The policeman kicked the ruined door out of the way and pushed his way in. I could see in past him, and heard him say, "No, there's no one here."

In the study, the desk and the chairs were still where they'd been.

So was the mirror.

George never came back.

NICOLA NEVER KNEW what happened to her father. But I took the mirror to a remote place. There I smashed it, then I buried it so that she would never again be able to drag anyone into the spot behind the mirror's silver eye: the spot where she eats their souls.

7

THE EATERS OF MEN

Amanda stared up. She couldn't help herself; the sky compelled her gaze. The desert air was so pure as to be almost not there at all. Way out here, the stars were brighter and stranger than she'd ever known. Amanda was the city girl, used to the cloudy skies of London. Here in the desert, the stars burned clean and cold like a tapestry sewn with diamonds. Time was different here too, not measured by clocks; instead, the heavens turned like a colossal engine shifting slowly on its predestined journey through the night towards the day.

It got dark early, and they were in their sleeping bags by ten. Amanda slept into the middle of the night but awoke suddenly. A sound came from outside the compound in the desert, a strange noise that left her with a feeling of unease. In the dark, it took her a second to remember where she was.

A hand's breadth away, Andrew lay sleeping. She heard his regular breathing. All was still apart from that, then the noise came again, breaking the deep silence of the desert. The sound was so strange that her brain couldn't fit it into any category; it wasn't the yapping of a desert fox nor the camels' shifting grumble. It was a dry sound, like a click followed by a hiss; like small dry fibres rattling together.

Amanda sat up and drew her hand out of the sleeping bag. She stroked Andrew's face as he slumbered. Like all rare and beautiful things, he had cost her a lot. She had given him all her time, stopped drawing, hidden her tattoos, changed her hair, and even given up smoking, at least as far as he was concerned.

She'd come with him to Jordan. Andrew didn't consider himself a tourist; he was a traveller. In daily life, Andrew was a rich man's dentist in Kensington, but a would-be Lawrence of Arabia in his time off. When he was a boy, Andrew wanted to be a soldier, but his mother told him to follow the money, and that had led him to look after the teeth of the impossibly wealthy—Arab sheiks, Russian oligarchs and Premier League footballers.

Amanda had to go to the toilet, but she didn't want to wake Andrew. She pulled her blonde hair impatiently into a ponytail and fastened it with a red hair tie. Amanda moved towards the door in the tented compound that led out into the desert. The Bedouin fire they had eaten around was now dead. The Bedouins slept in the tented area behind her. She heard their light snores. She stepped out, trying to be quiet. The sand was cold under her bare feet. She made her way to the door in the canvas wall. It was closed and tied with rope. She hesitated, remembering the noise, and then she shook her head at her stupidity.

She stepped out of the compound as if walking onto an enormous empty stage. The faint glimmer of the myriad stars barely lit the desert, and the massive sandstone bluffs were only visible as dark lines against the night sky.

Cold sand leaked between her toes as she ran to the

plastic Portaloo toilets the Bedouin had brought with them on the back of their jeeps. Amanda was halfway back to the camp when she heard the clicking, hissing noise. A shiver of fear flared in her again. It was such a dry rattling, something like she imagined an insect's carapace would make dragging over stones.

She peed and was nearly back when to her right, there was a movement. There was no doubt about it; there was something there. She stopped, then broke into a run. Her breath was coming in gasps by the time she got back to the compound. When she glanced back to where the sound had come from, she saw a darker shape against the desert sky. It was the height of a man, maybe six feet, and slender though Amanda could see no arms or shoulders. Then it swayed, a completely inhuman movement accompanied by the dry pattering of wispy fibres.

With shaking hands, Amanda pulled and tied the canvas flap closed tight behind her. She felt stupid to be this frightened of a shadow and a noise, but she trembled. Composing herself, she kneeled and squirmed into the sleeping bag. Still, Andrew didn't stir. Her eyes darted to the door behind her. It was tied tight; she had checked it. She knew that the Bedouin would laugh and tell her that it was something totally harmless.

WHEN AMANDA WOKE, the Bedouins had already lit the fire and were boiling water for tea. The worries of last night were now merely ghosts. She got up, the expensive sleeping bag, she hadn't paid for, falling away. Andrew slept on snoring faintly.

Amanda walked out of the compound into the sand outside where a young Bedouin man tended the fire and made the tea. He wore the long white thawb. His headdress was also white, kept on with the braided band that all the men wore. He was slim, even for the desert people, and his skin was dark from his life under the desert sun. His eyes were green like Malachite. He smiled. She knew it was his job to smile, but Amanda preferred to think he meant it.

The Bedouin called over, "Sabah-al-Kheir."

She answered, "Sabah-an-Nur." The green-eyed young man grinned at her for knowing the response.

Their encampment was in the shadow of rough sandstone heights, but in front of the camp, the desert stretched forever.

Another of the guides tinkered with the jeep while to the east, the sun's red orb hauled itself up in the sky like a beetle. Amanda wandered to a ridge near the automobile to watch the dawn, and there she noticed strange s-shaped marks in the sand. They were like nothing she'd seen before. She looked at them with avid curiosity and a touch of fear, bending down to feel the sand. The marks were about a foot wide. They circled the camp and then ran away into the desert over the dunes to the west. Something had definitely been around in the night.

The old Bedouin saw where she was looking. He called over to the man by the jeep. The other stared, and both frowned, but their eyes were blank. Amanda shrugged at them, inviting explanation, but none came. Instead, the men turned back to the jobs they had been doing and pretended that she was not there.

ANDREW DID NOT GET up for a while, even after he'd told the guides the night before that wanted to set off early. Amanda used the time to look at the rock wall behind the camp. She studied the cliff face, wondering whether she could climb it without equipment. Before she met Andrew, she dated a guy who was into rock climbing. He took her on holidays to Wales and the Lake District and, every Sunday if they weren't away, they'd hit the local climbing wall. She'd got good at clambering up sheer rock faces. She climbed. She went up far more quickly than she had expected. Her fingers searched out a handhold, and then another and made sure they were solid, then pulled herself up. Squeezing her small feet into notches in the rock, she climbed like a spider.

The young Arab with green eyes came running across the sand. He shouted up, "Lady, lady, what are you doing? It is dangerous."

She laughed and shouted down. "Not if you know how to climb." She had got up as far as was safe and so, to save his anxiety, she clambered down and dropped the last six feet into the soft sand.

She could tell he was pleased she was down, no doubt thinking of the impact on business if she fell. He said, "Lady, you are like a monkey!" But he laughed.

She laughed too. The exertion had driven away all of the terror of the night before.

"Soon it is breakfast," the man said.

ONCE SHE WAS DOWN, Andrew was still not up. Taking advantage of his absence, Amanda went into her fleece pocket and pulled out her secret cigarette stash. She lit one on a burning stick from the fire and sneaked it quickly before Andrew came out. He didn't like anything unhealthy. He was the most disciplined man she knew.

She sat on a chair brought by the Bedouin, the wood smoke drifting into her hair. An old, tarnished kettle boiled the tea that the locals drank at every opportunity. She had a packet of postcards she'd got at Jerash, a ruined Roman city north of Amman. Andrew had told her not to be so soft-hearted when she bought them from the rough-faced man who said, "Please, lady. I have five children." Andrew gestured for her to move on, but she couldn't help but think about her life compared with theirs, and so she'd secretly stuffed five dinar notes into the man's hand and taken the postcards.

The slim Arab man was struggling with the kettle and a tray of glasses. She said, "Here, let me help." Amanda went over and caught the wobbly tray. He looked embarrassed, frowned but thanked her. He took command of the dish, and she backed off. For some minutes, he didn't speak, and then he turned and offered tea in a small glass. She knew it would be almost unbearably sweet. "Thank you," she said.

He nodded.

"I'm Amanda," she said. "What's your name?"

He bowed slightly. "Hassan."

"Ah, Hassan! You're the one who will be our guide today?"

"Yes, just I—for two nights."

"I'm really excited," Amanda said. "Out there?" She pointed out over the dunes that were reddening as the sun's light hit them.

He nodded.

She sipped the tea. A mint leaf stuck on her lip, and she pulled it free and dropped it on the sand. "What time do we set off?"

The young man nodded in the direction of the tented camp. "When your husband wakes and eats. Can you tell him we should leave soon? We should travel before the full heat of the afternoon."

Amanda shrugged and tossed the butt of her cigarette into the fire. "Andrew doesn't listen to me, Hassan."

Today they were to go further into the desert. They would leave even the small comforts of the tented camp behind and journey into the wilderness with only one guide. Amanda watched as Hassan warmed bread to eat with hummus and dates and cheese. She thought his English was better than that of the others.

"Did you sleep well?" He asked, with the good manners of the Bedouin.

"It was cold." She wanted to ask about the noise and the tracks in the desert. Still, for some reason, she hesitated.

Hassan shrugged. "Of course, it is cold. We have made tents for you, but you sleep outside." He gave her a look that suggested that her bizarreness was beyond his understanding.

She laughed, "Hassan! The stars!"

"The stars are always there—every night."

"Not in London."

"Ah, London. Your husband, he is rich?"

She guessed that he thought everyone in London was rich. She said quickly, "He's not my husband. He's only my boyfriend." She looked over her shoulder over the vast red sands with their scattered rocks and odd patches of scrubby, dry grass. "What kind of animals live out here?" she said as if she was just making conversation.

Hassan looked puzzled at her question. "Snakes, birds, foxes, camels; that's all."

Amanda said, "It's important to protect regions like this and the unique creatures that live here."

Hassan shrugged. "The animals that live here are not useful. Some are dangerous."

"Anything especially dangerous?"

"Especially dangerous?" His eyes narrowed. Then he firmly said, "No, Nothing especially dangerous. Here is your bread. Eat. Also dates and cheese."

She ate from the plate he gave her and when she had finished looked at her watch. If Andrew was going to be much longer, she might have time to take out her sketchpad. The ochres and reds of these rocks were primal. She found time to write a postcard to her friend Kareen in Glasgow and asked Ahmad to post it for her back in town. Andrew still hadn't got up.

She got up and went towards the encampment to get her pens and paper from her big bag. But before she got to the canvas door, Andrew emerged, looking like he'd just been to a health club. He was wearing a khaki safari suit, and a red and white checked Arab headscarf around his neck. His body was a credit to his personal trainer, a beautiful Australian girl that Amanda was jealous of. He wore Ray-Ban aviator mirrored gold sunglasses, hiding his sky-blue eyes. He sauntered to the fire and took the tea from Hassan without acknowledging him.

"Today is where it gets interesting," Andrew said, sipping the tea. He curled his lip. He turned to Hassan. "Do you people ever drink tea without twenty spoons of sugar?"

"We put sugar in tea, of course."

"And this is breakfast?" Andrew pointed disdainfully. "Do you have any meat?"

Hassan shrugged. "Not for breakfast."

Andrew shook his head and smiled as if he expected no better. Then he waved Hassan away. "Thank you," he said without warmth.

Hassan left to go and help the other Bedouin dismantle the camp and stow it in the back of their pick-up trucks.

One of the others, Ahmad, was cresting the hill in front of them, leading three camels.

"Camels?" Amanda said.

Andrew showed his perfect teeth, his eyes were hidden behind the golden mirrors of his sunglasses. "For you," he said.

"For me?" Amanda didn't remember requesting camels. The sun was climbing now, and she felt its warmth on her skin.

"Where we're going today is trackless. I thought it was more authentic to go with camels. There's a hidden village that Lawrence of Arabia discovered and then refused to talk about."

"How do you know about it then?" She smiled.

Andrew frowned. He didn't like people challenging him.

She reached out and stroked his arm. "Just joking. It sounds exciting."

"Yes. It is. Go and get ready. I don't want you to make us late setting off like yesterday."

ONLY THE THREE of them went into the desert—Andrew, Hassan and Amanda. They had a camel each, and a fourth was tethered by a long rope to Hassan's beast. This last one carried their provisions—the lightweight tent, fodder for the other camels and other baggage.

Andrew kept his bag behind his saddle where he stowed his Zeiss binoculars, his Panerai flashlight and his Lumica chemical glow sticks. They were all the most expensive of their type.

They would be gone two nights, sleeping in the open. They were exploring the region known as the Hejaz, heading south toward Saudi Arabia. It was a vast, empty

area, supposedly full of djinn and efreeti, where the sand
blew up in dust devils on the barren plain.

As they rode, Amanda adjusted her cap, pulling the
peak down against the sun and yanking her hair through
the gap in the back. It was early still, but hot. She took a
swig of water. The camel swayed as they went on. Occasionally, it would blow air grumpily from the side of its mouth
and emit a deep bellow.

Andrew led the camel train. Hassan was their guide, but
Andrew demanded very little of him. Andrew had read a lot
of guidebooks before coming to Jordan. Sometimes Hassan
would try to explain about the desert and its people, but
Andrew would say, "Yes, I know," and proceed to tell Hassan
what the Arab had been about to say. Eventually, Andrew
didn't even look round when Hassan tried to point something out. After this, Hassan rode sullenly in silence, dropping back until he was behind both Amanda and Andrew.

After about an hour, Andrew abruptly spurred his camel
on, as if impatient at their slow pace. The beast grumbled
and spat but complied with the rough heels in her flanks.
Her hooves kicked up spouts of sand as she ran.

Amanda saw Hassan's green eyes were dark with anger.
He rode his camel past her until he was in hailing distance
of Andrew then yelled, "Sir, please do not hurt the camel."

Andrew slowed his camel and lifted his gold aviator
shades to make sure Hassan could see his disapproval. "How
much am I paying you again?"

Amanda came level with them. "Andrew," Amanda said.
He darted a glance at her, and she bit her tongue.

"How much?" Andrew repeated.

Hassan shrugged. He didn't meet the Englishman's eye.
"I don't know. I have nothing to do with the money."

"Well, let me tell you, sonny-Jim, it's enough to allow me

to kick a lazy camel." He waited for his words to register, then replaced his sunglasses, turned and drove the camel on as brutally as before.

Hassan spat in the sand and Amanda heard him mutter a curse.

They rode on over the dry ground. The desert here was rocky with taller stands of hills on the horizon. There were low dunes of sand in places, but otherwise, it was flat as a seabed.

The bad-tempered silence and the heat made the journey oppressive. Hassan didn't speak even to Amanda while, around them, the desert burned. The landscape rippled in the heat. There were no birds or animals, no clouds, just the burning air. Amanda felt sweat between her shoulder blades and under the frames of her sunglasses. She took a sip from her water bottle.

She saw Hassan was alongside her, still quiet. "I'm sorry, he upset you," she said. "He just gets carried away with his enthusiasm for whatever project he is on."

Hassan pursed his lips. He looked as if he were debating whether to say something. Then, without looking at her, he said," You are too good for him."

She gave a crooked smile. "Not really."

"You have a good heart."

"That's kind of you to say that, Hassan. Don't be too bothered by his attitude."

"The trip will soon be over. There will be new tourists." Hassan shrugged and swiped away flies from the neck of his camel. He gave the beast a stroke on its dry, dusty fur.

"It's scorching," Amanda said, changing the subject.

"We will shelter from the sun soon. We can eat."

"How long?" she said. She felt the heat like a physical assault.

Hassan gestured to rocks around half a mile ahead. They were about a hundred feet tall and made of broken red sandstone, carved into scoops and hollows by centuries of the desert wind.

Seeing that she was flagging, Hassan called forward to Andrew, "Mr Hayes."

Andrew turned. "Yes?"

"We eat by those rocks and rest."

Andrew followed Hassan's finger. For a minute, Amanda thought Andrew would disagree if only to show his authority, but he nodded curtly. "Fine," he said.

Within fifteen minutes, the camels had plodded their way to the rocks. In the shade of the red stone, it was only marginally more refreshing, but at least they were out of the sun. Hassan made Amanda's camel kneel, and he helped her off its back. He went to do the same to Andrew, but Andrew had already given the Arabic command, and his camel kneeled as directed.

Hassan had brought some sticks and the kettle on the back of the pack camel. He also had provisions for their meal, and he lit a fire to boil the kettle.

Andrew strolled up to Amanda and ruffled her damp blond hair in what he took to be a gesture of affection. "Magnificent, isn't it?" he said. "I could live out here."

Amanda smiled. "It's gorgeous; a little frightening, but beautiful."

"Frightening?" Andrew sneered. "What are you frightened of? I'm here to protect you."

She said, "It's just so immense. And we're so far from any help, should anything go wrong."

"Nothing can go wrong. I've prepared for this trip."

Andrew wandered away from her, over to a rock and stood there, gazing west. Amanda went to examine the stones. They were red and orange and stained with minerals into whites and blues. The colours entranced her.

Hassan called, "Come, tea is ready."

After she took the first sips of the sweet mint tea, she finally mustered her courage to ask about the previous night. She said, "Andrew, did you hear anything strange last night?"

He shook his head, looking uninterested, checking the dials on his watch.

Hassan frowned. "What did you hear?"

"Some creature outside the encampment; I went to the toilet and heard it."

"It probably was an animal," Andrew said. "Was little Amanda scared of the dark?"

"A bit."

"The desert is strange," Hassan said. "There are djinn and efreet here."

Andrew snorted with laughter. "And that, Amanda, is why the Arabs don't rule the world."

If Hassan understood Andrew, he chose to ignore the Englishman and warmed a vegetable and lemon soup for their lunch. He served it in ceramic bowls decorated with running deer and lions. It was delicious. Amanda asked him for the recipe.

Hassan laughed. "It is my mother's recipe—coriander, spinach, lentils and a lemon."

"I'll make it when we get home," Amanda said, looking at Andrew. They didn't live together, but she liked to spend as much time as possible in his wonderful well-equipped kitchen.

"Don't believe her, she isn't much of a cook," Andrew said to Hassan.

Amanda took a long look at Andrew. He was grinning at

his own joke. Her mouth tightened, and she stood up. Andrew didn't look at her as she stepped away from the fire. She walked over to the rocks behind the camp. There was some strange writing etched into the stone. It wasn't Arabic script.

"Hassan, what does that say?" asked Amanda, pointing.

Andrew glanced over. "He won't know," Andrew said. "It's Thamudic."

Hassan frowned. "I don't know."

"See?" Andrew said. "It's a proto-Arabic dialect. The inscriptions are scattered all over the remote desert."

Hassan shook his head. He looked like there was something he didn't want to say. Amanda watched him struggle. Then his dislike for Andrew won, and he told them something, which from his expression, he should not have. He said, "It is not old."

"Not old?" Andrew looked at him as if he were a fool. "Of course it's old. No one writes Thamudic now."

"You know this from your book?" Hassan snapped.

"I doubt you can even read," Andrew said.

Hassan walked up to the script on the stone. He rubbed the sandstone, which flaked away in his hands. "See, new— only months old, maybe a year."

"That can't be right," Andrew said.

Hassan busied himself with feeding the camels. Amanda went over. They were out of Andrew's hearing.

Hassan said, "Your husband, he does not respect the spirits of the desert. It is dangerous to be arrogant here. The djinn listen and punish those who disrespect them."

"He's a good man, really. His problem is that he had it all too easy."

Hassan busied himself with the camels, and Amanda

was about to turn away when he said, "Lady, the thing you heard last night."

"Yes?"

"It was one of the Kephroun. We saw the tracks in the sand."

She shook her head. "What are these Kephroun?"

"Be careful of them. They are worse than djinn."

She was about to ask more, but then Andrew demanded tea and Hassan went to minister to him.

AFTER HALF AN HOUR, the sun was past its zenith, and Andrew wanted to go on.

"It's still too hot," Hassan said. "We will get there in good time."

"It is pretty hot," agreed Amanda.

"We're going," Andrew said. He walked over to the camel. "There are things I want to see."

Andrew clicked his tongue; spoke in Arabic and his camel kneeled. He mounted and waited while Hassan helped Amanda up onto her animal.

"Where are we going?" Amanda asked.

"West," Andrew said.

Hassan nodded. "West."

Amanda said, "What's west?"

"The ruins are west," Andrew said. "The ones Lawrence found but didn't fully explore. The lost city of Irem. Abd Al Hazred found them long ago, and Lawrence was afraid to enter. No Westerner has been there since." He grinned like a schoolboy. "Think of the accolades that will come my way when I find them again."

Amanda frowned. "But the Bedouin know about them. Hassan is going to lead us to them."

Andrew said, "Bedouin don't count. These ruins are unknown to Civilisation like I said."

THE SANDSTORM HIT AFTER ABOUT an hour. Amanda pulled her scarf over her mouth, then realised it wasn't enough to keep out the sand. She pushed her sunglasses firmly back to minimise gaps and pulled up her fleece. She wondered if Hassan would make them stop and take shelter, but there was no shelter.

The storm thickened. Hassan became a grey, stooped figure riding slightly ahead of her, the baggage camel walking just behind. Andrew was only barely visible at the front. She hunkered down, her head tilted towards her chest. Soon she could not see Hassan through the whirling dirt. The camel's rhythm became her focus. The sand was in her nose and her mouth.

Amanda lost track of time as the camel plodded on through the rushing sky of dirt, and she could see nothing through the sandstorm. At first, she saw the traces of the feet of others' camels in the sand, but now she couldn't even see those because the storm blew them away. She had to trust her camel to keep with its companions.

And then the wind slackened. Suddenly, the sun broke through. There was blue sky again above; the heat of the sun stroked her, then burned her. Amanda pulled down her hood and took off her sunglasses.

The storm was gone. But so were Hassan and Andrew.

In a panic, she swivelled around on the saddle. Behind her, the desert was trackless; the storm had blown away all sign of their passing. She looked to her right and her left. The yellow and red dunes were punctuated with dead, dry plants. Further away, stands of hills stood here and there, but they were a long way off.

Where the hell had the others gone? She had no map of her own, no compass. She had some water in a bottle, but that would not last long. She was lost, and without help, and without help she knew she would die.

It was later in the day, and the worst of the heat was gone. She had no idea where safety was, no idea in which direction she should ride. Behind her, her camel's tracks led back forever, disappearing out of sight. Her knees ached. Her feet were sore. She pulled down the hood of her fleece and shook out her hair. It was dirty and full of grit. She ran her fingers over her eyelids and scraped off a layer of dirt, and then she turned and faced the sun, now two inches above the line that separated the pale sand from the pale sky.

So that was west. East was the direction of the Bedouin camp, miles away over the sand. She would not give up. If she gave up, she would die. She turned her camel and set off.

Another hour and the thirst was nagging at her. She imagined water in her mouth and throat, but there was no water. She'd finished the bottle though she'd tried to be sparing. Her lips were dry, she felt her eyes stick under their lids, and her tongue lay like a reptile in her mouth. She looked ahead and saw only sand. Her eyes didn't work right, and her thighs ached.

Amanda cried. She wiped away the tears with her fingers, then licked at them. What a waste of water crying was, especially if it was only for yourself. She was light-headed. She felt nauseous but had nothing in her belly to throw up. Every yard was hard. She sweated, losing more water until she could hardly move her tongue. Her lips stuck together, and when she pulled them apart, the skin came with them, breaking tiny beads of blood: more liquid she couldn't afford to lose.

Her strength was going. And then she lolled. She became delirious and fell from the camel, full length onto the hot dune.

She tried to rise, but could not. She lay there for a while face down in the sand. Her cheek pushed into the dune, and sand slipped into her mouth. She had an image of herself as becoming nothing but bleached bones with rags of wind-dried clothes flapping in the dry wind. And then her mind slipped into a dream. Perhaps this was the dream that preceded death.

She became aware that the camel was gone. It had waited a while, then wandered off. She was totally on her own now.

The sky was dark, and the wind rose, bringing with it more sand. It first inveigled and then intruded into her eyes, her mouth, and her ears. It was unrelenting; it came as half-liquid, half-solid; finally, it filled her mouth and filled her eyes. The wind moaned and buried her. She became a heap in the sand. No one would even know she was a person. And the sand blew, and it did not stop blowing even when it buried her.

When Hassan found her, she indeed did not have long to live. He turned her over. She was limp, and her arms splayed loosely against the enveloping dune. Hassan took the plastic water bottle from his cloak and pressed it against her lips until the dry, cracked skin absorbed the liquid and then she coughed, spluttering water. Her mouth opened and allowed more in. She woke from the sleep near death, and she took hold of the bottle, gripping it, drinking slowly, then more deeply. Her crusted eyes opened. It was early morning, the sun neither high in the sky nor hot. She had been unconscious through the night.

"Lady, you nearly died," he said when she finally had drunk enough.

She reached out and limply squeezed the tanned skin of his hand. "Hassan, thank you."

It took her long minutes to come from the daze that had held her. At first, she could not think straight, but then, when she did remember, it was Andrew she thought of first.

She sat up, then pushed herself onto her hands and knees and then rose. "Where's Andrew?"

Hassan said, "He entered the city of the Kephroun. I told him not to, but he said I was a stupid Arab who knew nothing."

I said I knew the Kephroun would kill him, but he only laughed.

"We must find him," Amanda said. She was unsteady. Hassan had to reach out to help her balance. She leaned against him until she was confident she could stand unaided. She said, "We need to find Andrew."

Hassan's eyes narrowed, and he said, "Your husband is gone. The Kephroun do not let any leave their city."

SHE SHOOK HER HEAD. Her hands trembled. Her head wasn't clear. She said, "I need a cigarette."

Hassan reached inside the jacket of his coat and pulled out a packet of Lebanese cigarettes. She took one without speaking and put it in her mouth as he lit it for her.

"After you smoke, we go back to the camp, please," he said. He had two camels, his own and the pack camel.

Amanda protested. "I can't leave him here."

"He does not deserve your help," he said. "He is a fool."

She drew deep on the cigarette and exhaled the aromatic smoke into the desert air. "You say Andrew went into the ruins?"

"Yes."

"And they are dangerous?" She imagined unsteady walls, rock-falls, uncertain pathways.

Hassan nodded.

"Which way are they?"

Hassan gestured with his hand.

She looked where he pointed. "How far?"

Hassan gently took her arm. "He is gone. Come. We will take the camels and leave." And for the first time, she realised he was frightened. It was in his eyes; it was in the wary way he stood, half inclined towards the weathered stones as if he expected to see something come from that direction.

"I can't leave Andrew. He may be injured. He needs me."

"Do not go, lady. You will die too. Come with me."

"No," she said. "Can I take a camel?"

Hassan sighed but helped her up onto the unwilling beast.

AMANDA HAD no idea Hassan was following her. He tried to persuade her not to go to the city of the Kephroun, but she wouldn't listen; all she could think about was Andrew. Hassan argued with her, but eventually, she rode off on the camel. Though she pretended to be brave, she was shaking. She didn't want to get lost again, but she couldn't abandon Andrew. He'd done so much for her.

She saw the ruins of the city from afar, among some dry, craggy hills. At first, she didn't recognise them as man-made, they were sculpted and eroded by the wind and looked ancient beyond the memory of man.

This was why Andrew was so excited. This city was apparently unknown to western science. The city that would make his name.

Amanda came to a rock wall. The camel could take her no further because the ground was so broken and rough. There were signs that there had once been a roadway here, but it was long worn away.

Amanda dismounted. She imagined Andrew with a broken leg or trapped under a rock-fall.

She swallowed nervously as she dropped down the steps, and then she went up over the boulders without giving herself time to think better of it.

She felt the cool of the shade as she entered the ravine. After it turned to the left, it went straight for a short while, where the bas-relief carvings were in the walls, then it turned again right.

She stopped and pushed back her blonde hair. She had lost her baseball cap hours before. The cotton shirt under the fleece was stained with sand and sweat. She thought she probably smelled terrible. It was days since she'd had a shower. Then she saw the blood on her fleece. It came from her hand. She had been so fixated on finding Andrew; she hadn't noticed that she'd taken off an inch of skin from the heel of her right hand. She sucked at the wound; and thought of how she was going to get into the ruin. The pain was just an annoyance. It wouldn't kill her.

She turned and went back to the ravine's entrance. From here, the walls went up vertically, but there were fissures in them and, in one place, a fig sapling grew. She could use that to pull herself up, but there were no footholds to get up that high. She scanned the rocks all around and then she saw it. About fifteen feet up were the remains of an ancient staircase that had fallen away in an earthquake long ago. It looked like it had once led from the ground level to the cliff tops.

Amanda stood beneath the first steps. They were out of reach, and there was no obvious way up.

She jumped for the first hold with both hands, and got it, one hand over the other in the same gap. Then she pulled her petite frame up. She had no fat on her, and she was grateful for that. Her muscles shook as they took the strain. She was close enough to swing for the next handhold, but if she missed it, she would fall onto the broken rocks below— not a fatal fall, but one that could cause serious injury.

She swung. And she got it. The leverage of the two hand-holds was better, and she hoisted herself so that she could force her left foot into a gap in the sandstone. The rock she gripped so desperately onto, fell away and she swung wide, holding on now with just one hand.

Amanda's fingers were rigid with pain. She was within a minute of falling. Gravity urged her down, but her will wouldn't let her release her fingers. She reached out again for the handhold that had betrayed her before. But this time, it was bigger because of the rock that had fallen away. She got a good grip. She pulled and moved and went right. And then, in a fluid movement, she went up again. She was within one lunge of the bottom of the antique staircase. She stretched and jumped, and she had it. With both hands, she pulled herself up. She dragged through the dirt and hugged the bottom stone steps. She was breathing rapidly. The sweat in her eyes stung. She wiped them and smeared blood from her cut hand. There was room to stand here, but she hung onto the rocks and looked back the way she'd come. Below her was a sheer rock face that no one could have climbed. Except she had. The only sign she had come this way were the smears of blood on the rock wall below.

Then Amanda turned and on her knees at first, but then standing, she made her way up the stone staircase to the clifftop.

THE SKY above was pure desert blue. The sun was hot on her face. On the exposed mountain edges, the wind was up. It contained only a fraction of the sand it did at the desert floor, but the ridge-path was so high that at any time she could be blown off.

The wind grew stronger as she came to the summit of the dry mountain around which this ancient city was built. Tumble-down ruins lay all around, and the the gusts of wind threatened to send her over the edge. She went on her knees and looked forward to the rocky climb in front of her. She risked standing taller, waiting to correct her balance with hands out if the gusts pushed her left or right. Standing, she could see further. She was on a long ridge, going north-south, at the end it climbed up and there were stone-cut stairs, weathered by the centuries since they were first built. The ridge was narrow and the rock crumbling. If she had an accident here, she would plunge into the gorges on either side.

And there was still no sign of Andrew.

To her right, she saw the rocks fall away into the ravine, and she saw how the narrow gap snaked towards what she guessed was the centre of the ruined settlement. To the north was a range of brutally dry mountains, their ridges etched like stone knives in the sere air. To the left, the hill she was on stopped and plunged sheer, two hundred feet into the sand.

She walked forward. Her plan was to find a vantage point from which to look down into the ruins and thus have a good chance of spotting Andrew.

The rocks were uneven, and she had to take care as she made her way onward.

The effort of crouching and walking as quickly as she could made her breathing ragged. The end of the ridge was in sight. She had hoped there would be an easy way down. Or at least some kind of vantage point. But instead of that, the ridge narrowed and a bridge led to a platform of red stone.

She shaded her eyes to regard the bridge; there were no sides to it. It was a flat projection of dressed stone, some six feet wide. It went straight forward to an open space, again clearly ancient and clearly artificial. This space must have been twenty feet square. Most of it was taken up by a circular bowl, carved from the sandstone. Something was moving in the bowl, she thought. She crawled closer on her hands and knees to see better, and she saw that there was more than one thing there. At first, it was hard to make out what they were. She thought they were heaps of rags. Yes, they were clothes, and certainly in rags. But then she saw bones among them, bleached white and broken. There were skulls with holes where their faces should be. Other bones were piled up unevenly: legs, rib cages, hips. They were all human, and some had scraps of flesh hanging to them. As her eyes untangled the scene, she saw that some of the bodies were almost whole.

And then, at the far side of the carved bowl, she recognised Andrew. He looked pale, his gold sunglasses twisted round his face, his blond hair caked in dark blood. She put her hand to her mouth and held onto a rock to steady herself. She saw his knee was bent up and he appeared to be lying on his side, one arm crushed beneath him. At first, he lay still, and she thought he was dead. But then there was movement. Despite herself, her heart turned over; Andrew was alive. Amanda broke into a run, balancing dangerously on rocks, desperate to get to him. She shouted out to him, but if he heard her, he didn't look in her direction.

When Amanda got close, she saw that all the bodies moved. Beneath their ragged clothes, she saw shifting and shuffling. She smelled the stink of death. Apart from Andrew, the other people who were still recognisable as people were local Arabs: a fat woman, a child, an old man. The child's belly was distended with gas. The foul odour was almost unbearable. As she got closer, a cloud of flies lifted into the air and then settled to feed again. The flies were on Andrew's face. His lips were swollen and discoloured, his eyes hidden beneath his broken glasses. Once again, she thought he must be dead and then she saw his chest move.

"Thank, God," she said. She rushed forward until she was among the corpses. Bones cracked under her feet and as she moved, her legs tangled in the torn clothes of the victims. Somebody had piled up these bodies here. They all seemed dead. But she couldn't believe Andrew was dead. His arm moved, and she went closer.

Amanda was above him now. His skin was a blue-grey, the same hue she'd seen on her dead grandmothers corpse. "Oh, Andrew," she said. "How ill you are." She kneeled down, pushing the bloated corpse of a child out of the way. She hated to do it, but the child was dead, and her Andrew lived. She kissed Andrew's forehead. It was cold. She gently removed his twisted golden sunglasses and saw his left eye was closed, and his right was blind and empty. She didn't understand. He had moved. How could he look so dead and still move?

And then his arm moved again. Amanda looked down and saw it wasn't Andrew's arm that moved but something in the child's corpse. She looked again and watched the child's flesh bulge and ripple. And then she saw the same movement in Andrew's belly. It wasn't Andrew's belly that was moving, but something in it. She stood back in horror.

She edged away. Then she turned and saw Hassan. He'd come across the ridge to her. His face was twisted in disgust and fear. He reached out to pull her away from the stinking bodies. But she couldn't come away. The movement in Andrew's corpse compelled her to look again.

Her mouth fell open. She turned in wondering terror to Hassan, "What is this?" she said.

"The Kephroun," he said.

Amanda turned back to look at Andrew. Her scream echoed among the dry rocks as the things burst from Andrew's belly; they were grubs, some kind of foul centipede young.

Hassan grabbed her hand and tugged. She watched, shaking, as five or six of the insects came out of Andrew's flesh. One came up his throat and forced its way out of his mouth. It waved its feelers at her. It was bright red. She heard the noise they made, and she knew these were the maggot forms of the things that had been in the desert. They varied in colour as they squirmed free of Andrew's corpse. The one from his mouth had black eyes and hundreds of tiny red feet. The feet rippled up and down as it pulled itself out of him. She spun around and saw the centipedes were erupting from the corpses all around.

Hassan pulled her away. "They will kill you," he said.

She stepped backwards and then her foot sunk to the

ankle. There was a hole beneath where she stood. The bones of the dead formed a lattice that supported her, but they were only debris at the mouth of a pit. Beneath the bones was a shaft sunk through the pillar that supported the High Place of Sacrifice. The bones cracked under her, and she fell into the pit, pulling Hassan with her.

As she tumbled down, Amanda expected she would fall the full height of the pillar, but she did not. She slipped around twenty feet and landed in a soft, squirming mass. It was dark in there and hot. The stink of putrid flesh made her gag. Hassan landed beside her, and she heard him retch. She put her hands out to feel what she had landed in. She and Hassan had fallen into the feeding pit of the Kephroun. The segmented, grub-like bodies of the insects were soft and warm. They resisted her hands and pushed back as they sensed her warm flesh. These were the young, and they stayed in the hollow heart of the pillar until their bodies had hardened into the carapaces that made the tracks in the sand. She pushed against them but only sunk deeper. She was waist-deep in the insects now. A noise came from her, but she hardly recognised it as human; it began deep in her abdomen and was born of deep, primal horror. The bugs moved around. Their thousands of legs tickled her flesh. They crawled over her arms. She pushed against them, and Hassan slashed them with his knife. He cut into their heads and stabbed their bodies, and they burst with a soft sound, and their yellow blood sprayed over Amanda and Hassan.

THEN SHE FELT them begin to bite her skin. To the insects, she was merely more food, live or dead, it didn't matter. They would worm into her, and the adults would lay their eggs. Amanda felt their searching mouths at her belly and her thighs. They crawled between her legs, seeking the warmth of her groin. Amanda screamed. She felt the tingling of the enzymes as they regurgitated bile from their stomachs to begin to digest her skin before they ate it.

Hassan stabbed frantically around him. Once he had cleared space, he found a foothold on the rocks that made up the inner wall of the pillar. He pushed himself out of the seething, wriggling mass and stood tall. Grubs were attached to his back, holding on with their feeding mouths.

Hassan reached down to Amanda. Blood was streaming from wounds on his arm, but he couldn't reach her. She was struggling, drowning. He stretched further, forcing his hand toward her and Amanda strained back but couldn't get to him. Hassan became unbalanced, teetering and almost tumbling back into the grubs. Amanda knew, if she didn't get his hand this time, she would go deeper. Then they would be at her face, around her eyes and writhing into her mouth. She closed her eyes in horror.

Hassan yelled, "Take my hand! Please!"

She opened her eyes and took one last chance at life and reached. Hassan's steady hand clamped around hers. She felt the power in his muscles, and he dragged her up.

"Try and get your feet on the rocks in the wall. They are uneven and will give you somewhere to stand."

She kicked at the Kephroun who clicked and hissed angrily as she hurt them. She kicked again, squashing some of the young. She kicked a third time, and her toes felt the rock wall. She felt up and down and then her foot lodged. This was enough. She pushed, and Hassan pulled, and she was half out. The bugs fell off her. The adrenaline that coursed through her meant she felt no pain from their bites. Hassan climbed higher. He reached down, again and again, she took his hand. He helped her, and her climber's instinct came into play. She saw the handholds and let go of Hassan. She climbed up under her own power, finding nooks and ledges to pull herself up with. She kicked back, and the remaining hanging Kephroun young flew off her legs, landing among their kin.

Above her, she saw the sun through the mouth of the pillar. Cracked bones and rags lay half across the opening. Hassan climbed up in front of her, one hand still holding his knife. He was first up. Amanda came after him but hesitated before pulling herself out of the pillar. The smell of the feeding pit rose up the shaft. Above her, around the feeding bowl at the top of the shaft in the open air, she heard clicking and moving. The larger Kephroun were up there, attracted by the commotion. She knew that they were fast and she might not outrun them, but when she looked down again at the sea of worming things, she knew she had no option but to climb out. Hassan was at the top, waiting. Her heart was beating like a hammer. She wanted a minute before she went up. She had to get emotionally ready to face what she knew lurked above.

Hassan was staring down. He was sweating.

Hassan knelt to help her, she found her courage, and together now they stood on the stone top of the Place of Sacrifice. Amanda could not help but look where Andrew's remains were. His death was apparent now; his torso and legs were disjointed, and two large Kephroun moved over him, eating where they went. One of them was draped in his bloodied shirt where it had caught on its segments. She was suddenly sick. She wiped away the bile from her lips. Hassan stood by her, "Please," he said. His voice shook. "They are coming."

She nodded.

He turned and ran across the high stone bridge that led

to the rock ridge. She was going after him when she heard
the clattering of the Kephroun as they scuttled after her.

Amandae turned and ran. It was dangerous crossing the
bridge at this speed as the stone was worn and there were
no sides. One misstep and she would fall. She slowed her
pace, shaking with the dilemma of going too fast and falling
or going too slow and being caught. She saw the hard stones
of the ruins many feet below her. Hassan was already over
the bridge. He was frightened, but he still waited. The
Kephroun were moving across the bridge behind her. The
adult Kephroun raised themselves up, so their heads were
about six feet high. They came at her in a strange swaying
movement. And they were quick.

She caught up with Hassan. Then they both ran. The
rocks were rough. He held her hand to steady her. She had
to let go of his hand; he was pulling her, and he was
tugging her off balance. She shook her head. He let her
hand drop and matched his pace with hers. He slowed
down for her. Amanda went as fast as she could. Every
atom of her concentration was fixed on where her feet
would land. She chose one footing, then the next, but she
heard the Kephroun behind her, and she knew they were
gaining. They were halfway down the ridge, but if they
could get to the broken staircase, the Kephroun wouldn't
be able to come after them. They were a hundred yards
from safety, when she glanced back and knew they
wouldn't make it.

He read the despair in her eyes, and he knew what she
was thinking. He nodded and stopped. She stopped too and
he shook his head. "No, you go. Go!"

She pulled at his arm, begging him to come.

He smiled. "No, I will stop them."

She looked at his knife. Then she looked back at the foul

centipede things. They were almost within touching distance. Their legs writhed at the air as they came.

There was no time. Hassan pushed her. "Please Go. I will see you when I have stopped these." He brandished his knife at them.

Amanda turned and ran. She was crying as she crossed the rocks of the ridge top.

Hassan yelled, cursed, and stabbed at them. Amanda heard a high-pitched shriek from a Kephroun as he pierced it. She was almost there—two-thirds of the way down the ridge. She would wait for Hassan at the top of the broken staircase and show him how to get to safety. The couldn't follow there. That was a plan. That was hope.

She got to the top of the staircase, turned ready to yell to Hassan to come to her, but as she turned, she screamed; Hassan had fallen and was being eaten by three of the centipede beasts. There were so many more of them more than she had thought. They were everywhere, and they moved so quickly in this their natural habitat.

She didn't see the Kephroun jerk as it hit her full in the face, but she felt its pincers lacerate her cheeks and felt the the gut enzyme scald as it spewed on her. Amanda pulled back, tearing her skin from its jaws. The Kephroun struck again, but she twisted to the side. This Kephroun was the one draped in Andrew's ripped and stained shirt. It had been the one that had come up through his chest.

Amanda backed off, dragging her backside over the rocks, scraping her elbows as she desperately tried to get away. She almost escaped.

The Kephroun darted forward again. This time it hit her in the belly, its teeth tearing through her shirt, and entering her flesh. She gazed into its insect face; its bright black eyes; its swivelling teeth and spiral mouth. Her blood foamed in her throat and her pretty painted fingernails pierced the palms of her hands. She was dying, but not dead, when the Kephroun placed its eggs in her flesh, from which, in several days, its hungry young would emerge.

THREE DAYS AFTER AMANDA DIED, Kareen McAvoy, one of Amanda's friends received a postcard in rainy Glasgow. Kareen frowned to see Amanda was on holiday with Andrew. She didn't like Andrew, but she hoped Amanda was having a nice time. Over her toast and coffee, Kareen studied the picture of the Roman ruins at Jerash and then flipped the card to read Amanda's words on the back.

> "Having a lovely time. Scenery is awesome. The wildlife is particularly interesting. They have all sorts of creatures here we don't have at home. Some of them very strange!

8

THE LIGHTHOUSE

إبليس
Sam Trafford got the Devil's name tattooed on his shoulder to let the Devil know he wasn't scared of him. It was like a taunt. Old Nick had tried to get him once and failed, and it was as if with the tattoo, Sam was daring him to try again. The curling black letters spelled إبليس 'Iblis', the Arabic for "he who brings despair."

The tattoo was because of Fallujah. In 2004, Sam was in the 3rd Battalion, 1st Marine Corp. The insurgents ambushed his platoon while they were clearing houses. Sam was on point. He'd gone in first but didn't see the booby-trap. The grenade went off his right side, injuring his hand, destroying his hearing in his right ear. For ten long minutes, he was alone in the house with the terrorists, and then Gene Nygard came and saved his life.

Later, Sam and Gene got tattoos done back in Chicago when Sam got discharged from the hospital. Gene got some lines from a Ryan Adams song. Sam got the devil.

Sam could still see Gene looking at the name Iblis, a big frown on his face as they sat in the bar on North Clark St.

He said, "Sam, my friend, having the devil's name on your arm is gonna bring you nothing but bad luck."

Sam laughed and bought him a beer. "I don't believe in luck, buddy," he said. "And the devil's got no hold on you if you have friends to watch your back."

In the end, Sam lived, but Gene died. He went back to Iraq and was killed in action. Another waste — a steadfast, loyal man that the country could have used instead of the self-seeking politicians who profited from the soldiers' sacrifice.

Every time Sam saw his tattoo, he thought of Gene Nygard and that house and how Gene never left him behind.

But now, six years later and a world away, Sam drove down the Pacific Coast Highway south from Carmel. His companion, Nadia, was in the passenger seat; hair combed back, Ray-Bans shielding her eyes. Her hand was out the window, feeling the wind, the charms on her hippy bracelet dancing, and gleaming. The fine hairs on her arm were turned gold by the California sun. She wore expensively ripped denim shorts, an American Apparel no-sweatshop t-shirt, and over it a blue floral kimono.

He guessed no one would have put the two of them together. Sam looked what he was; Nadia looked what she wanted to be. They were chalk and cheese.

Nadia happened to him like the sun rising on a new world. In the fall of 2009, he got a job as a technician in a lab at Berkley, and Nadia was an assistant professor of Transpersonal Psychology there. The first time he saw her was at a meditation class that his shrink told him would be good for his PTSD.

Meditation was more her scene: Nadia ate superfood açaí berries and had her chakras realigned every three months. When he saw her, he hesitated to speak; she was surely out of his league. But when you have the devil on your arm, and you should by rights be dead anyway, what do you have to lose? He struck up a conversation with her in the second session and got lost in her eyes by the third.

He knew she was the one. He glanced at her now as he drove. She was looking out the window, lost in the view of the ocean, and who could blame her getting distracted by that view? Heading south towards Big Sur, the ocean was to their right, the rugged cliffs dropping to azure water. Kelp forests floated under the wave tops; sea lions basked on rocks; Nadia was by his side. Everything in life was good.

Before he could react, the car entered the fog. It came up suddenly like a wall, and it enveloped them, making Sam hit the brakes, sending them sliding on the damp highway. He got control then proceeded slowly through the wet cotton-wool mist. He put the headlights on.

The temperature dropped ten degrees within a second, and Nadia pulled her kimono tight around her.

"Something to do with the water coming down from Alaska," he explained.

"I don't care what causes it," she said. "I want the sun back." She was shivering.

"Sorry, babe," he said as if it was his fault. He always wanted to make things right for her.

She laughed. Her voice was deep for a woman's and sexy. "I don't blame you personally," she said. She squeezed his right hand with its missing fingers. He wanted to pull it away, feeling like a freak, but she didn't seem to mind his injury.

A couple of miles further on the twisting road, they saw their goal — the lighthouse. The fog had settled into a bank

of low cloud, rolling off the ocean. The lighthouse tower
rose above it pearlescent and gleaming like a fairy-tale.

"There!" said Nadia. "That's it!"

"Yep," Sam grinned. When she was excited, Nadia was
like a happy little girl. She smiled at him and clapped her
hands in delight. "It looks like a dream!" she said.

"We need to get some provisions before we head there,"
Sam said.

"There's a town up ahead. it doesn't look big from the
map, but it must have a grocery store."

Sam drove on. The road took them away from the coast,
and the sun reappeared. The town was beautiful — fruit
trees in blossom, pink jasmine, wisteria, and laburnum all
around the houses. The wooden buildings painted blue
and white and ochre nestled on the edges of a forest that
led to the mountains of the Coastal Range. There was a
river at the edge of town winding from the mountains to
the sea.

Sam parked alongside a neat and clean sidewalk and got
out. Nadia watched him, smiling. She had her sunglasses on
again, and her teeth gleamed white between red lips. How
he loved her smile. Whenever she wanted him to do something, she just had to turn on that smile, and he melted. She
was impatient to explore. "Come on, slowcoach."

She beckoned, turned, and walked backward, grinning
at him. Then when he dallied, fumbling with his keys, she
strolled away, tall, tanned, young, and lovely.

He watched her go. His father beat sheet metal for a
living in Philadelphia; hers was a neurosurgeon in San Francisco. She'd grown up in the sunny suburbs of San Jose with
everything the good life could give her. He'd joined the
Army because it was a route out of the grimness of where he
was from. But she was here with him in the sun. On vaca-

tion. Who'd have predicted that happy ending for Sam Trafford?

Twenty yards from the car, they found a grocery store. It sold local produce, and they bought eggplants and zucchinis, olive oil, ripe tomatoes and onions, and fresh garlic. "I'll make a ratatouille," said Nadia. "My dad's recipe — it's the best."

They got milk, eggs, coffee, and bread. And wine. Six bottles of local wine. They'd taken the lighthouse for three weeks, ostensibly for Nadia to get quiet time to work on a research paper. Sam joked that he was there as her personal assistant.

"Yep," she said, "Cook, cleaner, and handyman during the day — red hot lover when the sun goes down. I'm gonna keep you busy."

He thought he was up to the task.

As they walked, she pointed. "Let's get a coffee over there before we head out to the lighthouse."

The coffee house was a white painted bungalow that fronted onto the main street. When they walked through the darkened bar, they found a sun-soaked veranda that looked out over an orange grove. They settled down in the low striped armchairs and studied the menus. Sam knew what he wanted. Just a coffee. He put the menu down and gazed at the fruit trees and gardens of the pretty little town. Swallows swooped and jinked overhead. Bees buzzed nearby. The day was warm.

Nadia took off her sunglasses and placed them on the dark wooden table in front. He admired her hippy bracelet again as it caught the sun. There was an iridescent sheen to the tiny metal disks, and they shushed and susurrated as she moved her elegant hand. He bought it for her in a tourist shop on Pier 39 in San Francisco. The shop was on one of the upper deck areas, run by a guy from Bombay. The man had held the necklace in his hand, twirling the charms that hung off it — pentagrams, and dream catchers—the kind of thing she liked.

Sam remembered how the owner's daughter had stamped Nadia's cheek with a star made of glitter after he got her the bracelet, and the girl turned to him and told him it would bring his wife luck. Then Nadia had kissed him.

She looked up from the menu and said, "You look like you've just seen something wonderful."

"I have," he said, not taking his eyes off her.

"You're so sentimental," she said, smiling. She squeezed Sam's hand. "Let's not get too serious, though." She was looking at him with an expression of studied care.

He tried to sound like he felt the same way. "Sure. Live each day at a time."

"That's right." She looked away at the darting birds over the garden. "I really like you, Sam. We're good friends."

"Of course. Absolutely."

Just good friends. That's how she wanted to play it. He gazed into the dark of the cafe, to see whether the waiter was bringing their coffee — flat black for him, chai latte for her.

She punched his arm gently. "Don't get moody."

The waiter came. Nadia ran her hand through her sun-bleached hair and put her Ray-Bans back on.

The waiter was a young guy, about seventeen. When he'd put their drinks down, he noticed Sam's tattoo, showing under his t-shirt sleeve, and took in the missing fingers and the scars on his scalp.

"Do you want to eat?" he said.

"Sure," nodded Nadia. "Can I get the chicken with the California Sunset Salad, please?"

The waiter wrote it down. "For you, sir?"

"Nothing, thanks."

The waiter hesitated, then he said, "Were you in Iraq?" he said. "Just the Arabic tattoo..."

Sam nodded. He felt awkward like he always did.

"Thank you for your service," said the boy with great respect.

Sam said, "You're welcome, but I was just doing my job." He turned his attention to the coffee.

The waiter seemed to want to mend the awkwardness. "You on vacation?" he said.

"He is," said Nadia, running her hand up the nape of Sam's neck and into his short blond hair. "I'm working." She flashed the boy one of her big smiles.

He flushed. "Where are you staying?" he asked.

"The lighthouse by Punta de Lobos," Nadia said.

A look came over the boy's face.

"What?" said Nadia, laughing. "You look like you've seen a ghost."

The boy waved his hand and smiled. "Just it's haunted."

Nadia teased the boy. "A fine young man like you scared of ghosts?"

The boy blushed more deeply.

"Leave him, Nadia," said Sam. He knew what a flirt she was, and he knew she didn't mean it, but she shouldn't play with the kid.

"Haunted by what anyway?" said Nadia.

"There was a guy who lived there in the 1920s," said the boy. "He was working for the Lighthouse Service. They say he did some bad things. He disappeared. Since then it's been full of evil spirits."

"Bullshit," said Sam.

"But it's a vacation rental."

The boy looked grave. "There have been deaths. A family drowned. Check it out."

Sam looked away. The boy was annoying him now. The waiter turned, but as he stepped away, he said, "You could get somewhere else."

"Why do we want anywhere else?" said Nadia.

"It's a bad place." The kid looked serious.

"Thanks for the warning," said Sam, fixing the boy with a cold glare. The kid finally disappeared.

Nadia squeezed Sam's arm. She said, "What did you think of that?"

"That load of horseshit? Not much."

WHEN THEY GOT to the coast again, the fog had lifted. Sam and Nadia drove off the main highway down a sandy track through dunes and saw that the tide had risen and covered the causeway that led to the lighthouse. Unable to go further, Sam got out of the car and left Nadia sitting inscrutably, looking at the ocean.

Sam walked up to the lapping waves. He could see the roadway underwater for the first couple of feet, and then it disappeared. He figured the tide was at least five feet deep. They would have to wait. How long he didn't know.

The convertible roof was still down. Nadia smoked one of her colored Sobranie cigarettes. Sam looked at it, burning between her elegant fingers, her bracelet catching the sun. He couldn't see her eyes through her Ray-Bans. "What?" she finally said.

He shrugged and said, "Nothing."

"I know you don't approve of this." She nodded at the cigarette.

"It's up to you what you do."

"Hmm," she said, flicking the cigarette out of the window. "See? Gone."

He smiled despite himself. "Until the next one," he said.

"It's a little victory. You should enjoy it. You won't get many," Nadia teased.

He laughed now and walked toward her, sitting down, leaving the door open. The breeze was warm.

"How long do you think until the tide ebbs and we can get across?" She said.

"Hours probably."

"How do you want to fill the time?"

"We could sleep."

"Okay," she said. She ran her fingers along Sam's knee and grinned. "Or we could fool around?"

"Somebody'll see," he said, but he was smiling.

She looked theatrically out of the car. "Well, there's a horse or two over there," she pointed. She looked up at the blue sky and pointed again. "And a couple buzzards up there. Don't think they care what we do, though."

Her hand came up his neck and into his blond hair. "Let's be friends," she said. "Or it'll be a long three weeks."

He leaned in and kissed her. The horses and buzzards watched for a while and then got on with their business.

The car was too cramped. They grew frantic and impatient at the lack of space. "Wait," Nadia said. She jumped out of the car, went to the trunk, and pulled out a blanket. "Come here," she said.

They made love on a blanket beside the car. It was a wild and lonely spot, and no one disturbed them. No one was even near.

Then they slept in the sun, her head on his arm, hair spread around like a waterfall.

When they woke, his arm was stiff. The heat was less. The tide had ebbed.

"Looks like we can get to the lighthouse now," Sam said.

Nadia looked sleepy still. He liked her like that. He put his hand out to help her up from the blanket, and she took his fingers.

"You drive?" she said, throwing him the key.

The causeway was still wet, maybe an inch of water in the far end. Storms had dug holes in it, and Sam had to negotiate the route carefully.

He saw Nadia laughing at him. "You're so slow and steady, Sam."

"That's what you like about me," he said, not sure if it was true.

That might be so," she said.

There was room to park the car outside the front of the lighthouse on a small concrete apron. The key was in an envelope nailed on the old wooden door. The door's green paint was flaking. Nadia ran her hand on the smooth white wall of the lighthouse beside the door. "The stone's lovely and warm," she said.

Sam opened the door with a creak. "Trusting," Sam said.

"Don't think anyone comes out here."

"Must be the evil spirits that keep them away."

He saw her shudder. He was surprised his joke bothered her. He apologized.

"Someone just walked over my grave," she said.

They entered the lighthouse. There was a chill inside the place, and it smelled of seaweed. A spiral staircase led up. They mounted it. The door of the first floor led into a kitchen. There was a small pantry. In it was a box of pasta spirals and some rice and a can of condensed milk and not much else. Sam brought the groceries from the car, and he put them on the utility top near the cooker. The cooker had a gas cylinder underneath.

"Looks dangerous," said Nadia, "that cylinder just sitting there full of propane or butane or whatever it is."

"Probably isn't. It looks like it's been here a while without causing any problems."

"I'll believe you. Want to look upstairs?" Nadia said.

"Of course."

"You go first," she said.

He checked her face to see whether she was joking. "Evil spirits?"

She punched him in the arm, right on his Iblis tattoo. "The kid creeped me out."

They went further up. Sam went first, and Nadia cautiously stepped behind him, looking like she was going to jump out of her skin at the slightest sound. It was weird that she was so unnerved.

On the next floor was a living room. There were wooden chairs and a sofa with cushions and throws with local Native American patterns on them. A big picture window faced the ocean, and a brass telescope set up against it on a tripod. Someone had decorated the room with fishing nets, and in the fishing nets were hung big shells and dried starfish.

"Oh, it's nice," Nadia said.

There was a bookshelf with some books about sailing and a couple of yellow novels: some thrillers and romances. Sam picked out a Western and flicked through the pages.

"I guess the bedroom's upstairs?" said Nadia. She stretched up her arms and yawned. The hippy bracelet jingled as she swept it down.

"I guess," said Sam.

"You go first."

He laughed. "Again? What's got into you?"

"Just go." She pushed him.

On the next floor up, the room had a big king-sized bed with crisp white sheets and a blanket. There was another window smaller than the one in the living room but with the same ocean view. Sam stared out and saw the ocean planing out to the horizon where its azure met the sky's powder blue. There was a ship out there, a long way from land.

"It feels isolated," she said.

"That's because it is. It's what you wanted. There's a table in the living room for you to put your laptop on."

"No cell signal."

"No land-line."

"Peace."

"You can get on with your writing," he said. "I'm going to beach-comb."

"You know, I think that life would suit you," she said.

He went back to the window. "When I left the Army, I didn't want to see anyone. I wanted to go to a place where I could walk all day on my own with just nature for company."

"So you chose Oakland," she teased.

"Yeah," he said. "I'm perpetually confused about what I want." He gazed at her. "Mostly."

She touched his arm and looked as if she was going to say something. Then she shrugged and chased the thought away. "The stairs keep going up," she said. "Go take a look."

He gave a mock salute. "Yes, ma'am."

He went out back onto the stairs. His feet echoed on the stone steps. He got so far, and then the staircase ended against a door. It was padlocked. He went and rattled the lock. No key. He turned and went back to Nadia. She was unpacking, putting her clothes in the armoire.

"It's a dead-end, locked door," he said. "I guess the light-house light is up there."

"They probably don't want anyone messing with it."

"I can see that," he said. "Want some coffee?"

"Sure," she said. "Go to the kitchen. I'll be right down."

He went downstairs and opened the door to let the sea air in. The coastal mountains reared up landwards beyond the road and the forest. The weather had changed again, and tendrils of fog were drifting in from the sea. It just felt so natural and free. Being here would do him good.

And then he saw a cat looking mournfully towards him, its ears pricked up and alert. What the hell was a cat doing here? What did it eat? Not much by the state of it. It was a skinny thing. It probably lived by eating rats or maybe even fish. It came right up to him and wrapped itself around his leg. He picked it up and felt its purr against his chest.

He took it up to where Nadia was coming out of the en-suite shower in the bathroom.

Her face broke into a broad smile when she saw the cat. "Oh, a little pussy cat! How thin it is!" She extended her arms, and he gave it to her. She cuddled it against her damp, toweled breast. "Listen to it purr! Poor thing. Let's give it some tuna."

They'd bought tuna amongst the other groceries from the convenience store. "I'll go open a can," Sam said.

"I'm going to call it Misty in honor of the fog that's always round this place," she said, still hugging it.

Later, Nadia cooked them a dinner of ratatouille — her father's recipe. It was good. They opened a bottle of Napa Valley wine. After dinner in the kitchen, they sat in the living room. Nadia had her laptop on and began to write. Sam started the Western *The Shootist*. They didn't put the lamps on for a long time, and gradually the day faded, and darkness grew over the ocean. Then, the first piercing beam of light came from above them, flashing out over the wine-dark sea.

"My God, what's that?" Nadia jerked her head up, pulling out the earphones.

Sam laughed. "Wait," he said.

"Wait for what?"

And then around a minute later, there was another beam of light.

"Duh, we live in a lighthouse," he said.

"Oh yeah," she said, annoyed. "Draw the drapes. That light is blinding."

He walked past her to do so. The curtains were heavy black-out material, designed to keep out the blinding light. They then lapsed into silence again. He went back to reading, and she went back to writing. The wind rose and soon drove the rain against the window like a lash.

Sam peered out through the drapes. "It's dark out there."

Nadia was engrossed in her writing, so she didn't hear him. He left the room and trotted down the stone spiral staircase to the front door. When Sam opened it, the wind blew in with a shower of salt rain, making him start back. He kept the door open against the wind long enough to see that the dark water had rushed across the causeway, cutting them off from the land.

"We couldn't get away now, even if we wanted", he thought. He closed the door, turned back, and was halfway upstairs when there was a loud banging. It seemed to come from high up in the lighthouse.

He craned his neck and yelled, "Nadia? What are you doing?"

She didn't reply.

He ran up the steps to find her at the door of the living room. Her face was white. "What the hell was that noise?" she said.

Sam frowned. "I thought it was you."

"Doing what? It sounds like someone kicking a door in." She was looking up the stairs. "It was from up there." She pointed.

"There isn't anything upstairs. Just the light."

There was another bang and then a repeated hammering. It was like something was trying to get out. Realization hit him. "It's from behind the padlocked door."

"Go check it," she said. She was shaking. "Please."

"Okay," he said. There was something unnatural about the noise, but he didn't want to look weak in front of Nadia.

Sam flicked the light switch, and the bulb came on above them. He mounted the steps slowly. His hands were balled into fists as if he expected to fight, but he told himself not to be stupid. What could be in there that could threaten them? He heard himself breathing. Nadia waited below. For a moment, he was halfway between Nadia and the padlocked door. It was the feeling he used to get when he was a small boy standing in the dark of his old house afraid to turn on the light in case of what he'd see.

"Is it okay?" she called from below.

"Yeah, just gimme a sec," he said.

He exhaled and went on. He turned the corner, one hand on the wall, the other clenching and unclenching. This was stupid, but the noise was loud, crazy loud.

And then he saw the door. The padlock was still hanging there, the steel rusty but serviceable. He went up close and reached out to the lock. Then there was an almighty slam on the door. It rocked on its hinges as if whatever was behind it was taunting him with its strength.

Then it stopped. The banging ceased, but Sam's heart still hammered. He stared at the door. He had no key. What could he do? Nothing till he found the key. Breaking the door down was foolish. It made no practical sense. In daylight, he would recheck it. He turned and walked down to Nadia. It was still quiet behind him, but he had seen the door shudder with each blow. Something was the other side.

He got down to Nadia. She came and hugged him, clinging on, but looking over his shoulder upstairs. "I'm scared, Sam."

"There's got to be an explanation."

"Do you think someone's got locked in?"

"Someone? No. How long since anyone was here?" Sam said. "They'd have starved to death."

The silence thickened as they stood there, waiting for the banging to start, and dreading it. Sam's heart was back to normal. He squeezed her to him. "Don't worry. It's probably a bird," Sam said. "A gull."

"The noise was too loud."

"They're strong. It could be banging its wings on the door to get out."

She said, "There must be a key."

"We'll find it tomorrow," he said. "Come on down."

"I won't sleep with that banging."

"It's stopped now."

They undressed and got ready for bed. Sam tried to make a joke of the banging, but she wasn't laughing. She was uneasy. She hardly spoke.

They lay there together in the big clean bed in the dark on the edge of the ocean. He pulled her to him, and she clung to him, frightened of the night. They had pulled the heavy drapes tight to keep the intense flash of the light-house out, but he felt its pulsing like a heart. Outside, he heard the wind that whistled and howled. He listened to the rain and the breakers smashing against the rocks below. And then the cat started to purr. He'd forgotten about Misty. The cat was nestled between them, and he leaned down to stroke her.

The wind dropped, and the ocean was quiet. Sam dozed. But deep in the darkness, a long while after the sun had disappeared, and an eternity before morning, there was a cry from above. It was the cry of a lost soul. Or something worse.

IN THE MORNING, it was as if the sun had driven away all her cares. They were downstairs in the kitchen.

"You okay this morning?" said Sam.

"Sure." Nadia looked embarrassed with an air of puzzlement that he knew was put on. "What about?" she said.

He was patient. "The banging last night."

"Oh, that. It was just a bird, like you said, but it's stopped now. You know I'm such a scaredy-cat sometimes. What a difference a day makes, or a night," she said.

He turned to the peculator. "Want a coffee?"

"No, I'm drinking Yogi Tea."

"Like in Yogi Bear?"

"No," she said —but she was smiling —"As in Brahmins and Hindu holy men." She did a little Indian dance with her hands in prayer above her head, waggling her head from side to side.

"That's good," he laughed. "Quite sexy."

"They're not interested in sex, Sam. Unlike you. And me." She winked and sipped her green tea. "I'm writing this morning. What are you doing?"

He felt dismissed. "I hadn't thought."

"You could go look at the beach. The storm is sure to have turned up something interesting."

"Yeah, I could." He nodded, convincing himself, he'd rather do that than stay with her. "I will."

"Good. See you later."

And that was that. Nadia went upstairs with her Yogi Tea to turn on her laptop. He put on his jacket and boots and stepped out. The sun was trying to burn through a wreath of fog. He could see it as a dim circle of fire, weak behind clouds. The ocean had thrown up flotsam and jetsam around the concrete square outside the lighthouse. He saw the storm had decorated the car with a shower of pebbles and some kelp on the mirror. He checked the vehicle over for scratches, but it seemed to have escaped unscathed.

He noticed a path of broken concrete steps, half-covered in wet sand, which led to the beach. Sam decided to wander that way, his boots sinking in and leaving his mark. The sea had gone back about thirty yards and was breaking in a white froth line on the golden sand. Sea pools studded the rocks across his route, so he veered and zig-zagged to find the easiest way, and he was soon lost in the journey from pool to pool. He didn't think of Nadia for a while.

Sam searched for and mentally cataloged the shells, crabs, and anemones that lurked under rocks and in the clear seawater. Time went by, and he didn't notice. He strolled along the shoreline away from the lighthouse.

Then, about a hundred yards up the beach, where the barnacle streaked rocks came down to the water and closed off any further progress, he saw something half-buried in the sand. It looked like a discarded satchel. Sam hurried up to the object and saw it was upside down. He pulled at it, and, with a sucking noise, it came free of the sand. It was somebody's old bag, but it wasn't empty.

The canvas hold-all had a name stitched on it — Hector Mendes. Sam undid the rusty clasps and looked inside. Half buried in wet sand, contained in the bag was a sculpture. It was shaped from stone and about the size of a bowling pin, but more substantial. The rock was white-brown and decorated with strange petroglyphs. It looked ancient, and Sam grew suddenly excited. It might be valuable, and he was sure Nadia would love it.

Then he looked at the sky. The sun was dim behind clouds that seemed to thicken as he looked out. The tide was turning. Tendrils of fog were reaching out from the ocean, cutting off his view of the land. As he looked down the beach, the sand became invisible behind it. Above the fog, the lighthouse still stood clear of the mist. Straight and tall as a beacon. That was his mark.

Sam hurried back, one eye on the incoming tide. It looked like the water was in danger of cutting him off from the steps he had come down. He broke into a run, paddling through the shallow waves as they rushed in. About halfway, the waves were bursting by the rocks, and there was no dry sand left for him to walk on. He sloshed through the water to get to the concrete. The sea came to his knees, but then he found the steps, and he was up above the ocean.

His sudden fear of being cut off ebbed away, and his excitement returned. He was bringing a prize back to Nadia.

He went in the door, kicking the sand off his boots, and then the boots themselves before he went in. He put down his little stone idol and hung up his jacket on the peg. He left the dripping satchel outside the door. Then he scooped up the stone carving and ran up the stairs. Nadia wasn't in the kitchen. She was probably in the living room. He yelled, but there was no reply. Maybe she had her earphones in again. He shouted louder. Still nothing. By this time, he was up level with the living room. Her laptop was open on the table by the window—her empty mug of Yogi Tea nearby, a stub of a Sobranie cigarette in the glass ashtray.

"Nadia!" he yelled.

He ran up the steps to their bedroom. When he got to the door, he glanced in the room. The window was half open, letting the sea breeze in, but Nadia wasn't there. He gripped the idol tighter, and then he glanced out of the window and saw the car still outside.

The ocean flooded around the lighthouse again, drowning the causeway. Nadia must be in here somewhere. Sam thought about the stairs that led up, but all they led to was that padlocked door.

He went up cautiously, shouting out her name. As he rounded the corner, he saw the door. It hung open. Something had smashed the padlock into two pieces, and it lay broken on the steps. Sam stooped and picked it up with his left hand. The shackle had shattered, and the ends of the metal were sharp. What the hell had done that? And when?

"Nadia!" he shouted sharply through the open door. His voice echoed dully up the stone staircase. She didn't reply.

Sam stepped forward through the dark doorway into the newly opened space. Stairs, not white like those below, but discolored by damp and algae, ran up further. Sam quickly mounted the stairs.

Nadia had her back to him. She was stooped over a pile of leather-bound books and had her earphones in so she couldn't hear him. Behind her was the gleaming metal and glass dome of the automatic light — quiet and dead now and waiting for dark. He went over and tapped her shoulder. She turned around with a start.

"Nadia! You didn't answer. I've been yelling."

She laughed, seemed happy. "I found these books. They're journals."

"I was worried," he frowned.

"Where did you think I'd gone?" She met his eye, and he saw mockery in her gaze as if he was stupid or a fool to care about her.

"You didn't answer. How did I know?" Sam said.

She turned back to her prize. "These journals are fascinating. Help me carry them down."

She picked up three of the books and held them out for him. Then she saw the stone thing in his hand. She raised both eyebrows and reached out for it like a kid at Christmas. "Where did you find that?"

"On the beach. It was half-buried. Looked like last night's storm had turned it up. It looks ancient."

She snatched it from him and turned it over in her hands, stroking the smooth stone.

"I don't know what it is. Native American?" he said.

"I know what it is," she muttered.

He raised his eyebrows. "You do?"

She nodded. She tapped one of the leather-bound tomes. "It's in this book."

"So, what is it?"

"It's a religious item. It's got magic power. He calls it the Idol."

"Magic power?" He snorted, "Yeah, right." Then he saw she was serious.

"Like what?"

She was impatient. "Let's take them all downstairs," she said.

Nadia made him wait for an explanation while she made more yogi tea. She took that upstairs from the kitchen to the living room, and he followed her. The books were placed on the wooden table next to the stone idol. She sat on the sofa and pulled up her leg with her hand. "This is really cool," she said. She couldn't resist picking up the idol and stroking it again.

Sam sat on the seat opposite. "How did you break the padlock?"

"I didn't."

"So, how did the padlock break?"

"I don't know. It was broken when I got there. The storm?"

"And nothing else broke?" He shook his head. "I doubt it was the storm."

"I don't know then. I got bored writing, so I went up to see the door. To see if the bird was still there."

"That was brave of you."

She didn't look up at Sam. She held the stone thing in both hands. "I know. Funny how you get scared of stupid things in the dark. Anyway, the door was hanging open, and the padlock broken. It just leads up to the light. We should have guessed that."

"I guessed it," he said.

"Clever old you," she said. "But I went up. The storm dislodged one of the wooden panels around the light chamber. I could see these old books in there. It looks like they've been there for years, but there were hand marks in the dust, like someone found them not so long ago, but had put them back. I've just skimmed a couple of them."

"I thought you were here to write your paper."

"I am." She narrowed her eyes. She took a sip of her tea. The atmosphere cooled. "I thought you'd be excited," she said.

"So who wrote the books?" he said.

"A guy called Clark Ashton. Turns out, he was lighthouse keeper here in the winter of 1926. That's what I got from the little introduction." Her voice grew quiet and dramatic. "But he really wanted to be alone here to practice magic."

"Magic? Like conjuring?"

"No, black magic."

"Well, there are lots of weirdoes around. I guess there were even then."

"I think he was odd — from his journals. That," Nadia pointed to the stone idol that sat innocuously on the table, "was something he used."

"He used it? What for?"

"I don't know yet. I have to read more."

"And how did it get down on the beach, buried in the sand? It was in a bag with the name Hector Mendes on it. The bag wasn't from the 1920s. It looked quite modern."

"Maybe somebody lost it?" she said.

"Or they were trying to throw it away."

She laughed. "You say that so dramatically."

He stood up and went to open the window. The sea wind came in with the mewling of gulls and the smell of brine. The yellowed pages of the journal she had open fluttered in the wind. She put her hand on them, shielding the old paper. "Close the window," she said.

He did so. "You writing some more?" he said, standing over her.

"No, I want a break," she said.

"Want to come to bed?" he said.

She shook her head. "No, I want to read more of Clark Ashton's journal. You go for a nap. Maybe I'll come up later."

.   .   .

BUT SHE DIDN'T. The day went on, and Sam tried to read but failed. He just watched the ocean a lot and then went out for another walk. He checked the oil and tire pressure on the car. He and Nadia ate separately. He couldn't tear her away from her journals, so he left her. Sam was asleep by the time she came to bed. He didn't know what time she finally turned it, but it was late.

He couldn't rouse her the next morning. She turned and got irritated when he asked her if she wanted a coffee. He got up, dressed, and ate some breakfast. It was 11 am. He went to the bedroom door and looked in to see if she was up yet. Nadia still slept. Sam turned on his heel and walked out. The cat came halfway down the stairs with him, and when she saw he wasn't going to feed her, she stopped and let him go.

Sam grabbed his coat from the peg by the door. He dragged it on and, standing outside, flicked the button on the key fob to open the car. The causeway was dry. He didn't know how long before the ocean came back and covered it. He would have to find a tide table. He stared back at the towering building, and he was angry.

Part of him never wanted to come back to the lighthouse or Nadia, though he knew from experience that the feeling would fade and he'd want her just as much as he ever did.

He drove faster than he should over the rough causeway, sending stones flying up from his wheels as they slipped and bit the gravel and got traction.

By the time he got to town, he calmed down. Sam knew Nadia never listened to anyone, least of all him. He wandered around a bit and had a coffee in a different place and glanced in the windows of the stores. Then he saw the town's neat little library — the Stars and Stripes fluttered on a pristine flagpole outside. The library was small and compact, and he liked it.

The librarian picked up her gaze from the book she was reading: *The Flora and Fauna of the Galapagos Isles.*

"Well, hi there," she said, with a big smile, taking off her reading glasses to see him better. "Stranger in town?"

He nodded in greeting. "Yeah, thanks. We're staying at the Lighthouse." He gestured to a place out of sight.

"Oh yeah, pretty spot." But there was something in her expression that didn't fit her words.

Sam said, "I just wanted to know something more about its history."

"Really. Any particular period?" She rubbed her chin. "I think it was built around 1910. We have a couple of books about the Lighthouse Bureau."

"Well, more recent than that."

There was an awkward silence. The librarian stared at him while he laughed unconvincingly. He wondered how he would bring this up without sounding like a ghoul. He said, "A kid in town said there were deaths there."

She nodded. Then she turned. "You'd be better looking at the local newspaper for that."

She got up and walked away from the reception desk, down through the shelves of picture books. "Down here," she said, pointing ahead of her.

He hurried to catch up. "You keep old copies?"

She shook her head and didn't turn round. "No, it's all microfiched. We have machines to read it on."

"Ah, okay." He was almost level with her now. She stopped by a metal box of a thing with knobs on either side. She flicked on the light switch and then busied herself, getting the right microfiche film. She put the cartridge on the reader. "It's all yours," she said.

Sam sat, and she directed him so he could search through the back issues and focus. The black and white words came clear on the screen, along with magnified hairs and scratches.

"It was July if I recall," she said over his shoulder.

There was nobody else in the library.

Then he found the story. There were only a few paragraphs with the names, a family of three called Mendes. He sat back and exhaled. She watched him curiously but didn't say anything, so he read on. The Mendes family was up from Santa Barbara, staying at the Lighthouse as a Vacation Rental. Just like him and Nadia.

"It doesn't say much, does it?" said the librarian.

Sam turned on the swivel seat and faced her. "Do you know more?"

"I can tell you what I know. Want a coffee? We aren't exactly busy."

He let her make the coffee. She came back with two mugs and beckoned him over to a more comfortable seat. Gesturing, she said, "We put these in the Library to make it look more like a coffee shop to entice more people in. Didn't really work."

They sat down together.

"So," he said.

"I'm Mary Jones," she said. She extended her hand, and he shook it. She said, "I'm chair of the local historical society."

"Ah, right. Thank you."

"So, the Lighthouse. You've heard its bad reputation?"

"Just what the kid told us in the cafe."

"Paulo? He's a nice boy. But you must remember that people mostly come and go without incident. They have for years." She took a sip but grimaced that it was too hot. She put the mug on the table. She was enjoying telling the tale. "But some people seem to have a bad time."

"What about the Mendes family?"

She sat back. "Mr. Mendes came in here. Like you, he was looking for the history of the Lighthouse."

"And?"

"He struck me as a highly-strung man. He certainly appeared very anxious."

"How many times did you meet him?"

"Just once. Then I read about the drowning."

"He just wanted to know about the history of the lighthouse? That's it?"

"Not quite. Mr. Mendes had an interest in a man called Clark Ashton. I spoke to him about Ashton."

"Clark Ashton?" said Sam, trying not to betray an interest.

"You've heard of him?" He couldn't tell whether she was surprised.

"A little. Not much. What happened to the Mendes family anyway?"

Mary Jones shrugged. "No one really knows. Their bodies were found separately. Washed up along the coast further north. No suspicious circumstances. A plain old drowning it would seem."

Sam sat forward. "But, you have a theory?"

Mary Jones, the librarian, picked up her coffee and braved a sip. She smiled self deprecatingly. "My theory is that the Mendes family got involved with what Clark Ashton left there. You see, Ashton was a minor occultist. He published a book on ritual magic. And Ashton was a friend of Jack Parsons."

The name didn't mean anything to Sam.

Mary Jones asked, "Do you know of Parsons? He was a

black magician who worked for the Jet Propulsion Laboratory. Anyways, Ashton spent time down in Pasadena with Parsons working on a series of summonings. Then they fell out. Ashton wanted to do more than they did. He wanted to call something more powerful."

"How do you know this?"

"Years ago, I wrote an article on him. I had an interest in the occult in those days. But there are some doors you shouldn't open, so I closed them." She looked uncomfortable. "I don't bother with things like that now."

"When you say 'summoning' — what exactly do you mean?"

"Spirits, of course."

"Evil spirits?"

"Some are."

"What happened to Ashton?"

"He just disappeared. In the fall of 1927, they noticed the light wasn't working, and when they went over, he was gone. The lighthouse was like the Marie Celeste. He was never seen or heard from again."

It seemed that was all Mary Jones was prepared to tell. She stood, taking her coffee. "Listen, I have to get back to my desk. You feel free to have a browse. We've got some great books on the wildlife of the area."

She walked away, and Sm finished his coffee in a gulp then he waved her goodbye and was about to go out, but just as he was at the door, the librarian said, "Don't meddle, and you'll be safe."

Good advice, he thought. He just hoped Nadia would take it.

·   ·   ·

WHEN HE GOT BACK, Nadia was up but still absorbed reading the journals. She was making notes on a big white pad that she'd brought for her academic work. He wanted to talk to her about what the librarian had told him, but she was too engrossed. He made her a cup of coffee and put it down beside her. She thanked him but hardly looked up.

Nadia wanted to be left on her own, so Sam went upstairs to the bedroom. The sky had cleared outside, and the sun spilled in through the half-open white curtains that revealed the vast blue ocean stretching away to eternity.

He picked up his Western. His eyes slowly made their way down the first page, and then he flicked that over and began the next. The story was good, but he made slow progress. Then his eyes grew heavy. He slept. He slept for a long time and didn't dream. When he woke, it was dark. He'd slept all afternoon and into the evening, and Nadia hadn't woken him to eat. As he slept, his book had fallen onto the floor beside the bed.

Sam's right arm had pins and needles where he'd lain on it. He picked himself up groggily and switched the light on beside the bed. The room was unchanged. It didn't even look like Nadia had been to bed.

He stood slowly. He heard the clicking of the mechanism from upstairs and then the flash of light. He was stiff, and he stretched out his legs to bring back the feeling in them.

The sound of the waves came through the open window. He shivered and closed it.

Sam went out of the room and down the cold concrete steps in his bare feet. The door of the living room was open. Through the gap, he saw a flickering of candlelight. Nadia sat cross-legged in a circle of tea-lights. In front of her was one of Clark Ashton's journals, a smooth pebble from the beach was holding it open at a particular page. In front of the book was the stone idol.

"What you doing, Nadia?" Sam hissed from the door.

She didn't hear him. His voice was quiet, and he could hear its uncertainty.

Nadia focused on what she was doing. Sam watched her mouth moving, speaking out what she was reading from the book. The words sounded like an archaic language. They were rhythmic and repeated like a chant.

"What are you doing, Nadia?" he repeated, louder this time.

She raised her left hand to silence him without taking her eyes from the book.

The candles flickered. A cold shiver ran up Sam's spine. If this wasn't meddling, he didn't know what was. He buttoned up his shirt while he watched her.

She often meditated, but this wasn't meditation. There was something sinister about the word; their hideous sibilants slithered around the room, creating the illusion that something was in the shadows.

Sam went closer until he stood just outside the circle of tea-lights. He saw a verse written in Ashton's spidery handwriting in the book in front of Nadia. It wasn't any language he recognized. Nadia repeated the ghastly words over and over, her voice louder and more insistent. The words hissed like snakes. The curtains fluttered, and the room felt suddenly cold and threatening.

"Nadia..." he said, but her face was blank now, her eyes closed. She was in a trance with just her mouth moving, and her words were alien and menacing. The atmosphere grew heavy as if a storm was brewing out over the ocean.

Sam saw sweat beading on her forehead. Her head lolled forward, and her hands were clenched in fists.

Then the banging started upstairs. It was more insistent than before — like whatever was up there could hear Nadia's chanting. It was like something wanted to come out; but it was still kept there by a more potent power than the door.

Sam went up the stairs. His heart hammered, but he was going to have to fix this. One floor up and their bedroom was empty. The source of the noise was further up, one floor higher.

The noise was relentless. Banging, banging. There was no sign of Misty. The cat must have gone to hide. Sam went up again. There was the door swinging like a broken toy — slamming on its hinges with no physical cause. The din of it crashed through the lighthouse and in Sam's head. The banging door was a sign that something was coming. The air was cold. An uncanny, numinous feeling filled the place like something was coalescing — as if Nadia's words were waking something that had slept for years. Sam felt its presence, just behind his shoulder: invisible, insidious, and evil. He spun around. And then it moved down the stairs.

He had a sudden fear for Nadia. He ran below. In the living room, the circle of candles was burning down.

Still inside the ring of tea-lights, Nadia's head was slumped onto her shoulder, her hair hanging down. She had stopped chanting. A thin dribble of saliva hung from her mouth.

A palpable presence haunted the room. Its evil filled the place.

Sam went over and shook Nadia. Her head rolled sideways, her eyes opened to reveal the whites. He half picked her up and dragged her from the circle. The tea-lights were swept out of the way, turning over, spilling liquid wax, and extinguishing themselves. The acrid smell of burned wick filled the room. He pulled her to the sofa and laid her down. He shook her awake, and she muttered something from deep within whatever dream held her.

"Nadia," he hissed. There was something in that room with them, but for some reason, it lacked the power to fully come through and manifest itself. It needed something more.

Then, he heard something from below. It was the unmistakable noise of the door opening. How was that possible? How could anyone be there on that dark night with the causeway covered by five feet of rushing ocean water? But it was definitely the sound of the front door opening. He knew it by the creak it made when you pushed your weight into the rain-soaked wood. He thought maybe the wind had blown it, but he knew in his heart that some intelligence had opened the door and come in.

Someone, or something, was downstairs.

"Hello?" he shouted. His throat was dry and his voice died off in a hoarse wheeze.

There was no reply. Sam kidded himself that it was the wind again. But he didn't move to check.

"Hello?" he yelled again. The greeting sounded stupid now. He must be mistaken. The door had somehow sprung open. He maybe didn't shut it properly.

The sound of the waves was louder from below. He needed to go down and close the door whatever he did, otherwise the wind and water would come in.

The sooner he did that, the sooner he could minister to Nadia. He took a step forward, then stopped, and his hands trembled. What was he becoming? He'd walked into booby-trapped houses full of men with guns who wanted to kill him so they could go to Paradise, but he'd never been as scared as this.

He told himself to man up. He hurried to where he would see the front door in one more step. His heart started hammering again. This is ridiculous, Sam: this is just dreams and whispers. And then he stepped toward the door.

It was so unexpected that Sam looked twice and still didn't believe it. There, in the harsh electric light was a girl. She was about twelve. At first, she looked healthy. She was drenched. So much that she looked like she'd been in the ocean. She had her back to him. Her long dark hair hung in wet locks down her soaked dress.

"Hello?" said Sam, "Can I help you?"

And then the girl turned. As her face came round, Sam saw raw holes where her eyes had been. She lacked lips, and wounds gaped in her cheeks where the fish had eaten through. Her old fashioned dress was ripped, exposing the bones of her chest, and there was a washed-out, ragged hardly-pink wound above her heart.

Sam heard his voice say, "Oh damn." He stepped back, hands holding the stone sides of the staircase. His heel slipped up a step. He swallowed. "Oh Jesus Christ protect me," and that was the first prayer he'd uttered since Gene died.

He stood his ground. "What do you want?" he muttered, willing the girl not to reply.

She stared at him, and her mouth fell open.

Sam heard a thump and noises from above. He glanced up as Nadia descended. She looked woozy and not woken from her unnatural sleep. Her hair was a mess, and her mascara had run. He put up his hand to stop her from coming further. "Don't," he said.

The dead girl was going to speak.

"What?" Nadia said. She couldn't see the girl.

The girl's mouth moved. It formed words, but they were slow and effortful; the dead forget the art of conversation.

"Don't come down," Sam said.

"Who's down there?" Nadia said, stepping down another step.

"I told you. Don't come down."

But Nadia came anyway.

At that instant, he heard the girl's voice. Her voice was dry as dead leaves whispering together. The girl said, "Call it."

And then she vanished, and the front door slammed shut.

"What the hell?" Nadia was level with him now. "The door just closed on its own."

He nodded. "There was a girl. A ghost."

He turned, expecting to see Nadia mock him, but she was smiling as she nodded frantically. Her smile was strange, and he did not like it.

"What's to smile about?" Sam said, his voice hoarse. He felt a shiver run through him.

Nadia said, "I summoned her. She was locked in upstairs, and I set her free."

"You did what?"

Nadia shrugged. It was apparent she was pleased with herself. She turned to hurry back up to the living room. He could hear her say, "I'm going to write a paper about this. It'll make my career."

Sam slowly climbed after her.

Nadia found the pad of paper and a pen and was about to come down to fetch him so he could narrate what he saw, and she could write it down. He came into the room after her. His face was stern. "This is messed up. What are you playing at Nadia?"

She smiled like what he'd seen was nothing. She said, "I've been involved in transpersonal psychology all my career. We do experiments to prove the existence of something 'other'. Mostly they prove nothing. And now..." She raised her hand in a mock punch of victory, like some privileged college kid. "I've summoned something. And you saw it."

"Something?"

"Technically, probably a projection of the collective unconscious."

Sam said, "I saw a dead girl."

She patted the couch next to her. "Come and sit down and describe exactly what you saw." He didn't move. "Come. Sit. Talk." She had her pen ready and looked like an excited teenager. "I can't believe it!" she said, her face wrinkled in delight. "This is so great! I've summoned a spirit!"

He sat down where she indicated. "I'm sorry I don't share your delight."

She ignored his anger. "So what did you see? Tell me. I want details."

"I saw a girl. Maybe twelve years old. It looked like she'd been stabbed in the heart then thrown in the ocean for the fish to eat. She was soaked through. Her flesh was pale and wrinkled. I can't believe I saw it, but I did." His hand was shaking.

Nadia nodded and started writing. "The fact that she's soaked represents the Unconscious. It comes from below."

His shock made him irritable. He grew impatient. "What did you do?"

She put the pen down, still smiling, still self-congratulatory. "Okay, well, this guy Clark Ashton was a ritual magician. You've got to understand that Western Ritual Magic is just the yoga of.the West. It's a discipline of manifesting the divine."

His mouth was a thin line.

She saw how pissed off he was, and she rolled her eyes. She put her pen down. One hand went up in a gesture of protest. "You mustn't take this too literally. It's all symbolic. The Unconscious is talking to us."

"Just pretend I'm stupid. I'm only a dumb grunt after all." He didn't blink. He was mad at her. But scared for her too. She was so arrogant she thought everything was her sandbox, but this was too deep; there was an old evil in this place, a predator, a hungry ghost.

She waved her hands expansively, and her bracelet shimmied. "Well, as I said— Western Ritual Magic. It's like yoga..."

He lost patience. "Skip the mumbo jumbo. What did you do to bring her here?"

She sighed. "Before I tell you that. I need to explain about Ashton."

"Go on."

"Well, Ashton devised a ritual to summon a sorcerer from Atlantis."

"Atlantis?"

"I know you're skeptical. Ashton maybe thought Atlantis was real, but to me, it's just a place in the Unconscious. It represents supra-human wisdom."

"Or demonic folly," he said.

"There are no demons, silly." She was gorgeous when she said it. She was vain, stupid, and shallow, and she still attracted him. She was so foolish. He had to protect her from her own sense of invincibility. The thing he'd seen in the little girl's form would devour Nadia, but her sunny upbringing, where she always got her way ,made Nadia think that she could do what she wanted, and all would be fine.

He tried to sound more conciliatory because if he came out against her, she'd just block him out. He knew her that well. He said, "You shouldn't mess with this, Nadia. Summoning things: You don't know what they really are."

"They're just parts of my psyche. I told you."

He was incredulous. "A dead girl is part of your psyche?"

"She represents sacrifice. A payment."

Despite himself, he almost guffawed. "A payment? For what?"

She narrowed her eyes. "A payment for wisdom. If I want to succeed in Ashton's footsteps, I must be prepared to make a sacrifice. I do the summoning. I write it up. Submit a paper to the Journal of Transpersonal Psychology, and my career is on an excellent footing. I might get a chair at Princeton or Edinburgh or Heidelberg."

"So for your career, you're willing to summon some god-awful demon?"

"It's not real, Sam." She spoke to him like he was stupid.

"It looked real."

"Simple folk all over the world believe in the realness of these apparitions. You have to be wiser than that."

Just then, the cat, Misty, came through the door. Sam guessed it had been sleeping on their bed upstairs. It walked right up to Nadia, purring. She stroked it, and it arched its back. "Hello, baby. Did you miss mommy?" Nadia said.

Sam stood up, exasperated, and angry. "You've got to stop this shit."

Her face was sour. "Just go to bed and leave it to me."

. . .

It was about 11pm when Sam went to bed alone. He woke in the middle of the night to find Misty in Nadia's place in the bed. In the morning, he got up and went down to the living room. She was asleep on the couch. One of Ashton's books open on her chest. He left her there. Sam went walking on the beach. He was out for hours, but when he came back, Nadia was in the living room. She looked at him. He didn't know if she was going to tell him to get out. Their eyes met. There was an awful pause, then she said, "Sorry, we fell out."

"Me too" he said.

"Want to go upstairs?" she said.

He nodded. They would make love, and after that, he would try to persuade her to throw those books away — to lock them where she'd found them. And he would put the idol in the canvas hold-all and hurl it out into the ocean so that it would sink beneath the waves and never be found again.

They made love in the big bed as the storm grew outside. The window rattled, and the rain lashed on the pane. They lay there in the semi-dark, her head on his arm. Misty came and started kneading Nadia's tummy. She stroked the cat. "She wants food," she said.

"I'll get it later," Sam said.

They lay in silence. Just the cat's purr and the sound of the wind and rain.

Sam looked at the ceiling. He began. "Nadia..."

"What?" She stretched and yawned but didn't move to get up. He guessed she knew what he was going to say.

"I don't like this occult stuff," he said.

"I know."

"I want you to stop. You didn't come here to do this. You have your work to do."

"But this has presented itself. It's a gift."

"Something bad will happen. It happened to Ashton. It happened to the Mendes family."

"I don't see that it was because of the idol. And if it was, it was because they couldn't control it." Her voice was steady and cold.

"What about the girl?"

"Ashton talks about the girl. I guess her spirit just got stuck here."

"Are you sure she wasn't a sacrifice to your entity?"

He felt her shrug.

Another pause. Sam said, "I don't want you to do it." He put his hand on her shoulder. "For me."

She was quiet for a long time. Sam could hear her breathing. "For me," he repeated.

"Okay," she said.

He'd never expected her to agree so he couldn't help himself smiling. "Nadia, I'm so happy you said that."

Then she said, "I've just one thing to figure out."

He sighed. He knew it was too good to be true.

She went on. "To summon the wise entity, Ashton says he used 'the red rose', but I don't know what that is."

Sam stayed silent. He wasn't going to help her figure anything out.

"It's not a red rose," she went on, "It's a cipher for something. Something obvious. I need to understand what it means."

"You said that you would stop with all this."

"I will. I want to know what the red rose is, then that's it. I swear."

"You won't do the ritual? You won't try to bring that thing?"

"Go feed the cat," she said.

Sam got out of bed. He was naked. There was enough light to see his reflection in the mirror; the devil's name was plain black on his shoulder — mocking him. The cat followed him, skipping down for her dinner. At the Living Room door, Sam turned and said to Nadia, "You've always got to get your way, don't you?"

"Just this time," she said. "Then, I'm done."

LATER AFTER THEY'D EATEN, he watched her work. She'd made a promise, and he wanted to believe her. She just had to work out what the red rose was, and then she'd stop. She'd have enough for her paper. She didn't have to carry out the ritual. But those were his thoughts, not hers.

He couldn't concentrate, and he knew she'd prefer to be on her own, but he wouldn't leave her. The cat came and nestled on his lap, purring. Nadia read and made notes. She brushed her long blond hair away from her face; she sucked on the end of the pen.

Nadia hardly looked up; when she did, it was to check he was still there. She forced a smile. At times she read aloud strange words from the book. As she spoke them, Sam thought something wicked pricked up its ears. Somewhere, something heard those words — he was sure of it.

Then Nadia sat up and smiled. "I've got it," she said. And that was that. There was no big celebration. Sam could tell she was pleased, but she was hiding something from him. "Bathroom break," she said.

While she was out, he got up and went to the book on the table. Ashton's handwriting was difficult to decipher at first. Sam didn't have much time before she came back. He traced Ashton's words with his fingers. He read:

"The wise entity is within the stone. The Nazuuth imprisoned it in Old Atlantis, fearing its power and its evil. But the strong can bend this thing to their will. And then they will have power undreamed of by other men. Any success in business or career will be theirs. To release the deity, I will use the words from the Atlantean language I have reconstructed. And then I will add the red rose. I have a red rose in mind."

He was still reading when Nadia came back into the room and caught him red-handed. He felt absurdly guilty.

"What are you doing?" she said from the door. Her voice was cold.

"Just reading your book."

"I thought you had no interest in it."

He shook his head. "It's all bullshit. You can't believe this stuff, Nadia."

She came into the room to the desk and waited for him to move out of the way. She picked up the book and held it away from him.

He stepped back. "So what's the red rose?" he said.

She gave a laugh that was conceited and smug, and he hated her for it.

"It was obvious," she said.

"What is it?"

She sat down and picked up the book. "It's blood, Sam."

"So to summon this thing —"

"—the wise entity..." she said.

"This thing. You need to sacrifice something?"

She nodded.

"So what blood sacrifice did Ashton make?"

"She was Victoria Gonzales. The daughter of a fisherman that Ashton befriended in 1926."

Sam felt bile rise in his stomach. "The girl I saw."

She nodded. "I summoned her. Her spirit still lingered here. There was a spell in Ashton's book."

He stood, stony-faced. "If you mess with this, you aren't the person I loved."

She smiled a mocking smile, her beauty taunting him. "Did you love me, Sam? That's sweet."

He looked at her as if he didn't know her. The demon might still be imprisoned in the idol, but its influence was already changing her. The evil words she had recited from the book had left their mark.

He took both her hands. He was begging her. "Nadia, can't you see what's happening to you?"

"Yes, I see it."

"This isn't you."

She turned away and put down the book. "Then, who am I, Sam?"

"I don't like what you're becoming. This thing is poisoning you. Let's leave. We can go now."

"Nothing is poisoning me, Sam." Her voice was sneering. She was looking down on him. "I'm engaged in academic research. I appreciate that's a world you know nothing about."

He nodded. "So I'm stupid. So be it. There are worse things than being stupid."

"If you can't support me in this, Sam. I don't know what you're doing here."

"I want to save you."

She threw back her head and laughed. "You? Save me? I don't need you to save me."

"Please, Nadia. Come away with me now."

She shook her head slowly. "Why don't you just pack your things and leave, Sam?"

It was like his heart stopped beating. He was torn between his care for Nadia and the wound she'd cut in him. She'd pushed him away like he was nothing. He stood, his love wanting to grab her and drag her to safety, and his pride telloig him to leave her. His pride won. He turned and walked down the stairs.

Sam opened the creaking front door with his right hand. He pushed the door open, and the night-wind hit him. It was dark. There were no man-made lights except a boat way out and a house about two miles away to the south. The gusts grabbed at him. Grief filled him. He walked over to the car and leaned heavily on it. He had the keys in his pocket. For long minutes he stood there, his head spinning.

The lighthouse flashed high above, bringing the country about him into sharp contrast of light and shadow. The tide was coming in again, the way it had done twice a day forever. He heard it sucking across the stones and the sand, trailing the seaweed, bringing in the crabs.

She hadn't followed him to beg him to come back. He gave her a minute, five minutes to realize what she'd done and run after him. He looked at the door he'd closed behind him and he knew she wouldn't come. She wanted to be left alone to play with her demon.

Damn her then; she'd made her choice. Sam squeezed the key, and the lights on the car flashed in welcome. He pulled open the door and sat down, closed out the howling wind, and fired the engine. He turned on the headlights, and a world of water was revealed. He put the gearstick into reverse and hit the gas too hard, sending stones flying, banging the car against a rock. He cursed. He jerked it into drive and accelerated down the slip-road, and hen he was up at the main road.

He turned north, up Highway 1. He drove too fast for the

narrow road, hitting the curves at high speed and almost losing control. The pain in his chest was unbearable — it was like frost burning out his heart. He pulled over on a rough piece of ground by the road that tourists stopped at to take photographs when it was daylight. He sat there in the car, the car engine still running.

He was sweating. He was sweating because he couldn't leave Nadia. He had allowed his pride to make him walk away. And he knew if he left her, she would die as Ashton died and the Mendes family died. When she called the thing, it would kill her. The only mercy was that she had nothing to sacrifice and so she couldn't call it. He would be in time.

He gazed down the coast and saw the lighthouse's distant flashing, then he put the car in reverse and turned it. He was going back for Nadia because he had to save her from herself.

THE LIGHTHOUSE DOOR HUNG OPEN. He called upstairs, but Nadia didn't answer. He would have even welcomed the hungry cry of the cat, but there was nothing. The silence was hollow; it seemed like everything wholesome had been sucked out of the air. He stepped up the stairs, the water dripping from the fingers of his hands.

There was no one in the kitchen. Sam went up further. In the living room, the desk lamp was on; the laptop had gone to sleep. Several of the Ashton diaries were on the desk. Where was Nadia?

He heard the waves breaking outside. The wind's voice howled; it moaned, keeping company with whatever was being summoned.

Sam turned over the pages of the books. There were five

volumes of Ashton's diaries there, and he flicked to the last pages of the final one.

It seemed that Ashton had become afraid of what he was doing— of what he had done. He spoke of the stone idol with great fear. The entity had been in the stone idol.

Instead of the wise entity, he hoped would help him, it was a ravenous, cadaverous thing. No longer did Ashton believe it had any wisdom. He had summoned it with the Gonzales girl's blood, and when he had called it and fed it, it had come indeed.

Ashton spoke of how it lurked like a twisted shadow — a black shape in the corner of the room. And how it prowled around him. It had not been satisfied with the girl alone. Now it wanted him. It wanted to come inside him and take over his body — to eat his soul and move into his flesh like a hermit crab does the empty shell of a whelk.

Sam read how Ashton had tried to protect himself from the thing he'd called. Ashton revealed that the thing could not cross saltwater. He said saltwater burned it and was a barrier. Ashton planned to leave, but the journal petered out, and Sam guessed the thing got him first.

After Ashton, the thing, having nothing more to feed on, must have retreated inside the stone idol. It was like a foul eel — hiding inside its stone home and waiting for fresh souls to devour.

Then at the back of that journal, Sam saw a folded note. Nadia had not found this. Sam opened it up with shaking fingers. The handwriting was feminine, not Ashton's, and it was written in a ball-point pen, not Ashton's fountain pen. The name at the bottom was Mary Jones — the Librarian. She told how she had come to the Lighthouse after the Mendes family drowned. She found the idol on the table, and she found the sacrificed body of a bird.

She wrote that Mendes must have called the thing and then tried to escape over the salt-water. But he had failed. The Mendes family drowned while trying to escape the lighthouse. Jones put the idol in Mendes' canvas hold-all and flung it out from the tower into the ocean, hoping it would not be found again.

But Sam had found it and brought it back to Nadia.

He felt sick. He dropped the note onto the table. What-ever happened to Nadia was because of him. If he hadn't brought the idol back, none of this would have happened.

Sam left the books on the desk, turned, and went to the stairs. He looked up. The light was still on, one electric bulb burning feebly, without a shade in the pale stone surround. "Nadia," he called again.

He heard a noise. It was a voice, but it wasn't like Nadia's voice, the words were odd. It wasn't any kind of reply. Sam yelled up the stairs.

This time it was more distinct. Sam heard a gurgling noise so vile and unnatural that his stomach heaved. He steadied himself against the wall. But whatever she had done, it was his fault. Despite herself, she needed his help. He had to have the courage to go to her.

Slowly, he forced himself upstairs. He checked the bedroom. Nadia was not there. He even went in to check the shower. He went back to the stairs, his wet boots scraped on the stone steps. "Nadia?" His voice sounded hollow among the damp stones.

This time the gurgling sound was more audible. It was as if someone was trying to speak with a mouth full of water. He went up. The broken door was now still. He saw the rhythmic pulsing of the light from the chamber above: flash, then pause, then — flash.

"Nadia!"

Sam knew she was there, round the staircase, just out of sight.

And then he saw the flood of blood running down the stairs, dripping, starting to congeal as it came down step by step. He heard himself grunt, and his head spun. He staggered forward; his boots smeared into the blood, and from then every step left crimson footprints.

He turned the corner and saw her. She was standing there — her chest a sea of red. Blood ran from her hands that were clutched to her breasts. Blood ran down her shirt and over her jeans and onto the floor. She was covered in crimson, and the light flashed behind her throwing her into black and white, then crimson and white.

Sam stood there, his breath hanging. Words wouldn't come. She was standing upright, and he knew she still lived. Finally, he said, "Nadia," he said. "What have you done?"

And then she dropped it. The limp body of the cat fell with a thud. She had held it to her chest, and now it dropped dead to the stone steps.

"My God, Nadia."

"The red rose," she said in a whisper. "It was what I needed."

"Did it come?" he said, dreading her answer.

She nodded. Her face was turned down, and Sam couldn't read her expression.

And then he saw it.

Behind her, a black shape stood, tall as a man, twisting in place. It flickered and moved like it was projected from a silent movie. And there was the stink of chemicals; sulfur and saltpeter. It wasn't just a shape; it was a feeling too. It stunk of wickedness and hunger. Sam felt the hairs on his neck rise, and his hands clenched. He swallowed hard, and he couldn't look at it. "Come now," he said to Nadia.

She didn't move. "Help me," she said.

He extended a hand, but she didn't take it.

"Come closer," she said.

He shook his head. "Come to me. Let's leave."

Her face was still turned down.

His hand was still out. He took a step closer, hesitantly, but Nadia didn't move. He took another step until he was very close.

She turned her face to him, and she beckoned. He shook his head and pulled away because something moved in her eyes; something flickered like a black candle behind her irises. There was something in her. The thing had entered in.

"Sam," she said.

His mouth was dry. "What?"

"Hold me."

He still didn't move. "Please," he said. "Let's get out of here."

She was covered in blood, but even like this, Sam loved her. He wanted so much to go and hold her, to make things better. He took a half step.

But her eyes were wrong. A primeval urge to run rose up in Sam. She was wrong; it was there behind her eyes, and he backed away. He could swim, and if he didn't drown, he would be free of it; the saltwater would keep it from him. But he would have to leave Nadia.

"Come to me," she said. Her voice was strange. The demon was already in her like an egg laid by a blowfly. It just needed more blood to pop out, like a maggot dropping free from a cadaver.

The entity would walk our world as it had all those millennia ago when the Atlanteans worshipped its dark kind under hostile stars. It had waited patiently, tricking fools like Ashton and Nadia into opening doors from other worlds to enter in.

Sam stepped back toward the door. His fear was winning. "We need to get a doctor. You're not yourself."

She looked at him and grinned. The black shadow was half in her. She said, "I don't need a doctor because inside me I have a butcher. And he is going to show me how to cut you open."

Sam looked and saw she had a knife folded in her hand. It was the knife she had used to kill the cat.

Sam was at the door. She didn't follow him. She stood, unmoving, with the knife still in her hand, her hippy bracelet at her wrist. Her mouth opened again, but the voice was not hers now. The thing was taking her over. It was a voice full of whispering snakes and the crepitation of dead leaves. It said, "Leave Nadia. She is mine."

Sam's voice shook. "Nadia, come to me. I'll take you from here. It can't cross the water."

She stepped toward him, knife brandished. "I will eat you too, Sam," she said in a voice as old as hell. She was close enough to stab him. Sam saw the flickering in her eyes, and he knew he could flee and save himself or let it come and fight it for Nadia.

One step. Two steps closer. Nadia dragged her feet. Blood was smeared all over her, and all the time, shadows shifted in her eyes. Sometimes he thought he saw her, but mostly it was the thing. Her mouth drooled, and her hands were streaked red with the cat's sticky blood. The knife blade glittered as the lighthouse beamed its warning.

And then he punched her. Nadia grunted and slumped back, half-falling, and the knife went limp in her hand.

Sam grabbed her wrist and, with desperate strength, bent it back until she dropped the blade. Then he seized her by the waist and picked her up. The thing in her struggled. It writhed and fought. It rippled out of her and came at him.

Sam slammed her against the wall and knocked the wind out of her.

Then he had her over his shoulder and went down the twisting stone steps with her slumped over him. Nadia's strength was gone, but the thing inside her reached out. He felt its tendrils coming from her body. They were as cold as the space between the stars, cold as the fog, colder than dreams. The thing came from a place that had been without light and heat so long that it was frigid. He felt its incorporeal limbs creep over him. He felt its thoughts as it tried to enter his eyes and his ears.

He felt himself stumble. Falling, but he caught the side of the wall with his right hand. His remaining fingers held him up. He stood there, breathing heavily and thought he wouldn't make it. Then Sam remembered Fallujah again. Gene didn't give up. Nor would he. Every second he lingered there in that stairwell, was a second closer to it taking him over. He steadied himself and breathed. It was in his chest now. He stepped down and felt it stir in his stomach, reaching for his heart.

Nadia felt heavy on his shoulder. His knees sagged under her weight. She stirred and spoke, but he didn't understand the words. And then he was at the door. He kicked it open, and the sea wind stung him. It woke him from his daze, and the gulls called in the darkness. The fog was all around like a blanket, and he could see nothing, but nearby he heard the rushing of the waves.

He saw the beginning of the concrete road down to the causeway until it disappeared into the mist. The tide was full in. There was no way the car would get over. He would have to swim with her. Sam staggered down and thought he would drop Nadia. But if he dropped her, that would be the end.

He got a few more steps, and then his knees gave way and he slumped into the damp sand. The fog stroked them with its deathly fingers, waiting like a ghostly carrion bird for him to die. Nadia struggled and tried to get free of his grasp, but he seized her with a grip of iron, and he would not let her go.

He was breathing heavily. He had to rest, just a minute and then he'd be ok. Just a minute, and then he'd get up. But the minute stretched to five minutes and then ten. Sam's head fell onto his chest as he felt the monster moving in his viscera. Soon he would be nothing more than a lifeless bag of guts.

He forced himself to stand, but he slumped again. Nadia began slapping at his back, trying to break free of him. But he knew it wasn't her; it was the thing that possessed her, so he gripped her tight and prevented her moving.

Sam stood, steadying himself, getting his breath. His knees shook, and he locked them so he wouldn't go down again. He was cold and numb.

From the landward side, a bird called. Sam couldn't name it. His gaze was fixed on the Lighthouse and between him and it, an arm of the ocean. A current that could take him to Carmel or Santa Cruz and break his bones against unseen rocks. The Lighthouse flashed. It synchronized with his pulse.

Sam stood on that cold shore one minute more, and then stumbled on. He waded into the tide. He thought he'd be used to the cold, but it hit him like wringing hands on his thighs and then his hips and then his belly. Soon he stood chest-deep in the brine. He felt the ocean tug at him, pulling him away. He knew it wanted to drag him fathoms deep where he would die and drift with the jellyfish and the cold-blooded eels.

The ocean would take him and drown him if he let it. And if the sea didn't swallow him, the ancient evil inside would devour him for sure.

Sam couldn't swim properly with Nadia on his back. He flailed, splashed, and threatened to take them both under. She shouted and fought against him, but he only gripped her tighter.

The thing reached spectral fingers and wrapped around his throat. It tightened its grip.

The saltwater was burning it. It was frightened. The monster didn't want to devour him now; it wanted to kill him quickly to get out of the water. It pulled him down, but he wouldn't give in. He was under the water. If he drowned, he would take it with him. And then it relented. It weakened. Sam felt it withdraw from his body, hissing and resisting.

Seizing his chance, Sam struck out into the tide. As he swam, he felt the current pull him. Nadia was burdening him. He had survived the entity, but now the water threatened him.

He felt his love for Nadia fill him. Not the Nadia that the thing had twisted, but the real Nadia he had fallen in love with.

He thought of Gene Nygard pulling him from that house, his ears ringing, and his strength gone. Sam would not let the ocean take them.

He kicked, and he swam. Above them, the clouded sky. The dark ocean around them.

Always in his eyes was the pulsing of the lighthouse. He used that as a marker. He kicked against it — straight back towards the land.

And then, after long minutes, he felt a rock hit his back. Then another. He felt the slimy weed around his hand. He pushed backward, and then he felt the land rise under him. He half stood and pulled Nadia with him, dragging her limp form. With all his strength, he lifted her from the sea.

And there they stood on the landward shore. In front of them, the ocean surged, and behind that, the lighthouse stood tall and dark, its one bright eye flashing a message to the endless sea beyond.

Sam saw the haunted shape of the thing Nadia had let free standing on the shore by the lighthouse, twisting and turning, waiting for them to return.

No one entering that lighthouse would ever be safe from it, but without a body to inhabit, it could never come the landward side on its own. Sam and Nadia would soon be gone. Sam cradled Nadia tight and stroked her blond hair turned dark from the water. The demon would take someone again. That was its nature. But at least it wouldn't be her.

9

SKIN WALKER

A ngela Houghton ran a B&B. The B&B was in the pretty Cumbrian village of Askham, not far from Haweswater. It was October, and business was slack. Angela's husband Liam, an engineer, was away for the weekend on a project to do with the restoration of a stretch of the Lancaster Canal. The money was good and, though he said he'd rather be with her, she knew both the money and a weekend with the lads were things he relished. Angela and Liam loved each other to bits, but still it was healthy to do things separately sometimes. Angela hoped the extra money could be put to something nice like that holiday in Bali they'd talked about. That would be lovely, and make it worth spending the weekend on her own. At present, she was enjoying a cream tea with her friend Kath when she got a phone call from Penrith tourist information.

There was a bloke in who was asking specifically for her B&B, Rose Cottage. They said he'd seen it on the Internet and wondered if there was a discount if he booked directly.

She grimaced over her fruit scone at Kath, phone to her ear, listening to the woman. She couldn't really be bothered.

The summer had been busy with visitors and she was looking forward to a winter rest. She had some bookings for Christmas and the New Year, but she'd hoped to slack a little until then. Then she thought of Bali.

"Okay," Angela said, "but no discount. If he won't come without the discount, then that's fine."

But the man came anyway, full price. He'd be there at 5 pm.

"I suppose it's all extra money," Kath said.

Angela shrugged and reached for the floral china teapot. "Let's finish this pot then I'll get back."

He was a strange looking man, long black, spade-like beard streaked with grey. Long hair, similar. He could do with a haircut. His clothes were black too, some heavy material like moleskin, and he had a backpack rather than a suitcase.

"Hello, what a lovely place," he said, looking around as soon as he was in the main door.

"Just sign here," Angela pointed to the visitors' book. "Find us all right?"

The man nodded as he signed his name.

"You can park round the side. You're the only one here this weekend. Staying long?"

He smiled. "I don't know yet." He had a foreign accent. Polish maybe?

"Well, let me know when you decide. Full English tomorrow? We serve between eight and ten on a Monday."

Sunday was a funny night to arrive, come to think of it. She hoped he wouldn't stay the week; there was something about him she didn't like.

She showed him to his room and he professed himself delighted with it.

"I hope you'll be comfortable."

He put his backpack on the bed. She didn't like that either. He said, "Do you run the B&B on your own."

That was technically true, so Angela said, "Yes."

"You live here alone then?"

She frowned. That was a queer question, a distinctly unnerving question. "No. My husband lives here with me."

"Ah. But he's not here now?"

"He'll be back shortly," she lied.

She would lock her bedroom door tonight and not make this stranger too welcome. He gave her the creeps and she shuddered as she left him there.

In the makeshift office, she checked the booking: a Mr Jacob Golyadkin. He was on holiday and gave his last address as a B&B at Cabus, near Garstang. He he was definitely foreign.

The next morning, Golyadkin sat there like a prince waiting for his breakfast. She prided herself on the neatness of her breakfast room with its shiny silver cutlery and starched white linen tablecloths. He was a big bearded mess in it, a blot on the landscape.

"Full English please," he said. He had the works: bacon, sausages, beans, black pudding, mushrooms, fried bread and hash browns. The hash browns weren't technically English, more American, but that's very similar. They speak the same language, even if they murder it.

After he'd finished, she collected his dinner plate and left him with the small plate where he buttered toast. He asked for another pot of tea. She'd rather he just hurried up and went out for the day.

"Did you enjoy your Full English?" He obviously had; he had bean juice in his beard.

He smiled. "Beautiful. My compliments to the chef."

"You like our food then?" She was fishing. She knew he was foreign.

He shrugged.

"You ordered it though."

"Well, you didn't have a full Russian breakfast."

Very sarcastic. Then he said, "I didn't hear your husband come back last night."

"He was very quiet."

"I see." It looked like Golyadkin might say more, but she interrupted. "How long are you planning on staying?"

He said, "I'm not sure yet."

"It's just that we have a group coming in tomorrow. We're full up."

"That's a pity. Still, it's good to be so busy midweek in October."

"Yes, can't complain." She picked up his plate and hurried off. She really didn't like him now and wished Liam would come home.

Liam arrived back around 11 am. Angela heard the car crunch up on the gravel outside and she was so pleased to see him she ran out and they embraced. He looked exhausted. As she helped him with his coat and the lighter bag when he brought his big suitcase from the car, she glanced up and saw Golyadkin staring out of his bedroom window at them. He'd caught her out lying, so what? Liam was home now and that's all that mattered.

As she put the washing on, she saw that Liam had left the door to the cellar open. He always did that. The light was on, and she called down but he didn't answer so she flicked it off. That usually brought a yell if he was still down there, but no reaction came echoing up the stairs from below, so he must be in their room.

She got Liam his lunch. He sat in the kitchen looking dazed. Angela said, "You work too hard."

Liam laughed and ate his cheese and pickle sandwich.

"Honestly, love, you look dreadful."

"Thanks,"

"I worry about you."

"That's nice."

"Still, let's look forward to Bali."

"Let's."

Later she cajoled Liam into going out for a walk. She told him about Golyadkin before they went out, not that he seemed to be listening. Then they bumped into the Russian in the hall.

"Going out Mr Golyadkin?" She said. Most of their visitors were out all of the time. This bloke just stayed in. He was weird.

Golyadkin seemed more interested in Liam. "I understand you are an engineer?"

Angela tilted her head. How did he know that?

Liam nodded

Golyadkin continued. "Working on the Lancaster Canal restoration."

"Yes, that's right."

"You're familiar with the Gota Canal? In Sweden?"

Liam shook his head. Angela thought that was weird, because Liam was obsessed with canal engineering, she thought he knew everything about every canal in the world.

"Well," Golyadkin said. "It's interesting because the Swedes used English and Russian engineers, and then after that, some of the Russians came over to England and worked on your canal system. Including the Lancaster Canal, that tunnel you're working on."

"You know a lot about canals, Mr Golyadkin." Angela said. "Are you an expert, or something?"

Golyadkin stared at her. "I'm a writer."

"So, you're writing a book about canals?"

Golyadkin shook his head.

"Anyway," Angela said, "We're off out now. If you do go out please lock the door."

She hurried out with Liam, linking his arm and glad that Liam was six foot two and a lot meatier than that damned Russian weirdo.

Their walk was lovely. Sun broke through the clouds and all the colours of late autumn displayed themselves, reds and golds and oranges. Angela loved the smell of the woods in Autumn. They walked down the bank of the River Lowther and the river was in full flood, the water hurrying busily towards where it would join with the Eamont and then the Eden before finally reaching the sea. She was grateful that she lived in such a wonderful place. Liam didn't say much. He was really working too hard. He had a sheen of sweat on his forehead. "I hope you're not coming down with flu," she said.

They walked home through the village. It was Halloween the next week, but the cottages where kids lived were already decorated and had pumpkins outside them.

When she got home and went to their bedroom, she knew something was wrong. "Somebody's been in here..."

Liam slumped on the bed. "How do you know?"

"I just know."

"Is there anything missing?" He asked without looking around.

She busied herself turning things over, looking in drawers. All her jewellery was there, and £200 in cash. There didn't appear to be anything missing. "I'm going to call the police."

"Don't," Liam said. "It's a big fuss. They'll ask if anything has been stolen, and if not..."

"It's him." Angela hissed. "That bloody Golyadkin. I want him gone."

"On what grounds? He's a paying guest."

"I just want him out of here. I don't like him. I bet he's taken something."

"What?"

"I don't know. Something valuable. Something I've overlooked."

Angela waited until she heard the door click and Golyadkin went out. Liam had fallen asleep on the bed. She rushed through to Goldyadkin's room. It was locked but she had the master key. She laughed to herself when she turned it in the lock. He needn't think he was getting the better of her.

The room was pretty much the same. He'd been lying on the bed reading by the look of it.

She had a search, and in his backpack there was a bottle labelled Aconite: Poison. It even had a skull and crossbones on it. She left it well alone and after all her rummaging about could find no stolen property, then she turned to the book Golyadkin had been reading. It was titled:

The Doppelgänger, a Study by Montague Summers.

She leafed through the pages, reading odd bits. It was all occult mumbo-jumbo; she knew he was a freak.

'In its natural form, the doppelgänger resembles nothing so much as an overgrown slug.... It has a natural adhesive so it sticks to ceilings and tunnel roofs, waiting to drop on unsuspecting victims."

She sighed. He honestly needed locked up, reading this crap, but she still read on.

'The most famous cases come from France, and of course St Petersburg in Russia...'

And the next section made her uneasy.

'We do not know how the doppelgänger assumes the shape of its victim. We presume it studies the victim before it consumes him, though we are unclear how long a period of study this might require. There are reported cases from Sweden and Poland where the doppelgänger apparently researched its victim's life and haunted his steps before finally consuming him and taking his shape. '

Angela's mind whirred like fruit machine dials and then stopped. That's what this was. Golyadkin was a doppel-gänger, or at least he thought he was. More likely he was a crazed lunatic, but if he believed he was a doppelgänger then he might do something threatening. She remembered that Golyakdin's last known address was Cabus, not far from where Liam was working. He was stalking Liam. God knows what he intended to do to him.

Angela hurried out of Golyadkin's bedroom door, making sure it was locked behind her. She shook Liam awake. He gazed at her out of bleary eyes. "What?"

"That Golyadkin, he's crazy."

Liam shook his head. "I think you're overreacting. You've never liked foreign visitors."

"No, he's crazy. I think he might be dangerous. We should call the police."

"And tell them what?"

"That he's crazy."

"They'll just ask you what crime has been committed."

"None, yet."

"So, don't ring the police."

She bit her lip. "Well, maybe the doctor?"

"What, Birkbeck Surgery? What will they do?"

"They're doctors. They'll know what to do."

"They're not his doctors."

She was exasperated. Liam wasn't taking her seriously. She was really worried this man was dangerous. He might kill them in the night. "Then there must be a mental health emergency line."

Liam said, "It's the same as the police. What will you tell them?"

"That he's insane, schizophrenic or something."

"And how are you qualified to make that diagnosis?"

Liam was sweating. He looked really unwell. She put her fingers to his forehead. He was burning up. "Liam, you're not well," she said.

"Probably a hangover. I had a rough few nights on the drink with the lads."

"No, you look feverish."

He shrugged. "Probably picked up a cold. Don't worry."

"But I do worry," Then she remembered the poison aconite in Goldyakin's bag. What if Goldyakin had poisoned Liam? He could have done it in Garstang unseen, on the site. Who knows what access he could have, he could have put it in Liam's food, or even his car door handle, God knows how poisonous the stuff was.

Angela's heart raced and her mouth went dry. "Liam, I think he's poisoned you."

"In the name of God, Angela. You need to calm down. Please, or I'm going to be calling a doctor for you."

Liam didn't want to eat anything, and neither did she. She guessed Golyadkin had gone to the pub for his evening meal. She heard him come back about ten, and Liam went to bed early and slept, which wasn't like him at all. Angela spent the night googling aconite and doppelgängers until she'd read every click-bait article on the internet, but there wasn't much real information in them, just a series of cases, copied and repeated from website to website all intended to put advertising in front of your eyes. In the end, she wore herself out and started to calm down. It probably all was in her head. She'd told Golyadkin she was full tomorrow, so he'd be gone. And if Liam didn't get better, she really was going to ring the doctor.

Angela didn't know what woke her, maybe it was just the absence of Liam from their bed. She turned on the bedside lamp. Liam's side of the bed was cold. Instantly, she remembered the aconite. "Liam!" She called and ran through to the ensuite bathroom. The light was off and there was no sign of him. Her heart hammered and her hand was to her throat. The night was cold now as the heating had been off so she pulled on her dressing gown and hurried out.

Golyadkin's bedroom door was closed. She eyed it suspiciously, but her priority was to find out where Liam was. She imagined him lying dead, poisoned by that awful Russian.

The house was still, just the ticking of the landing clock. No lights were on. Angela hurried down the stairs two at a time. She couldn't control her panic. She rushed through the house: dining room, living room, office, kitchen, and from the kitchen she saw the cellar door was open and the light was on.

What the hell would he have gone down there for? She grew scared and drew a long kitchen knife from the knife block. If Golyadkin was around, and he'd hurt Liam, she'd stab him.

Cautiously, almost unable to breathe, she stepped down. She didn't care shout out, in case Golyadkin was down there with Liam and her call alerted him so he would hurt Liam further.

At the bottom, there was no sound at all.

"Liam?" She hissed.

No response came.

"Liam, please!"

But there was only silence.

Her heartbeat hammering in her ears and throat, she stepped off the stairs into the cellar proper. The old stones were cold under her bare feet. There was a door and a lath and plaster wall, but through there was where Liam did his little projects. That's where he would be.

She stopped and looked through the door. She saw a heap of clothes in the middle of the cellar room, Liam's clothes. The knife fell from her hand and rattled on the flag-stones. "Oh, my God!"

Both hands flew to her throat as a wail broke from her lungs.

In the middle of the heap of clothes were the be-slimed remains of Liam's skin and hair. It was as if he'd been opened up from the inside and his skin peeled from him.

She rushed over, still not believing what she was seeing. She couldn't breath, the room span out of control. She thought she'd faint, and then she heard someone coming down the stairs behind her.

Golyadkin emerged into gap of the door.

"You!" She screamed running and snatching the knife.

He backed off, "No, Mrs Houghton, please; this is not what you think. I am not who you think I am."

But those were the last words Golyadkn ever spoke. Angela plunged the kitchen knife into his chest and he staggered back, his lifeblood spouting from the fatal wound. Angela would have stabbed him again, stabbed him a thousand times, but her grief overpowered her. She want back and stood over Liam, his clothes, his skin and his hair.

And then something dripped on her. Involuntarily, she touched her cheek and felt the strange slime. Then another drip. Angela glanced up and saw a slug-like thing attached to the ceiling. Then a third drip, and what the hell was that?

The doppelgänger dropped from the ceiling, right onto Angela, and it ate her all up. And then, when it was finished, it stroked itself down, admired its new long hair and pretty gel fingernails and smiled, ready to receive the B&B's next guest.

10

THE HOUSE OF BONES

It was Sabine who wanted to buy the old children's home. Personally, I wouldn't have gone near the place. It needed so much work, and it was so far from the main roads; no landline, no internet, no cell phone signal, but the rent was cheap, and it was huge.

Sabine wanted to run a therapy centre with workshop rooms and space for people to stay for the duration of their courses. She did hot stones, Hopi Ear Candles, reflexology, meditation, all of that.

She thought the customers would flock to her out there —to that rural stillness. For the three years I'd known her, she'd always wanted to do something like this. They do say you need to let someone go free if you want to keep them, and I wanted to keep her, so I just said yes to everything. Secretly, I hoped she would soon realize how hard the work would be, and we would go back to Berlin.

THAT DAY, Sabine had her phone plugged into the car stereo and was singing and dancing in her seat as we drove along.

We turned off the autobahn onto the straight two-lane road that would lead us, after many kilometres, to the old children's home. I didn't like the music she played, but I'd never told her that.

We still had a long way to go. With my right hand, I reached over and stroked her long blonde hair. She took my hand and kissed it, then she rubbed my raspy chin. "You should have shaved."

I said, "Why? Who are we trying to impress?"

"Lukas, this is going to be my dream come true." She tried to sound like she was open-minded. "But I promise you; we'll take an honest look at it before we decide we're going to live there." Her eyes sparkled, and her mouth smiled. Sabine was beautiful even when sad, but when she was happy, she looked like an angel.

"That's wise," I said in my measured, grown-up tone.

She tilted her head and drummed her fingers lightly on my forearm to emphasize each point she made. "I know you're not sure about this, but it'll be fantastic. You'll love doing drama workshops. You're so good at them."

"Sure. Of course." I never took my gaze from the long straight road.

She said, "I love you, Lukas."

ALL AROUND US, the marshlands stretched away flat and endless. The evening sun caught on pools of water, making them shine like gold. Birds called, their cries haunting the landscape. I half-turned to look where Torsten, Sabine's son, listened to music through his headphones in the back seat. He looked bored, but at least he smiled at me. Torsten and I always got on—I knew he liked me better than his real dad —Sabine's ex. He said it was because I was more chill and way funnier. I'm not sure that's true, but I was pleased he thought it.

AND THE ROAD WENT ON. The car ate up the miles of that long highway as it lay straight as a ruler across the swampland. While we drove, the minutes turned into hours, and the day fled, and night descended.

"How far do you think it is now?" My legs were stiff from the long time cramped behind the wheel.

Sabine consulted the map that Martin had provided. We had no GPS in my old car and no internet data to use the map on the phone.

"Martin's marked it here in pencil," she said. "The house doesn't appear on the big road map."

"How close is it to the town?"

"About 10km."

"Better make sure we get all our supplies in before winter," I joked, hoping that we'd be long gone by then.

About a half-hour later, I saw a group of dark trees silhouetted against the red of the dying sun.

"Here! Here!" said Sabine, pointing. She clutched my arm in her excitement, and I had to take it back gently to twist the wheel.

I TURNED off the straight road, and we crunched along the gravel track to the house. The building itself was hard to make out against the trees initially, as it had no lights on. When we got close, I saw it was a three-story building that stretched way back into the shadows. For some reason, I knew there were lots of outbuildings behind. I had the most curious feeling like I'd been there before, but I shook it off; it was just déjà vu—just a misfiring of the neurons in the brain. It couldn't be anything else.

As we pulled up and the car turned into the parking place, Martin was standing outside to meet us. He held an oil lantern in his hand. Sabine pushed the door open and leapt out to give him a big hug, but Torsten was less enthusiastic. I gave Martin a half-hearted handshake.

"Long drive in your old banger?" he said in his usual smug manner.

Whatever beef we'd had in the past, I let it slide for Sabine's sake. "You bet," I said.

"We're thrilled to be here," said Sabine.

I saw Martin's eyes linger on Sabine's breasts. He knew I'd seen him leering, but instead of getting embarrassed, he flashed me a challenging smile. My hands curled into fists, but I left it. If I started something, I'd be the bad guy in her eyes. Us all getting along would make her happy.

I remember at a party at her old place near the Hakescher Markt, Martin sneered at me over his beer: "How does it feel to have ruined man's life?"

He was right. I'd ruined Sabine's husband's life by taking her from him. But I loved her, and I wanted her more than anyone else I'd ever known. And she loved me too. I told myself that her marriage was already over—that any feeling she'd had for her husband was long gone. But it was something that didn't make me proud.

The divorce was how come she had the money for this place. Martin had been her husband's childhood friend. They'd all met at university. Martin had chosen to keep friends with Sabine because he wanted her. I didn't kid myself. He always had. When I said it, she laughed it off, but it was obvious. And if Martin could take her from me with his funny jokes and his outdoorsy style, he would.

I watched them talking. Sabine was precious to me, and I wouldn't let her go without a fight. Loving her made everything in my life beautiful, and, after all, don't all the songs and books say that love is the higher law?

Torsten stood back. From his body language, I knew he didn't like Martin any more than I did. The boy finally spoke. "So, what was this place?"

"It was a home for disabled kids," said Martin.

"Like mentally subnormal children?"

Sabine hissed at him. "Torsten, we don't use words like that."

"But that's what it was."

Martin nodded.

"What happened to it?" I asked.

"The owner went bust ten years ago. All the kids got moved out. It's been empty since then."

"But, you have a connection with the owner?" I said.

"Something like that," he said. "Let's get in; it's getting chilly."

INSIDE THE KITCHEN, someone had attempted to clean up. The light came from two oil lamps and some candles stuck in old wine bottles. There was bread, milk, some vegetables, and as Martin talked to Sabine, I looked in the cupboard and found tinned meat and soup and a jar of sauerkraut.

"Where do we sleep?" asked Torsten.

"Easy cowboy," said Martin. "I'll show you when I've finished talking to your mother."

Torsten frowned and looked at me for support.

I didn't like how Martin kept touching Sabine's arm or putting his hand on her shoulder as they talked and laughed. She was so excited and enthusiastic about this new venture that she didn't realize that his zeal for her project was only to get into her pants. As we stood in the kitchen, he still looked at her like he wanted to lick her. Out of politeness, or maybe spite, he turned to me and said, "How's the acting going, Lukas?"

"So-so," I said.

"You're still doing the living history thing? Going round the schools?"

I nodded. He let it hang long enough for it to sting, then he said, "Never mind, I'm sure you'll get a real role one day."

I grunted.

Then, he said, "Anyway, let me show you to your rooms."

The rooms stood off a long drab corridor that ran the building's length on the second story. They didn't have much in them. In mine and Sabine's, there was an oil lamp, which I lit, and two mattresses on the floor. Torsten was next door to us, but there was no connecting door; you had to go out onto the corridor and along a bit to get to him.

"Where do you sleep?" I asked Martin.

He waved vaguely behind him. "Along there a way and then up."

The further the better I thought. I waited for Martin to leave, but he didn't. He was too busy chatting with Sabine. I said, "Torsten, you look tired. Why don't you go to bed?"

Torsten nodded at me but didn't move. He was waiting to say goodnight to his mother, but Martin monopolized her, talking about nothing and anything, filling her head with plans of what they could do with the house. And she lapped it up.

In the end, I took Torsten to his room myself.

"I'll come and kiss you goodnight," said Sabine as we walked past her and Martin.

Torsten's room had a mattress but also a chair and a

bookshelf in it. There were even some yellowing paperbacks on the shelf. I lit Torsten's lamp.

"Can I keep it on all night?" he said.

"Sure," I laughed. "But why?"

He looked embarrassed. I'd caught him being the little boy when he wanted to pretend to be a man.

"I just don't like the feeling here."

I joked, "So, you think the place is haunted?"

He shuddered. "Full of the ghosts of murdered kids."

I laughed. "Why murdered?"

"They always get murdered in places like this," he said. "And these books," he pointed to the bookstand. "Are all about reincarnation."

I went and peered over. He was right. I said, "I guess someone had an interest in reincarnation. Maybe the last owner. Listen, I'll leave you now, but I'll send your mother in."

"Good night, Lukas," he said. "And let's hope we're back in Berlin soon."

"Fingers crossed." I winked at him, and I paused before going out the door. "Have you taken your medication?"

"You're not my dad, Lukas," said Torsten sulkily.

"I know, but take your medication, anyway."

BACK IN OUR room Sabine was alone and undressing. I told her Torsten was waiting to say goodnight. I knew I shouldn't show my jealousy, but I said it anyway: "I thought Martin was never going to leave."

She stood there in her white bra and panties. I felt a familiar surge of desire, and I went over and placed my hands on her hips. She didn't stop me. Instead, she leaned in and gave me a soft kiss. "You're silly to be jealous of

Martin," she said. "You know I love only you." She hesitated. "Is it because he was my husband's friend?"

"No, it's not that at all," I said.

We made love, then we slept.

IN THE MORNING, the sun spilled in through the curtainless window and shone into my eyes, waking me up. Her blonde hair was tousled and spread over her pillow like a golden storm. "Good morning, my gummy-bear," she said sleepily, leaning over to kiss me. I sat up and rubbed my eyes. "Wonder what we can find for breakfast."

"Where do we wash?" she said. She stood, and I watched the sun caress her naked body, her skin golden brown from her habit of sunbathing nude on the roof of her old apartment in the city. "You know I had the weirdest dream," she said.

"Oh?"

"It felt real." She shuddered.

"A nightmare?"

"Kind of. In it, I was called Kristen, and I lived in this very house. And Martin was there too."

"I like him even less now," I said.

Sabine laughed, but I wasn't joking.

LATER OVER TOAST in the kitchen, with Torsten slumbering and Martin still absent or up to something somewhere, I said, "Let's go to town. We need some provisions. I'm going to get some meat and buy some flashlights and batteries. We can't rely on the electricity supply from the look of this place."

Sabine grimaced.

"What?" I said.

"I've got lots to do here."

"Like?"

"Just I need to look over the plans with Martin. The plans for the therapy rooms."

It was my turn to grimace. I picked up the car keys trying not to let the irritation show. "Fine," I said. "I won't be long." But then at the door, I couldn't help it. I said, "I knew he'd try to get you to himself—just didn't know it would work so quickly."

She blushed. "You know it's not that." Then she put on the look that was supposed to make me ashamed for thinking wrong of her. The truth was, I didn't want to think badly of her. But she'd been unfaithful before with me when she was still married; why wouldn't she be again? I tried to shake it off. "Is Torsten upstairs?" I said.

She nodded. "I don't think he slept too well. I could hear him moving about all night."

"I'll ask him if he wants to come, anyway." I went to the bottom of the stairs and walked halfway up, my feet causing the bare wooden boards to creak. I shouted, "Torsten, want to come to town?"

He didn't answer, so I went to the top of the stairs. For some reason, looking at his closed door, I got a rush of anxiety. That was very odd. I yelled again—still no reply, so I walked to his door and rapped, pushing it open and peering round.

Torsten was lying in his bed, wrapped in his sleeping bag. I could see his hair plastered over his forehead. He looked sweaty, so I stooped to touch him. He felt clammy. His eyes flicked open, and he started back from my touch.

I smiled, "Easy, it's only me! Want to come to town?"

He rubbed the sleep out of his eyes with the back of his

hand. "I'm not feeling so well, Lukas. My hips and legs really ache," he said.

"Hmm, could be the damp. We are in the middle of a swamp. Might make the inflammation worse."

"I do want to come with you," he said. He half sat up, and then he winced. I saw that his knees and hips looked swollen, as they did when he had an attack.

"Maybe you should stay here. You look tired," I said.

"I had some awful dreams."

"So did your mother."

"This place is creepy."

I mussed his hair. "Take it easy. Want anything from town?"

He shook his head.

"I'll see you later," I said. When I got back to the kitchen, Sabine wasn't there. I imagined she'd gone to find Martin.

As I GOT in the car, clouds covered the sky, and it looked like it would rain before long. The drive took about twenty minutes, back on the main straight road through the swamp country then a turn off to Emmelsdorf. There was a straggle of houses as I approached along the road that turned into a miserable looking main street. The houses were made of wood and needed painting. I could see there was a general store, a garage, and a hairdresser. Parking wasn't a problem.

I got out and walked over to the general store. The shop was small but had newspapers, a fridge, rows of tinned food, chocolate, bread, et cetera. An older woman with thin dyed hair that looked like it was meant to be blonde but had turned out a pale orange stood talking to a decrepit farmer. I wondered what crops grew well out here in the swamp country. Then again, who cared?

I got what provisions I needed and then went to pay for them. The woman shovelled them into a plastic bag while I stood there with my cash in hand. She didn't make conversation. When she spoke, it was only to name the price. Her accent was thick, but I could understand her fine. When she spoke, I saw she had no teeth. This was a town of inbreds and ingrates.

Outside, I thought I'd go for a walk along the main street, bag in hand, just to get the measure of the place. There were only a few people about, and none spoke or looked up. I quickly exhausted the main street and saw that there was nothing but more swamp beyond the small Lutheran church. The dull, wetland lurked a hundred meters beyond the village, looking like it was waiting for its chance to smother the whole place and its people.

I stood there for a minute, and then when I was about to turn round, the church door opened and a woman came out. She was the most normal-looking person I'd seen so far. That is to say; she didn't look like her mother would have also been her aunt.

She wore a clerical collar, so I took her to be the town's pastor. She met my eyes and smiled. This was the first smile to cross anyone's face since I'd arrived in Emmelsdorf, and I smiled back. She walked down the stairs like she wanted to talk. She looked strangely nervous.

"Hello," I said as she arrived on the sidewalk beside me.

She didn't waste time with pleasantries. "You are the new family at the old Children's Home?"

I nodded. "You're well informed."

"People here knew you were coming. Martin's mother told them."

"Is Martin from here? I didn't know."

She raised an eyebrow. "You didn't know? His father was caretaker there until he died."

"Oh, really? But Martin lives in Berlin now."

"Yes, but he visits his mother often."

The pastor looked like a bird. She had a puckered brow and a sharp little face, but for some reason, I trusted her. I did some fishing. "The Children's Home went bust, didn't it?"

She nodded. "And the children all disappeared," she said.

I hadn't heard that. "Disappeared? What do you mean?"

She shrugged. "They were probably sent to other homes. They weren't the kind of kids who had anyone to miss them. 'Broken biscuits' they used to call them."

"So who owns the building? Sabine never told me their name."

"I think Martin's mother does."

For some reason that surprised me.

"Martin's father was a powerful man around here. Dead now. He died in 1981."

1981, the year I was born; it seemed a long time ago now. I was puzzled, and I wondered why Martin had been so cagey about his close connections with the old children's home.

"This is an out of the way community," she said quietly. "I still count as a stranger here even after ten years, and we strangers should stick together." The way she fixed me with her gaze struck me as odd. She was a nice woman, but she made me uneasy.

Suddenly she put her hand on my arm like she'd been working up her courage to tell me something, and it was now or never. "Come into the church," she said.

"What? Now?"

I glanced at my watch then back down the road towards my car.

"Please?" She implored me.

I shrugged. "I don't have a lot of time."

Her hand was still on my arm. I looked down at it. "Sure, okay. But I can't be long."

We walked up the steps into the old wooden building. Inside, it smelled of Bibles and damp. Glancing around, I commented about its history or architecture, trying to be polite, but she ignored my pleasantries.

She said in a low voice, "I need to tell you something important."

"Okay," I said warily.

"What do you know about the Grail Movement?"

I shrugged. "Nothing."

She nodded." They call themselves Christians, but they're not."

"Okay..."

"For one thing they believe in reincarnation. For another, that you really have to eat the flesh and drink the blood to be reincarnated. Only if you eat the flesh and drink the. blood can you be born time and time again and achieve a kind of eternal life."

"Isn't that a common Christian belief?"

"No," she said, shaking her head as if I was stupid. "Not just the idea of the blood and flesh. Not even the transubstantiated mystical idea that the Catholic Church believes."

"I don't get it."

"They eat flesh and drink blood."

"Oh," I said as the penny dropped. "So instead of wine and bread, they drink and eat real blood and real flesh? Like from the butcher's shop?"

"Yes," she said like I was a slow kid who finally got it. But there was still something she was holding back.

I was incredulous. "This cult ate raw meat? Really? "

She didn't answer.

I narrowed my eyes. "But why are you telling me this?"

"Because the Children's Home was one of their places."

I stared at her. No, she was one of them, after all. She seemed far from normal, possibly deranged. It was time to leave. I stepped away and walked towards the door of the church.

She whispered, "But maybe you shouldn't stay long there in any case. That would be best." As I walked toward the church door, she said, "I've said too much. Don't tell Martin I told you anything about the Grail Movement." She looked genuinely frightened.

"Can you let go of the door, please?" I said coldly.

The parson woman moved back. As I was going out the door, glad of the fresh air, even if it did stink of the bog-land around, she called after me, "They're waiting for their father to return."

And what the hell that meant, I didn't know.

WHEN I GOT BACK, Sabine was in the kitchen with Martin. She beamed at me as I walked in. Then when I was close, she stood up and kissed me. He just sat there and nodded.

"Want a beer?" said Sabine. I saw they'd been drinking.

I shook my head. "Too early for me." I put down the supplies on the table and said, "What have you two been busying yourself with?"

I saw a smirk on Martin's face, but Sabine's face was innocent. "Just talking through the plans. If we can get the place fixed up in two months, we can start advertising the courses. Do you think you could get the acting classes prepared by then?"

"Sure," I nodded. "But making this place welcoming is going to take more than two months."

"Such a negative attitude," Martin sneered, meeting Sabine's eye, thinking he was funny. I peeled Sabine off me but kept holding her hand as I sat down, her fingers twined through mine. I ignored Martin. "Where's Torsten?" I said. "He wasn't so well earlier."

"He took some anti-inflammatories, and that seemed to work. He went off exploring the house."

"Okay." I was still trying to please her. I said, "Maybe I'll have that beer." No one moved, so I went and got it myself. I took a pull on the beer while I put my arm around her waist and listened to Martin's ideas for fixing up a hot tub for the visitors around the back. Sabine was full of the new life she planned and enthralled by Martin's schemes.

After about an hour, Torsten came into the kitchen. Dust stained his jeans, and he had cobwebs in his hair. "Lukas!" he said. "Man! You gotta come! I've found a secret room!"

"Calm down!" I laughed. "What secret room?"

"It's full of bones. Skulls and leg bones and ribs—all sorts. They're only small, like kid's bones."

"That's disgusting, Torsten," said Sabine. "Please don't go there again. You've probably disturbed a burial area for the children who died here."

Torsten was excited. "The kids aren't buried. Their bones are just piled up like somebody threw them away. Come with me, Lukas, come on."

"Let me finish my beer," I said. Torsten had always told tall stories ever since I'd known him. Despite being thirteen, he was childish in lots of ways. I didn't doubt that he was exaggerating to make his mother pay attention to him.

"I don't want you going back there," said Sabine. "It's not respectful. Go and get a bath, you're filthy. Then come back down."

"I got the boiler going," said Martin. "There should be hot water."

Torsten's face twisted into a sulk. He looked anywhere but at his mother, seemingly angry for her treating him like a child in front of grown men.

"I'll come with you later," I said.

Torsten grinned at me, pleased he had an ally.

Sabine flashed me a look of disapproval and said, "No, you will not go back there. Neither of you."

Torsten scowled.

"Go get a bath!" I laughed at him. "You stinker!"

He giggled, and when he'd gone, I said to Martin. "So what's this with the bones? Is it real?"

He took a sip of his beer and shook his head. "How would I know?"

"I thought your father was caretaker here."

He looked like I'd caught him out. Recovering his composure, he said, "Who's been talking to you?"

"The pastor. In town."

He scowled. "That busybody. No one likes her. Probably only talked to you because everyone else shuns her."

"Maybe it's an ossuary," said Sabine. "This was a religious establishment. Martin told me."

"What religion?" I said, wanting to see how honest he'd been.

"The Grail Movement," said Martin.

"I don't know that one," I said. "What do they believe?"

"Nothing special," he replied, not meeting my eyes.

"Who would pile up children's bones?" said Sabine.

Martin said, "He probably just found animal bones."

But there was something in his voice. He turned back to Sabine. "You were going to give me a demonstration massage."

"When we've set the place up," said Sabine. She turned to me. Even she sounded embarrassed. "With the hot stones. You've had one before, Lukas," she explained.

"Oh yeah, very therapeutic," I said. "I'm sure he'll love it."

I WENT UPSTAIRS LOOKING for her son and found he wasn't in his room. I shouted his name. No reply. I thought he'd decided to go and look at his bones without me. I walked along the corridor a little way. The house was big, and I hadn't explored it. I hadn't even been upstairs or down into the cellars. I walked in the direction where Martin had indicated his room was. I yelled again for Torsten, but still, no reply came.

It was still light outside and would be for a few hours. In the end, I couldn't find him, despite my shouting. I thought he'd come back eventually when his resentment towards his mother had cooled off. This situation could even work in my favour. If Sabine saw both Torsten and I were pissed off at her, she'd maybe give up on her ridiculous plan to make this god-forsaken dump into a therapy centre.

I made my way back to the kitchen. Martin was gone, thank God, and Sabine was standing by the open door looking out. Midges from the marshland buzzed around my face.

I said, "Torsten's not in his room. I guess he's gone back to see his bones."

She didn't turn round. I felt warm towards her again, and I was ashamed of my jealousy, and I wanted to make up with her. "He'll be back soon enough, don't worry."

But still, she didn't speak or turn round.

"Hey," I said, "I'm sorry if I was a jerk before. But you've got to see it from my point of view."

She still didn't move, so I stepped in front of her.

"Sabine?" I said

Slowly she said, "I'm not Sabine. I'm Kristen."

"What?" I said, confused.

"I lived here before," she said.

A chill pricked up my spine. "This is weird, Sabine."

She kept on. "I was Kristen. But I died."

I shook my head. "What are you talking about?"

"Something terrible is going to happen here," she said. She stared at me with eyes blue as a china doll's. "Like it did before with Kristen."

"Then let's leave. We can go now."

"But my therapy centre..."

"We can hire somewhere in Berlin. It'll be far more accessible. It'll be better."

"I wanted to be in the country."

"This isn't the country; this is a wasteland."

I walked her over to the table and sat her down on one of the wooden chairs. She looked dazed, ill even. She said, "It came to me in a flash. As real as my life now. In my last life, I was a child here. I know I died. I can't see how—but I know it was awful."

"You said that Martin was in your dream?"

She wasn't listening. "There was a father—the Holy Father."

"Your father?" I screwed up my eyes in disbelief. "Martin was your father?"

She nodded. "He's the father of all the children. He's the Holy Father." Then she shook her head. "I don't know if it was Martin".

I looked at her long and hard. She'd always been fragile. I knew she'd had a nervous breakdown when she was a teenager. And I knew we just had to get out of that place. I said, "I'll go get the bags. You didn't unpack?"

"I didn't have time."

"Okay, I'll go get them. I'll shout for Torsten too. Where's Martin now?"

"He went back to his room. I think. I don't know."

"Doesn't matter. I'll get the car. We've got to leave; you get that, don't you?"

She smiled, the tears still running down her cheeks. "You're probably right. I'll do what you say."

"Good. Just wait here."

I WALKED OUT. I'd parked the car around the side, but it wasn't there when I rounded the corner. The tire marks were there, but no car. I couldn't believe it. I'd left the keys on the dash because there was no one in that place but us. No one for miles.

And then I saw the woman.

She was old and tired looking with stringy light brown hair. Her face was slack. Her eyes held a kind of watchful resentment.

"Who are you?" I said abruptly.

"I'm Frau Kaminski," she said as if that should mean something to me.

I said, "Where's my car gone?" She didn't answer. She made as if to go. I went over to her and put my hand on her shoulder to spin her around. I looked her in the face. "Did you move my car?" I demanded.

She looked back at me; there was more resignation than anger on her face. "I know you," she said quietly.

I grunted. "Well, I sure as hell, don't know you. Where is my car?"

"It's safe." She looked at me with a weariness I'd rarely seen. "Who are you anyway?" I said.

"I'm the caretaker's wife."

"There is no caretaker now, not for a long time."

"His widow."

Then the penny dropped. "Are you Martin's mother?"

She nodded, but I saw fear deep in her eyes, like the light of a candle from another room—a flickering, uncertain light.

"You're frightened of him," I said.

"And so should you be."

"I just want to leave. We'll all leave—me and Sabine and Torsten. You and Martin can keep this place."

"Martin wants you to stay."

A mix of anger and cold apprehension filled me. "I doubt that."

She nodded. "I wanted to see you as you are now," she said. "Just one time."

"What? Anyway, why should I be scared of Martin? Tell me!"

She turned and walked away, and I let her go. When she said I should be frightened of Martin, she certainly meant it. But I could stand my ground. I would force him to give me my car back, and that bullshit about him wanting me to stay. He didn't want me; he wanted Sabin, but I wouldn't let him have her. She was coming home with me to Berlin. If we had to fight, then we had to fight.

Sabine wasn't in the kitchen even though I told her to stay there. Why the hell would she go wandering? Unless she'd gone to find Torsten. I shouted for her, but there was no reply. I hurried along the corridor, trying the doors, but neither Sabine nor Torsten were in any of the rooms.

At the end of the corridor was a door that was locked. I tried the handle and knocked on it, shouting their names. I even yelled Martin's name, but when I listened, there was no sound from inside. Finding no one on that floor, I climbed the stairs and called out there, here again, there was silence.

I went to Torsten's room. There was no sign that he'd been back. It was still light outside, but heavy clouds were massing in the west, and the wind looked as if it was bringing the bad weather our way. From the window of the passageway on the second floor, I saw flat marshland bleeding away in all directions like a muddy bruise as the light drained out of it. It was as if the light knew something was coming.

Alternately, I called out for Torsten and Sabine, but there was never any reply. I hurried along the passageway, opening doors of rooms I'd never yet entered. They were mostly empty. Some had rusty bed frames; others had broken bookcases and chairs, and there was dust everywhere.

Something in that house frightened me. It was as if something waited at the edge of memory as if in a second, I would remember what I had always hidden from myself.

All this place seemed weirdly familiar, though I'd never been here before.

I found rooms filled with dust and rot. At the far end of the corridor was a further room. I stopped just before I entered as a flash of memory struck me, but so quickly that I retained nothing.

In the big room, someone had daubed a painting of a skeleton in red paint on the wall. Around it were other skeletons, skulls, and ribcages, drawn by different childish hands. The big skeleton was raising a bone to its roughly sketched mouth.

AT THE FAR end of the house from the kitchen, I made my way through the downstairs rooms. Eventually, I stepped into the big one that Sabine had wanted to use for her yoga and my acting workshops.

I heard the wood creak and then split under my shoes. The floorboards were rotten, and I was in the centre of that big room. The wood ahead of me looked in a worse state than that behind.

I stepped, but too late, I saw my foot go through, and then, almost in slow motion, my shoe sank through the rotten wood. I lost my balance and went careering forward, and the whole floor collapsed under me.

I fell in a cloud of splintered wood and dust into a cellar. I couldn't see as I toppled, but as my hands went forward to protect myself, I knew they'd sunk in a pile of bones. I jumped up from the mouldy, cold things, and felt an excruciating pain in my right leg. I rolled, and I heard skulls break and ribs crack under my back. I put my hands down to my ankle. I tried to get up onto my knees and then stand up, but the pain was like a stab of electricity. I felt the ends of my bones rub—the crepitations that told me that I'd broken it.

Even in the poor light, I could see the piles of bones in the room. And they were small—definitely children's bones. This place was no ossuary—there was no grace or dignity here; this was a charnel house. Scraps of rotting flesh clung to childish femurs and tiny skeletal hands. Some of the small skulls retained leathery rags of skin and hair. The smell of old decay and damp was still as strong as if the last of them had died only months before. It made me gag. I limped and stumbled to the door.

Stone steps led up from here, and I took them, careful to avoid aggravating my broken ankle, but as fast as I could to get away from the bones. I went on my knees at one point, pulling myself up by the railing. Hopping and limping, I got to the front door. I had no idea what I was going to do. I could hardly walk to the town like this.

And where were Sabine and Torsten? I shouted for them again, but still no answer. And then I remembered Frau Kaminski. I made my way to where I'd seen her. The care-taker's house had to be nearby. I followed round behind the main building, and there was a smaller house; it must be hers.

There must be a phone in Frau Kaminski's house. No one could live way out here without any means of commu-nication.

Frau Kaminski's front door was wide open. I went in.

She lay on the floor of her front room on her back. Her entrails were spread out from a cut in her gut that ran from her pubis to her sternum. Her face was twisted, and her swollen tongue protruded from between broken teeth. From the marks on her face, it appeared she had been clubbed to the ground and ripped open. And then I saw that her liver was lying beside her. It had been cut out in pieces, and the bits were strewn across the floor. It took only an instant to take the sight in, but that instant was enough to make me violently sick.

And then behind me, I heard Martin calling my name. He was shouting from the main house. I stepped back into the yard, and, looking up, I saw Martin's grinning face at the window.

"Your mother," I said, horrified. "She's dead."

He was up on the top floor of the house, way above. "My mother? I know she's dead," he answered. "It's my father I'm waiting for."

FROM THE CRAZY look on his face, I guessed now he had killed her. She had been frightened of him, and now I knew why.

I HAD to find Sabine and Torsten because Martin was so crazy he'd kill them too. I stepped, and pain jolted through me. It was so intense I thought I might pass out, and for a second, I took my eyes from Martin. When the wave of dizziness passed, I looked up, but Martin was gone. I feared Sabine and Torsten were in the house with him at his mercy.

"Sabine," I yelled in the door, hoping that she would answer and that she and Torsten would run out. But the only reply was the sudden sound of heavy rain breaking from the clouds above and puddles formed on the ground around me.

"Sabine," I called again, and when there was no answer this time, I stepped through the door. Slowly and painfully, I went to the kitchen drawer and took out a knife. It was about 20cm long and sharp and made for gutting fishes. Then I stumbled to the foot of the stairs leading down into the room of bones.

I descended into hell. The hammering rain outside made the room darker than it had been before. Shadows lurked in every corner, hiding behind the ruined heaps of bones. Children's skulls grinned from empty eyes and broken teeth. The pain in my leg flashed with every step, and I held the knife out in front, shaking like a leaf.

MARTIN JUMPED FROM A CORNER, his bony hands twisted around my neck. He dragged me, and I collapsed into the pile of bones. He kneeled on me, his thumbs like steel pegs either side of my windpipe. He squeezed so firmly that I began to pass out. I dropped the knife. The knife intended for revenge. I heard it clatter out of sight and knew I was lost.

Martin's insane face leered at me as my vision went red then began to fade. Blood and saliva ran over his lips, and it seemed I was going to die, and then I remembered nothing more.

I DIDN'T EXPECT to wake up, but I did, crumpled on the floor —still in the room of bones.

MARTIN HADN'T KILLED ME. Sabine was kneeling near me now, a look of tender concern on her face. She stroked my cheek. I was aware of the agony of my broken ankle. Martin must have kneeled on it because it looked and felt displaced further out of shape. My throat throbbed where his fingers had choked me.

Sabine said, "Father, you are awake."

I was groggy. "What? I'm not your father, Sabine."

She smiled sweetly. She wasn't well, but I still lived, and so I still had a chance to save her. My throat rasped and burned like fire with every word. "Sabine, we need to leave. Get Torsten, and we'll leave."

I struggled to get up, and she helped me. She even supported me as I stood because I couldn't bear weight on my broken leg.

"Sabine, come on," I said. "Hurry; he'll be back soon."

But why hadn't he killed me—why he hadn't cut me open as he had his mother?

Sabine smiled at me. "I'm not Sabine anymore. I'm Kristen."

That crazy story again, the name from her dream. I stared at her to try and divine how much she believed this.

Sabine kept smiling. "And you'll remember who you are too soon."

I tried to drag her towards the stairs. The knife gleamed on the floor where I'd dropped it.

Sabine saw it too. "You want this?" she said.

I nodded, and she bent down and picked it up. She offered it to me, handle first, and I took it; I would kill him with this.

At the bottom of the stairs, I said, "Where is Torsten?"

"My son?" She looked puzzled, holding the word in her mouth as if it tasted strange.

"Your son, yes."

She nodded, her brow knitted, as if remembering. "He's close. In the house."

"Is he safe?"

"He's with Martin," she said.

Horror flooded through me. What was going on? I yammered, "What did Martin do to you? Did he hurt you?"

She tilted her head. "Why would he hurt me?"

"Sabine! Because he killed his mother. He nearly killed me."

We were going up the stairs, slowly, one by one. She

propped me up as I strained and gasped with pain. I said, "Did Martin tell you where he put the car?"

"Yes. It's in the barn. Behind the house."

"Can you show me?"

She frowned. "It's better you stay here with us."

"I don't think so. Sabine, you've got to shake this off."

We were at the top of the stairs now. I could see the open door that led to the kitchen and beyond that the door outside, still open. I could hear the pattering of the rain. My leg was too painful. "Can you drive us from here, Sabine?"

She said slowly, "Sabine can. But Kristen belongs here. Kristen doesn't want to leave. Neither should you. You'll remember soon."

This was madness. "Sabine, you must come with me. You have to get Torsten. We've got to go before Martin kills us all."

She grinned. "Martin won't kill us."

I said, "I don't think you realize how crazy he is. Martin killed his mother."

She shook her head. "No, she offered herself up." She leaned in and kissed my cheek. "You know, she waited a long time for you coming. Once she'd seen you, she knew it was time."

"Time? What do you mean?"

She stifled a giggle. "You'll see!"

I started to pull her with me through the kitchen. She came up to the door with me, but then wouldn't go any further.

"Please, Sabine," I said.

"Please, call me, Kristen."

My hand shook as I put the knife on the table. This was all going crazy. I pushed my hand through my hair as if it helped me think, feeling the moisture of my own sweat on my palm. I said, "Let's just go for a little drive to town. I need a doctor, Sabine. Look at my leg."

She looked down and nodded. "It's broken," she said.

"So, drive me to town. Please?" My voice was raspy, and I began to cough.

"No, we need to find Martin. Torsten's with him."

She was right. I couldn't leave the boy. "Okay," I said. I grabbed the knife again.

She took my hand and led me. She walked, and I hobbled down that corridor. I held onto the blade for dear life. I knew that the only way out of that house for the three of us was to kill Martin.

AT THE END of the corridor was the door that had always been locked. The one I'd knocked on, but couldn't open. Sabine opened it. Someone had unlocked it.

Martin crouched with his back to us. He bent over the body of Torsten. At first, I thought maybe Torsten had had an attack, and Martin was helping him, but then I realized Martin was doing something terrible to the boy.

I roared, and switched the knife into an overhand grasp and broke free from Sabine. I raised the dagger and rushed to stab Martin in the back while he was still so terribly preoccupied with whatever he was doing. And then Sabine knocked the knife from my hand, sending it flying and landing dully against the bottom of the wall.

"No, Father," she said, putting up a finger in admonition.

Martin turned round in greeting, a massive smile on his face. "Ah, you're here at last," he said. "Welcome to our sacrament."

Blood drenched his hands. In his right fist, he held a small saw. On the floor was the naked body of Torsten. I could see now what they'd done to him. Martin had sliced off part of the boy's rump. He'd also put out his eyes and cut off his penis and testicles. He'd kept these snippets aside. They lay heaped in a bloody mess like delicacies saved for later.

Blood covered Martin's chin. I was late to the feast, and his hunger had overcome him. He hadn't waited. Sabine went over and picked up my dropped knife.

A bottomless pit of terror opened. I felt remembrance come over me. Just at the edge of consciousness, I knew I had been there before, just as Kristen had. The sense of Deja Vu I'd had was a real memory.

I had been a member of the Grail sect. We were reincarnated as the creatures we had once been, sly carnivores that feed on our own kind.

With the last vestiges of Lukas, I looked at Martin. I forced the words out, "I wish you'd killed me. Why didn't you kill me?"

Martin smiled. "Because you are our Father. We have long awaited your rebirth."

I remember his father had died in 1981. The year I was born.

To my right, Sabine dug her knife into Torsten's skull. She peeled away the scalp and the crust of bone, and then she used the knife's flat blade to spoon out the grey gobbets of her son's brain. She offered it to me and said, "As soon as you eat, you'll remember."

I looked at Martin as he bent and cut out Torsten's heart with his knife. He bit into the heart like a dog savaging meat. With blood running down his chin, he urged me. "Eat, Father, eat."

11

KILLER CLOWNS

I t was 7 pm on Halloween. Jacob slipped his coat on and hovered by the door. His grandmother was watching TV, and his dad was out, but mom was in the kitchen.

"Where are you going?" asked his mom, lifting her head from making pumpkin pie.

"I'm going to a Halloween Party with Tyler."

His grandmother perked up. She said, "Oh, you be careful on Halloween! Halloween's an Irish thing, you know, so I know what I'm talking about."

His grandmother was from County Mayo in Ireland. She still talked real Irish too, it was embarrassing.

"Sure, grandma," he muttered.

She continued. "And especially don't take any food or drink from any spirits you come across. That's their way of snaring you and dragging you into the underworld."

"I don't believe any of that stuff, grandma."

Grandma snorted. "You kids think it's all computers and motorcars, but old spirits still wander, even if they wear modern faces these days."

His mom interrupted. "So, you're going with Tyler."

"That's what I said."

She frowned. "I thought you didn't like Tyler."

Jacob said, "He's okay."

Now her suspicion was roused. "Where's the party anyway?"

Jacob shrugged in his teenage way. "Not sure. Tyler knows."

"Hey, Jake, wouldn't you rather stay home with your mom on Halloween, and watch scary movies? I've got treats."

He shook his head awkwardly, and she ruffled his hair. "Only kidding, you go and have a good time. I'm pleased you're going out rather than sitting at home with your X-Box like you normally do."

Relieved at getting her permission, Jacob hurried out. At the door, he called back, "Don't wait up, mom; I'm going to be late."

"See that guy over there," Tyler pointed. "The one standing by the side of the road."

Jacob gasped. "He's got a clown mask on!" He stepped back into the shadows so the clown couldn't see him. The clown stood in a light pool, though the streetlight was too dim to really see the figure. The lamp cast a glowing circle in the clinging dark that hung around the lonely road junction, and the freak stood in the middle of it like he was showing off. Time to go. An owl hooted from somewhere in the trees, and the air tasted of oncoming rain.

"He's got the whole clown suit on!" Tyler laughed and strolled off, cradling his beer keg to his round belly. His curly hair bobbed as he walked.

"What a loser," Jacob muttered. The clown had freaked

him. He had a particular phobia of clowns but tried to hide the fear in his voice because Tyler would mock him for it.

"He's only a clown. It's Halloween, dude. What do you expect! I think it's great."

Jacob shook his head. He had a bottle of vodka taken from his dad's secret stash in his bag that he hoped would ingratiate him to Tyler, but his hands were clammy as he drew the bag straps tight. In his heart, Jacob didn't think coming out here to this out of the way place was such a good idea, but Tyler insisted there was a party at one of the houses, and Jacob didn't want to seem scared or uncool.

"Come on," Tyler said. "The house is down here." He scratched his head. " I think anyway." Tyler moved off.

"What about the clown? Do you think he'll follow us?" Jacob cast a wary glance over his shoulder. The figure still stood in the light, studying them with his evil clown eyes.

"Fuck the clown," Tyler said. "We've got a party to get to."

They trudged along the deserted country road. The town and their warm homes were behind them. As they'd passed along the main street, it had been crazy with all the partiers dressed up and drinking. Jacob had wanted to stay there, but Tyler always thought he knew best. He said he'd heard of the sickest party, and it was down here past the edge of town, in a house in the middle of the woods. Wasn't that cool?

As they entered the first trees, Jacob asked, "Are you sure it's okay? I mean, these woods are huge. We could get lost."

Tyler shook his head. "You're such a wuss. Of course, it's okay. There's this girl. She's calling herself Elvira, and, man, she is red hot. Smokin'..."

"You saw her?"

"No, not in actual life. But I mean from her pic. Like she was wearing a revealing costume, you get me? Dude, she's offerin' it up." Tyler guffawed like a dirty old man. He jabbed his thumb towards his chest. "If she's offerin' it, I'm takin' it."

Jacob gave a half-smile, then a broader one. He liked the sound of that. Jacob wasn't the most popular kid, but neither was Tyler. As a matter of fact, Tyler was more than a little annoying at school, but Jacob didn't have a massive choice of friends, so he tagged along.

"Here." Tyler pointed down a dirt track that ran deeper into the woods. As they stopped to take stock of where they were, the tall pines on either side shushed and moved in the wind.

Jacob paused. "You sure?"

Tyler nodded. "Yeah."

Jacob brushed his straight brown hair away from his forehead. His voice wavered. "Okay, if I use the flashlight? It's just kinda dark down there. Moon's behind the clouds tonight."

Tyler grinned. "Sure, if it makes you feel braver, mommy's boy."

Jacob flushed at the insult. He was close to his mother and his grandma too. Mom still tucked him up in bed at night, not that he would be telling Tyler that.

"Come on, I'm getting cold," Tyler said, holding his keg and walking off.

Jacob flicked on the flashlight, and the beam caught the dirt road and the tree trunks. Tyler walked fast, and now he was a little way ahead. Jacob hurried and glanced into the gloomy forest that crowded in on both sides. He heard the moaning wind, and for a second, he hesitated, worried about getting lost among these trees, but Tyler wasn't wait-ing, so he ran to catch up.

Out of breath, he came level with Tyler at last, and they trudged on. Jacob's flashlight wavered feebly in the darkness. They were way out in the wilds now. Jacob heard their feet crunch on the dirt, and he changed his grip on the bag to put it over his shoulder. Beside him, Tyler cradled the beer keg like a baby.

"So, there's gonna be girls?" Jacob's voice sounded shrill. Truth to tell, he wouldn't know what to do with a girl if he found one, but he hoped showing interest in girls would make him seem more manly.

"Yep, hot chicks." Tyler nodded. "And all waiting for us. Not many people will come out this far, so we've got a better chance. The male to female ratio will be in our favor. Sex is a sure thing for us. Well, for me."

Jacob forced a laugh. "Cool." He turned. He thought he glimpsed a shadow to their right, just inside the forest edge. Seeing something move was so startling that he snapped the flashlight beam around as a jag of fear ripped through him.

Tyler stopped. "What are you doing?"

"There's something in the forest."

"Yeah, like a squirrel. Don't be a pussy," Tyler snorted, walking on.

It wasn't a squirrel. It was way bigger than that. The flashlight beam couldn't unpick darkness from deeper darkness, but Jacob felt something was watching them. Spine prickling, he scurried to catch up with Tyler. Tyler might be a dick, but Jacob didn't like lagging behind on his own. "How far down the track is this party?" he said.

"We're near now."

"How do you know?"

"Don't ask me how I know. I just know, okay?" Tyler said it without looking round. He walked purposefully, fixed on his goal.

They came to a crossroads. There was no moon and no stars to light their way, just a dark crossroads in the wilderness. Dirt trails went four ways. The trees were tall and met above their heads. Jacob flashed his beam this way and that, but it all looked the same.

Tyler paused. He put down the keg and thoughtfully considered each alternative.

Jacob said, "You know where you're going, right? You did get directions?"

"Sure, from the WhatsApp Group. Elvira told me."

"So, which way?"

Tyler scratched his head. "Hmm."

Jacob knew the way back was down the track about half a mile, and then he'd reach the highway. Then he shivered, worried about what lurked in the woods between him and home.

"Okay." Tyler picked up the beer keg confidently and walked off to the right.

"You sure this is correct?"

"Of course I am," Tyler called back.

Jacob stared down the track that went the opposite way. It was too dark to make much out, but he still had a feeling this was wrong.

"Come on," Tyler yelled. He was some way ahead now. Jacob lingered and shined his flashlight into the gloom. The whispering of the trees disturbed him. It was almost as if they were muttering together.

Then among the shadows, Jacob saw a man-sized shape. It moved. His heart nearly jumped up his throat, but then he thought maybe it was another partygoer who could give them directions.

He stared into the dark, and the shape moved again. As it got closer, Jacob saw it was another clown. He jumped backward. This wasn't the same clown as the first one, the face was different, painted in hideous, jolly colors. Leaving the clown behind, Jacob sprinted down the path to where Tyler was still going, head down.

Jacob panted. "There's another clown. Behind us."

Tyler said, "He's probably going to the party."

Jacob was silent, catching his breath. Yes, that's what it was — another partygoer in fancy dress.

JACOB AND TYLER walked on for another mile until they reached a further crossroads. Tyler hesitated only briefly this time before plunging down a path through the woods. But now the trails were far from straight; these weren't loggers' tracks anymore but felt more ancient. They might even go back to the days before the Europeans came—when the Continent dreamed, and spirits haunted the endless groves.

After a further twenty minutes, they got to a branch in the track. Tyler stopped and looked around while Jacob blurted, "We're lost, aren't we?"

Tyler grunted. "I wouldn't say lost."

"But, you do know the way to the party house?"

Tyler sucked his lips audibly. He put down the beer keg. "Sure. I'm just a bit disorientated."

"So, what about the way back to the town? Do you know that?"

Tyler flapped his hands. "Of course I do."

"Which way then?"

"Just straight back. Obviously."

"We've made about five turns, and it's so dark, they all look the same." Jacob gestured to the rows of trees that lined the path, dense on both sides. "This all looks the same."

"Okay, let's go back," Tyler picked up his keg.

Jacob shook his head. His flashlight beam was getting faint, so he clicked it off. It did no good, anyway.

They slouched their way back the way they came. Neither of them spoke now, and the bad atmosphere between them got worse.

"It was maybe bullshit anyway, the party," Tyler muttered finally.

"What? You tell me that now?" Jacob heard the anger in his voice. It wasn't like him to lose his temper, but Tyler had brought him to the middle of the woods on Halloween and got him lost.

Damn it, he could have stayed home and watched Halloween XIII with his mom and grandma.

A branch broke in the woods to his right. Tyler heard it as well, and they stopped dead. Jacob scrabbled for his flashlight, but the weak beam only lit up the tree trunks and did nothing to illuminate the inky blackness behind them.

"What's that?" Jacob hissed.

"I dunno. A bear?"

"Don't be stupid. There's no bears near here."

"A cougar?"

Jacob tried to calm his frazzled nerves. "No. Maybe a deer. It's more scared of us than we are of it."

He didn't believe it. He exhaled, and Tyler rubbed his forehead, then they began to walk again.

They heard another noise. Jacob thought there was definitely a creature of some kind in the forest to their right. They hurried, not speaking, heads down until they were running. Ahead of them, they saw a shape and stopped dead.

"Oh, shit," Tyler whispered. "It's the clown."

Jacob's heart beat so hard he could almost feel it bouncing out of his chest. "Ask him the way?"

"Are you fucking kidding? Come on. Hurry."

The two of them broke into a jog. That clown was to their right, but Jacob turned to see another clown emerge from the woods behind them. He sprinted, almost weeping until they got to a fork that looked like every other fork in the trail. He sobbed, "Which way?"

"That way," Tyler nodded his head to the left.

"You sure?"

"Yes, yes. Come on."

The two clowns still walked behind them on the track. Jacob heard Tyler gasp. "There's one ahead of us too. In the middle of the path."

"Two behind."

"Oh, God."

They stood paralyzed as the clown shapes shuffled towards them with a strange dragging gait.

Jacob and Tyler huddled together. Only the right path was clear, but that was definitely not the way they came. Going down there only risked getting lost deeper in the woods.

Almost miraculously, from that direction, Jacob saw the glow of car headlights. Then he heard the engine. A car was coming down the track. He sighed in relief.

"We can hitch a ride," Tyler said eagerly. "Get out of here."

Jacob nodded. "Sure. They must stop. They couldn't leave us."

The car got closer, and the clowns huddled away into the shadows. When it arrived, they saw it was a beat-up Ford, and they stood in the middle of the track so the driver couldn't avoid seeing them. The vehicle braked heavily, and its wheels crunched in the grit. The bright lights blinded them, and Jacob shielded his eyes, then the driver's window wound down, and someone stuck their head out. The face was in shadow because of the brilliant beams.

Tyler went forward, and Jacob followed him, still hugging their alcohol. Jacob got close enough to see the driver and brought a hand to his mouth, staggering back. The driver looked just like a cabbage patch doll. The cabbage patch doll smiled.

"Great costume, dude," Tyler said.

The driver grinned. "Thanks. You must be Tyler and Jacob. You want to get in, and I'll give you a lift to the party."

Tyler went straight to the car and opened the rear passenger door, but Jacob hung back. Something about the cabbage patch doll unnerved him. Tyler pushed the keg of beer onto the back seat and turned. "C'mon man, get in." But Jacob hesitated. He gazed at the Cabbage Patch doll staring at him out of the driver seat window, its smile fixed on its face, its painted-on eyes bright blue. He couldn't read its expression. The doll saw him looking and said, "Hi, Jacob, I'm Chubby."

Jacob stepped back. "How do you know my name?"

The doll said, "I know you. You're Tyler's friend. You're coming to the party."

Jacob held his bag like a shield in front of him. He said, "No, I don't want to go to the party. Can you take me home? Maybe to the road road into town?"

Chubby continued to smile. He could actually do nothing else with his fixed cloth face. "No, Jacob. I can only take you to the party. Hop in."

Jacob heard the annoyance in Tyler's voice. "Hurry up. Let's go."

Jacob sighed and got in the car, and Tyler shuffled over to make way for him.

"That's it," Chubby said. "Close the door, and we'll be off."

Jacob didn't.

"Close the door, doofus," Tyler snapped.

"I'm not sure about this," Jacob said, but browbeaten as usual, he pulled the door closed behind him, anyway.

The car moved, turning neatly in the crossroads until it faced the direction it appeared from. Chubby hit the gas, and the vehicle sped off. On an impulse, Jacob turned and gazed back through the rear window. There at the crossroads where they'd been, stood three clowns.

Tyler's shoulder pushed painfully into his as they bumped along the track. Chubby at the wheel said nothing. It was almost as if he had sunk back into being an unanimated, lifeless doll.

"Good costume, huh?" Tyler said.

"Who?"

"Chubby."

Jacob said warily, "I'm not sure it's a costume."

"What?"

"I wonder maybe if he's not a real person."

Tyler laughed. "What? What the hell have you been snacking on?"

"The way he moves his head, it's not natural."

Tyler snorted. "What a freak." Then he added for clarification, "You, not him."

Despair pooled in Jacob's stomach. "We're going deeper into the woods. I want to go home."

Tyler shook his head. "If you wanted to bail, you should've bailed back there. Now you're along for the ride."

"I didn't know my way home on my own. And there were clowns there. I didn't want to be left with the clowns."

Tyler snorted. "What is fucking with you and these clowns? It's fucking Halloween, what do you expect? Of course, there'll be clowns. Anyway, shut up. You're getting on my nerves, you whiner."

Jacob lapsed into silence, and Chubby still said nothing while the atmosphere grew awkward. Trapped there, Jacob felt horror swallow him. He wanted to be away from here, but the car carried him deeper into the vast forest, and from any chance he could make his way home on his own.

Finally, Jacob saw vague lights ahead. He could hardly make them out because the back of Chubby's headrest obscured the windshield, but then the car braked and pulled in to park. The wheels threw up a scrunch of grit, and Chubby's cheery, monotone voice said, "Here we are, Jacob and Tyler. Here we are at the party. Time to get out!"

Tyler's head snapped up from where it had lolled in half-sleep, now energized by the thought of the party, and all the hot girls he imagined would be there. "Come on, come on, let me out," he said.

Jacob sighed. He put his hand on the door handle but didn't pull it until Tyler jabbed him with his elbow. "Come on, it's gonna be freakin' awesome."

Having no other option, Jacob shoved open the door. He swung out and planted his feet onto the rough grass at the edge of the forest road. He didn't forget his bag with its vodka.

Tyler eagerly shoved past him, holding his keg in front of him. Jacob shivered. It was cold here. Standing on the grass, Jacob took in the house. It was made of wood but half-dilapidated. The logs in its walls were covered in moss, and where the wood could be seen, it was rotten with damp. Pumpkin lanterns sat outside on the deck, their jagged mouths and eyes leering at them as the candles within flickered through their hollow heads. The cabin door hung open, but there was no sign of any party.

"I don't like this," Jacob said.

"Yeah, we got that already. You're such a pissy little freak." Tyler pushed past him and lumbered towards the house.

Kerosene lanterns hung inside. In their orange light, Jacob made out the silhouettes of figures standing there. He felt a prickle of fear at his throat. They didn't look right. They were clowns, standing silently.

"Bring the vodka," Tyler called back.

Then the driver door opened, and the Cabbage Patch Doll, Chubby, got out. He swayed slightly until he got its balance and stepped forward with the gait of something clockwork. Jacob stared. Chubby didn't move like a person at all. Chubby turned and, with his painted smile and plastic button eyes, he beckoned. "Come on, Jacob. There's fun inside."

Jacob glanced again through the windows. It didn't look like fun. There was no music, no party lights, just the pumpkins' flickering candles, and the silent standing clowns.

His voice wavered. "I'm not sure."

Then, a figure appeared at the door. It was a young woman dressed like Elvira with long black hair, pale face, and lips painted luscious crimson.

"Well, hello!" Tyler said.

The woman grinned.

"You must be Elvira!" Tyler said. "I got your Snapchat." He looked her up and down like a piece of meat hanging in an old-time butcher's window. "I follow your Tik-Tok channel."

"Thank you, kind sir," she said.

'No need to thank me." Tyler leered. "You're hot!"

"So are you, big boy," Elvira said. Then she looked over

to where Jacob stood still in the shadows away from the
house. "And it's Jacob, isn't it? Why so shy?"

Despite himself Jacob blushed. He was not used to
talking to women, other than his mom and some of the
teachers.

Elvira extended an elegant hand, the sharp fingernails
painted bright red. "Come on. I'll show you inside."

Jacob hung back, but he heard a shuffling noise behind
him and spun around. Appearing from the darkness, shuffled three figures, three more clowns with blank, shiny eyes,
brightly painted smiles, and round red noses. They moved
with a jerky gait, coming closer. Jacob gave three backward
steps then turned from staring at them to find the smiling
face of Elvira right behind him. She grabbed his hand and
pulled him toward the door. "I see you've met some of the
other partygoers."

"The clowns?"

Elvira laughed. "Yeah, they're strong silent types. But,
come and see the house."

Tyler had already disappeared inside. Elvira yanked
Jacob with her, and the boards creaked under Jacob's feet as
Elvira's tight grip dragged him in. He smelled the damp and
the rot of the house. He tried to hold back, but she yanked
him with her.

Once inside, Jacob stopped. The rows and rows of
clowns stood silently with their painted smiles and button
eyes. He pulled back, dragged his hand free, panic rising. He
backed to the door.

Tyler spun around, seeing him try to leave and said,
"Where are you going, asshat?"

Jacob yelled, "Can't you see all these fucking clowns?
This isn't a fucking party. This is something else." Jacob
cursed so infrequently that anyone who knew him would

realize how scared he was, but Tyler shrugged and said, "Go if you want, loser. I'm staying here with the lady. Her sexy friends will be here soon."

Jacob was too scared to leave on his own and walk back home through the gloomy woods full of who knew what, so he sat on the old leather sofa. Tyler found himself in a Lay-Z Boy recliner, which was pretty out of place in a cabin in the woods. The pumpkins watched them with shifting evil eyes.

Elvira brought Tyler a glass of a bubbling green drink that gave off smoke. "We call that Zombie Juice," Elvira said when she saw Jacob looking.

Tyler grabbed the drink from Elvira. "Has it got alcohol in it?" He asked.

"Sure," Elvira grinned. "This is a party!"

Jacob thought the drink looked disgusting, but Tyler knocked back his Zombie Juice, the green liquid running over his chin, then wiped his mouth with the back of his hand. "More!" he grunted.

"Your wish is my command!" Elvira said in her husky voice and went to fetch Tyler more Zombie Juice.

Tyler turned his head. "You should try it," he said. "It's extreme. It'll lighten you up some because you really are a boring jerk."

Jacob shook his head. He remembered what his grandmother said before he came out about how you shouldn't take food or drink from the spirits on Halloween, or they'd be able to keep you in their realm. "You shouldn't be drinking that stuff," he muttered.

"Pussy," Tyler said.

Just then, Chubby appeared at Jacob's shoulder, making him start with fright. "You want a Zombie Juice?" he said, his voice hissing like a snake's.

"No, thanks. I want to leave."

Chubby kept on. "Maybe a Witch's Brew? It's yellow."

"It makes no difference what color it is. I don't want it."

Chubby said, "Suit yourself, Mr. Tetchy."

Jacob watched them. There was something not wholly human about these two. Chubby definitely not, but Elvira was also not what she seemed to be either, for all her taffeta mini skirt and black velvet basque.

She came back with a tray of cookies in the shape of spiders. Tyler took one greedily. "When are the girls getting here?" he said munching.

"Soon, big boy," Elvira said. Elvira brought the plate of spider cookies. "Can I tempt you, Jacob? They're delicious."

"No, thanks."

"You sure?"

"Yes."

"Did you see my Tik-Tok channel, Jacob?"

"No. I don't like Tik-Tok."

"Even with girls dancing, not wearing much?"

"No."

Tyler yelled, "Jacob's scared of girls."

Jacob sat tight-lipped.

"Really? You shouldn't be scared of me. I'm soft to the touch," Elvira said in her softest, sweetest voice. "Mind if I sit next to you on this couch?"

Jacob said, "I'd rather you didn't."

She sat down anyway, and he budged over, so he wasn't touching her. She whispered, "Hey, why don't I give you the password to my special Instagram account. You do have an Insta account, don't you?"

"Yes."

"Good, because, you know, I've got some special pics on my account, just for fans."

"Very special!" Tyler said.

Jacob glanced over to Tyler, who had finished his second glass of Zombie Juice and was looking for more. There was something really weird about him. Tyler's face had gone very pale, but his lips and eyes seemed bigger and brighter, somehow.

Chubby came from his left and thrust a plate with little fondant cookies in his face. They were shaped like black cats. "Eat a cookie," Chubby said.

"I don't want one."

"You've got to eat something, Jacob," Elvira wheedled, stroking his arm. "You'll waste away. Hey, can I get you a Bloody Mary? They are luscious!"

Elvira gazed into his eyes with her big blue peepers, but Jacob thought her eyes had an odd glint; they were glassy but didn't look like glass, more like the glaze on a tile. Elvira's voice was low and sweet. She sat closer, and Jacob felt conflicting emotions. She looked maybe, twenty-three, but she must be older than that, though her tight clothes showed off her remarkable figure.

He cleared his throat. "No, thank you."

She pressed her shapely thigh against his, but her leg wasn't warm; it felt cold as old wood.

Chubby reappeared with a chunky glass of foaming yellow drink. "Take a sip of Monster Mash, Jacob. You'll love it."

Jacob looked over at Tyler. He was already drinking Monster Mash, and, by the look of it, he was drunk. His head lolled forward, and a string of drool hung from his lips. Jacob saw his face was definitely whiter now, and his lips were red like paint. He had bright red circles on his cheeks, and his nose was growing round like a button mushroom.

Jacob jumped up.

"What's up, sport?" Chubby said.

Elvira tugged at his wrist, trying to pull him back down. "C'mon Jacob, sit next to Elvira, then we can get real friendly."

Jacob shouted, "Tyler, wake up! They're turning you into a clown!"

He rushed over and yanked Tyler up, but the other boy was heavy and slumped back with a stupid smile. Tyler waved Jacob away. "Nah, I'm good." Then in a thick voice, he said, "Hey, Chubby, fetch me some more Zombie Juice, will ya?"

"Sure thing, Tyler," Chubby said. "Anything for my little buddy."

Tyler lifted his head. His face was now entirely made-up like a clown. He even wore long banana shoes and suspenders holding his pants up. He said, "Elvira, baby. What about that private show you promised?"

Elvira got up from the sofa, walked past Jacob to where Tyler sat. She put her shiny high-heeled shoe up on the Lay-Z-Boy, so her skirt rode up to reveal she was wearing nylon stockings and a garter belt.

"Tyler, come on! This isn't safe!" Jacob yelled.

Chubby stood at his shoulder. "Hey, Jacob. You need to relax. You know where we're from, the birds sing a pretty song."

Elvira smiled a sweet smile. "Yeah, Jacob. If you come with us, you can have that gum you like; the gum your momma won't let you have."

Jacob felt dizzy with panic. He backed away to the door. "Tyler, please. Come with me."

Elvira just watched him, a curious but unfriendly look on her face.

Chubby stood in his way, his cabbage patch head tilted quizzically.

"Can you give me a ride home?" Jacob blurted.

Chubby said, "No, Jacob. The trip is only one way."

Jacob looked back at Tyler, he was almost totally a clown now, almost totally asleep, almost totally gone. "Tyler!" he yelled.

"It's too late for Tyler," Elvira said. "We can only take the ones so deep in their lusts that they were doomed even before we met them."

"You're too innocent," Chubby said.

"Too innocent," Elvira said, almost sadly. "But we've got Tyler."

"Yeah, we've got Tyler," Chubby said, "and we can't have you."

"No," Elvira said. "We can't take you with us, and that's a pity because we live in such a pretty place. "

"Yeah," Chubby said. "We've got birds and bees and cigarette trees, and lemonade springs where the bluebird sings. You must have heard of it?"

"Yes," Elvira said, "It's called Hell." An evil cackle broke from her lips.

Jacob went for the door. Chubby stood between him and the exit, but Jacob barged past and got out.

Chubby called after him. "We can't take you to Hell, but we can sure kill you here."

Elvira yelled, "Clowns, get him!"

Jacob burst out of the cabin and onto the grass outside. He yelled back, "Tyler, come on!"

He was breathing heavily now. He was miles from home and didn't know the way through the forest in the dark. And then he saw the shadows. Hundreds of clowns emerged from the dark woods and started moving toward him.

Jacob was a weedy kid, but he could run, and he ran with all his might, sprinting into the night, along the forest track, not looking back, heading into the dark. His heart hammered, and his breath came in ragged sobs as his feet pounded the earth, taking him away from that house.

The clowns followed, but they were slower than him. After a hundred yards, his breath came in sobs, but he forced himself on, the muscles in his calves burning like fire. After another hundred yards, he had to stop. He stood, hand on a tree trunk, gasping for breath.

He looked at the log cabin. He could still see the ring of pumpkin lanterns, small and faint now. He shouted with all his might, "Tyler!"

The clowns shuffled along the forest trail toward him. He saw their painted funny faces, huge startled eyes, and their big laughing mouths. And Tyler was among them. He didn't recognize him at first, but then he knew the potbelly and the curly brown hair that escaped from behind his pork-pie hat. It was Tyler, all right.

"Tyler! It's not too late," he yelled again, but Tyler didn't answer. Turns out, it was too late for Tyler; there was nothing he could do now. Tyler had wanted drink, and he'd wanted girls, but instead, he got Halloween cookies and Zombie Juice and a one-way ticket to the Haunted House of Horror.

Jacob's grandma had been right, don't take the spirits' food and drink, because if you do, they'll drag you down to hell with them.

The clowns shuffled closer, so Jacob turned and ran. Eventually, he was exhausted; his sprint became a jog, and then a walk. It was way after midnight. The clouds cleared, and a half-moon burned like pale fire.

After many further desperate wrong turns and retracings of his steps, Jacob finally exited the forest, but it was dawn before he reached the road that led to town. There had been no clowns for a long time now. He trudged along the highway, and an early morning driver, a friend of his dad's, stopped to give him a lift.

When he got home, he had to knock until his dad woke up. He made sure his dad locked and bolted the door behind them. "What's got into you, Jacob? Halloween's supposed to be fun!"

Tyler disappeared. No one at school knew what had happened to him. Jacob tried to explain, but no one believed him. Then, about a month later, Jacob googled 'Killer Clowns' and found an article from a German newspaper with Chubby and Elvira's pictures. He hit the button and translated the page. It was an urban myth about a traveling circus of ghouls and freaks that tricked kids into going to parties, then killed them and resurrected them as creepy clowns. There was a joke at the end of the article that read:

Q: What do you do when attacked by a group of clowns?
*   A: Go for the juggler.*

12

ALIEN MUSIC

The yellow sunlight slanted down as Shane Parker sped west on the 101, heading for a suburban street in Winnetka. It was October just before Halloween, but it was California, the land without seasons, and the weather stayed pretty warm all year.

Shane had a degree in Astronomy from the University of Texas but had ended up in Panorama City. In the car with him on this fine evening were his co-conspirators: Jake, the engineer, in charge of sound, and Carl, who had no particular expertise in UFO hunting, but plenty of money. Carl had a small business repairing washing machines that did well. He had a thing about aliens, so he funded the Valley UFO Research Group.

They pulled up outside the modest house and got out. Jake wanted to bring his two-spindle tape machine with him, but it was so big he needed both hands to carry it and what with the enormous earphones round his neck, Shane thought it would freak Sandra out.

"Softly, softly," Shane said, "We don't want the woman to think we're a bunch of freaks."

Carl laughed softly to himself, but Jake shrugged and put the apparatus back in Shane's 1974 Ford Pinto trunk.

A troubled-looking middle-aged woman appeared at the door. Shane, ever the showman, made a big fuss. "Hey! Sandra, I presume?" and went in for the handshake. She nodded, her forehead creasing. "Glad, you could come," she said. "God knows we need some help."

"Sure, sure," Shane said. "And we're here to help. Okay, if the guys come in?"

She looked at Jake warily. He was a rangy ginger guy with long curly hair and a beard wearing a Grateful Dead t-shirt. Carl, in his short-sleeved shirt and clean slacks, was more presentable. "Of course," she said. "I'll show you through"

The house was small, but it had a back yard with some parched looking grass and some chewed dog toys lying about. It turned out the dog was dead, but they hadn't got around throwing out its toys. Halloween decorations were festooned about the front room.

As the UFOlogists sat, Sandra said to her daughter, "Hey, honey, will you go and fetch some lemonade for our guests?"

Kathy brought three bottles of 7 Up, cold and beaded with moisture from the refrigerator. Kathy, nine years old with long dark hair, hovered around until her mom said, "Okay, Kathy. You go and play in the yard. I'll call you in when I need you."

The three visitors sat around expectantly, sipping their chilled 7 Ups while waiting for Sandra to talk.

"I didn't want Kathy to hear," she said.

"Is her dad home?" Jake asked abruptly, 7 Up bottle to his bearded lips.

Shane shot him a glance.

Sandra said coldly, "Kathy's father doesn't live with us."

"Oh, right," Jake said.

Carl rolled his eyes.

"Please, when you're ready," Shane said with a sympathetic, comfortable smile.

Sandra sighed. The room was warm. A fly buzzed around. Shane glanced up to see glue paper hanging from the light fitting with the dead bodies of twenty flies stuck to it.

"It all started around her birthday in June. She was nine."

"Seems like a nice kid," Jake said.

Carl nudged him.

"She started having nightmares."

"Go on." Shane nodded.

"Well, she kept saying there was a black hole in her wall. I couldn't see it, but it brought back memories."

"Memories?" Shane said.

Sandra nodded but ignored the question. "Anyway, she said things came through the hole. People. Grey people with shiny black eyes like glass."

"Interesting," Shane said.

Sandra said, "She said they told her they wanted to come through to our world and work with us."

"Work with us?" Shane said. "What does that mean?"

Sandra shrugged. "I'm not sure."

"What do you think they were," Jake said. "Aliens?"

Sandra shot him a piercing glance, and he visibly sat back.

"Aliens? From outer space?" she said.

Jake glanced around at his companions as if for support. "I guess."

Shane looked thoughtful. "You were saying something about memories, Sandra. What did you mean by that?"

Sandra went pale. She studied her hands. "Just that the same thing happened to me when I was her age."

"Exactly nine?" Shane asked.

Sandra nodded. "And my mother too. When she was nine. She told me."

"Where is your mother now?" Carl asked.

She looked at Carl for the first time. "She lives nearby."

Sandra said, "Kathy says they took her through the spinning black hole in the wall."

"Wow! And what happened there?" Shane asked.

Sandra shook her head. "She says she can't remember."

Carl sat forward. "Excuse me for asking this, Sandra, but did they ever take you through the spinning black hole when you were a kid?"

Sandra gave an empty smile. "Thing is, I don't remember either."

Shane said, "Listen, Sandra, are you okay if I get Jake to record this conversation? Just for our investigation report?"

She shrugged. "No, sure. That's fine."

Jake got up, and Shane nodded to give him permission to go fetch the tape recorder.

At that point, Kathy came rushing through from the kitchen. The door to the back yard was open. "Come quick! There's a ball of light."

Without waiting for further explanation, the investigators rushed through the kitchen and piled out into the yard.

"Well, I'll be..." Shane said.

"Holy shit!" Jake exclaimed.

A golden globe of light about six inches in diameter was floating across the back yard about ten feet up from the parched grass. It wobbled slightly as it moved slowly in a straight line.

Shane turned to Carl. "Did you bring the polaroid?"

Carl blustered, "It's in the car."

"Go get it! Hurry!" Shane barked, but as Carl ran to the open kitchen door, the ball of light stopped. Later Shane said it was as if it was watching him, just taking stock of who he was. Then abruptly, it darted up in a straight line hundreds of feet so fast it was like a reverse bolt of golden lightning. Then it was gone.

They stood around, stunned. The girl Kathy was freaking out, crying, and her mother had to go and comfort her.

"Did you see that thing?" Jake asked.

"Of course I saw it," Carl said.

Shane went over to console the mother and tearful daughter. "Are you both okay?"

Sandra nodded, tears streaming over her cheeks. The girl Kathy was inconsolable. Sandra said, between her sobs. "They followed me for years. Sometimes they followed the car and sometimes they came into the house. When they did, the lights would go off."

Shane could see Sandra was too distraught now for further questions. "Listen, Sandra," he said. "We didn't manage to record anything this time. Is it okay if we come back another day and ask you some more questions?"

Sandra stared into his eyes. "Only if you help us, Shane. Please, you've got to help us."

Shane nodded gravely. "I'll do my best, Sandra. I promise I will."

IT WAS two weeks later that Shane managed to get back to Sandra. He brought along Jake and Carl in the Ford Pinto, but additionally, squeezed in the back was Dr. Andrew Morgan, a hypnotherapist. Shane knew Andrew from a past-life regression workshop the previous year, and they had stayed in touch.

They pulled up outside Sandra's house, and Jake went to the trunk to get the tape recorder. Before he hefted it up, he glanced at Shane for approval.

Shane nodded. "We want to get this recorded."

"Pity we didn't tape the last session," Carl said, biting into a peach he'd brought along. "There was some good stuff."

"We'll go over it again," Shane said.

Sandra seemed apprehensive about Dr. Morgan, even though Shane had explained about him on the phone beforehand.

Morgan smiled. He was a lean-faced man with thin lips and shoulder-length hair. "There's nothing to worry about, Sandra," he said. "Hypnotic regression is perfectly safe. You need to understand that the mind tidies away certain memories, particularly if they cause anxiety. We call it disso-ciation."

"Maybe it tidies them away for a good reason," Carl said.

Dr. Morgan shot him a sideways glance but continued preparing Sandra.

Shane got out a piece of paper, wrote on it in ballpoint pen, and slipped it to Carl. "Not helpful," the note said.

Carl sighed.

"So, if you're ready, Sandra, we'll begin."

"Ready as I'll ever be."

"Okay, if we tape this?" Shane asked.

"Sure."

Shane nodded to Jake, who put his earphones on and got ready to start the tape recording. He shifted the micro-phone closer to Sandra's chair, grinning at her as he did so.

"Right, Sandra, sit back, relax, and I want you to visualize what I'm telling you." Morgan turned to the others. "And it's important you all keep quiet."

Jake gave a thumbs up, staring at the rotating tape spool.

Carl shrugged, and Shane gave Morgan an encouraging smile.

"So, Sandra, I want you to imagine you're at the top of a long flight of stairs. You look down the stairs and see them disappear into the darkness below. But it's a comfortable darkness, all right?"

Sandra nodded, eyes closed, settling back into her chair.

"I want you to slowly slowly take a step down the staircase. And each time I count, I want you to step further down."

He paused, waiting for her to relax further into her chair. "And with each step, you are getting more and more relaxed."

Sandra nodded, her eyes twitching under her eyelids.

"Step down, one, two, three, step, getting more and more relaxed..."

Morgan modulated his voice to be low and slow and calm. Sandra seemed to be falling into a hypnotic trance.

Morgan went on. "Now, at the bottom of the steps. It's ten years ago. You are ten years younger, all right?"

Sandra nodded, still without opening her eyes.

"And there's another flight of stairs going even deeper. And as you step down, and go deeper and deeper and deeper, you get more and more relaxed. You're relaxed. Relaxed. More relaxed, the deeper you go. Down, down and down. Deeper and deeper and deeper."

Carl had closed his eyes and appeared asleep. Jake, with his headphones on, was looking perplexed. He frowned and twisted some of the knobs on his tape recorder.

Shane looked back at Sandra then at Dr. Morgan.

"So," said Morgan. "You're nine years old now, Sandra. You're in your old house as a kid. You're in your bedroom."

Sandra grew visibly more disturbed. She started trembling, and sweat broke out on her forehead. Her eyes fluttered like she was seeing something.

This looked promising, she was deep under. Shane glanced at Morgan, then at Carl and then at Jake. Jake was unhappy about something with his machine because he kept turning knobs and frowning as the tape spooled. Carl breathed lightly in a slumber of his own, and Morgan was fully concentrating on the hypnotized Sandra.

"What do you see, Sandra?" Morgan said.

Sandra twitched and became increasingly agitated. "He's here, in my bedroom."

"Who's here, Sandra?" Morgan asked.

"The alien."

"Hmm. Can you describe him for me?"

"He's not tall. Maybe five feet. Glowing, with black skin, and eyes like glass, like dark glass. He's standing by my bed."

"Is he scaring you?" Morgan asked.

"Yes."

"What is he saying?"

"He doesn't talk. He makes noises, like music."

"But is it a language? Can you understand it?"

"Yes," Sandra nodded. Her fists were clenched now, grasping the material of the chair arms. She grew rigid with muscular tension.

"What do they want from you, Sandra?"

Her voice cracked. "He wants to use me like he used my mom."

"Why?"

"Grandfather brought him. Mom's dad."

"Grandfather?"

Sandra said, "He wants to insert himself into this world."

"Insert himself?"

"Like music."

Shane raised his eyebrows and looked at Dr. Morgan, who shrugged. Jake was increasingly unhappy with the tape machine, shaking his head and muttering as he fiddled with it.

Shane whispered, "She doesn't look well. Do you want to bring her out of it?"

"Sure, sure." Morgan leaned forward and took Sandra's pulse. "A hundred thirty."

"Bring her out of it, Andy."

Morgan nodded.

Abruptly Sandra's nine-year-old daughter Kathy came screaming into the room. "Stop, stop, they say they'll kill my mommy if you don't stop!"

Carl woke up abruptly, and Shane shot to his feet. Sandra's eyes opened suddenly, and she looked disorientated. Shane spoke first, "What's up, Kathy? Your mommy is fine. She's just helping us—"

"No, no!" the child yelled. "You've got to stop. He said so."

"Who said so, Kathy?" Shane asked.

"The glowing man. The man who comes through the spinning hole."

Carl said, "The alien?"

Morgan was leaning over Sandra, but she knocked him away. "I knew I shouldn't have contacted you, but we were their prisoners. I just wanted to be free. I hoped you could help."

"Well, we're trying..." Shane said.

Just then, Jake started making strange noises. They all looked around and saw the ginger sound engineer slump back in his chair, his tape machine still spinning. As he fell back and started to convulse, Carl got up. "He's epileptic, but he hasn't had a seizure in years."

Morgan looked at Shane wide-eyed. "What the hell's going on?"

The room was in an uproar. Sandra went to console her daughter, and Carl and Dr. Morgan were trying to help Jake, who was still in the throes of his seizure. He kicked out and knocked the tape recorder off the small table. Shane ran over to pick it up off the floor. It didn't look broken, but he didn't want to lose that tape. That was a stupendous session.

Later at Wendy's, Shane bought burgers for everyone except Dr. Morgan, who only had a coffee. Jake wolfed down his cheeseburger and fries, then asked for another.

"Sure, of course," Shane said. When the waitress brought the order, Shane said, "So what was going on with that tape?"

Jake exhaled. "Man, that was some weird shit."

"Did you get it? The transcript of what she said?" Morgan asked.

"Yeah, sure. But it was the other noises. They were like something from The Exorcist."

"What?"

Jake nodded rapidly. "All the time you talked to her, there were electronic noises, like a synthesizer, but weirder than that. They kept bleeping and interfering with the signal."

"So, that isn't normal?" Carl asked. He shrugged apologetically. "Just I don't know anything about tape recording."

Jake gave Carl a stare. "No, man. That isn't normal. It was unnatural."

"Can you let me have the tapes for analysis?" Shane asked.

Jake nodded. "Sure, I'll listen to them again at home, and then bring them round."

THE NEXT DAY, Jake just put the tape reels in a thick envelope and stuffed them into Shane's mailbox. He didn't come in or even knock, which was odd because Jake always came to see if he could get something to eat. Shane took them over to his friend Mario who worked as a technician at UCLA. He didn't say much, just asked Mario for his opinion on some strange noises on the tapes. He didn't say it was urgent.

Nothing more happened for two days.

At five minutes past three on November 16th, 1976, a crazy hammering on his front door in Panorama City roused Shane Parker from a dreamless sleep. "Who the hell is that at this hour?" he said as he climbed out of bed. Alarming thoughts flashed through his mind as he pulled on a dressing gown and hurried, barefoot to the door where the hammering continued as if someone was desperate to come in.

He opened the door warily, still on its chain, knee behind it to push it back closed if necessary. "What?" he yelled before he saw it was Jake. Jake stood there, crazy-eyed, bubbles at the corner of his mouth as he shouted, "I saw them."

"Saw who?"

"Let me in. It's not safe out here."

"Jake, what the devil has got into you?"

Jake pushed his way into the house as Shane removed his knee, and they stood there, the electric bulb making the scene even starker.

"What are you talking about, Jake? Who did you see?"

"I saw the things from Sandra's house. The aliens. The glowing men who come through the spinning hole."

"Take a second, pal. Do you need a drink? I've got some Bourbon."

"No, no. I need to warn you."

"Warn me?"

"Warn us all. I know what they're doing with the tapes."

"Okay, come sit down."

"No, I've got to get away."

"You've only just arrived."

Jake was agitated, pacing in the narrow entrance hall. He had his large hands to his face.

"You need to calm down, buddy," Shane said. "Start making sense."

Jake visibly stopped himself. He stared at Shane. "Shane, the noises on the tape. I couldn't figure them out, but they are like a key."

"A key? You've lost me."

"But you didn't hear them, that's the thing. Once you hear them, they get into your brain. You've got to promise me, you'll never listen to them."

"But why?"

"Because if you listen to them, the key will turn, and you'll know. And if you know, you can never un-know."

Shane rubbed his brow. "Are you sure you don't want a drink because I think I do."

"No, I've got to leave. I heard the music. I just came to ask you to give me the tapes back. I'll destroy them to stop anyone hearing that noise."

Shane shook his head. "I don't have them."

"You don't have them?" Jake was incredulous. "I've got to destroy them, Shane. You don't realize. If anyone hears that stuff, it'll turn the key."

"Yeah, yeah, you keep saying that. But what does it mean?"

Jake looked at Shane like he was stupid. "If you turn a key in a lock, what happens?"

Shane shrugged. "I don't know. The door opens?"

Jake nodded. "The door opens, and then what?"

"Listen, man, you've really lost me."

"The door opens, and they come in."

Shane frowned hard. He was maybe going to have to call a doctor for Jake.

"Who did you give them to?"

"Mario. You know him. He works at UCLA. I wanted him to give a second opinion on the tape noise."

"But you never listened to it?"

"I don't have the equipment."

"Good. But I'm going to have to go and get Mario to destroy the tapes."

"Jake! Think about what you're saying."

But Jake hustled out the door. He paused just outside and said, "Sorry, Shane, but at least you never heard that music."

Shane heard the rough engine noise of Jake's old car, and then all was quiet again.

ABOUT NOON THE NEXT DAY, Carl phoned Shane, who was working on an article at home.

"Hey, man, what's up?" Shane said.

Carl said, "Listen, Shane, I don't know how to say this..."

"What?" Immediately, his thoughts jumped to Jake, and that state he'd been in last night. He should have called a doctor, but he didn't know where Jake went after he left, presumably home.

"It's Jake," Carl said.

"What?"

"He hung himself. Left a crazy note, lots of stuff about music and keys."

"Is he dead?"

"Yeah. His brother found him this morning. I'm really sorry."

"Oh, my God."

That afternoon, Shane drove up to UCLA, to the technical building in the Humanities Area where Mario worked. Mario wasn't in his office, which was strange because it was mid-week, and he worked regular hours. Shane saw a woman he vaguely knew. "Mario about?"

She shook her head. "No, he was in on Monday, but not since."

"Is he sick?"

"Sorry, I don't know."

TWO DAYS LATER, the police phoned Shane. They'd found a note with his address on in Mario's apartment. Mario had gone missing.

"So, did you find the tape?" Shane asked.

"No, no tape," the detective said. "That's what was in the envelope?"

"Yeah, he was a sound guy. I sent him an audiotape to listen to."

"Okay, well, there were plenty of tapes and stuff there in the apartment, hard to say which was which."

"Mine had my name on it. Shane Parker."

"Do you want it back?"

"Well, yeah, ultimately. Let me know how he is when you find him."

"You'll be told," the detective said ominously.

It turned out that Mario had driven up Highway 1 up to El Capitan, then headed into the hills and hung himself off a black walnut tree. He left no note, and no one knew why he'd done it. Despite a search of the apartment, the recording Jake had done of Sandra in her house was never found.

It all made no sense. A week passed after the funerals, and Shane decided to go back to Winnetka to Sandra's house to ask her more about the music and the key. He couldn't help feeling she and Kathy knew more than they let on. But when he turned into the close, he saw a For Rent sign.

He parked up and sat there with his window down. The house looked empty, and he could see no furniture in the front room. A neighbor wandered over, a big guy with a striped t-shirt. "Yeah, she went," he said without being asked.

"Moved out?"

"Hm-hm."

"When?"

"Last week. Thursday."

That would be the day Mario killed himself. A couple of days after Jake's death. "Okay."

"Yeah, it was weird. Left in the night. She and her little girl were there when I was going to bed, but in the morning, the house was empty. That afternoon, the realtor came round and put the To Rent sign up."

"That was sudden," Shane said.

"Yeah. You know where she went?"

Shane shook his head.

"So, you aren't a friend of hers?"

"Not really. I'm a... journalist."

"A journalist, eh? You looking for a scandal?"

"No, no scandal."

The guy would have talked more, but Shane started the engine and drove off.

AND THAT WAS THAT. Shane continued to research, and he wrote a couple of books and became an expert on a couple of low-budget UFO films. He even did a speaking tour or two and got married and had kids of his own.

One day, forty years later, he was sitting in his house in Pasadena with his grown son Martin. It was October again, and Shane was reading a book called *The Labyrinth of Time*. His son, Martin lifted his head. "Hey, dad, I found an article about you."

Shane looked up from his book. "Oh, yeah?"

Martin came over and showed Shane a blog post. The blog was entitled: *Alien Music Discovered*.

Shane listened with mounting horror as his son read it out.

Martin said, "It turns out an old fashioned spool-to-spool audiotape was discovered in a deserted cabin in the mountains back of El Capitan and some notes made by some sound expert. Apparently the tape was produced by The Los Angeles UFO Society in 1976." He looked up. "That was your gang, wasn't it, Dad?"

Shane's mouth dried up as Martin read on, "The blog author claims the tape contains backward talking in English."

"What did the talking say?" Shane asked. He felt himself trembling.

Martin shrugged. He traced the article with his finger to find the exact words. "Apparently, the alien voice said, erm,

'Turn the key in the lock and let me in." Whatever that means.'

Shane couldn't speak. Martin read on. "There were weird sounds on the tape that the blog writer claims are authentic alien music. He's going to release the tape on Youtube, so anyone and everyone in the world can listen to the alien music. So he says."

Martin grinned at his dad. "It's so fake, but he's built up interest. He says he's going to upload the tape at 8 pm. That's round about now. Oh, yeah, here it is. Want to listen?" Martin's finger hovered above the play icon.

With a quavering voice, Shane said, "For God's sake, Martin, don't listen to that music."

13

THE MAN IN THE TREE

Ryan Dodds slipped in from work about 11 pm. He locked the door behind him and quietly hung up his coat, first sniffing it to make sure it didn't smell of Saskia's perfume. It did. He did. Careless, but he would blag that one of the women at the University was wearing too much scent. He also smelled of alcohol, some fucking cocktails Saskia made him drink, but that was helpful, because as far as his wife knew, he had been to the pub with the lads.

"Hey!" he said and slipped over to where his wife Alice sat watching the TV with a glass of red wine in her hand. She looked up with a faint smile. "Good night?" She asked. He sat close.

He shrugged. "You know, Barney's always going on about the stock-market and David drones on about golf, but you know..."

"I'm sure you enjoyed it," Alice said. "Want some wine?"

Ryan smiled. "Sure, why not." As she stood up he went and cuddled her and planted a kiss on her wine-stained lips. "I'd have rather been with you."

"Sure you would," she laughed.

"No, really. It was boring. Much more fun with you."

He sat down as she filled his glass. "Much on TV?"

She shook her head. "Just that German series, Dark. It's good."

He shuffled over as she collapsed next to him.

"Hard day at work?" He said.

She gave a lop-sided smile. "Always hard as a primary teacher, Ryan." Then she sniffed. "Barney's taken to wearing Daisy?"

He had the glass up to his nose. "Eh?"

"Daisy. It's a woman's perfume."

"What? No. It's probably Linda. She wears loads of perfume at work."

"She's sixty. Daisy's a young woman's scent."

Ryan forced a grin. "Tell her that."

Later, as they undressed for bed, Ryan saw a business card on his bedside table. It was a thick card, embossed, with a black border and the name, *Asmodeus Matheson: Kabbalist* on it. He lifted it. "This yours?"

"What?" Alice squinted, then shook her head. "Not mine. Never seen it before. It's on your side of the bed."

He frowned. "It's not mine."

"What's a Kabbalist anyway?" Alice asked.

"A kind of demonologist."

"Well that's definitely up your street."

"I teach Gothic Literature, not the same thing at all."

"It probably fell out of one of your books."

IT GOT dark early at the end of October and Ryan had a date with Barney at the Olde Starre on Stonegate, but first he had to nip to the University Library to look up some references in old literary journals that hadn't yet been indexed online.

The library was busy with undergraduates and some postgrads. One or two of his own Gothic students milled about and looked awkward when they saw him. Luckily, Saskia wasn't there. She been haunting him all day but he'd managed to give her the slip. He sat down on a table in the corner shielded by long bookshelves. When he was working, he didn't like to be disturbed. There was only one other person in sight, an older man. Weird, he didn't look like a postgraduate. He was dressed in black, like some kind of older Goth. Gothic Studies tended to attract people like that, but Ryan didn't recognise him. The man sat at a table reading.

Ryan got on with his reading. He checked his watch. He only had five minutes then he'd need to get off to meet Barney at the Starre. As he glanced up, he saw the black-clad man was staring at him. Ryan looked back to his journal, made some notes then lifted his head again. The man was definitely staring at him. He was really rude. Ryan ignored him, stood, got his coat and took the journals back to the box file on the shelf nearby.

As he walked, the man followed him with his eyes, very dark eyes, with irises almost black.

Ryan was going to say something. As he went past the man's table, he said, "Do I know you? Sorry."

The man smiled. "The name's Matheson. But I don't think you do know me, Dr Dodds."

Ryan was taken aback. "How do you know my name?"

Matheson smiled softly. "I follow your work. You are quite the authority on Gothic literature."

"Ah, okay. Just you were staring."

Matheson's smile widened. "I was hoping you'd say hello."

What a freak, Ryan thought as he walked away. He was going to be late for Barney.

Ryan hurried through the streets of York. The city was dressed up for Halloween. It wasn't till the weekend but the shops and pubs were making the most of the Americanised festival. Ryan remembered his youth when it was apple bobbing and turnip lanterns rather than Elvira and Trick or Treat.

Barney was waiting in the Starre. The old pub was packed.

"Old Peculiar?" Barney asked.

"Yeah, a pint."

"Naturally, proper Yorkshiremen don't drink halves."

They both laughed. Barney paid. Ryan would get the next one.

"You look knackered," Barney said, wiping dark froth from his lip with the back of his hand.

"I am, mate."

"Burning the candle at both ends," Barney said.

"Hmm."

"At least dipping your wick at both ends."

Ryan snorted and took a drink.

"How old is she, anyway?" Barney said.

"Old enough."

"No, really."

"Twenty-one."

"Fucking hell. I don't know where you find the energy."

"She's very tasty. Crazy, but tasty. I'm going to have to get rid."

"Then there'll be another one," Barney said.

"You're just jealous."

"Not really."

"Oh, Mr Happily-Married."

"As it happens."

"Each to their own. Want another pint?"

"You sank that fast."

"I was thirsty."

Ryan went and got another two pints and sat down.

"She's a good woman you know."

"Saskia? She's a girl."

"Alice."

"Oh, yeah, of course."

"You shouldn't do it."

Ryan sniffed.

"Really," Barney said.

Ryan groaned. "Oh, Christ. I don't go looking for them. They throw themselves at me."

"Well, you're a big deal to them. Way above the boys their own age."

"Listen, Barney, I feel bad enough. I don't like deceiving Alice."

"You don't feel bad enough not to do it."

"Please. Don't go moral on me. I was thinking of getting rid of her, anyway. Then no more. Honestly."

Barney sat back. The pub was noisy. "Do you think she knows?"

"Alice?" Ryan pondered. "Hard to say." Then. "Nah, I don't think so. But you know what? There was a bloke watching me in the library just before. He was so out of place in there. But, for a minute, I thought he might be a private detective Alice had sent after me, just following me about."

"You really thought that?"

"Well, she might. She's more vindictive that you know, Barn."

"I find that hard to believe. Anyway, who was he?"

Ryan shrugged. "Some middle-aged student dropout, I think. Fairly weird, but harmless."

Ryan was late home from the Starre, half-cut, but Alice didn't seem to mind. She was watching more TV. "Hi, babe," he said, leaning down to give her a peck on the cheek. "Got any wine?"

She nodded and went to fetch the bottle she hadn't finished the night before.

Ryan needed to pee. He went up and stood there, gazing out of the bathroom window. He should have closed the blind, but there was no one about. And then there was. His golden stream plunged steaming into the toilet bowl as his eyes unpicked a solitary figure by a tree. It was a man dressed in black. Ryan finished, shook, zipped and was about to wash his hands, when the man in black slithered, that was the right word, slithered up the tree and disappeared into the branches. Ryan stood, bewildered, frightened even. It was such a weird thing that he didn't know if he'd really seen it. He stared harder and saw a man there crouching on a bough of the sycamore. But what was worse, the man was looking straight at him.

He backed off, heart thumping. Outside the bathroom, he pulled the door securely shut and stood for a minute. He rubbed his eyes. "That can't be right," he whispered. "What the fuck?"

He was tempted to look again, squeezed the door handle, got ready to turn and push, but didn't. Instead he went downstairs where Alice had poured him a big glass of wine. He was sailing on a sea of alcohol anyway, a little more wouldn't hurt. It might help in fact.

"You all right?" Alice asked, looking concerned.

"Me? Yeah, why?"

"You look like you've seen a ghost."

Ryan forced a laugh, took a sip. "Just overworked."

She laughed out loud.

He felt hurt. "I work too, you know."

"I thought you just stood there and pontificated in front of your adoring students."

"They don't adore me."

"You say it like they should."

He buttoned his lip. At least someone should.

They watched some French series about a forest dubbed into American. It was some folk-horror crap. That stuff was done to death these days. It lacked the psychological depth of the Gothic. He turned and told Alice that, but she hissed for him to shut up.

He wasn't sure when he fell asleep, but when he awoke, the TV was still on but Alice had gone. This often happened. He had a few pints with the lads, came home, fell asleep on the couch and awoke to find Alice already in bed.

He checked the clock on the wall. He never liked the ticking since one time Alice said it was ticking away the seconds of his life. That gave him the shivers. But it was one a.m. Time for bed. He thought about stirring, drained the last of his wine and then the picture on the TV changed. Some kind of weird logo formed of lines and curves with an arrow tail and cross bars: very odd indeed. He thought he'd seen something like that before.

He stared for a second or two, wondering what it was going to advertise. But it didn't advertise anything, at least nothing commercial. There were no words, no music, just that damned glyph thing.

He took a photo of it on his phone then did an image

search. It was the Seal of Asmodeus. He read that in the Malleus Maleficarum this seal was the logo of a demon. Apparently Asmodeus was Prince of the Nine Hells and the demon of lust.

What weird shit to be advertising on TV.

Halfway up the stairs, he recalled the business card that Alice had denied dropping. That had been for Asmodeus Matheson. Maybe she'd been looking him up on the TV browser. Smart TVs could do that. At the top of the stairs he remembered the old man in the library. He'd called himself Asmodeus Matheson. At the door of his bedroom, he remembered the man in the tree.

Ryan didn't sleep very well. He put it down to the alcohol.

Next day, as usual, even with a mild hangover (they got easier with practice), he hauled himself out of bed, into the shower and was at work bright and breezy. Well, he was at work.

He flirted with Leslie the secretary he fancied. She wore lovely fitting skirts and black tights, or maybe even stockings. He wondered about that because sometimes they had seams. Leslie didn't fancy him, he knew that. She'd called him a lecherous old bastard that time at the Christmas Party. Still, he liked the idea of taming a woman's scorn; it made the prize all the sweeter.

He grinned at her. She scowled back and he thought that every dog would have its day. Even a dirty dog like him.

Lunchtime and Saskia knocked on his door. He didn't like her coming to his office, even on a pretext. People could guess what was going on, and then he'd get in trouble. "Saskia!" he said. "What's up?"

She didn't look happy. She was gorgeous, but sulky,

though, on reflection, he quite liked that. He felt a familiar stirring.

"You didn't call me," the girl said.

He pretended to frown. "When?"

"Last night. The night before. The night before that."

"I've been so busy, babe. Close the door, we don't want anyone hearing."

"I don't mind anyone hearing."

"Don't be like that, Sask."

"You told me you'd leave her."

He grimaced. "These things aren't easy." He lowered his voice. "We've been married a long time. It's complex."

"You told me she was boring."

He huffed. "Yeah..."

"You told me you didn't love her."

"I mean, I care for her. Of course, but, it's not the same."

"I'm fitter than her. I'm younger. I've looked on Facebook."

He was surprised. "Really? I don't think you should do that." He wondered if you could see who'd checked your profile on Facebook. He didn't really use it. It was too proletarian. Twitter was more his thing. But if Alice could see some strange girl had checked her profile out, that might make her suspicious. That wouldn't be good.

Saskia stepped forward. "So when are you going to tell her?"

Ryan sighed heavily. He had to get rid. "Listen, babe. I mean, I'm a lot older than you. You want things a young woman should, kids, going to clubs. You want a good-looking young man on your arm, not an old duffer like me."

"I think you're handsome. I love you."

Oh fuck, thought Ryan.

She started to unbutton her blouse.

"Saskia! What are you doing?"

"Do you want to do it here? It would be fun. In your office. With your secretary and colleagues all round."

He put up a hand. "Saskia, really. We can't. I think this has gone too far."

She sneered. She buttoned the shirt back up. "I knew you'd be like this. I was just testing you. You never loved me. It was all just lust. Well, Mr Dr Ryan fucking Professor Dodds, world expert on The Gothic, you can fuck right off. She's welcome to you."

And with that, she left, slamming the door behind her.

Leslie came in, "All okay, Dr Dodds?"

He forced a grin. "Just a student."

"I saw. Saskia Williams, wasn't it?"

"Yes. Got a mark she didn't like. You know how they are."

Leslie grinned at him. "Oh, yes, we know how they are. Funny, I thought she was one of your favourites."

He tightened his jaw. "I don't have favourites, Leslie."

"Of course, Dr Dodds. You're very professional."

Ryan sat at his mahogany desk behind the iMac. That was a lucky escape. He'd known he was going to have to end it, but she'd ended it for him. Very convenient. He reached into his desk drawer and pulled out the bottle of whisky and glass he had stashed at the bottom. Very convenient. Then he saw that someone had scratched a pattern of lines and curves in the side of his beloved desk. He touched the pattern with his fingertips. He loved that desk. It was a sign of his status. As he ran his fingers over the pattern, he knew it. It was the seal of the demon Asmodeus.

Ryan went straight home, No after work drinkies for him that night. He was pretty shaken. It was like someone was trying to get into his head and freak him out. He unlocked his front door and called out, but Alice didn't answer. He heard her talking to someone. He wasn't sure she had heard him so he waited at the door and listened.

She must have some visitor. It sounded like a man and he wondered who the hell it was, a deep voice, older. For a second a jealous impulse flashed through him, then he thought no: he'd always trusted Alice. She wasn't the type to stray. But still, who had come calling? He listened harder. He heard the man say, "...he needs to up his game. He's done well, but he must do more before we can be proud of him."

Alice muttered something. The man spoke again. "If he doesn't redouble his efforts, we'll have to get someone else. I've favoured him so far, helped him with all sorts of opportunities, but he just isn't premier league material. My patience will eventually run out."

What the fuck was all this? Was the bloke talking about him? Ryan got the distinct impression that he was the subject of this conversation.

With outraged dignity, he shoved the door open, ready for a full-blown row with whoever the hell thought they had the right to come into his house and put him down with his own wife.

But there was no man in the room, just Alice, sitting watching the TV.

Ryan's brow creased. "Who were you talking to?"

Alice indicated the TV.

"You were talking to the TV?"

"No. I wasn't talking to anyone. I knew you were listening outside, but it was just the TV. The news has just finished."

"No, really, who was here? I heard a man."

She frowned hard. "There was no one here, Ryan. I was just listening to the TV."

"No, I really heard a man, and he was bad-mouthing me."

"I'm worried about you, Ryan."

He shook his head. "I need a drink."

He went through and opened a bottle of wine. He poured himself a glass, offered Alice one but she declined.

"I think you're drinking too much."

He blew out. "I'm a social drinker, Alice. Plenty of people drink loads more than me. Anyway, who's this Asmodeus?"

"Who?"

"This Asmodeus Matheson. Is he a private detective? I know his card said he was a Kabbalist, but what is that? A detective?"

She looked at him hard. "What? I have no idea what you're talking about, Ryan."

He gave a hollow laugh. "Sure, sure. You're not a stupid woman, Alice. You never were. You've maybe let your intellect slumber..."

Alice's face grew hard. "You're very offensive. I won't hold this against you because I don't think you're well, but really, Ryan, you should go and see a doctor."

He smiled at her over his glass. "I don't blame you. I haven't been the best husband."

She snorted.

"I'm guessing you checked your Facebook? Is that how you got it?"

"Checked my Facebook? I only use it to keep in touch with my mum and sisters. I post a few photographs whenever we go anywhere, which isn't very often. I advertise your fucking public lectures to get you more punters. What do you mean, I checked my Facebook?"

Ryan was puzzled. Alice's denial was pretty convincing, but it had to be that. She'd found out about Saskia, maybe some of the others too, and she'd got a private detective, that old bloke to follow him, and scratch his little symbol in his prize desk. That was unforgivable.

"Ah, leave it," he said.

Just then there was a knocking at the door. "Is that him back?" Ryan said.

"What?"

"Mr Asmodeus. Is that him back?"

It's fucking Halloween, Ryan. It's fucking trick-or-treaters."

Ryan swallowed more wine. "I hate that American shit. Trick or fucking treat. Little fuckers can fuck off."

He was about to get up but Alice yanked his arm down.

"Hey!"

"How much have you had?" She asked.

"What?"

"Drink."

"Hardly any. Had some whisky at work, but I needed it after the stress I've had."

The knocking came again. Ryan went to get up but Alice kept him down, then she rose and went to the door. He heard her being nicely-nice with the stupid kids. She gave them sweets and pretended to be scared by their Halloween costumes.

She came back and stood at the living room door, her dark hair on her shoulders, her blue eyes cold as sapphires. "Ryan, you need to stop drinking. Really."

"Sure, sure," he said. "You go to bed and leave me to watch something that might challenge the intellect of a frog."

"Fuck you, Ryan." And she left.

He was raging. How dare Alice treat him like that? After everything he'd done for her. She was a primary school teacher and he was on track to be head of English at York University and then probably Dean of Humanities.

He went to the kitchen and filled his glass. The damned ticking of the clock mangled his nerves. Ticking away the seconds of his life. That's the kind of shit Alice was always saying. And now she'd got a private detective onto him. He remembered his mother saying that if trust was lost in a marriage then the marriage was over. Well, Trust was absolutely lost then, to get the black-clad freak to follow him around York sniffing at his heels to see whether he was shagging his students.

As if shagging your students meant anything? It was a perk of the job. It had as much meaning as a cup of coffee. Then he remembered the man in the tree. That was freaky. Maybe he was drinking too much. Ryan went to the front door and opened it. The cold night air flooded in. He heard the sounds of excited children and boozy laughter of fancy-dress clad revellers walking down the streets.

He just had to step onto the street and he could see the tree through a gap between the houses. He just wanted to convince himself no one was sitting in the tree. Who the fuck would be sitting in a tree on Halloween? I must be the drink. Or maybe he'd been spiked. Maybe Alice had put LSD in his wine as some kind of payback when she found out about Saskia?

But he just needed to see the tree to see there was no one there.

But there was. A man, or something approaching a man, crouched on the big branch. It wore a black cloak and a hood, but he could see his face. Ryan stood rooted with fear. The face was bony with black eyes and holes instead of a nose. It looked like Nosferatu from the black-and-white film.

He stared and started trying to convince himself it was

an illusion, but whichever way he looked, it refused to become anything else but a man crouching in a tree. Ryan ran back inside and slammed the door behind him. He pulled the chain across and turned the key in the dead lock. He was breathing heavily.

He needed another drink. Luckily, he still had half of the balloon glass full of red wine. And there was a trickle in the bottle and a then another two bottles of cheap supermarket red in the kitchen. He rubbed one hand across his forehead as he gulped the wine. Then he went and opened another bottle, glugging it into the huge glass.

What the fuck was going on? Must be acid. What a bitch. He'd never touched her, never laid a finger on her all their married life, though God knows she'd deserved it plenty of times, but he was better than that. He just wanted her to admit what she'd done, then he'd forgive her. Then they'd make up.

He mounted the stairs slowly, glass in hand, rehearsing what he was going to say to her, "Alice, what ever you think I've done, it's time to forgive. If we want to move forward, we need to let go of any bitterness you may have towards me..."

The bathroom door was opposite the top of the stairs. The door was ajar. The light from the window was blocked by the shape of something in the bathroom. Someone was in the bathroom. "Alice?" He said tentatively. The light wasn't on, but maybe... Then he heard Alice's breathing through their open bedroom door. It wasn't Alice in the bathroom.

Ryan swallowed hard. The wineglass trembled in his hand. With the toe of his foot, he pushed the bathroom door. Slowly, it shifted open. There was something in the bathroom. Something stood there. It had a bald white head, bone-white skin pulled tight on its bony cheeks.

Eyes like black holes. A mouth full of teeth. It rushed at him.

Ryan lay dying on the bathroom floor, blood flooding out like a red Gothic flower all around and in his hair. Just before it gnawed off his head, it hissed, "We expected more of you Ryan."

When Alice woke and stepped out of the room, Ryan was already dead. His head was eaten off. The police came, investigations were made, and they said it must have been a maniac, and that Alice had a lucky escape. They couldn't explain what it had done to Ryan's head. The Superintendent looking at the pictures said it looked like his head had been eaten off, but of course they didn't tell the grieving wife that.

The York Press was full of stories of the tragic death of a beloved University Professor, killed by an escaped lunatic. There were pictures of Alice, cheeks red with crying, wearing black at the funeral.

As the reporter respectfully snapped the photographs for the paper, Alice stood inside the crematorium, shaking hands with everyone as they filed past in a dignified shuffle. Beside her, was her best friend, Janie, who'd never liked Ryan since he'd made a pass at her on Alice's wedding night. Countless people shook hands, an inordinate amount of tearful young female English students, but one didn't shake hands, just walked past without a word. Alice whispered, "Who's that? Do you know her? That pretty blonde one."

Janie shook her head.

At the exit door, Saskia turned, watched Alice shaking all the funeral goers hands, thought of Ryan, and smiled.

14

THE TWISTED WOOD

I t had rained for days, endless Biblical days of downpour that came relentlessly as the wind; the deluge that threatened to break all banks and rise all rivers had arrived, while I was at work, shuffling between meetings and managers from Newcastle to Barrow, all the time in my car, listening to Mahler and Sibelius and Iggy Pop. Driving, driving, driving, windscreen wet, drenched by torrents, becks in spate overflowing the road.

You may know the road; it runs straight through an extended cut of pines? Not far from Soulby? No matter if you don't. I hardly know it. The motorway had been flooded and foolish as I was, I thought maybe this was a way through, back home to Barrow, or Baradise as the wits have it. Actually, Urswick, Great...

THERE WASN'T much traffic on the road that night as the darkness blossomed in from the east like a cancerous flower and gobbled up the day.

The water sheet shone in the headlights. It stretched

right across the road, illuminated in my yellow beams as I slowed. I paused. Perhaps I could get through it? It looked like a stream had diverted with the heavy rain and now channelled its way from wood to wood across this narrow asphalt corridor, upon which my fate and my fortune, or at least my chances of getting home in good time, now hung.

The engine idled, I havered, and then took my chance. I wanted to be home with my wine and warm, not out here in the middle of a nowhere made yet more null by this wind, this wet, this wuthering. I gunned the pedal and plunged into water that was deeper than I thought. The wave surmounted the bonnet with a hiss and then a sudden stop as though the car were poleaxed and left dead in the wayward water.

"Bloody Hell!" I slumped over the wheel. What was I to do now? I couldn't wait here. I saw the headlines: Community Arts Manager Found Drowned.

No indeed, I couldn't wait in the car, even now the water seeped in, dark and frothy around the soles of my shoes, soon threatening my mid-foot, then my ankle. This would not do.

I grabbed my gaberdine and hat from the back seat, reaching over with a grunt, pulling it all to me. I snatched the strap of my black rucksack and checked it was closed and nothing spilt out. I have a habit of checking things more than once, so I opened the rucksack, making sure I had everything, my bag, my phone whose battery was long dead, and my Tupperware box of uneaten sandwiches: hummus and rocket.

I opened the door and saw the flood. I had no option but hopped into it, and it came up to the knees of my elegant trousers. They always say I'm dapper. No bother, the trousers would dry, and the car was leased. I waved it goodbye. I have heard you should stay by your vehicle and await rescue, but I couldn't wait here, the waters would overcome me, or I'd die of hypothermia.

My plan was to walk back down the road I'd just driven. There must be a farmhouse somewhere. I vaguely recalled seeing a field of wigwams on the west side, but that was a summer's day years ago, probably the last time I'd travelled this way. They were for tourists, and there were no tourists now.

I trudged along the cheerless highway, face into the driving rain, with a wind that lifted and fretted at me, so I kept my hand on my hat to prevent it from blowing away. I walked for a quarter of a mile, that felt like a hundred miles, until at last, gratefully, the rain went from pouring to drizzling then to merely dripping from the overhanging branches of larch trees. The wind lessened as well from a roaring to a moaning, and I could take my hand from my hat and look around. No moon sailed the sky, or if it did, it was entombed behind thick miles of black cloud.

The forest hissed and rustled on either side. On every side, the gurgle and rush of floodwater. After another ten minutes, I reached a broken bridge. In the dark, I didn't I hadn't seen it as I drove across before the car went into the flood, but now I saw the stones of the bridge were carried away in the torrent that flowed the height of a man and more, driving all in its way, from broken boughs to agricultural barrels to dead sheep.

There was no possibility I could cross that. I thought of walking back to the car and trying to wade through that flood, but I knew that was suicide. I was stuck, trapped between two torrents of water in the middle of a dark and trackless wood. I would have to await rescue.

And then it came to me that perhaps in the poor visibility when the rain hammered down, I had missed a turning into the wood. Maybe there was a lesser way that led to a farmhouse or a cabin. God knew, a cabin to wait out the night would do me. In the morning things would be better.

I shuffled my weary way back along the single-tracked road. It was still dark, but somehow a tenebrous glow gave vague illumination, and I wondered if it were some phosphorescence from a strange fungus or rotten wood. After ten or fifteen, minutes--I lose count—I stopped. I peered to my left; the shadows seemed somehow thinner there.

I listened to the dripping of water and the rush of unseen watercourses. No animal moved in the wood. I stepped closer, yes there was a track, probably a forestry track, but did foresters need shelter? I told myself they did. Maybe a little way into the forest I would find a cabin or even a lean-to. I told myself it was healthier than standing out on that damned road all night until dawn. Such a shelter might also be dry.

I walked along the rough forest track, damp trees leaning in on either side and crowding in overhead like gossiping hags. After four minutes or so, I came to a clearing. Here were piled cut logs, rows and rows of them, stacked on each other maybe three times my height. In the dismal wood, I also saw a building. My prayers were answered. It was a rough hovel, not what I expected foresters to use, it looked older and more idiosyncratic than anything they would build. It looked just the kind of house a witch might have buried in the wood. I laughed at my fears. What was worse, the irrational fear of midnight witchery, or the real risk of death from hypothermia?

I went to the door, rattled the handle and yelled, "Anybody home?"

The weird cottage was lightless, the windows blind and blank. It smelled abandoned. It sounded as if it were asleep. The door was unlocked. I pushed it open. With a deep breath, I stepped inside.

If anyone had ever lived here, it was a long time ago. The furniture was made of wood and could not be dated. Any primitive might have cobbled together this rough stuff at any time from the Dark Ages until today. The windows were glazed but fusted with spiders web. Huge mats of cobweb, looking like they were centuries old, and dust on the floor so thick that my feet left inch-deep impressions. The place smelled damp, but the rain was not in.

It was not somewhere I relished being, but as the rain began again outside, I pushed the door closed and made myself as comfortable as I could. I had only to wait until dawn, then everything would become normal.

WHEN I AWOKE, it was already day, or at least that's what I thought. It's true, the light came in the mildewed window, but the quality was odd, like a neon grey, brighter than it should be but also less penetrating. The cottage door was still shut, though I could see light seeping through cracks in the boards. I went out to peer at the weird day. I was where I had been, in a clearing with logs piled up amongst the churned-up ground. The tyre marks of heavy vehicles were evident, and oil-stained water glimmered blue and gold and black in the ruts. The cottage was even more ramshackle than I had taken it for when I arrived last night, but at least it had afforded me shelter, and I would not curse it for its lowly look. It had been useful. Hail to thee, cottage, and thanks!

Standing there, at the door of the hovel, I looked up.

There was no sun, neither was the sky full of clouds. In fact, it seemed that light suffused the sky, rather than emanating from any one spot. It was spotless as a summer's day, but instead of blue, the sky was spread with a self-luminating grey.

And another thing was the trees. They looked ordinary enough, spruce and larch and pine, but they were festooned with hanging threads and webs as if enormous spiders spun gossamer between their branches. And if the spiders were this big, I quailed to imagine how large were the flies.

I'd never seen anything like it, and I wondered whether it was a local phenomenon. Perhaps this forest here was struck by a strange blight? As I listened, I heard no birds. The familiar sounds of jackdaws and pigeons were absent. No blackbirds called alarms, no wrens clicked their displeasure at my presence. Instead, the air was filled with clicks and whirrs and other noises stranger to describe and unrecognisable to me. Where had I ended up?

It didn't matter, for I knew the main road wasn't far hence. The rain had subsided, and so soon, I guessed would the floods. My car would stand high and dry and likely immovable in the middle of that straight road that cut through this mysterious wood. I would wander back and leave this weird woodland behind me with its diseased webs and odd ticking and snapping noises.

But first, by habit, I checked whether I'd left anything in the hovel. I'd lost a hundred hats that way and countless sets of gloves and now always reminded myself to look again before moving off.

I shoved the door and glanced around the grim downstairs of the cottage. Rickety stairs led aloft, but I had no inclination to explore. I wanted to get home and comfort myself with familiar surroundings.

None of my possessions was mislaid, but as I looked around the room, I saw a glistening object on the floor, under the hollow legs of a rude wooden bench, looking as if it had been deliberately stowed to be out of sight, but my stumbling around in the dark had budged the bench and disturbed it. What was it? It was multicoloured with rainbow hues, an imperfect oval like an overlarge fruit, bigger than a coconut or pineapple slightly. I went down on one knee and with fingertips reached and scrabbled to bring it forward so I could snatch it. It was wonderfully smooth and warmer than I had expected.

It felt organic, perhaps wooden, but as I handled it and felt again its mysterious heat, its smooth material; it seemed living almost. The thought occurred to me it might be chitin, the fabric that makes up the skeleton of insects. And the heat seemed self-generated as if a strange process were going on inside, a composting, or an alchemical fermentation. Instinctively, I tapped it.

It sounded hollow, or at least not solid. And then, as I examined it, I saw a seam, a crack and getting the edge of my thumbnail into it, I worked it, and it came open.

Inside, the most wonderful glittering thing was revealed. It was a cocoon of diamonds that sparkled by their own inner fire. They hinted red and yellow and blue sparks of light. I was amazed, what wonder was this? How valuable a thing to find in an abandoned house in the middle of a deserted wood in the heart of an empty county.

The colours were vibrant, vaguely eastern, though whether from the Hejaz, Samarkand or far-fabled Malabar, I did not know.

I wanted to take it more than I can express. Its iridescent beauty, as bright as a peacock feather, had captured my heart, and I coveted that rare thing even though I did not know what it was. But it was not mine. I placed it on the floor. I stood, went to the door, but then turned and stared at my lacquered container. It lay, glimmering in the gloomy surroundings, blue and yellow and red and gold. It must be lost. It must have been stashed here years ago when this place was inhabited and since long-forgotten, its true owner beneath the sod many a year. In truth, it belonged to no one. No one owned it, and so it could belong to me.

In a rush, I knelt down, picked it up and stuffed into my black canvas rucksack where it was hidden among the Tupperware and notebooks, a jewel amid trivia.

I hurried out of the door, not looking back, though I was careful to close the door firmly behind me. Who knew, perhaps another traveller would need shelter, and it would be better to leave the spot as dry as possible.

I strode down the forest trail back, as far as I could tell, in the direction I had come the night before. All the time, despite the inhospitable surroundings, despite my aches from a night on a wooden bench, despite the cold and damp and my broken car, I felt the fire of triumph kindle in me. I had found this wondrous thing, and I knew it indicated a change in my fortunes. I had laboured with my talent unrecognised, a minor director of a community arts project in Barrow of all places. I deserved better, and now I would get it! I would tell the story of the box's finding, but with details concealed that its true owner could never prove from whence I obtained it, if they lived, if it had an owner. I suppressed feelings of guilt and even began to whistle with happiness.

But the trees were not right. They were not healthy trees. I had taken them for those that grow in an ordinary forest plantation, but that was not so. These were the oddest trees I had ever seen, and though I am no arboriculturist, I knew they were wrong. They glistened and were bulbous, and where leaves and needles should be, they had growths. But the trees, even in that ghastly grey light, were not the most unnerving thing. It was the sounds. I didn't know if the trees themselves made those odd whirrings and whisperings, or the clickings and chatterings, or whether whatever lurked amid their twisted boughs did it, but I hurried my pace. Soon, I would be back at the main highway and normality.

But I found I had somehow lost my way. The wood was not as I remembered it. This path was twistier and stranger, and soon I stopped and looked and tried to orientate myself with growing panic.

It was a minute before I noticed him. He was, I would say, a tramp. His clothes of brown and green were old and stained and much mended. His boots were sturdy, but not new. He had wild hair and a beard of brown but twisted with grey. His eyes were brown too, and he watched me.

"Ah!" I said, starting, for he had surprised me in his silent watchfulness. "My car broke down, last night... The flood."

'The flood," he said. "The weather was bad."

And then something moved in the tree over his head. My glance darted up, and I saw a spider as large as a big bird, scurry across a thread of silk into a funnel of web. I jumped back. "My God!"

He raised an eyebrow. "The spiders?"

I felt my stomach lift. I imagined its spindly legs crawling over me, and its huge faceted eyes peering into mine. "I've never seen one so big. And these trees. What species are they?"

He studied me. "You don't know where you are, do you?"

I shrugged. "I've never been here before, but I presume—"

"Don't presume. You are lost, and you will never be found again if left to your own devices."

My brow creased. I accepted I needed help. "Do you know where we are?"

"I do indeed. I come here hunting."

"Hunting? What, foxes?"

"Stranger prey than foxes," he said. "But don't you bother about what I'm after. I can show you the way out of here."

"Would you? I'd be very grateful. I find myself most disorientated."

He laughed. "Many do. But most who come here, never leave."

"Never leave? Whatever do you mean?"

"I mean what I say."

I had to be practical. All this jibber-jabber wouldn't serve. I said, "I'd be grateful if you could show me the way out."

He nodded.

I offered, "Do you need payment? I have some cash..."

He shook his head. "I don't need payment, I'd be glad to help you as a good deed."

"That's very generous of you. Very Christian."

"I'm not that," he said, "but then again, neither are you."

Something fluttered across the clearing behind us. I swivelled my head around and saw to my amazement, a moth around six feet long with whirring wings much broader than that. This was the cause of the strange whirring I'd heard.

The thing flew with its huge goggle eyes and, feathery antennae and powder white fur.

"A day-flying moth."

"I've never seen one so big."

He nodded. "It's late in the season. Most are at the pupa stage now."

"Right," I agreed as if I knew what he was talking about.

He said, "You find the pupae lodged in safe places, inside a chrysalis, awaiting the change to turn from caterpillar to moth. They liquefy and reform in the most wonderful alchemical process."

"You're quite the naturalist," I said.

"I'm a hunter," he reminded me.

As we walked down the forest trail with the brown-clad man as my guide, the path was wholly unfamiliar, but I trusted him, mainly because I had no option. Also, why would he try to trick me? There was no advantage for him in doing so that I could see.

As we walked, I asked, "Is the road close? Just, I am anxious to be on my way home."

"Of course, everyone wants to get home."

"So, the road?"

"Ah, yes. Very close."

We walked on. There was still no sign of the highway. I said, "I don't recall walking this far last night."

He smiled. "This wood is very strange, as you have noticed. Its ways are not those of other woods, you know."

And I struggled to remember which woods I knew, precious few, but even those I had a passing acquaintance with, were nothing like this.

As if making conversation, my brown-clad guide said, "You slept in the cottage?"

"The abandoned cottage? Yes. It was the only place I could find shelter."

He nodded thoughtfully. "It's been abandoned many a long year."

"Did you know the people who lived there?"

He shook his head and without looking at me, said, "It's empty now."

I shrugged. "Yes."

"Nothing of value in there now," he said, but something in his voice suggested he was testing me. I pride myself that I can read people. I cleared my throat. "I didn't see anything of value, it was a poor, run-down place."

"Indeed." And he said nothing more for a while.

By this time we should have seen the highway, but there was nothing but twisted, misshapen trees in every direction, strung with webs woven by loathsome spiders with massive bloated bodies. I was only glad they didn't leave their trees. I had no idea that spiders so big lived in my own country.

Then a sizeable day-flying moth flitted in front of us drawing a gasp from me, a shudder and a step back.

"You don't like them?" He grinned.

"Do you?"

He said, "I'm used to them. They're harmless."

"They're huge."

A thought occurred to me. "You say you're a hunter. Is it the moths you hunt?"

"Oh, no," he said most definitely. "The moths are interesting, though."

"Really?" I was unconvinced.

"They're big as moths, but they come out of a much smaller chrysalis. It's only about the size of a coffee flask, but multicoloured, very beautiful."

"Oh."

"Have you ever seen one?"

I shook my head vehemently, perhaps too emphatically I said, "How could I? I've only just ventured into this place."

"Of course, and you haven't been anywhere to see anything like that."

The moth still hovered around, and I saw it drinking from huge arum lilies with a long proboscis that curled at the end.

He saw me gaze at it in fear and said, "They have a curious life cycle, those moths."

"Oh," I said, though I wasn't really interested. I just wanted to escape that damned wood.

"Four stages, not three."

"Well, that's all very interesting, but I'm sure we must have got lost. None of this is familiar."

He wasn't listening. "Caterpillar, chrysalis, and moth are normal, of course." He laughed as if enthralled with his own story. "But there is a stage between the chrysalis and the moth."

I stopped. "I appreciate this is your special interest, and I'm most obliged for your kindness in showing me out of the wood, but actually you haven't shown me out of the wood. Perhaps I should find my own way."

He shrugged. "Suit yourself."

I had hoped he would just shut up and show me the way out, but if he wanted to play it like that, I didn't need him. Eventually, I would find a road or even a field. There would be some end to these damned twisted trees.

I paused waiting for him to relent and say he had been teasing me and he would now show me the road, but he didn't.

"Fine," I said. "Well, thank you for your company."

He nodded. I began to walk away. This track must lead somewhere eventually. The big tyre tracks were long gone, and the only marks were strange slithering shapes in the mud and tree mulch.

From over my shoulder, I heard him call. "Just one thing."

He was going to change his mind. I stopped, smiling, then cleared my smile before turning to face him so he wouldn't see my look of triumph. "Yes?"

"I was thinking that the reason you can't leave the wood is that you have something that belongs to it."

"What?" I blustered. What did this even mean? How could a wood own anything?

"Yes, local stories say you can't take anything from the wood. It won't let you. If you want to leave, you will have to give up what you found."

"But I haven't found anything."

"No, of course not."

"Really!" Like all liars, I protested my innocence long and loud.

He just smiled.

I turned on my heel and hurried off.

As I walked, I thought of the beautiful coloured thing in my canvas rucksack. So that's what it was, the chrysalis of one of those alien moths. Such a beautiful thing of buttercup yellow and poppy red and lapis lazuli blue-veined with gold, and when I had cracked it open, inside was a thing of living diamond that sparked red and blue and yellow with its own inner burning. It was just bluster. I wondered if he had been looking for the chrysalis. Maybe that's what he was hunting. I was sure they were worth a fortune, and I was only surprised I'd never heard of such things before.

He had led me a circuitous route to bewilder me. He must have suspected the chrysalis was in the house and was probably seeking it himself, but I got there first. That's what his questions were about. He suspected I had it, but of course, he couldn't know for sure. I laughed softly to myself. And this last desperate comment that the wood wouldn't let me take anything that belonged to it was undoubtedly intended to persuade me to surrender the chrysalis, and then he would point the main road, out a hundred yards away beyond the trees, beyond which he had led me such a merry dance.

I looked at the path. There were no boot marks here, and that proved the trail was little used. No foresters came here because it led nowhere.

I turned, and the brown-clad tramp was out of sight. I sucked my teeth; this path led nowhere, so I would strike cross country. I looked up at that infernally grey sky. It gave me no directions then I remembered that moss grew on the north side of a tree, but there was no moss, only damp wads of cobweb hanging down. I shuddered again, imagining the spiders that wove them.

I glanced left. The trees were not thickly clustering together. I could walk through that wood. There was nothing in these trees in England that could harm me. I gathered my courage, and stepped off the path, heading, as best as I could tell, for the road.

I walked, at first light-heartedly, then less so. I found no road. I found no further path. I saw no sign of mankind, just the scuttling of the spiders and the whirring of the moths and the clicking of God knows what else in the depths of the trees. I shuddered and hurried on.

And after an hour, I was weary and sat down.

I made sure I sat on a rock away from the trees, so no enormous spider could scuttle down behind me, unseen. I put the rucksack on my knees and fished in it for my useless possessions. Strangely, I was not hungry, and neither had I craved food since I first entered this weird woodland. But the real goal of my rummaging in the rucksack was the marvellous chrysalis. Even in the folded dark of my bag, it glowed with its fantastic array of gleaming colour. I took the chrysalis out and held it in my hands. So light, and still warm. Now, I knew it was organic; the lightness of the material made sense. Not wood, nor plastic, but a living insectile material, sturdy, durable and so wonderfully coloured.

There along the side of it was the crack I had already cracked open. That must be the larva of the moth. As I sat, I felt drowsy. I struggled to remember the life stages of a moth: larva, chrysalis, adult. But the tramp had said these giant moths had four steps. This was the chrysalis, and I had seen the adult, and the larva was the diamond thing inside, but I had no idea what the intermediate stage was: the stage between chrysalis and adult.

My head lolled. Dreams weaved around me. The forest clicked and whirred and whispered, and I slept.

When I woke, I was lying on my back on soft beds of cobweb. I must have fallen from my rock and with no tree to keep me up, was now lying flat. Something moved on my arm, something, glittering, glimmering, sparkling, as it shuffled along with little heaves of its diamond body.

The grub had emerged from the chrysalis, which lay cracked and discarded on the forest floor nearby. I peered to see the little thing that was busy eating its way through my jacket and shirt. I saw smears of blood and drool on its quartzite mouth. Its head was halfway into my flesh, but I felt no pain. I looked blear-eyed: I was anaesthetised by the secretions of its chomping, grub mouth.

Standing nearby, closely observing was the brown-clad tramp.

"You!" I said, but I could hardly lift my head, so drugged was I by the little diamond thing.

"Me," he replied.

"But what....?" I was making little sense, I could scarcely form the sentence.

"You asked me what I hunted in this twisted wood."

If he expected a response, I could give none. The moth larva ate into me. I felt it burrow into my chest cavity, its crystalline angles chewing through muscle, sinew and fat. But it didn't hurt.

The hunter continued. "I didn't answer, because if I'd answered, it would rather give the game away."

"I don't understand," I said.

The hunter smiled. "Well, the truth is, I hunt people." He pointed. "And I use those little things as bait. It's the glitter and the colour, I think." He grinned. "The glitter and the colour. They never fail to hook men like you. The hook catches the fish, and the fish feeds the fisherman."

I raised a dying eyebrow. "You're going to eat me?"

He winked. "I should say so. But I'll hang you up for a few days so you're nice and ripe. I like 'em ripe."

PART I

SCHLOSS VON HOHENWALD

1

Ralph Waters-Wyn sat in the passenger seat beside his friend, as Gerald Anderson pulled his Rover 10 in by the Schönbrunn Palace. He left the engine idling because he said he wouldn't stop long and because the Rover was a bugger to start again. He helped Ralph retrieve his luggage from the boot while the horse-drawn carriages and other motors filed past.

"You're still going the long way round?" Ralph said, valise in hand.

Gerald nodded. "Via Styria."

"Backwoods country there. Make sure you don't break down, or we may never see you again. It's a very superstitious part of the country. I don't think they see many foreigners."

Gerald laughed. "Don't worry about me."

Ralph frowned. "Seriously. Why don't you go a more direct way – through more civilised parts?"

"You know me, old man. I like an adventure."

"That's all well and good, but don't get involved in anybody else's problems, and — I know you — don't try to fix things that are not your to fix. Remember you never know who you can trust in foreign parts."

"And you sell lots of paintings so you can buy me dinner in a nice little place by the Blue Mosque."

They said goodbye, and Ralph, who was spending time with wealthy clients in Vienna, promised to meet Gerald again in Istanbul, although that would not be for several weeks.

Ralph stood on the pavement as Gerald pulled the Rover off onto the road. He saw him wave through the window but then lost him sight of him in the traffic.

THE TWO FRIENDS PARTED, and Gerald took the road south. He planned to take the long route to Istanbul to while away the time until he met his friend, and divert south through the ruins of the Austro-Hungarian Empire, sight-seeing across Styria until he crossed the border into the new country of Yugoslavia, and from there he would thread his way south-east through the Balkans to Turkey and Thrace.

The weather was not in his favour, though Gerald should have guessed late October was not the time for plea-sure-touring, but he wanted to return to England in time for Christmas, so it was October or never. He crossed the regional boundary into Styria and found the mountainous, heavily-forested land strange and forbidding. The leaves in the lower deciduous woodlands had turned iron, gold and bronze. The drizzle pattered on his windscreen, and the wind smelled of winter.

It was a beautiful country, but a mysterious country, and a country where each vista through the woods and each glimpse of a rustic village suggested secrets long kept. Since the War, the area received few visitors, most inns were boarded, and such rural folk as Gerald spotted from his speeding Rover 10 looked poverty-ridden and downtrodden.

Gerald drove through village after village, seeking somewhere to stop, but settlements were few among the mountains and forests, and villages with inns fewer still. Nowhere did he see anything like welcoming accommodation, and so he pressed on hoping the next town, or then the next, would offer something appropriate, but by the tenth hour of driving, he would have happily stayed anywhere with a roof.

Gerald arrived at Geistthall as darkness fell, and with the darkness came vicious, squalling rain. The gloomy pines all around the village thrashed in the wind, and as he scanned the narrow main street, he despaired of finding somewhere comfortable to stay. To be sure, there was a small inn there, called *Zum Schwarzen Wolf*, but when Gerald stopped to enquire, collar up against the shower, a middle-aged woman with dark hair answered his knocking. He had trouble making her understand his German at first, but then she seemed to get it and shook her head with a smile. She told him the inn sold beer and wine but had no rooms. "Sorry, Mein Herr, better luck somewhere else." She was mid-sentence when a mutton-chopped man with a sour face came up beside her.

He glared at the woman who winced as if expecting a blow, then he said in English, "No rooms! No rooms!"

Gerald bit his tongue. It looked as though the woman were afraid of this man whom he guessed to be her husband, who snarled at his wife to get in.

"Hang on a second..." Gerald said.

The landlord stuck his index finger up in warning. "You mind your own business, or you will have more trouble than you imagine."

Gerald fixed him with a stare. "Treat your wife decently, or you'll have me to answer to."

The man's face dropped, and he stepped back. It seemed he was a coward, as most bullies are.

But Gerald decided to mark his card. "I will be back, and I will ask, and if you have laid a finger on her, I'll lay more than a finger on you."

The man hurriedly pushed the door closed. With a final scowl, Gerald turned. The wind blew the rain in his face. His Rover was parked about fifty yards away, and as he approached, he saw a man in a raincoat and hat admiring it. It looked like he was stroking the bonnet, and he stepped back guiltily as Gerald approached.

"Rover 10?" The man said in German, then he said, "English?"

Gerald nodded. The man wore a clerical collar: a priest. "She runs well, yes. Just doing a bit of touring."

"Bad weather for touring."

"You're telling me. Do you know of anywhere to stay hereabouts?"

The priest shook his head. Bizarrely, he had white powder on his coat sleeve; it looked like he'd caught it in the sugar bowl. He said, "No, sorry. The *Schwarzen Wolf* doesn't have rooms."

Gerald gave a bitter laugh. "So, I understand. Anyway, off I go. Perhaps I'll find somewhere further on."

"Perhaps you'll find somewhere," the man said.

"I'm just passing through, anyway."

The man nodded. "Styria is old and full of secrets. Best pass through."

Gerald laughed. "I'm all the more determined to keep going then."

"Good luck!"

Gerald got in the Rover as the priest walked away. It struck him that this was the second time he'd been wished luck in a short space of time. He hoped he wouldn't need it.

AND SO, Gerald was forced to drive on. The road from Geist-thall was narrow and steep with huge boulders at the margins that had clearly tumbled from the mountain to block the way but were since cleared to allow passage. The Rover's engine laboured as it took the slope, the road twisting like a corkscrew on a steep climb through wildly moving pine trees. The car began to misfire long before he reached the top.

"Damn, just what I need," Gerald muttered. He had a set of spanners to do minor running repairs, but he was no mechanic and did not relish trying to fix anything in this weather. As he leant forward over the steering wheel, urging the car on yard after yard, the engine sputtered and coughed and lost power, once, twice, three times, just to surge on before coughing and sputtering once more.

The road went on and on, and up and up, and round and round, spiralling into the mist, and on each twist, Gerald hoped he was nearing the summit of the pass. If the engine failed after he reached the top, he could simply coast downhill and thus escape being marooned on this damned mountain.

What a ridiculous time of year to drive through these Styrian Alps. Why hadn't he taken the usual route to Istan-bul? Why hadn't he waited for Ralph in Vienna? But rest-lessness and a need for novelty had always been Gerald's downfall. He couldn't resist pushing everything a little further than anyone else.

Well before the top, the engine backfired mightily, like

something had blown and quickly lost power, the engine noise suddenly dying away. Gerald cursed and prayed. "Just get me through this, Lord, and I promise I'll go to church every Sunday for the next month." How frequently how men find faith in times of crisis.

As if the Lord heard him, the engine caught and resumed feeble traction, and the Rover climbed on. However, Gerald was still far short of the crest of the pass when the car spluttered and died, standing motionless on the side of the wild Austrian road, the only sounds a faint ticking from the engine and a slow hiss of steam. Gerald gazed through the fogged-up windows, but no sign of human habitation met his eye; even the road looked rarely used.

The heavy rain had formed rivulets that flooded downhill over the pitted tarmac. Slumping on the wheel, he remembered he had seen no traffic since long before Geistthall, so he hardly expected rescue now.

Just then, to his horror, the asphalt road surface shifted under the car. Gerald shoved the driver door open and leapt out. The road underfoot was moving as the rain undermined the surface, and as he stared, the vehicle began to slide. It shifted a few feet sideways but didn't tip off the road. Gerald feared that if he stayed the night in his car, he would wake to find himself tumbling down the mountainside.

But if he didn't stay in the car, where would he find shelter? He looked around, getting steadily drenched standing there. For a few moments only, he considered going under the trees, but he would be soaked within minutes and never sleep. In great trepidation, as if it were a dog that might bite him, he approached the car, snatched open the rear door and grabbed his mackintosh from the back seat.

Gerald was already wet-through under the coat, but the

mackintosh absorbed some of the downpour as he trudged up the dismal road, making sure to keep away from the edge. Grey fog hung in tatters across the highway and drifted through the trees. The only thing that raised his spirits, and that not by much, was his hope that there were sometimes inns at the top of passes in these countries.

2

In the end, it was not an inn he found, but a castle: a Styrian Schloss buried behind serried ranks of trees. The old fortress was ruinous in parts, but lights gleamed through the mist: two of them, one on the ground floor but one through a smaller window high up in the left-hand tower.

A castle! It was like something out of a penny-dreadful story, and the Gothic grandeur of it set him back and made him even fearful, but what choice did he have? He would have to knock on the great oak door.

Cautiously, Gerald approached the dark building. Its battlements loomed above, and its windows watched, all of them dark except the two showing lamps, and those two he imagined concealing peering eyes of persons keen on keeping their secrets, and keen on knowing his.

A foreboding came over him as he crossed the draw-bridge. He guessed at one time, the bridge would be drawn up for defence but looked now as if centuries had gone by since it last lifted.

Finally, Gerald stood before the huge oak and iron door.

In this massive door was cut a smaller entrance, sized for a man. This was a door cut for convenience of human buildings, so no matter how monstrous the place appeared, some human lived here, and surely no human could turn him or anyone else away on such a night as this?

As if to emphasise the sharpness of his predicament, lightning cracked the sky behind him, flashing white on the ivy-draped walls in front.

His mouth was dry and his hand trembled. Why was he so nervous? But then, of course, the car breaking down, his aloneness in a strange land, the weather, the cold, his shivering, these were surely enough to explain his anxiety. The sight of this place and the dread it had caused him were due to his overwrought nerves, not to any real threat.

Overcoming the seeping unease, Gerald reached and gripped the heavy iron knocker in the shape of a wolf's head. He lifted it and rammed it down three times, and the heavy blows echoed deep within the building, but no one came.

He reasoned: there were lights here, so there were people. Why did they not come? Perhaps they hadn't heard his forlorn knocking, so Gerald lifted the iron wolf's head again and beat it a further three times. Nine times now, he hammered down the wolf's-head knocker, and nine times the echoes went forth, summoning whoever was within while nine times the lightning cracked behind him, sparkling and dancing against an ominous background of clouds.

Still no one emerged from the fortress, and Gerald was about to retreat into the night and go who knows where, when he heard a sound. Bolts drew back, and chains were unshackled, and the door groaned open to reveal a hollow-faced man in servant's attire, standing with a golden candelabra in which flared seven candles. The flames fluttered, the wild wind threatening to extinguish them, as the servant glared coldly.

Gerald spoke in German, "Excuse me, my car broke down. I have nowhere to stay, and the weather..."

The man looked at him a long time as if digesting the words. Gerald wondered whether he had made himself plain and cleared his throat to say more, but before he could speak, the servant said, "My master does not receive guests."

Gerald stood bewildered, one arm gesturing to the storm. More lightning split the sky to support his entreaty. "But the weather....?"

The grave-faced man repeated himself. "My master does not receive guests." At the door, in despair, Gerald begged the servant, and the man finally sighed and went to his master. It transpired that his master was kinder, or more curious, than the servant and Gerald was allowed in out of the rain.

GERALD STOOD DRIPPING in the vast entrance hall of the castle, and the door closed behind him to keep out the storm. He stood, head back, amazed. It was as if he had been transported back to the Middle Ages. Faded tapestries hung on the walls and substantial black-iron candelabras dangled from the ceiling, their crowns of candles unlit but dripping with stalactites of frozen wax to show that once, perhaps long ago, they had burned with life. But what life was here now? Staring around, all seemed gloom.

The only illumination in the hall came from the triple candelabra the servant retrieved from the top of a scarred oak bookcase. He'd placed it there so the gusting wind did not extinguish the light when he closed the door.

The servant led Gerald through stone passages past open doors that showed shadowed rooms but did not permit enough light to enter to unmask their secrets. As they walked, Gerald imagined centuries worth of heirlooms — priceless antiques mixed with worthless junk, unsorted and left long alone. He followed the servant who strode down passages and stalked along hallways, Gerald walked behind and the servant didn't speak while Gerald hoped for a fire, and possibly food.

Finally, they came to a great hall. The hearth was ten feet wide and eight feet tall and blazed with massive logs, culled, Gerald supposed, from the trees that encircled the schloss like a besieging army awaiting their chance to throw all of this down and restore the land to wild nature. He craned his neck. The ceiling of the Great Hall rose to the height of two rooms, but the enormous fire was enough to heat it, and even from here, the flames scorched Gerald's cold cheeks.

Turkish carpets lay one upon the other on the stone floor in vibrant patterns of red and green and black and yellow. They too looked ancient as if they dated from the time, centuries ago, when the Turks harried the borders of Austria. The stone walls were dressed in tapestry, all faded, all showing hunting parties, all except one strange scene that appeared to depict a wedding between a man and a wolf standing on her hind legs.

Baroque suits of armour huddled in corners, too rococo surely ever to have been worn in a fight, and above them, racks and rows of broadswords and halberds. Ancient muskets and fusils decorated the other walls and everywhere stood tables and tall cabinets overstuffed with china and porcelain. Items from the orient: China, India and Japan filled gaps around the hall's edge, and then there were heaps of books, old books, shelves of books, hundreds of books, leather books, cloth books, paperback books, but none looking as if they had been read in years.

The flickering light in the Great Hall came from the wide iron crowns of candles hung on black chains from the ceiling. Unlike the dead candelabras in the entrance, these danced with rippling flames, shifting in currents of unquiet air. A long table ran along the centre of the room for almost its full length.

But the chief wonder of the room was the host. He sat in a tall chair, dressed in black, silently observing Gerald's entry, and Gerald could not tell his age, fifty at least, maybe older. This noble-looking man sat, thin, and high-cheekboned, with black hair pulled from his forehead in a severe widow's peak. He watched Gerald with eyes as blue as glacier ice compressed for ten thousand years and his face was unnaturally pale as if sunlight never fell upon it.

"Allow me to introduce myself," Gerald said, as soon as his astonishment at the room and its contents subsided. He had been in castles in England of course, but none so grand or ancient-looking as this.

His host nodded to acknowledge Gerald speaking but did not get up from his wing backed chair.

"I'm Gerald Anderson, from Sussex, England. I live some of the year in London." Gerald jerked a hand in the direction he supposed his lonely car to lie abandoned in the howling storm. "My car broke down, you see."

Gerald spoke German. The man answered in English. "I see, Mr Anderson. Thank you for your introduction. I do not normally receive guests, but the hour is late and the weather most inhospitable. Because of this, I have made an exception for you. We have ancient laws of hospitality in this country. I'm sure you can have your car repaired tomorrow and be on your way. Vincent in the village is an excellent mechanic."

"I thank you, sir, but you have the advantage over me..."

He nodded. "I am the Graf von Hohenwald. My family have lived here for many centuries. My brother was Graf before me, our father before him, and so on, *et cetera, et cetera, in saecula saeculorum.*"

Gerald was dripping and inched closer to the fire, and soon steam rose from his clothes.

"You are cold and wet," the Graf said. "Do you have dry clothes?"

Gerald had dry clothes in his suitcase, but that was locked in the boot of his car, and he didn't relish going out to fetch it. Gerald's hesitation caused the Graf to mutter to his servant and order him to set out some dry clothes. The Graf then turned to Gerald, and his glacier eyes pierced the Englishman like a moth on a pin. "Change, then I will ask Tobias to provide food. At this time of night, it will be cold meat, cheese and bread only, and wine, if you drink alcohol?"

Gerald smiled. "I do. That is most kind of you."

"Go now."

THUS DISMISSED, Gerald followed Tobias from the Great Hall, dripping still. Gerald's room was in the tower. It was clean, but felt cold and damp as if no one had lived in it for a long time. There was a window shuttered in dark, varnished wood, and the wind screamed outside, so he did not open it, though he thought there might be a beautiful view from this room in the morning as it was so high.

But he had no plans to stay. This old place felt strange. Whatever mysteries it held were of no concern to travelling

Englishmen: let the Styrians keep their secrets. As soon as his car got fixed he would be gone.

The clothes set out were plain and old, but in good order, no holes or wear. There were even soft leather shoes that looked Victorian in style but were a reasonable fit.

Someone had laid out towels, and someone, possibly the same someone had put a warming-pan in the bed to air it. The linen smelled fresh. There was another bookshelf, but Gerald had no time to peruse the volumes after drying and changing before a soft knocking came on the door. It was the hollow-faced servant, Tobias.

"Your dinner awaits you, sir." He said.

Gerald wasn't sure whether it was his imagination, but Tobias seemed slightly warmer in demeanour as if he'd seen his master be courteous towards Gerald and decided to follow his lead.

GERALD TROTTED after Tobias and arrived again in the Great Hall with its blazing fire. Now, the long wooden table was set for dinner with only one place. Silver candelabras brightly polished with new white candles stood lit on the table, the flames gleaming in the varnish. The Graf sat in the same chair by the fire and told Gerald he had already eaten.

Gerald didn't speak while he ate, and the Graf's silent gaze, as he stuffed his mouth, made him uneasy, but he quelled the anxiety with the Graf's excellent red wine, sipping from a fine crystal glass. From the quality of the cutlery and the excellence of the wine, Gerald didn't doubt that someone living here had once had a lot of money, maybe not now, but certainly then.

When Gerald finished, he sat back and dabbed his

mouth with the crisp linen napkin, his wine-stained lips left traces of red on the white. Still the Graf sat silent.

To make conversation, Gerald said, "I thank you for your hospitality. I must admit I feared I would die of cold out in the storm."

"The weather here in October is terrible. We are high, you see," the Graf said.

Silence. After several minutes of awkwardness, Gerald said, "You say there is a mechanic in the village?"

The Graf nodded. "Vincent. Yes. He has a workshop next to the inn. I will ask Tobias to take you in the morning."

"Good. Well, I am very obliged you let me stay." Gerald felt a little impertinent as he added, "Especially given that you do not normally receive visitors."

The Graf studied him. Finally, he said, "I must admit I was curious."

Gerald was taken aback. "Curious? About what? Me?"

"Yes. You."

"Me? Why on earth would you be curious about me? If my car hadn't broken down, I wouldn't be here at all."

The Graf smiled a slow smile. "A strange coincidence, don't you think? That you should break down almost outside my door, when there is no other house for miles. It was as if by magic."

Gerald frowned. "Whatever can you mean by that?"

The Graf kept staring. "Just that we have been expecting a visitor. Someone who might not be honest about who he really was."

Gerald's frown deepened. "What?"

The Graf considered his long fingers. "We are not wholly certain in what guise our expected visitor will come."

Gerald shook his head. "You are expecting someone, but you don't know who they are?"

"Exactly."

'That's quite strange."

"We have known about them for years, but the visit becomes imminent. I wondered perhaps if our long-expected visitor was you."

"Me? But I had no intention at all of stopping here."

"But he would say that."

"We English are plain-speaking folk. So forgive me if I ask you plainly, why do you expect this visitor now? And more especially why do you think it might be me, given that I assure you my arriving here is pure fluke?"

"The answers to these questions are all my business, not yours."

How rude the man was. Gerald forced a smile and thought it best change the subject. He cleared his throat. "It's a big place. It must be odd living in a castle."

"Must it?"

"It's so large and old for one person."

The Graf nodded. "It is large and old."

"You live alone here, I presume?"

"You presume?"

"Ah. So you have a family. But I see no sign of anyone else."

The Graf pursed his lips. After five minutes more of silence, Gerald decided he would go to bed. The sooner he was away from the Schloss Hohenwald, the better.

3

The next morning, after getting out of bed, Gerald drew back the wooden shutters of the circular tower room, revealing ancient and irregular glass panes, and through them, as he had guessed, a most beautiful vista over the Styrian Alps. The forest stretched miles and away in all directions, cladding the hills and valleys and giving the impression there was no other world than that blanketing overcoat of swaying green. Again, he had a feeling of unease, but still, Gerald felt better for his rest. There was even blue sky; the dawn had washed away the rain, leaving a pleasant Autumn freshness. The forests hereabout were pine and spruce, and Gerald guessed the hills kept this aspect of foreboding green, so dark as to be almost black, from season to season, and season to season after that. What mysteries must be concealed in these forests? What had they seen over the centuries and what tales and folklore had they given rise to? But he was letting his imagination run away with him, a thing most unlike him. He was usually a practical man.

Startling him from his reverie, crows rose cawing from

the closest trees across from the window, and Gerald felt his stomach rumble—time for breakfast.

He wandered down the stone spiral stairs from the tower room and encountered no one. His footsteps echoed on old stone, and he paused to admire the ancient suits of armour dotted on landings and in halls and wondered whether they had belonged to the Graf's martial ancestors.

Eventually, Gerald saw the door to the Great Hall and strolled in there. His watch told him it was after 10 am. He had slept late.

The fire was burning. The smell of woodsmoke met his nose but also the aroma of food. Someone was cooking bacon. He saw the long wooden table had been laid for breakfast, but just one place. Gerald shrugged. It must be for him, so he went and sat down. There was a napkin, antique-looking silver knives and forks that weighed more than any modern ones. He waited, and within minutes, Tobias emerged, as expressionless as always.

"The Graf asked me to give you breakfast. He said you would enjoy this." In his hand, held with a serving cloth, was a large white china plate and on the plate, a heap of bacon and eggs and black bread with butter. There was also a silver pot of coffee and a smaller, china pot of milk decorated with blue flowers.

"Please, thank your master. Is he around? I feel I left abruptly last night, but I was exhausted."

"The Graf is indisposed this morning, but I have, on his instructions, telephoned the mechanic, Vincent, and asked him to collect your car for repair."

Gerald raised his eyebrows. "You have a telephone?" He found the idea surprising in that vast, ancient fortress; it seemed out of place, somehow too modern in a place that reeked of time.

Tobias nodded. "Yes, sir."

"Well, that's very kind of you. And did the mechanic collect the car?"

Tobias nodded. "I should imagine. I rang him much earlier."

"And did Vincent have any idea when the car would be fixed?"

"He did not, sir. He had not examined it at the time of our conversation."

"But I could phone him, I suppose."

"As you wish, sir."

"Will you show me the telephone? After my breakfast, of course. It smells delicious."

"After your breakfast." And Tobias departed.

TOBIAS LEFT Gerald alone in the large room with the blazing log fire. The fire gave off pleasant warmth on that cold morning, and the wood smoke smelled sweet as if the logs were hewn of cherry or apple. Gazing around, Gerald took in again the tapestries and banners and oriental ornaments and antique bookcases filled with leather-bound, gilt-embossed books, and then the halberds and pikes and shields. For the first time, he noticed their heraldic designs. He guessed they bore the heraldic arms of the Graf's family and their allies in marriage. The Von Hohenwald family emblem seemed to be the snarling head of a black wolf on a yellow background.

That the Graf was not there, did not concern him. The Graf didn't seem much of a man for company, and perhaps he preferred to avoid dealings with Gerald. Still, that strange story of the long-awaited visitor, a visitor whose actual identity was still unknown was intriguing. If odd. Gerald chuckled. It was all very rich, a peculiar adventure indeed, and a story to dine out on when Gerald returned to England, but the sooner he was in his trusty Rover and away on the next leg of his travels, the better. He planned to get to Ljubljana as quickly as possible and then spend a day or so doing nothing much.

Gerald finished his breakfast. Tobias hadn't come back to clear up or show him the telephone. In any case, there was little likelihood of the mechanic having fixed the car yet, so Gerald decided to explore the castle. He wandered to the suits of armour and ran his finger over the old metal: no dust, so someone cleaned them scrupulously. He idly perused the bookcases filled with tomes about history as well as German classics. Then he sauntered out of the Great Hall and went to see what of interest he could find to fill the time until his Rover was repaired.

He wondered whether he might even run across the telephone or Tobias in his travels. As he wandered, he found a wide oak staircase of polished wood with faded stair carpets held by brass runners. Gerald scratched his head. The place was enormous. He knew his room was off one of the towers, and he did not remember using this staircase. There were two towers, and one was in ruins, at least at the top. It was unlikely this broad stairway led to either of them, so it seemed most likely it led to the main body of the Schloss. Having nothing better to do and enjoying the excitement of exploration, he mounted the stairs. If he bumped into the Graf or Tobias he would merely tell them he was looking for the telephone, after all, there was no one around to show him and if he was not allowed in these areas he could easily claim to have got lost.

Gerald was struck by the dearth of servants. There was Tobias, but surely such a huge and draughty pile as this needed maids and gardeners and whatever? Still, there was no one around, and as he explored the first floor, Gerald's excitement changed to a less pleasant emotion. There was an atmosphere to the place, haunted almost—and he didn't mean by ghosts—though by rights there should have been plenty of these, but by a certain air of despondency as if something unresolved hung over the place.

Gerald grew tired of wandering the passages that led endlessly on to other rooms, mostly featureless. Most were locked, some were not, but those that were not had shuttered windows, dust-sheets draped over furniture and beds stripped of linen, just bare mattresses. No one came here, he saw that now, and it seemed the Graf lived all alone, despite his hint of family, but whether his solitariness was by choice, or because no one sought out his company, it was hard to say, but not so hard to guess.

And as Gerald wandered, the weather, as he observed it from the windows of those rooms that were not shuttered, or from the panes along the passages that ran parallel with the outside of the building, or even from the odd ornate skylight, changed and grew altogether darker; the blue sky was gone, replaced by smothering cloud. Gerald sighed. He had taken against the place; it was too old, too dark, too haunted by alien memories that hung heavy in the air, impure, implicit and impenetrable. He now wanted to find the telephone, ring the mechanic and leave.

But it was not easy finding his way back. By accident, he came across a part of the schloss that seemed almost set apart. There was something in the furnishings and decoration that suggested it had been used by someone else. Gerald couldn't exactly say why it was different, but it *was* different. There was a plain wooden door, and there had been many of those of course, and this one was closed,

as were most of the others, but there was something that
set this door apart, an aura, unseen, but noticeable. It
almost had a taste—acrid, and animal, unusual and
unpleasant.

Curiosity aroused, Gerald tried the handle, but it was
locked, again nothing novel in this, but as he was about to
turn and leave, he heard something or someone move
inside. Halting and pressing his ear to the door, he listened.
There was definitely someone inside. He considered
whether this might be the Graf's private apartment, but if
anything, this part of the castle seemed too feminine for
that austere gentleman.

Finally, "Hallo?" he called out.

"Hallo," came the reply: a woman's voice.

"I'm sorry to disturb you," Gerald said, in place of any
other sensible response.

The anonymous female voice whispered, "Please, don't
leave."

Gerald cleared his throat. "I'm Gerald Anderson, an
Englishman. I stayed here last night as a guest of the Graf."

"A guest of the Graf?" Her voice grew suddenly anxious.
"Are you then a friend of his?"

"No, I came upon the place in last night's storm. My car
broke down. He was kind enough to let me stay."

"So, not his friend?"

Gerald shrugged. "I owe him a debt, but, no, I wouldn't
consider myself his friend, nor, I guess, would he consider
me a friend either. We hardly know each other."

"You must help me," she said abruptly.

Gerald stood back. Help her? What with for Heaven's
sake? But he paused. Last night it had been he who needed
the help and now some resident of this castle was
requesting his aid.

The woman blurted, "I am Amaris. The Graf keeps me prisoner here."

"Prisoner?" How bizarre, but the girl went on.

"The Graf is my uncle. He keeps me locked up."

Locked up? What kind of a tangle was he getting himself into by coming here? Gerald said simply, "Why on earth would he do that?"

"The Graf is a wicked man. He fears my birthday."

"He fears your birthday? Why in Heaven would he fear your birthday?" This grew odder by the minute.

Amaris said, "Because when I am twenty-one, I come into my estate, and this castle will be mine. It is not his, never his. It was my father's, and Alexander is only Graf here while I am a minor, and soon I will have my birthday, and he will be deposed, so that is why he fears me, and keeps me locked way, but you—you can set me free."

It occurred to Gerald that the Graf might have locked this girl Amaris away because she was insane. Such things happened, even recently, even in England. He hesitated, unsure of how to respond.

"There is a key," she said. She was driving the situation faster than he could think.

"A key?" He hesitated. He should speak of this to the Graf, or, easier still, walk away and never mention it to anyone. Equally, her story might even be true and she might indeed be the victim of a great wrong. How was he to truly know?

Gerald Anderson was not a dishonourable man. He had fought bravely in the war, and would never let down a friend or a comrade, but this peculiar situation was far beyond his experience, and it left him uncomfortable. He sighed deeply. Where did his loyalty lie—to the Graf whom he hardly knew, but who had showed him hospitality, or to this strange girl, whom he did not know at all and who might easily be mad and locked away for her safety and the safety of others?

Amaris continued. "Yes, behind you, is a rosewood cabinet. In the top drawer, is a key to the outer door here. Unlock it, and we can speak more freely."

"It only unlocks the outer door?"

"Yes, sadly. But still, even with one door opened, we can talk better."

At least he could give her the benefit of an honest hearing. His sense of fair play wouldn't let him leave a woman locked up without hearing her out.

Gerald turned and saw the cabinet—it was a chest of drawers more properly and seemed designed for the keeping of linen. He approached it and again feeling he was been driven by the girl's demands and not knowing how reasonably to refuse her, he dragged open the topmost drawer. In it was indeed a key. Slowly, as if it might bite, he took it. He rubbed his chin and looked at the key in his right hand. Ah, well.

Gerald unlocked the door. His heart beat a little faster as he opened the door. He didn't know whether he expected her to rush at him, but he needn't have worried. This outer door now opened onto a suite of rooms. There had been a door at the end of the short corridor, but that had been removed, and now there was an iron grille. Behind the latticed iron stood a young, black-haired woman. She looked around twenty and was, to all appearances, in good health. It seemed the Graf did not starve her at least, and her clothes, though plain, were clean. She was also extraordinarily beautiful.

She said, "I am Amaris Von Hohenwald, the rightful heir

of this castle. Thank you, Mr Anderson, for opening the door."

Gerald could see from where he stood that there was a lock on the grille. It seemed another key was needed to free her completely.

Yes, she was rather striking. The sort of woman you could look at all day and not grow tired.

Amaris smiled. "I sense my freedom is at hand." She paused. "I had expected another to come and rescue me. He long ago promised he would come on my twenty-first birthday, but perhaps he has been killed. I cannot think he would abandon me if he still lived."

He gestured. "The iron lattice here is locked as well."

"Yes, Mr Anderson, that is the next step." Amaris Von Hohenwald had the face of an angel and a voice was as sweet as Alpine honey made from the brightest and freshest wildflowers in the highest, cleanest meadows.

"Will you help me?"

The least he could do was to wait while she told him her tale of woe.

4

Gerald stood, one step away from the iron grating that imprisoned Amaris. Not that he suspected anyone so slender and lovely could do him harm, or even reach her hand through the grille. As he stood, she told him her story.

"My father, Joachim Von Hohenwald, was the rightful Graf and owner of this castle. He was the elder of the two brothers. The current Graf that you have met is Alexander, the younger. The family disapproved of my father's marriage. My mother was a commoner, in trade, and a Hungarian. Her father was a watchmaker and far below the Von Hohenwalds in social standing. This was just before the end of the last war when the old empire was dying and the country was in turmoil. Alexander saw a way of gaining an advantage over my father, and he poisoned my grandparent's minds against my mother. I believe Alexander killed my mother, and my father took his own life because of grief."

"The Graf murdered your mother?"

"With poison, yes. There is no proof. Still, I believe it."

"But your grandparents?"

"Are now dead, but they agreed that Alexander would be my guardian. He was kind enough to me while they lived, I remember him being sweet, but once they were dead and he was Graf, he put me in this suite of rooms, installed the cage, locked the door, and I have been here since."

Gerald paused. "But why didn't he kill you? If he was wicked enough to poison your mother, why did he simply not do away with you, once your grandparents were gone? I'm sorry to be so blunt, but perhaps you are mistaken, and your mother died of natural causes."

Her eyes blazed. "So, you are on his side?"

Gerald gestured helplessly. "No, I didn't say that."

"If he was innocent, why has he locked me up here?"

It struck Gerald that he didn't actually know that the Graf had locked her up here, or for how long, or indeed whether she was really his niece. But she was locked in, that was for sure. It certainly seemed like devilry. He said, "I don't know."

She implored him. "Please, Mr Anderson, you must help me escape!" Her eyes were blue as spring crocuses with a yellow star flare around the iris, unusual and fascinating

"But how do I do that?"

"My uncle has a key," she said.

"If your story is true—"

"—it is true, I swear."

"Then surely, he won't just give it to me."

She shook her pretty head. "Of course not. But he keeps it in his room."

"I don't know where his room is."

"It's up the broken tower."

Gerald frowned. "You can't expect me to go into his room and steal it."

Tears flowed from her eyes and ran down her cheeks. "Of course, you are right. For a second, I had hope. But clearly, it is too much to ask you to do for me. I am a stranger to you after all."

Then a thought occurred to him. "What if I try to reason with him? Find the facts and point out other courses of action."

"My uncle Alexander will not see reason on this matter. He is my gaoler. Please do not expect him to listen to you." Her voice went quiet as if she was afraid. "Please, do not even mention my name. If he knows you have found me, and that you have given me hope, I fear for my life."

This was all too strange. Gerald knew he should turn his back on this. Who knew the truth of anything here? But some Chivalric impulse pulled at him. "So, you want me to go and get the key?"

"And then take me away, to Vienna, to anywhere."

"I thought you wanted to claim your inheritance?"

"In time, but first, I need to be safe from his murderous rage. Once he realises I have escaped, he will seek to destroy me, and you for helping me. So we must get safe, then speak to a lawyer."

A lawyer! At last, the real world intruded. Gerald would undoubtedly trust the mundane workings of the Law. He said, "So, you say it's in his room?"

"Yes, but please, be quick. Then we can leave."

Gerald noticed the emphasis on 'we' as if she had twined his fate with hers. All of a sudden he imagined them together, years from now, remembered their daring escape from her wicked uncle. Then he shook his head. What was coming over him? He needed some space to think. "His room's in the ruined tower?"

She put her hand up to the bars of her cage. "Yes, please hurry back with the key."

GERALD LEFT Amaris in her prison. He had no idea what to do. Or rather he clearly knew he should leave all of this well alone. But that would mean leaving her to his fate, and he struggled to do that—a poor young woman like that must be innocent. She seemed too pure and, indeed too beautiful for it all to be a lie. He would speak to the Graf, hear his side of the story. Surely something could be worked out.

He retraced his steps to the Great Hall with a heavy heart. The fire had been banked up, and the plates cleared away, but of Tobias or his master Graf Alexander, there was no sign. This was a very strange place.

As he looked around the hall with its ancient weapons and its even more ancient traditions, there was no sign of anyone. Gerald thought on what Amaris said: that the Graf would fly into a mad rage and kill them both. A nobleman such as the Graf could probably do whatever he wanted out here, and get away with it.

He wasn't frightened of that, but there was no point walking straight into a fight.

He sat on a chair. Gerald considered going to the village and finding the local policeman. But then, of course, any police officers in this isolated neck of the woods would be deferential to the local lord, so he could expect little from them. He held his head in his hands. Maybe, he actually would have to rescue her himself.

Gerald decided to go looking for the Graf's room. He hadn't actually made his mind up to ransack the room looking for the key, that would be such a gross trespass on the Graf's hospitality to him. First he would find the Graf's chamber, and decide what to do then.

GERALD SPENT over an hour wandering over the vast, many-roomed schloss, getting lost, retracing his steps, finding himself and losing himself multiple times until he had the glimmer of a clue of his way around the castle and where the broken tower could be found. The broken tower was the twin of the tower where his room was, and the schloss was broadly symmetrical, though there were particular idiosyncrasies and he guessed each Graf had added a little bit to the place, some more than others.

But finally, he had it. He knew where the Graf's room was. He didn't know where the Graf was though, and it was very possible he was in his chamber.

Gerald stood, like a novice burglar with stage fright outside the door on the long, empty corridor. No one came. He stood there five or six minutes. Gerald put his hand on the crystal doorknob. Shaking his head, he turned it.

If the key were in the Graf's room then Amaris's story rang true and the Graf must be complicit in her imprisonment. Then he would go back and unlock Amaris. He wasn't a cad and he wasn't a coward. He would find out the truth and then act accordingly.

The knob turned, and the door clicked open. Gerald thought anyone within twenty yards would hear the hammering of his heart, but there was no sound from within the Graf's room. He pushed the door gently and coughed. Again, if the Graf was inside, he would say outright that he'd found Amaris and do him the courtesy of asking him for his side of the story.

No alarm was raised at the opening of the door and

thereby emboldened, Gerald pushed it open the length of his arm, expecting some cry or shout, but still, no words were yelled or even whispered. The Graf wasn't there. More confidently, Gerald opened the door and peered around.

The room was panelled in walnut. There was a four-poster bed with silk hangings in yellow with a stylised wolf's head emblazoned on them. The sheets were undisturbed. Either the bed had just been made, or the Graf hadn't been sleeping here. Perhaps he'd got the wrong room? But in any case, where the hell did the man spend his days?

Gerald scanned the chamber. A window looked out onto the rainswept forest, and grey light percolated in through undrawn curtains. It was a dull day, and would soon be dark again. The room had more bookshelves, armoires and chests, more porcelain and brass oil lamps with frosted glass globes, but no Graf.

He went to the first chest of drawers. All the while, he looked around the room, on the nightstand and the top of the bookcase to see if there was any sign of this key. Nothing was visible, so he dragged open the top drawer and found old clothes that stunk of camphor. He yanked the next drawer, and saw yet more ancient clothing that looked like it had not been worn for decades.

This was like looking for a needle in a haystack, but, as he hovered, ready to search another drawer, some sixth sense prickled the hairs on the back of his neck: someone was coming.

As quietly, but as quickly as he could, he pushed the drawer closed. Gerald hadn't shut the chamber door properly behind him, and it sat about six inches open. He slipped behind the door so he would be hidden behind it should anyone enter. Of course, if they came fully into the room, he would be exposed, and the Graf was sure to come into his own room.

Gerald heard steps along the passage outside. The stone was carpeted, but the tread was heavy enough for him to know it belonged to a man and that he was coming this way.

Gerald stopped breathing. As he waited, eyes closed, to be revealed.

Then, whoever it was stopped. Gerald heard him pause and put his hand to the door, and the door moved slightly open. Then, he pulled the door shut from outside. Closed, but thankfully not locked. And he left.

It must have been Tobias walking past, thinking the Graf hadn't shut his bedroom door properly. But what if he wondered why and came back to check the Graf was well? Gerald needed to get out of the room right away, key or no key. All this skulking wasn't his style. He didn't know what had come over him to be so shifty.

He gave it five minutes then opened the door, listened and heard nothing.

It was impossible to find a hidden key among all the items in that overstuffed bedchamber. He would have to try something else. Gerald left the room, making sure to close it tightly behind him.

GERALD HURRIED DOWN THE CORRIDOR. He found his way back to the Great Hall. This time Tobias was there.

"Ah, sir, I came looking for you, but you weren't in your room."

"I went to the library. I presume it's a library, there are lots of books!" He had seen a library on his travels, but not entered. He might not be a cad or a coward, but here and now he was a liar. What was this place doing to him?

Tobias studied him as if he knew he was lying, then said, "The mechanic telephoned. He told me he ordered a part from Graz this morning and is expecting it this afternoon. He fully anticipates having your car fixed ready for you to leave this evening."

Tobias clearly didn't want him to stay another night. He had to find a way of releasing Amaris before then.

Will you require food before you leave?" Tobias asked.

Gerald said, "Is the Graf around?"

"No sir, he is currently indisposed."

Gerald put his hand to his mouth the said, "Tobias, does anyone else live here in the castle?"

Tobias cocked his head. "Have you found anyone in your wanderings?"

He wasn't going to give his master's game away. Gerald felt foolish for even trying to wheedle the information out of him. Whatever he was, Tobias was not disloyal.

Gerald thought he would get his car and bring it back and then figure out another way or releasing Amaris or at least get better directions to where the key might be kept. There might even be a locksmith in the village. He couldn't expect the locksmith to help, but he might be able to get a loan of his tools and hope he could figure out how to use them in lieu of a key. Gerald said, "I suppose I can get food in the inn?"

"Of sorts."

"I'll do that then. I'll get the car and fetch it back up. Is there someone who can take me down?"

"I can, sir. We have a horse and trap. But I have some jobs to do first. If you would be happy to wait half an hour?"

"That'll be fine."

5

It was getting dark as Gerald sat in a borrowed fur coat next to Tobias on the Graf's carriage pulled by two black horses. They clip-clopped down the pass at an amiable speed. From a distance, Gerald heard a deep baying howl, and started in his seat.

Tobias chuckled. "The English herr is frightened at the sound of a wolf."

"A wolf?"

"More than one. There are still wolf packs in Styria."

"My goodness." Gerald glanced all around. "Will they bother the horses?"

"They are usually timid." Then he smiled. "Unless they are hungry."

They kept on going down the pass, the way was steep, and Gerald nervously glanced at the tree-line on either side of the road just in case wolves emerged. They didn't, but as they trotted along, the wind blew the clouds away, and a large moon rose. The orb seemed bigger than usual and tinged with red.

"Full moon," he said.

"The Hunter's Moon, they call it," Tobias said. "It makes the wolves brave."

He knew Tobias was teasing him. How these people liked to manipulate his emotions. Gerald heard the wolves again, but they were calling a long way off. Still, he had no idea how fast they ran. In his Rover, he would have felt safe; there was a metal door between him and them, but here he was sitting on an open trap. He willed the horses to trot more swiftly, but they just kept the same steady pace.

They were about halfway to the village when Gerald finally worked up his courage. "Does the Graf have any family, Tobias?"

Tobias nodded. "He has only one niece. She is his only living relative."

"His sister's or his brother's child?"

"Brother's, but Graf Joachim died, and Graf Alexander has looked after her since."

"What do they call her?"

"That would be Lady Amaris."

So Amaris had told the truth, she was the Graf's niece. But why would he lock her up, unless she was telling the truth about the inheritance?

"Tobias, where does Amaris live, if the Graf looks after her?"

"Why she lives in the castle with us," Tobias said. "I believe you may have met her. Amaris's mind wanders. I wouldn't give credence to what she says. She likes to play with our guests."

They had arrived on the village street. Gerald's mind whirled. Who actually was telling the truth here?

Tobias dropped him off by the inn: *Zum Schwarzen Wolf*.

Gerald desperately wanted to know more. "Will you

come in for a beer, Tobias?" Gerald said. "I'll treat you for bringing me all the way down."

With the same expressionless face, Tobias declined. "No, I must hurry back to the castle. The Graf will be waking soon and I must attend to him."

"Waking? But it's evening!"

"The Graf is an aristocrat. His ways are not our ways." Tobias flicked the switch over the horses' backs and they turned to head back up the pass, the way they'd come, and Gerald's chance of finding out more was gone.

GERALD LOOKED AROUND. So, they knew he'd met Amaris. But who'd told them? Perhaps Amaris herself, perhaps she and they were part of some strange conspiracy. But why? And then the Graf getting up at this time of the day? Even if ancient aristocratic families always felt above bourgeois conventions, getting up at this time wasn't natural. And where had he slept all day? It certainly wasn't his chamber.

Gerald yanked open the rough door of the inn and stepped into the aroma of tobacco, goulash and beer. A gipsy-looking man fiddled wild airs on the violin and villagers played backgammon and laughed uproariously. All that stopped as Gerald entered. He was clearly foreign, but after the obligatory gawp, the locals had the manners to continue with their revelry. Gerald was hungry, but first he needed to get his car. He asked the mutton-chop whiskered man, the landlord, who was cleaning pewter tankards with a clean linen cloth where he could find the mechanic, Vincent. The man clearly remembered Gerald too and was overly deferential.

With a fawning smile, the landlord told him the mechanic's workshop was three houses down; he couldn't fail to see the petrol pump outside it, he said. Gerald hurried back to the door, and with his hand on the doorknob, he hesitated. Inside, it was warm and convivial; the food smelled good, and the dark beer that foamed from tankards on the long wooden tables or held in the hands of the chattering men had great appeal. Outside, it was cold where the clear skies and sanguineous moon had sucked away any warmth that lingered under the clouds. But there would be time for a beer once he had the car fixed. Gerald turned up the collar of his borrowed coat.

As he pulled tight his coat, he remembered it wasn't his. Damn, he was not rid of the Graf just yet.

Once he retrieved his car, he would stop at the castle again. He would find a way to free Amaris. As he walked from the inn to the mechanic's shop, strange imaginings filled his mind. Gerald certainly wasn't given to wild fantasies, yet with each step he pictured himself confronting the Graf, appealing to his humanity, or threatening him with the law, and taking the beautiful Amaris with him. He imagined them in Ljubljana or Istanbul, she so young and beautiful and so very grateful.

He shook his head to try and clear it. He even wondered whether they had bewitched him, the Graf and Amaris together.

GERALD FOUND the mechanic's workshop. The door of the garage was open, and electric lamps lit up his work. The bonnet of his Rover was open, and the blonde head of the man he presumed to be Vincent was studying the engine. He hailed him, and the mechanic looked up, surprised.

"Gerald Anderson," Gerald said. "This is my car you're working on."

"Ah, Herr Anderson." Vincent grimaced. "I'm sorry, it's not ready yet."

That was a blow. "Oh? I thought you ordered the necessary part."

Vincent took off his gloves a finger at a time and pushed back the blond forelock that fell over his creased forehead. "I did, I did..."

"So, didn't it arrive?"

He sighed. "It needed new filters. One arrived, but it was not quite the right one. English parts are hard to get here. I thought it would do as it was the closest in size, but the thread is the wrong way."

"Damnation. So, when do you think it'll be ready."

"I am afraid, Herr Anderson, that it will not be tonight. I will send for the replacement first thing tomorrow. It could arrive tomorrow night, but more likely the day after tomorrow."

Gerald felt like he'd been punched. "The day after tomorrow? Oh, no! Can't you do it sooner?"

Vincent seemed a decent man. "I will try, I promise you, but it's better to be realistic."

"By the way, do you have any bolt cutters?"

"Bolt cutters? No, why?"

Gerald frowned. "Or is there a locksmith in the village? Someone who would lend me his tools?"

Vincent stared at him a second then said, "No, no locksmith in Geistthall. Is there anything I can help you with?"

"I just need something that can cut metal."

Vincent scratched his head. "I have some shears. I use them for slicing through the bodywork of wrecked cars."

He went and fetched some heavy black metal shears about three feet long with leather handles. The blades were big and sharp. They looked like they might do the job.

"Can I borrow them?"

Vincent said, "I don't use them all the time. I'd need them back. But yes, I suppose. What do you need them for?"

Gerald sucked his teeth. "I really can't say. Please honour my confidence. I'll bring you them back when I'd done with them."

"Do you want them now?"

"No. Can you put them in the back seat of my car? I don't need them until my car's fixed."

Vincent looked genuinely bewildered but promised to do as Gerald asked.

They talked briefly, but there was no point in lingering. It was cold and Gerald's belly growled. At the door of the mechanic's workshop, Gerald turned. "You said the car needed a new filter. I had all the filters changed before I left England."

Vincent shrugged. "I think there was something wrong with your fuel. It was sticky and congealed, blocking the filter."

GERALD WALKED DESPONDENTLY BACK to the inn. He needed some beer. Back in the busy tavern, he smiled at the innkeeper's wife. She didn't greet him but he got the impression she remembered him. Probably they had so few tourists that he stuck out like a sore thumb. Gerald found a table by the fire and ordered a *stein* of dark beer, a plate of beef goulash and bread and butter. He was despondent at the thought of returning to the castle, and because he'd dismissed Tobias and his ponies, it looked like he'd be walking. He certainly didn't relish that long walk up the pass in this cold with those wolves howling all around. Then halfway through his beer, Gerald remembered that the castle had a telephone. He would ring and ask Tobias to come and fetch him!

Goulash finished, the innkeeper's wife came and collected his pewter dish, and Gerald ordered another dark beer, and gave her a tip of a few groschen.

"I hope you found accommodation," she said.

He nodded. "Yes, at the castle."

"The castle?" She seemed alarmed, but she took away his dish without further comment and went to fetch the beer. When she returned with it, she whispered, "Is the kind *herr* staying still at the Schloss Hohenwald?"

He nodded sadly. "For longer than I anticipated."

She shook her head, and continued in a low voice as if she didn't wish to be overheard. "It is a bad place, the Schloss Hohenwald."

He had formed the same opinion himself but he imagined the local peasants were in awe of the Graf, so he smiled indulgently, "And why do you say that?"

She shook her head. "It is cursed. The Von Hohenwald family are all cursed."

Gerald sat back. He could at least fish for information about Amaris. "I heard there was a tragedy in the family. The late Graf died."

"Graf Joachim. Yes, a good man. He killed himself, yes. He could not bear what he had allowed."

"Allowed?"

"His daughter."

"And her name was?"

"The Lady Amaris. It was not her fault. It was in her blood."

"The Graf's blood?"

"No, from the other side—her cursed mother!"

Gerald decided to risk asking a potentially explosive

question. "I heard Graf Alexander killed Amaris's mother, is that true?"

The woman seemed taken aback. "No! That is a lie! For all his faults, Alexander did not kill her. Her father Joachim killed her himself. For the child was not his."

"Not his?"

"Amaris was conceived in fornication, out of wedlock, in adultery."

"And Graf Joachim killed his wife for that?"

"Aye, and for other sins. And then he took his own life in grief."

The mutton-chopped husband was calling her back. The fire burned and the chatter ebbed and flowed in the tavern. The woman hesitated then took the crucifix from her neck. "Please, will the kind *herr* take this cross? It is for protection."

He frowned. "From what?"

"From the evil that lurks there."

"It's very kind of you," Gerald said, "But it's yours." He thought her superstitious gesture wouldn't help him much, as well-intentioned as it undoubtedly was. He pushed it back. "Thank you but I can't take your crucifix."

She looked at him with what appeared to be a genuine concern as she backed away and then turned to go to her tasks.

The tavern owner was increasingly impatient. He yelled over. She had been wasting time talking to Gerald when there was work to be done. Then he recognised Gerald. A look of fear came over his face and he stepped back into the kitchen.

6

A s the innkeeper's wife walked away, the door opened, letting the cold in and a slender man entered wearing clerical garb. It was the priest who had admired his Rover—a priest coming for his pint of ale, well why not?

Gerald watched him scan the bar. When he saw Gerald, he gave a smile and came over. Gerald sat back. What did this portend?

The priest spoke in English, "Hello, you are Mr Anderson?"

Taken aback, Gerald said, "I am. Nice to meet you, Father, but how do you know me?"

"We met briefly."

"I remember, but you know my name."

The priest said. "Foreign visitors are not common. Word gets around, even to the ears of the parish priest."

The priest shook his hand limply. He was very pale and his hair dark. Gerald saw that though the man had clearly shaved, he had a shadow of stubble on his chin. His hair was so dark he probably had to shave twice a day to get rid of that shadow.

The priest pointed to the table. "May I join you?"

Gerald shrugged. Why not? He would phone Tobias when he'd finished his beer.

The priest sat. "I am Father László János."

Gerald said, "You sound Hungarian from your name."

"Very observant. I am. I am a stranger in Styria. I've only been here a month."

"A month? And how do you find the locals? I hope they've welcomed you."

The priest smiled, and Gerald took it they hadn't. When when the the innkeeper's wife came back, János ordered a beer. Father János sipped it when it was brought. "It's fine. I didn't expect them to wholly see eye to eye with me. I think they find some of my ideas too modern. I'm from Budapest, so I have an urban mentality, perhaps." He shrugged.

"So the story of my car breaking down is common knowledge?"

"It's not a big community. That and the story of your stay at the castle soon got around, and I was curious. Not many people stay at the castle. Few indeed of the villagers have been inside it."

Gerald smiled. "A strange place, the castle."

János said. "I've never been invited."

"No, the Graf doesn't strike me as particularly pious. You know he disappears during the day?"

"Perhaps he's a vampire?" Father János said with a smile.

Gerald said, "Well, I haven't yet discounted the idea."

János said, "I've never met him, or even seen him. He doesn't come to the village. I hear he goes to Vienna, or even Venice but never Geistthall."

Gerald was guarded. "The Graf has been hospitable enough. I wouldn't want to speak ill of him."

"Many do," Father János said.

Gerald raised an eyebrow. More fishing. "Really? Pray, tell."

János said, "Have you met his niece?"

He tried not to let his surprise show. "His niece? He has one?"

"Apparently. His brother's daughter. She's called Amaris Von Hohenwald."

"Ah," Gerald said.

"So, you've met her?"

He couldn't lie to a man of the cloth. He was always uncomfortable lying anyway. "Yes, I met her."

"They say she's quite beautiful."

Gerald wondered what interest a priest had in beautiful young women, but shrugged. "I suppose she is." He decided to keep quiet about her being locked up for now.

"You've heard the story?" János said.

Gerald shook his head. "What story?"

János sat back. "Ah, well. The locals say his brother Joachim's wife was afflicted with a strange disease. It was in her bloodline. The wife fell pregnant, and Amaris was born. Apparently, Joachim realised his wife would die slowly and in pain from this mysterious illness. It was said her mother suffered from it too, and so would Amaris. Joachim strangled his wife."

"He strangled her?" The story of Amaris's birth and her mother's death seemed to change with whoever was telling it.

János said, "Out of mercy."

"A strange kind of mercy."

"Joachim's wife asked him to, so it's said, but his heart was broken. They say that this illness comes out in adulthood and there was every chance that Amaris would carry it too, and Joachim knew he should destroy his infant daughter, but he couldn't bring himself to do it. He left Amaris outside one cold winter's night, expecting her to die quietly of cold, and then Joachim took his own life."

"And Alexander found her?"

"Made her his ward."

"So what was this disease?"

"Some congenital defect of the blood that curses certain families."

"But if that's the case then Amaris is heir to the castle."

"I imagine so. I'm sure she is of age now, or soon will be to inherit. Would you like another beer, Mr Anderson?"

Gerald sighed. "I have to get back to the castle eventually and I have no transport. I will need to phone the Graf's servant for a lift, or walk."

János said, "I can drive you."

Gerald raised his eyebrows. "You have a car?"

"I do."

Hearing that, Gerald agreed to another beer. The thought of a lift cheered him, even if the anticipation of another night in the castle didn't. Into his third pint, Gerald said. "He locks her up, you know."

János looked shocked. "He locks her up?"

So the priest hadn't heard that. Gerald nodded. "Behind an iron grille."

"How strange. And is there a key?"

"Apparently."

"Do you know where it is?"

Gerald shook his head.

János peered at him. "But why does the Graf lock her up?"

"She says that he keeps her prisoner because he doesn't want her to inherit the castle and turn him out."

Father János shrugged. "Perhaps it's true. But maybe he keeps her prisoner because he is afraid of this illness she is supposed to carry."

Gerald frowned. "Surely, he should seek treatment for her."

János said, "You're right, but he doesn't sound like a forward-thinking man. Maybe he doesn't think there's a cure."

Gerald said, "How would he know? He's no doctor." He took a gulp of beer. He had an idea. Gerald said, "We should persuade him to let us take her to a hospital."

"Should we?"

"Well, if she is sick, then she needs medical help."

János nodded thoughtfully. "I understand what you're saying."

Gerald rubbed his eyes; the smoke from the fire made them sting, and the beer was made him woozy, but he still knew the difference between right and wrong. "I was planning to have a word with the Graf."

"Really? Good luck."

"But, I suppose a man like that can do what he wants and get away with it."

"Especially if he's a vampire."

Gerald blinked. "Of course he's not really. Vampires don't exist." Gerald thought quickly. János could be a good ally, if he could persuade him to help. It made sense to use the power of the Church— confront the Graf and shame him into freeing Amaris. He wouldn't dare kill a clergyman.

Gerald nodded. "What if we two go and have a word

with the Graf and if he doesn't release her, we will threaten to call the police."

"I would imaging the police here would be deferential to the Graf. They would take his side rather than that of a foreign tourist."

"But what about you? You're a man of the Church."

"And a foreigner too."

"But still, the parish priest. You must have some standing."

"Less than you'd think."

Gerald said, "But we can't leave her. It's immoral."

"I agree."

"Then will you help me?"

János gave a strange smile. "I'm not sure the Bishop would be too happy about me calling the police on the Graf."

"But you're a Christian, you must do what's right."

János grinned. "I must."

"Then will you help me?"

"To try and talk sense into the Graf?"

"Yes, just that. We won't come to blows. I can't imagine you're much of a fighter—no offence."

The priest shrugged. "Well, I'm happy to come. It's a very humane idea of yours. I approve."

And if talking didn't work, Gerald had the shears in his car.

THEY DECIDED NOT to have another drink. Gerald waited inside the inn door while Father János fetched his car. As he stood there, the innkeeper's wife who had served him beer came up. She had something in her hand, and, thinking it was the crucifix, he turned to refuse it, but it was a small glass bottle.

She held it up. "If you will not take the holy cross, take this herb."

"A herb?" Gerald peered at it. In his warm drunken fuddle, he took the bottle from her to see it better.

The woman said, "It is aconite. It is poison," and with that, the woman gave him a sad look, turned and went back into the smoky inn. The glass bottle remained in Gerald's hand as he wondered what he was meant to do with it. Poison? But whom to poison?

Father János pulled the tavern door open, revealing the dark night without. "Ready?"

Gerald was going to ask him about aconite, but János seemed in a hurry, so Gerald stuffed the glass bottle with aconite in it into his inside pocket, planning to ask the priest what he thought about it later.

"Do you mind if we go by the mechanic's shop? There is something I need to fetch from my car."

János shrugged. "That is not a problem."

VINCENT HAD GONE to bed when Gerald called. He came downstairs, in his vest and opened the door a crack. "Ah, it's you."

"Yes, sorry. But you know those shears?"

"Yes."

"I need them now."

"Now? But it's late."

"Honestly, I need them. Can I get them?"

Vincent shrugged. "I guess. The garage is open. But bring them back tomorrow."

"I will. I'll fetch them back when I get my car."

The garage was indeed open—such a trusting village.

GERALD BUNDLED the shears in his coat and placed them on the back seat. In the dark it would just like the coat was just a coat.

The trip up the pass in Father János's Hungarian Magomix was quicker than the trip down in the pony and trap. Gerald hadn't expected a Catholic priest to have a car, but it seemed Fr János was extremely interested in motors, and they chatted about Rover and Vauxhall and Rolls-Royce. Halfway up, Gerald peered out of the window. "At least the weather's improved." There was no rain, and the red moon sat halfway across the sky like an enormous Chinese lantern above the dark Styrian forest. Once again, the wolves howled. János saw his alarm and laughed. "Don't be frightened of the wolves, Mr Anderson. They call all night to their friends."

They pulled up outside the Schloss Hohenwald. Gerald hesitated; his idea of trying to make the Graf see sense and let his niece go now seemed rather doomed to failure, even with the priest on board. These aristocrats were too used to getting their own way, probably even a priest would make him hesitate.

"Listen, father," Gerald said.

"László, please. I think we are friends, no?"

Gerald nodded. He still felt drunk. "Yes, of course. But listen. I am guessing you've never come to blows with anyone."

"Oh, I don't know. I was a boy once and like all boys had a few scraps."

"But you've never been in combat."

János sat in the car, his leather-gloved hands gripping the steering wheel.

"You see, if the Graf is the tyrant we think he is—"

"—and we do."

"It seems that way. You know, it's possible he may not give Amaris up without a fight."

"Ah."

"So, I think: don't fight. If he cuts up rough. We back off."

"Back off?"

"Yes, retreat. Pretend he's won."

"I see. And then what? If he 'cuts up rough' as you say, then surely that proves he is indeed a tyrant and Amaris will suddenly be in greater danger once he knows the game is up."

"I've thought of that." Gerald reached over and pulled up his coat. He took out the shears. The moonlight illuminated them.

"Goodness," János said.

Gerald smiled grimly. "We retreat and use these to snip the lock off. Then we get her out."

"It seems like you've have it all planned out."

Gerald shrugged. "Desperate times. We can't leave her to that monster."

"No, indeed."

"And now the castle."

They were parked just outside. "I've never been inside," János said. He smiled. "But now's the time."

"It's pretty much what you'd expect, I suppose," Gerald said.

János patted Gerald on the shoulder. "You're a good man, Mr Anderson, very honourable."

"I hope so,"

János seemed keen. "Let us begin."

Gerald nodded. Tight lipped, he walked over the draw-bridge to the castle door, and János followed as the old walls stared down at them. János grinned standing at the door; there was something about him, not like a priest at all. Gerald frowned; and it was odd the priest was so keen to go in, but Gerald pounded the door with the wolf's head knocker as János stood beside him, almost expectantly.

After he knocked, Gerald stood back, holding his coat that concealed the shears.

Eventually, Tobias answered. He registered no surprise to see Father János in his clerical garb beside Gerald.

Gerald muttered, "The car wasn't fixed."

"I'm sorry to hear that, sir."

"It leaves me at a disadvantage. I would have taken a room at the inn—"

"—But there aren't any," Father János said.

Tobias regarded the priest for the first time. "Indeed."

"So," Gerald said."I'm afraid I need to put upon your hospitality again."

Tobias nodded gravely. "I will ask the Graf, sir."

They waited there, the light of the baleful mood washing the forecourt of the schloss in blood orange.

"Very decent of you to come with me," Gerald said to János.

"Not a problem. Glad to be able to help." The priest smirked. Inexplicably, he seemed to find the situation amusing. Gerald felt suddenly dizzy. He rubbed his eyes.

"Are you quite well?" János asked.

"Probably just the beer."

"It's strong."

"Yes."

They waited.

Eventually, Tobias returned. He nodded and said, "Please come this way."

Once inside the Entrance Hall, Tobias stopped and chained the doors behind him. He shot the bolt and turned the heavy key. "Let us go," he said.

Gerald hung back. He put the shears behind one of the chairs that flanked the hall. They weren't hidden, but there was no one about to find them anyway.

Gerald and Father János followed Tobias to the Great Hall, where the fire blazed. The Graf sat inscrutably in his wing-backed chair with his black hair and his piercing blue eyes. "Mr Anderson, I thought we had lost you."

"My car didn't get fixed."

"That's a pity."

"It leaves me without anywhere to stay."

The Graf nodded. "I see. And I expect you will need breakfast also."

"If you don't mind."

The Graf studied the two of them silently. He did not greet the priest until Father János said, "I am László János, the new priest in the village."

Without looking at him directly, the Graf said, "I have heard of you. You have modern ideas, not suited to Styria. We are an old-fashioned people here who like old-fashioned things."

János said, "With due respect, Graf, I believe that if we are to rejuvenate the area, we need to be bold."

"And you are Hungarian."

"I am."

The Graf said, "I do not like Hungarians."

"That is unfortunate."

Gerald thought he'd better get it over with, so he said, "Before we retire, Graf, I would like to speak of Amaris."

The Graf said, "Of Amaris?"

"Your niece, whom you have locked up in a room of the schloss."

"Sequestered. Yes."

"Whatever you call it, it's not right."

"You know nothing about it. Best keep your nose out of this, Englishman."

"You can't just lock someone away."

"Apparently I have."

"Such things must be against the law, even here."

"What would you do with her? You seem to know it all, so please enlighten me as to what other possible course of action there could be? Should I have killed her?"

"Of course not. She's your own niece."

"I'm not sure about that."

Gerald thought he was referring to the tale of the adultery the innkeeper's wife repeated. Gerald said, "Please can we stop playing word games?"

The Graf stared at him with his ice-blue eyes. "Perhaps you'd like a drink? I have some good Zweigelt, so fruity, fresh and soft. It is quite the success story in Austrian winemaking. Did you know the grape was produced first in 1922 at Klosterneuburg?"

Gerald ignored the diversion. "What is your reason for locking this poor girl up?"

"Why not have some wine?"

"I'd rather sort this out first. Explain yourself, please."

"I'll have some wine," Father János said, sitting down in one of the leather chairs.

Gerald glanced at the priest, once again János appeared enormously amused. But Gerald was uneasy, though he knew János was an ally. He said, "Very well, I'll have a glass, but then tell your tale, and we can get the poor girl free. Even if she is ill, she shouldn't be locked up. I'll take her to a hospital, even if you won't."

The Graf laughed. "You'd take her with you in your little car?"

"If necessary."

"You amuse me."

Gerald saw János laughing too. What the hell was going on?

Tobias came and brought a decanter of red wine. When he poured it, he withdrew, leaving the three around the blazing fire.

"I was always suspicious of you, Mr Anderson,' The Graf said, lifting his heavy crystal goblet to his full lips. The wine stained them crimson as blood, and he wiped his mouth with the back of his pale hand.

"And me of you, Graf," Gerald said.

"Of me? Why?"

"You're a strange man. You are completely absent during the hours of the day for one thing." A chill ran up Gerald's spine as the Graf studied him.

"I sleep during the day. I am awake all night, but when the first rays of dawn break in the east, I retreat to my bed."

Gerald said, "But I entered your bedroom earlier today, and you were not there."

"Because, Mr Anderson, I do not sleep in my bedroom. I sleep elsewhere."

"Elsewhere? Why do you not sleep in your chamber?"

"Because where I sleep, it is quieter, and I get better rest."

All this while, Father János sat quietly. At a pause in the conversation, János said, "You don't like Hungarians. As a Hungarian can I ask you why? Please explain how my countrymen have offended you."

"My brother's wife was Hungarian."

János folded his arms. "I believe you were not well disposed towards her."

The Graf studied his two visitors. "Are you two in league? It makes no difference, I merely ask from curiosity."

Gerald shook his head. "I hardly know Father János. He gave me a lift. We only just met in the tavern." Then he remembered, "Ah, yes and once before, just before my car broke down."

The Graf kept his silence, but János continued, "And so your niece is half Hungarian."

A shadow crossed the Graf's brow. "Half something. Maybe more than half."

Gerald blurted, "She will take the castle from you, that's why you lock her up. You want to keep what you got from your brother."

The Graf gestured around him. "This? I care not for this. I only stay from duty."

János said, "Why don't you leave? Leave it to her. Go to Vienna or wherever you want to be. Right the ancient wrong you have perpetrated, seeking to block the natural order."

The Graf snorted. "Do you know who the Von Hohenwald family are, Hungarian? We have been in these mountains and valleys for always, all down the centuries, always carrying out our ancient duty to the Emperor and the Church. I, Alexander Von Hohenwald, will not be the one who lays down his sword and lets evil in."

Gerald pleaded, "But Graf, you can't keep a young woman locked up against her will."

The Graf shook his head. "What do you know, Englishman? Your country knows nothing of the ancient evil that plagues this land."

"I know the difference between right and wrong. You must let Amaris go."

The Graf said, "I see you have fallen under her spell. Tell me, does she look hungry or dirty?"

"No, but that still doesn't justify false imprisonment. As a gentleman, as a nobleman, I appeal to you to see sense."

This wasn't working. Gerald's suspicions of the Graf's evil intent now seemed well-founded.

The Graf sighed deeply and drained his goblet. "I cannot, and I will not let her go."

"But surely, whatever your reason for this—"

But at that moment, Father János stood and put his hand on Gerald's shoulder. "Come, Gerald. We shall free Amaris."

And then realisation dawned in the Graf's eyes. "I know who you are now."

Father János seemed amused. "Do you?" But he had little interest in the Graf now and turned to Gerald. "Show me the way to Amaris."

Gerald stood from his chair.

The Graf stood too. He rubbed his forehead. "I have been foolish. I have allowed the enemy in through my front door. Mr Anderson, do you know what you are doing?"

Gerald shrugged. "I just know it's not right to keep someone locked up behind an iron grille."

"Isn't it?" The Graf stared coldly at Gerald.

János said, "Come, Gerald, we must be quick."

As they hurried out of the Great Hall, Gerald heard the Graf calling for Tobias.

· · ·

GERALD SHOWED Father János the way. The priest seemed
unnaturally eager now to free Amaris. Gerald put it down to
some natural sense of justice and mercy that we guess must
be in all churchmen. Hurrying along the ancient echoing
halls, Gerald got lost once, then he found the way.

They were in the entrance hall. Gerald saw the shears
and darted across to get them.

János grinned. "Ah, your shears."

"Yes, we'll need them for the lock."

János reached out a hand. "Can I borrow them?"

Gerald frowned but handed him them anyway.

János went over and nipped through the chain that held
the castle doors closed. He gave Gerald the shears back and
then for good measure turned the huge black key and drew
back the huge black bolt. The outer door was now unlocked.

"Come," János said.

Gerald followed the priest up the stairs. They had not
got far when suddenly the electric lights were extinguished.

János laughed. "He may think that will stop us, but he's
wrong."

In the dark, János's eyes gleamed strangely. "Are we
near?" Then he said, "No matter, I smell her."

Gerald frowned. "Smell her?"

János said, "Perhaps you would like to leave now? Our
kind is not lacking in mercy, whatever tales they tell of us."

"What? Your kind? I'm sorry, I don't understand."

Red-tinged moonlight flooded in at one of the windows
that opened onto the exterior of the Schloss. It was enough
to show Gerald that János's eyes glittering like rubies.
Gerald put his hand to his throat. Who exactly was János?
What exactly was going on?

János said, "And I am grateful to you, Gerald. Without your help, gaining entry to the castle would have been harder, and the Graf would have been alerted if I had simply come on my own."

Gerald said, "Should I come with you? Do you need me to take Amaris away in my car?" He was still holding the shears.

János shook his head. "That won't be necessary. Just take me to her prison, then, if you know what's good for you, leave."

They turned and strode down the passage to where Amaris's prison was. János had a strange loping gait, and as the moonlight struck him, his appearance rippled, like the moon on water on a winter's night. There was something very strange here. It all seemed planned and Gerald began to suspect he had been duped.

János arrived at the iron-grille that kept Amaris prisoner.

Gerald yelled, "You'll need these!" He thrust out the shears to János, but János did not need them. With enormous strength, he rent the latticed iron from its frame, and heard Amaris yell in triumph, "Father, you have finally come!"

As Gerald looked, he saw man and girl transform in the moonlight. Their forms altered until they were human no more; they were wolves — huge werewolves.

Gerald turned and fled.

Running, and almost out of breath, arriving outside the Great Hall, Gerald found two armoured figures. They wore two suits of armour that had recently lined the halls. The visors of both helmets were up, and he saw the Graf, with the Wolf Head shield of the Von Hohenwalds and beside him his squire, Tobias.

"Are they coming?" The Graf said.

Gerald nodded, unable yet to speak.

The Graf drew a longsword that glinted in the yellow flames of the fire. It gleamed, not as steel would, but with a softer glimmer, as from more noble metal: it seemed the Graf's sword was of silver. "You are far from safety, Englishman."

"They turned into wolves!" Gerald stammered. "Monstrous wolves." As he spoke the words, he still couldn't quite believe them.

"You should leave. This isn't your fight."

Gerald said, "I can't abandon you. They played me for a fool, and in my foolishness, I helped bring this upon you."

The Graf nodded. "Yes, you have been very foolish. But so have I. You have been their Trojan horse, but I let you in. And I was so stupid in letting that Hungarian into the castle. I thought that because he worse a priest's garb he could not be one of them."

Tobias said, "The power of the Church is not now what it was. They mock it now where once they cowered in fear of it."

The Graf's mouth tightened. "You still have time to go, Mr Anderson. Not much, maybe minutes."

Gerald shook his head. "I can't go. I will fight."

The Graf said, "That might also be an act of foolishness."

"I was foolish to trust Amaris."

The Graf gave a wry smile. "But she is fair while I am grim. That is why you were deceived."

Suddenly Tobias spoke up, "Evil comes in like a serpent, often wearing a mask of beauty."

The Graf said, "Tobias speaks truly. For beauty is not always truthful and the truth is rarely beautiful. Men down the ages have made the same mistake as you and trusted poisoned words spoken by a fair mouth, rather than listen to truth that wore a less appealing face."

"I will make up for my gullibility. I will stay and fight," Gerald repeated.

"Very well. I accept your offer of service. Take a weapon and stand ready. You will be tested—perhaps unto death."

Gerald selected a halberd from the rack and returned to the two steel-clad warriors. He took his place beside them.

The Graf said, "The Von Hohenwalds have protected these lands from the werewolves for centuries. It was our sacred duty handed to us by the Emperor and the Pope—to cleanse these mountains from the ancient plague of lycanthropy. And we nearly succeeded, but then, as a cruel jest, or perhaps by wicked design, my brother fell in love with a Hungarian woman who was one of them. She seduced him, and they had a child, but the girl was not his, it was fathered by the male wolf.

"Joachim was cuckolded and tricked. I tried to talk to him, but he wouldn't believe the girl wasn't his. He was so convinced, he even half convinced me. I knew she was half-wolf, but until tonight, I persuaded myself that my brother's blood ran in her veins and so she was kin to me and deserving my protection, even while I protected others from her. I should never have been so merciful."

Gerald watched the Graf's handsome, anguished face in the flickering firelight.

The Graf went on. "Before she died, my brother's Hungarian wife taunted me and said the wolves would come to rescue Amaris. And that is why I awaited the stranger." He gave a soft laugh. "For a while, I thought you might be he— an Englishman! How foolish I was, of course, it had to be a Hungarian."

Then a great howling came from outside the schloss. A great howling and pounding on the massive castle door.

The Graf said, "Our minutes are gone."

"I'm ready," Gerald said.

"Their pack is outside the main door," the Graf said.

"Do not worry, my lord," Tobias said. "I made sure I locked the door and bolted it and chained it with a heavy chain of iron. Nothing evil can enter that way."

The growling grew closer. A sad smile played on the Graf's face and he snapped down his visor. "Then at least we only have to face the two werewolves. Though that is enough. Remember your honour, gentlemen. To the fight."

With a sickness in the pit of his stomach, Gerald remembered János unlocking the door and snipping through the chain as if it were butter, snipping through the chain with the shears that Gerald had gone to such pains to bring here and leave handy for János to breach the castle door.

He was about to apologise once more for his misplaced trust when a noise of quick paws clattered down the stairway. Amaris and her true father were descending, muzzles snarling, dripping teeth, eyes blazing. Unholy fire filled their gaze, red as if the bloody moon had sunk deep within the amber orbs and now shone with fierce glee.

"There they are, lord," Tobias yelled.

"At least the pack is kept outside," the Graf muttered.

Then the castle door smashed open and the pack of cur-wolves poured in.

"TO ARMS, AND OUR SACRED DUTY!" The Graf called and drew his silver sword.

"I don't understand!" Tobias cried. "How could they get in through the front door? Forgive me, lord. I bolted it."

"It doesn't matter, Tobias," The Graf said. "Stand firm."
He glanced at Gerald as if to steady his nerve. Gerald was
about to tell them about the door when the Graf snapped,
"Stand firm, Mr Englishman. Whatever mistakes you have
made do not matter now."

Gerald turned to see the wolves come in at the door;
they poured in like the froth of the sea on a wave of moonlight. The Graf and Tobias formed an arrow point, facing
out on two sides with Gerald behind, inexpertly holding his
weapon in front of him.

The wolves leapt, and the swords struck them down.
The mortal wolves yelped as the blades cut them and their
blood flowed, making the ground sticky and wet. The air
filled with growls and yelps and the grunts of the fighting
men. Gerald jabbed the wolves with the point of his halberd
to keep them at bay. He felt, useless, superfluous. More than
that, he felt duped. His gullibility was the cause of this
disaster.

Amaris and János advanced and the wolf pack cleared a
path for them and stood back snarling while their masters
prepared to attack.

Tobias ran forward, but the Graf called him back. "You
only have a steel sword, Tobias. Remember that only silver
will cut these abominations!"

But rage filled Tobias, overpowering his reason,
sweeping away his rationality, and he lunged at the Amaris
wolf looming above him, standing seven feet tall. Lazily, she
swiped him with her claws and knocked him to the floor.
Tobias rolled on the stone flags, clutched his blade and
didn't let it drop, and his armour prevented the worst hurt,
but his steel sword couldn't hurt her.

She advanced for the kill.

Instinctively, the Graf went to protect his servant and

took his eyes off his adversary, the wolf János. János roared and leapt, knocking the Graf off balance and sending him reeling. János followed up and smashed the wolf's head shield from the Graf's grasp.

Now the Graf gripped his silver sword in a double-fisted hold and faced off János while Gerald stood, helpless, the halberd keeping the natural wolves at bay, but little more.

Tobias struggled to his feet, desperate to help his lord, but as he fought to rise, the Amaris wolf seized him with her arms and with inhuman strength bit into his neck, Tobias's head lolled back to reveal an enormous gash at his throat from which arterial blood pumped in rhythm with his slowing heart.

"No!" the Graf yelled. János attacked. The Graf recovered composure enough to parry the darting claw, but he was off-balance and the János wolf knocked the silver sword from the Graf's hands sending it spinning into a corner. The wolf pack covered the dropped blade and to go among them to retrieve it would mean certain death.

Tobias lay dying in a slumped heap. There was no hope for him.

"Come!" The Graf yelled, and Gerald followed him as they retreated.

The wolves, natural and otherwise, could not overcome their bestial hunger. First the werewolves ate, and they sated themselves on the corpse of Tobias, ripping off his armour and burying their muzzles in his bloody flesh, snapping and bickering between themselves as to which of them took the tastiest organs.

After they had eaten, the wolf János and Amaris allowed the pack to take their food. János seemed so confident of his final victory that he allowed the Graf and Gerald to flee the scene of their defeat.

G erald and the Graf ran down the corridor, and then up the stairs. They ran fast.

"Let me catch my breath," Gerald said, gasping.

"Hurry. We have little time." The Graf, though older and wearing armour, paused for Gerald to recover.

"What have I just seen?" Gerald said, leaning on the wall.

"The truth! What has always been! People pretend such things do not exist and believe by turning their eyes from stranger truths, the stranger truths vanish. But they do not. There are creatures foul and dark in these woods."

Gerald heard the howling beasts not far off. Without another word, he and the Graf ran on.

The Graf said, "In my chamber is a silver dagger. It is the only other silver weapon. But I must be honest with you, our chances are slim."

As they ran, they came in sight of the Graf's room. "In there, I'll get the dagger, we can barricade the door. If we can make a stand until dawn, we may survive."

Gerald nodded, and they ran, but as they were within

yards of the door and the silver dagger that lay within, the Amaris wolf appeared from the other direction, and she blocked their way.

Gerald spun round. Behind, he saw János with the full wolf pack.

Gerald knew they could not reach the Graf's door before the wolves were upon them.

What a strange and unexpected way to end his days. He had been warned not to interfere, he hadn't heeded that warning, and now it seemed he would pay the ultimate price.

The Graf hissed. "Quickly, the broken tower. We can perhaps escape over the roof."

To their left lay the dark stone steps that led up to the ruined tower. This tower struck by lightning in years gone by was open to the skies. Only a flimsy door sealed it off from the rest of the schloss.

They leapt up the stairs two at a time, but the wolves snapped at their heels. Rubble covered the ancient stone steps, and Gerald seized a stone and hurled it backwards at the pursuing wolf pack.

His aim was excellent, and he struck a wolf on the head. The beast cried out in pain, and its yelp caused the others to hold back. The werewolves were not in sight, but they couldn't be far behind.

"Hurry, Mr Anderson. Up."

Gerald hurled another stone but with less effect. Hurling rubble wouldn't save them.

"Where to now?" Gerald said as the Graf put his shoulder to the thin wooden door, bursting it open and letting in the cold October night. They climbed up the stairs and stood in the glimmer of the blood-red moon. Below them yawned the stone spiral up which the wolves and worse still, the werewolves would emerge.

Gerald looked out over the moon-drenched tiles. That was their way of escape. He prepared to step out and then, skulking, growling, baring their teeth, he saw wolves on the roof. There must be ten of them. If he stepped onto the roof he would be caught in the open between these in front and those that came up the tower behind him.

"No escape then," The Graf said. "At least we will make a noble end."

Gerald and the Graf stood side by side, the ruined tower above them like a broken tooth. The broken fragments of a stained glass window remained in its frame, jagged shards showing smashed pictures of lords and ladies long dead.

The Graf looked sadly at Gerald. "I die doing my duty, the duty my ancestors have always fulfilled, but unlike them, now I fail—a disgrace to my line. I spent my life in this isolated prison waiting for this he-wolf. And in the end, for all the years of vigilance, I let him in, duped by his clerical collar and black cloth coat."

He sighed. "You know, I would have rather have spent my years in Venice or Vienna or New York. I wanted to be a poet, not a warrior, but it was not to be." The Graf shook his head. "And you, Mr Anderson, this is not your rightful fate. I am sorry you have to die here."

Gerald shook his head. The wolves were seconds below them. "Surely, there must be some other way to kill them?"

The Graf said, "The werewolves? They are not natural creatures and can only be harmed by certain things—"

Gerald said, "—Silver, I saw that, but surely that's not the only thing that can hurt them."

The Graf shrugged. "Silver or wolfsbane."

"What's that?"

"Wolfsbane? A herb. They call it Monk's Hood, or

Aconite. I am of the Von Hohenwalds. We disdained such womanly poisons and trusted instead to our silver blades."

"But your blade is lost to you now."

"Ah, yes. My pride has brought me low. What I would give now for aconite."

Gerald produced the glass bottle given to him by the barmaid. "Like this?"

The Graf's eyes narrowed. "You have aconite?"

Gerald shrugged. "I didn't know what it was. It was a gift."

"A great gift indeed. You have a good friend in whoever gave you that herb."

Gerald handed him the bottle. With shaking hand, while the wolves waited warily outside on the roof and below on the stairs, still not sure of their kill, still awaiting the coming of Amaris and János, the Graf broke off a shard of glass from the shattered window with his mailed gauntlet and, opening the bottle, squeezed the herb to produce its juice then smeared the wolfsbane on the sharp edge of the glass.

Seeing him do this, Gerald took off his jacket and using the doubled-up material to protect his hands, he too took a sliver of glass. It was not much of a weapon, but it was better than nothing. The Graf gave him the aconite, and he daubed it on the broken glass.

Then the wolves came.

The beasts could not speak. They did not bother themselves with taunts, but launched straight into the attack, thinking there was nothing now to stop them, thinking the Graf had lost his silver sword, thinking that Gerald never had anything that could hurt them anyway.

But with a full stretch of his arm, the Graf jabbed the aconite anointed glass into János's chest. The werewolf screamed as the herb seared it and seeped poison into its lupine heart. It fell back, amazed, baffled and stupefied, its amber eyes rolling, stumbling into the wolf-pack who recoiled, retreated, and ran back, dismayed at their leader's fall.

János died screaming as the wolfsbane destroyed his magical form. Soon he lay, a burned and leaking human corpse: wolf no more, merely now a thin man in priest's garb.

Amaris saw her father's death and raised her muzzle to the sanguine moon and howled.

And Gerald struck. There could be no mercy given to the wolves. Such as they would never give quarter to such as he. With shaking hand, he stabbed Amaris with glass smeared in aconite, and she died, like her father: seared and burned by the sacred herb, turning to a scorched bag of human bones, washed in the pale light of her mother the moon.

And with that, the wolf pack lifted their heads and howled, and having howled, fled.

RALPH WATERS-WYNN SIPPED his Turkish coffee under the awning of a street cafe by the Blue Mosque in Istanbul. The day was already hot although it was just morning. The street was full of the hubbub of Turkish chatter and the sweet smell of tobacco from the hookah pipes of the customers around him.

He saw Gerald Anderson's Rover 10 appear down the road behind a donkey cart, two motorcycles and a car. Gerald was grinning through the window.

He pulled the car up and hopped out. Ralph thought his friend looked well, but he had that excited grin that Ralph knew meant he had stories to tell.

"Lovely to see you, old boy," Ralph said.

"You too, Ralphie. Anyway, did you have a nice time in Vienna?"

"Capital. Did your travels in Styria provide you with any adventures? I know how you like adventures."

"You warned me against them, Ralph!"

"Ah, yes but did you listen?"

"Not exactly, no."

ALSO BY TONY WALKER

London Horror Stories

Cumbrian Ghost Stories

The Haunting of Dungarvan Castle

Made in the USA
Middletown, DE
26 October 2022

13547020R00205